HALF-MOON RISING

BY

TRACY TAPPAN

ALSO BY TRACY TAPPAN

The Choose A Hero Romance™
reading experience

JUSTICE

Keith Knight's Story

Brayden Street's Story

Pete Robbins's Story

The Community Series
Paranormal Romance

PREY (free novella)

THE BLOODLINE WAR

THE PUREST OF THE BREED

BLOOD-BONDED BY FORCE

MOON-RIDERS

Wings of Gold Series
Military Romantic Suspense

BEYOND THE CALL OF DUTY

ALLIED OPERATIONS

MAN DOWN

For more information, go to www.tracytappan.com.

Sign up for Tracy's author updates and find out about FREE books today!

JUSTICE
A Choose A Hero Romance™ Novel

"I've completed reading all 4 stories, &, boy, what an adventure! I really had a good time reading all these endings, ultimately surprising myself on which one I liked the most."
~ Cathy C.

"I just finished all three endings and I'm blown away… This was amazing. I actually cried a little when I finished. I wasn't ready for it to be over!"
~ Kat A.

"I was Team Keith 100% of the way but now Brayden is laughingly taking the lead slightly. Damn you for that :-)"
~ Anna H.

"I laughed more with Brayden's story, but I'm still Team Keith. I guess I like the protector type more than I thought. I've only got Pete's story left to read…
 Wow, totally changed teams. Now I'm Team Pete."
~ Chelsea F.

"I just finished Justice and OMG you had me right from the beginning! I have chosen Keith to be her hero…
 Just finished Keith and Justice's story and, wowza, that was amazing. I have decided to read Brayden's story next because I just can't help myself and want to compare."
~ Sandra B.

"I just finished Justice's main story. I. Am. Blown. Away! It is incredible. My hands are shaking. Not a bad kind of shaking though. It's the kind that happens when you're so immersed into a good book your adrenalin gets pumping [and] your emotions are at a heightened state."
~ Tricia R.

Time Note

HALF-MOON RISING begins 5 months after the end of book 4, MOON-RIDERS, in 2018. So even though the publication date of this book is 2022, all times referred to in HALF-MOON RISING are referenced against 2018. For example if something happened "five years ago," that means the year 2013, not 2017.

CHAPTER ONE

May
Topside
San Diego County Courthouse, Dept. 10
Night court
6:50 p.m.

ON THE DAY CORKY DISDALE found out her boyfriend was an utter and complete asshole, her underwear fell out of her pants leg while she was on her way up Department Ten's main courtroom aisle.

"Psst" sounded behind her.

Corky stopped and turned around.

A woman in the gallery caught her eye. She had rich, radiant brown skin, eyes of an even darker brown with wide, deep pupils, and black hair caught in a bun at her nape. She was petite, but her small stature was offset by a power suit.

The *power* part hit a note of recognition. "Ria Mendoza!"

Ria was a San Diego prosecutor, known for being ferocious in a courtroom. Corky had never had to face off with Ria in court—Corky worked mostly civil cases—and good thing. Ria would've eaten her for lunch.

Not that Corky was a bad lawyer. Just new.

"How's life as an ADA?" Corky asked.

"I left that job, actually, and hung out my own shingle. My partner and I want to create an all-service firm, so we've been vetting some civil attorneys. We're looking for young blood—lawyers we can mold. Your name came up."

Corky nodded pleasantly, barely managing to keep the

double-whammy reaction off her face. Excitement was right up there, her pulse leaping at the implied job in the offing. A joyful picture of not having to chase down the odd onesies and twosies of clients just to pay the rent—but instead leaving client recruitment to someone, *anyone*, else—was already dancing in her head.

The *being molded* part was excitement number two. Corky still had a lot to learn. She'd graduated from law school only four years ago. And even though she was in the top five percent of her class at Loyola, and six months after graduation she passed the bar on her first try, she met nothing but rejection when she started pounding the pavement for a job.

For some reason she'd never been able to figure out, she made people uncomfortable.

Uncomfortable…hah! Be honest.

She outright repulsed people.

She changed her brand of deodorant four times and practiced three different types of smiles during her job hunt. *Nothing.* Every interview ended with, "Thank you, we'll get in touch."

No one ever did.

She finally gave up on everyone else and opened her own small law firm—*small*, meaning a one-woman show.

Who knew that would be such a *hilarious* solution to her unemployment problem, but apparently it was. Her boyfriend, Hunter, laughed his ass off when she told him about her practice, giving her all sorts of verbal pat-pats on the head…like her firm could only ever be a hobby, nothing more.

You'll see, Hunter.

Although the truth was, her lack of a track record *did* make it difficult to drum up clients.

But now here was a hotshot former ADA wanting to mentor her. It was a dream come—

Okay, nervousness was creeping in now, her pulse hammering even faster. Because Ria was clearly here to evaluate Corky…although Ria couldn't have picked a better case to observe Corky argue than this evening's pretrial hearing.

Corky was on the side of good and honorable, protecting Small Citizen from Big Corporate.

And she was about to serve up an ace.

She offered Ria a wide smile. "Congratulations on the new firm. I'd love to hear more about it. Maybe we can grab a drink after court tonight."

"That would be great. And, oh, um…here." Ria checked behind her, then lifted her hand. "I think these are yours."

Women's panties were dangling from her fingers.

Heat flooded Corky's cheeks. Those *were* hers. Pastel pink, the panties were identifiable by the one-inch strip of lace sagging by mere threads off the right leg opening—a casualty of Hunter ripping them off her one night last week.

"They dropped out of your pants leg," Ria added in a low tone.

"Oh, Lord." Taking the panties, Corky quickly stuffed them in her blazer pocket. "They must've gotten stuck up there during the dryer cycle." And chose *right now* to come tumbling out. She forced a laugh. It sounded airy and tight.

"These things happen." Understanding crinkled the corners of Ria's eyes.

She was being nice about it. Would it be weird to hug her? *Yes.* It would be weird. Corky settled for a professional nod. "I'd better get situated."

Ria returned the nod. "Good luck."

Corky continued up the aisle and pushed through the low, swinging gate. Her client was already seated at the plaintiff's table.

Mary Sills was a spry fifty-five, with short, never-quite-styled gray and brown hair and kind, careworn brown eyes. She'd emigrated from Romania at the age of twenty—her maiden name was Zugravescu—after marrying an American scientist. The two moved to Pine Hills, a wilderness town located about an hour and a half east of downtown San Diego, and built a big house, planning to have a large family. Except Mary's husband died too young during a research expedition. Following that tragedy, Mary converted her large house into a group home for foster children.

Corky set her briefcase on the plaintiff's table and patted Mary's hand in greeting. Pulling out a manila folder, Corky glanced at the opposition's table and—

She snapped erect. "Hunter."

Her boyfriend gave her an urbane smile.

She stared at him for two hot ticks of her pulse, then stepped over to him.

Hunter got to his feet, buttoning his blazer as he rose.

He was six-two, with a lean, athletic body, and a photogenic grin as big as a Cadillac's grille. His handsome face was built from strong bones that were actually fool's gold when it came to an accurate depiction of his character.

Hunter was, in truth, a man given to bouts of querulous whining.

Things one did not challenge Hunter Scott about included: where to go out to dinner; how to properly wash his Mercedes; which tie best matched his suit; why he practiced lack-of-orgasm reciprocity in bed; and whether he'd been faithful to Corky during the course of their four-year relationship.

Oh, and whether or not her small, personal law firm was a joke.

"What are you doing here?" Corky asked, struggling to remain calm. Actually, *calm* was out the door. She was struggling to *appear* calm. "Why are you sitting at the defendant's table?"

Please tell me you're just keeping the seat warm for a colleague.

"I'm representing my client," Hunter said.

"You're…?" A weird brittle alarm rang in her. "But—"

The bailiff arrived. "All rise!"

Corky scooted back over to her table.

"Oyez, oyez, oyez," the bailiff blared. "Civil district court for the County of San Diego is now in session, the Honorable Jonathon Katsu Hirota presiding. God save the state and this honorable court."

The robed figure of Judge Hirota entered the courtroom and climbed the steps to the bench. Hirota was of Japanese-American descent, stoutly built, wore bookish glasses, and was known to be fair. He was a good judge to draw.

"Thank you, bailiff." Hirota took his place on high. "You may be seated," he told the rest of them.

They sat.

"Case number two-two-zero-five-one," the bailiff broadcast. "Mary Sills versus Rand Resources."

Hunter stood. "Hunter Scott representing Rand Resources, Your Honor."

Corky shot back to her feet, banging her knee against the table leg with an audible *whack!* She managed not to make a face. "Catherine Disdale for the plaintiff. With the court's permission, I would like to make Your Honor aware of a possible conflict of interest in today's proceedings."

The judge peered at her over the top of his glasses.

"Mr. Scott and I are in a romantic relationship."

"Untrue, Your Honor." Hunter smoothed his silk tie. "Ms. Disdale and I have parted ways. Opposing counsel just refuses to accept facts in evidence."

The gallery of spectators snickered.

Corky's face burned. Lord, Ria Mendoza heard that.

Judge Hirota sat back in his chair. "Care to change your complaint, Ms. Disdale?"

Well, Your Honor, I'm not sure what to say about it because Mr. Scott and I were still in a relationship as of last night, when, ahem, I was on all fours, taking it from behind. As I recall, Mr.

Scott was pumping away to his heart's content while simultaneously spanking me.

Corky wasn't a big fan of sharp, stinging pain while trying to get her pleasure on, but she'd rather be spanked than deal with Hunter's grousing about *not* being able to spank her when he wanted to.

The judge set his elbows on his armrests and interlaced his fingers. "*Are* you and Mr. Scott in a relationship, Ms. Disdale?"

Corky unnecessarily adjusted the front button of her blazer. If she said *yes*, Ria would think Corky was some parasitic hanger-on unable to accept *facts in evidence*. "I guess not, Your Honor."

More snickers.

Corky moved her lips together. Points to Hunter for breaking up with her in a totally inventive—and cruel—way: in open court.

"Then let's proceed." The judge pulled some papers in front of him. "Motions?"

"Yes, Your Honor," Corky rushed right back in. "At this time, we request permission to add charges against Rand Resources. Should Rand Resources succeed in driving Mary Sills off her—"

"Object to the term *driving*." Hunter was back on his feet. "Rand Resources has done nothing but offer fair recompense to Ms. Sills for her land."

And harassed Mary in the most disgraceful fashion imaginable over the past three months, with things like calling her home multiple times in the middle of the night, dumping a two-ton pile of garbage on part of her land, cutting the electricity to the main house—a *group home*, for crying out loud. All so Rand Resources could get their grubby mitts on Mary's coal-rich acreage in Pine Hills.

When the noise of a jackhammer roared at the edge of Mary's property all day and all night, preventing the children from sleep, Mary finally ran to Corky for help.

Corky filed a harassment suit against Rand Resources, alleging "emotional distress."

Problem was that in an emotional distress case, Corky had to prove "extreme and outrageous" conduct on the part of the defendant, and she was, um, a tad light on proof.

She'd subpoenaed Rand Resource's phone records and found evidence of the late-night phone calls, but she couldn't prove Rand was the one who dumped the trash or cut the electricity or operated the jackhammer. And she wasn't wholly confident in her ability to make harassing phone calls stick as "extreme and outrageous" conduct, even with a therapist waiting in the wings, standing ready to testify to Mary's level of upset.

Corky had done more digging and—*Aha!*

She stumbled upon an old statute designed to protect the richness and integrity of the water supply. Didn't matter what it was designed for—the statute would serve her purposes just fine.

And Ria Mendoza was here to watch Corky serve up her ace.

Judge Hirota flicked a gesture at Hunter, clearly unhappy to be interrupted for a deliberation on the semantics of the word *drive*. "Sit down, counselor."

Hunter unbuttoned his blazer and sat.

Corky extracted a piece of paper from her manila file. "Should Rand Resources succeed in driving Mary Sills off her land for the purposes of coal mining, Rand Resources will be in breach of environmental statute five-five-three-four." She held up the paper. *Her coup de grace. Her ace.*

Her way to save Small Citizen from Big Corporate.

"No for-profit business," she announced, "may operate on land in Pine Hills if a waterway is on said lands. Eagle Peak River runs through the edge of Mary Sills' property."

"That is a criminal charge, Ms. Disdale, not a civil one."

"Yes, Your Honor." Corky kept her focus on the judge, although her next sword thrust was directed at Hunter. "We would like to drop the civil case in favor of a criminal action."

Take that, Hunter! I'm going for your client's jugular.

CHAPTER TWO

Judge Hirota reached for his gavel. "Very well."

"Your Honor." Hunter stood. "Before we waste any more of the court's precious time, might I be heard on this issue?"

"This is now a matter for the criminal courts, Mr. Scott."

"I beg to differ." Hunter held up a sheet of paper in the same manner Corky just had. "Here, I have evidence to contest Ms. Disdale's claim."

Corky whirled toward Hunter. Even with him in profile, she could detect a gleam of malicious victory in his eyes. *Oh, my God. What are you up to, you penis-faced poser?*

"Early this morning," Hunter continued, "a Mr. Reuben Meyerston—Ms. Sills' direct neighbor—bought an eighth of an acre of Ms. Sills' land from Ms. Sills herself."

This morning…? Corky locked her molars together to keep from stuttering out a protest. *B-b-but…*

"Eagle Peak River no longer runs through the property in question." Hunter elevated his papers. "I have both the land survey and the deed of sale right here."

Oh, no… Last night's romantic bath together came back to her with sickening clarity. *I found an ace in the hole!* That's what she'd trumpeted to Hunter while they were relaxing in sudsy bubbles, drinking wine.

Corky's stomach went wormy when Judge Hirota gestured for the bailiff to collect the documents.

While the judge read Hunter's papers, Corky bent toward Mary and whispered urgently, "*Did* you sell land to Reuben?"

"Yes," Mary admitted, her forehead knitting. "I'm sorry,

but I didn't think it mattered. I'm dealing with a leaky roof and plumbing problems, and Reuben offered me a great deal of money for only a small portion of my land."

"And that didn't strike you as odd?" Corky tried not to sound judgmental, but she was sinking fast here.

"No." Mary gave her head an adamant shake. "Reuben would never resort to foul play. He and I have been friends and neighbors for too many years."

Except that everyone could be bought. It was just a matter of finding the person's price.

"Ms. Disdale," Judge Hirota called for her attention.

Corky straightened with a jerk, her face numb, her hand crunched around the copy of environmental statute five-five-three-four.

"Unless you have anything to refute this"—the judge brandished Hunter's evidence—"I'm going to have to dismiss this case."

"Um, I…in the matter of emotional distress, we…uh-uh…" Her lips shook. Her mind spun away from her…

There was a crooked man, and he walked a crooked path. He found a crooked defense while in a crooked bath…

Hunter made a noise with his tongue, like he was trying to unstick a glob of peanut butter from the roof of his mouth. "Counsel has already dropped the civil case, Your Honor, opting to do so because there is *no* evidence to support a charge of emotional distress." He regarded the judge with a smirk, as if the two of them shared the opinion that Corky was a dunderhead of the highest order. "Phone records of a few erroneous calls?" he drawled. "Testimony from a therapist with a dubious record?"

"Objection!" Corky thundered. "Opposing counsel is lambasting my case before I've even had a chance to put evidence before this court."

Hirota's hand came up. "Yes, Mr. Scott, that's enough. However, he has you, Ms. Disdale. You made a motion to turn this into a criminal case, and Mr. Scott just took the legs out from under you with his evidence."

"Move for a continuance," she spewed.

Judge Hirota shook his head. "I don't see a viable suit here for an emotional distress case either." He indicated the papers in front of him. "From what I've already read, Rand Resources has done nothing extreme and outrageous." He shuffled the papers together, then extended the pile to the bailiff. "If additional evidence comes to light at a later time, you may refile. Otherwise this case is dismissed." Judge Hirota slammed his gavel down with a resounding *wham*.

Corky flinched.

Mary turned her face up to Corky. "What does that mean?"

Hunter adjusted the knot of his tie. His perfect, gorgeous teeth were set on full smug.

Mary tugged on Corky's sleeve. "Did we lose?"

"Um, we… Yes," Corky rasped out. "For now."

"But Rand Resources will keep on bothering me." Mary's lined face crumpled. "I've got six foster children to think of."

Corky's heart went dead in her chest, and her face ached from spending so much time at a temperature equal to the surface of Mars. *What have I done?*

Hunter tucked a yellow legal pad into his briefcase, closed the case, then sauntered through the swinging gate and down the aisle. He didn't once glance at Corky.

"What are we going to do?" Mary waited a moment, then—"Corky?"

"We're going to…" Corky couldn't go on, choking up over Mary's use of her nickname—the very nickname Mary herself gave to the waif with the mop of blond curls who'd been abandoned on Mary's doorstep, a simple note tucked in her baby basket that said, *This is Catherine.*

Mary herself invented the last name Disdale.

Now Corky's hair was only wavy—and today, tamed into

a tight bun for court—but the nickname stuck.

"We need to…" Corky stopped again. Her emotions toppled. Mary had saved Corky from destitution thirty years ago, and Corky owed her foster mother everything for that.

This evening she was supposed to repay Mary. And she failed.

On top of that, she had no idea what to do now.

Tears burned at the backs of Corky's eyes.

The bailiff stood. "Case number six-nine-four-four-three. Newbury versus Sizemore Automotive."

Two male attorneys headed down the aisle.

Corky stuffed her manila file into her briefcase, then took Mary by the elbow with care and led her outside the courtroom.

Across the hall, Hunter was using the drinking fountain.

"Why don't you go to your car," she told Mary, "and I'll meet you outside?"

While Mary ambled blinkingly toward the exit, Corky aimed for Hunter.

When her boyfriend—*ex*-boyfriend—saw her approaching, he waited.

She searched his face. If she'd seen even a hint of uncertainty or regret in his expression—if there'd been any sign of the damaged man she knew Hunter was—she would've forgiven him on the spot, without reserve. She might even have tried to patch things up.

Think only good thoughts… That's what she would've tried to do, as always.

But Hunter just dished up more smug.

She squeezed the handle of her briefcase. "Rand Resources gave Reuben Meyerston the money to buy that eighth of an acre, didn't they?"

Hunter laughed. Like it was a stupid question. Like *she* was stupid. "Of course."

God, how she despised it when he found her ineptitude

oh-so-funny. She felt her lips pulling back from her teeth. "You stole my idea for a defense and used it against me in there."

"Yes," Hunter admitted without remorse. "And thank you. I've been trying to land a job with Shoemaker, Firth, and Nolan for some time. When I approached them this morning with this surefire defense for their client, Rand Resources, they hired me."

Tears smarted again. She'd given *everything* to this man. She'd held him through all his dark emotional spirals, letting her heart bleed for the ten-year-old boy who'd lost his father in an airplane crash, making sure she never added to his pain by asking too much for herself.

And this was the thanks she got? "I-I'm going to report you," she quavered. "This is a…a breach of…of…"

Hunter snorted in disdain. "There's been a breach, all right, but on *your* end, Catherine. You broke client confidentiality. I knew how to undermine you because you *told* me your strategy."

"You weren't opposing council last night, you sleazebag!"

"Doesn't matter. You broke privilege." Hunter's right nostril wrinkled, like he just caught a whiff of B-grade caviar. "A nibble on your ear, a flick of your nipple, and I've got you ignoring every attorney-client confidentiality rule in the book just so I'd go clam diving."

A sharp breath fell out of her wide-open mouth. "I-I can't believe you said that. You're absolutely awful at oral sex!"

"Really?" He tidied a cuff link. "That's news to me. But then you never complain, do you? Ever. You're pathetic."

"*I'm* pathetic? Me?" This was too surreal to be happening. "*You* are so pathetically needy, Hunter, I didn't dare complain. You couldn't handle anything unless I babied you!"

He flicked that aside with a wrist-flip, like a king dismissing a serf. "It's a little late for excuses, isn't it?"

A prostitute strutted by with her attorney. The woman

was crammed into a poison-green spandex miniskirt and a neon pink tube top.

Hunter watched her pass. "The only reason I stayed with you as long as I did was because you're so pitifully eager to please that you let me do anything to you. If I'd wanted to stick your head in the toilet while I fucked you up the ass wearing a barbed condom, you would've let me."

Corky pressed a forefinger to her lips. *Don't cry. Do. Not.*

"Have you ever stopped to consider what kind of woman that makes you?"

Scream—that's what she needed to do. Throw her briefcase down on the floor and stomp around and smash things at random for emphasis.

What kind of woman did it make her that mere seconds ago she'd been willing to reconcile with this jerk?

"But hey…" Now Hunter leered at her. "At least I got laid one last time. You *are* hot. I'll give you that much."

Her cheeks burned for about the tenth time in so many minutes. "And you're an utter and complete asshole."

He barked out a laugh, then his eyes frosted. "And you're really fucking weird, you know that? I can't put my finger on what's wrong with you, but… You creep me out."

Her insides shrank and slunk away, her self-esteem curling into a fetal ball from having Hunter touch a live wire to her biggest self-doubt. She was pretty sure she creeped out most of the human race, and the only thing she knew for certain was it damned well wasn't her brand of deodorant.

Hunter checked his watch. "Rand Resources will put in a final offer on Mary Sills' land by four o'clock tomorrow. I recommend you advise your client to accept it." He brushed past her.

Corky's nose prickled. She fumbled in her purse for a tissue and pinched it around her nostrils. Fighting to collect herself, she turned toward the—

She drew up with a jolt.

Ria Mendoza was standing just outside Department Ten.

Any litigator worth her weight knew how to go poker-faced in the wake of hearing unwanted or surprising information. Ria's rep for that skill was champion class, but everything she'd overheard go on between Corky and Hunter was clearly enough to shake some of that talent out of her.

The smile Ria aimed at Corky was lopsided and awkward.

"Oh, Ria, uh…" Corky took a couple of halting steps forward.

"I'm sorry, Catherine, but I can't go out for a drink tonight after all." Ria held up her cell phone. "Something's come up."

A twitch jerked at the corner of Corky's mouth. *Of course it has.*

"I'll get back in touch," Ria promised.

Sure you will.

Chapter Three

Same day
The underground community of Ţărână
Weekly meeting of the Community Council
7:17 a.m.

Vasile Lazăr set his ankle on his opposite knee and scratched the flesh beneath his ankle shocker band. He heaved a great breath, then complained to his younger brother in Romanian. "<This is a bore.>"

Nicolae was seated next to him on a pew-like long-seat in the room reserved for discussions of stately importance. There were eight rows of long-seats made of glossy wood—this was where all the *Călăreţii Lunii*, or Moon-Riders, sat.

Moon-Riders were Vârcolac, although different from those vampires who lived in this small community built in an underground warren of caves.

Not different by blood, but by culture.

Moon-Riders had been born and raised in Old World Transylvania, and none of them knew much of anything about what these modern townspeople knew.

Vasile knew the land, and he knew the moon—and down here, there was little need for knowledge of either.

Vasile blew air out of his nose. "<Do these people think to make us talk by putting us to sleep? I would rather have my arm stuck inside a cow than be here listening to this twaddle.>"

Back home in Transylvania Vasile had been in charge of forty-two dairy cows, a job that contributed in a vital way to the survival of his people—the Moon-Riders earned the majority of their income through the sale of the traditional Romanian cheeses they made with this wholesome milk. Thus, supervising the valuable kine was a way for Vasile to make himself important among his brethren, in addition to his duties as lead Protector.

His people eked out a bare existence from their dairy trade and could ill afford to lose even one cow. So it was a time of great upset for everyone when the best of their milkers fell into peril for her life while trying to bring forth a calf. The calf was striving to come into the world in the wrong manner, threatening to tear its mother asunder due to a hoof caught on her hip bone. Others more learned in husbandry warned that the mother was immedicable, but Vasile did not forsake her. He reached inside her womb and, over many hours, maneuvered the calf into the correct position.

The calf was born hale and whole, and the mother survived.

It took two days for the feeling to fully return to his arm. Yet he would go back to that discomfort in a moment—his arm inserted inside a bovine uterus up to the armpit, the whole of him covered in mucus and blood, and his arm going more and more numb under the unrelenting crush of contractions—if he could only be removed from sitting here, forced to listen to topics he little understood and cared about even less.

But the town chiefs required the Moon-Riders to attend every council meeting, no doubt hoping that at some point during the communing and conferring one of them would rouse himself to speak.

None of them ever did.

The concept that those of them in the middling class of Vârcolac were no longer ruled by their royal betters but now had a *say* in their own governance, lay too far outside of their habits and beliefs.

Syrian Popovici now raised a hand to be heard.

She was seated on the left-side arm of a table shaped into a U that was set up at the front of the room.

At the head of this table were the two chiefs of the community, Roth Mihnea and Dr. Toni Parthen, who sat with a hand resting on her belly—she was five months gone with child. The other ten council members sat along the sides, distributed in even numbers, five people on each arm.

Syrian Popovici was a blood donor. Not donor to Vasile. To Nicolae. His younger brother fed from her when he needed blood, and she was tolerant and patient.

The donor to Vasile, Ectarina Vlas, offered her wrist to him by stretching her arm out as far as she could from her body to avoid getting too close to him. This was an offense and an insult. To prevent her rudeness, Nicolae advised Vasile to smile at Ectarina prior to feeding. But there was nothing to smile about. Her blood was strong to his body, yes, but tasted of gruel made from something a sick goat might have expelled from its arsehole.

Roth Mihnea gestured for Syrian to speak, and so she did. "Do we have an update on the ___ of new Dragons due in for training?"

Frowning over the unfamiliar word, Vasile leaned toward Nicolae. "<Update on what?>"

Nicolae sliced him a look. "You need to practice your English, Vasile."

Vasile shut his lips. And give himself more of a headache?

After five months of living in this community, he now, finally, understood a great deal of the English language—his first weeks in Țărână had been as pleasant as living in the armpit of a witch. Howbeit he still could not speak the language very well. He should have followed the example his brother made and watched more American television while living in Transylvania. If he had done that, maybe he would not feel so lost in his new life.

Although if truth be told, he had never felt well-placed in his old life either.

"<Just tell me,>" snapped Vasile.

"<The *batch* of new Dragons,>" Nicolae translated. After five months of living in this town, Nicolae could speak English almost without flaw. <Batch means group.>"

Vasile straightened. "<For the love of the Zâne, why not just say *group* then?>"

Jacken Brun set a fist on the table. "I object to the male Dragon, Reese Terrella."

Hard-faced, black-eyed, and lethal, Jacken Brun was seated to the left of Syrian. He was the mate of Toni Parthen.

Toni arched a brow at him now. "What's your objection?"

"I've read the man's record," responded Jacken. "He's trouble." Jacken sat back and crossed his arms. His forearms were marked with black tattoos—not circular in nature like the warding tattoos adorning Vasile, rather more like swooping tusks or teeth.

Jacken was leader of the Warrior Class, making security his utmost concern.

He was also boss to Vasile.

Five months ago, on the day after Christmas, those Moon-Riders who accepted the invitation to stay in Ţărână were led from their temporary home in the community hospital into a maze of tents.

Each tent was a designated "station" in charge of dispensing information to the Moon-Riders in a way that would help them navigate the transition to community living more easily.

At the first station Vasile was given a plastic card used for purchasing items and services. He was also issued a cellular phone, the workings of which were still somewhat of a mechanical bafflement. The whole idea of using a phone to talk to someone in a small town was ridiculous at any rate. If he had something to say to someone, why not just seek him out and say it to his face? The concept of *emojis* did not even warrant addressing.

At another station he was allocated a living space to share with another man—a *community* Vârcolac, for Moon-Riders were not allowed to live with other Moon-Riders to ensure that they practiced English and learned community culture. Vasile was assigned Amza Tófalvi as a house partner.

Amza knew how to move water and sewage through pipes, and although he acted in a friendly manner toward Vasile, he spent much of his time in a foul state about not having a woman. Vasile knew nothing about how to engage women, but it seemed to him that Amza pursued them with a method that was altogether too assertive. Vasile could recognize a disagreeable expression well enough—having borne the brunt of them for most of his life—and whenever Amza talked to a woman, her facial flesh pinched.

At the station labeled "makeover tent," two women were in charge of repairing the appearance of each Moon-Rider. It was here that Vasile watched in horror while a Vârcolac-Dragon woman wielding a *bzzzzing* instrument sheared off the sloppy mane of hair Nicolae wore, making his hair very short all over except in the very front. At first Nicolae was not sure about this hair butchering, but then the Dragon-Witch he liked, named Hadley, gave him cow eyes, and Nicolae was glad.

All the same, the devil if Vasile wanted his head shaved. So it was a lucky happenstance that the hair-cutting woman just snipped a bit off the bottom part of his long black hair, leaving it to fall just below his shoulders, then did something called "layering" to the rest of his hair. Now his hair flowed back from his face without him having to do anything to make that happen. It just did.

Finally he was given several sacks of fresh clothing, shoes, and boots by a Human-Dragon woman called Beth, who determined his correct size with a mere visual inspection of his body.

At the second-to-last station he was provided a schedule of the classes he was required to attend. Daily English lessons, of course, but also courses on how to eat a meal with proper manners, to socialize politely, to dance with a woman, to feed from a donor in a certain, gingerly way—lunging at a female and tapping into her vein when the mood struck was strictly forbidden—and how to treat females with respect and care.

And then there was something called sex education class.

Disastrous.

Catastrophic.

It was in this class that the Moon-Riders were turned into "true men," but their untoward reaction to this process ultimately earned them their shocker bands to be worn around their ankles always. Like they were no better than animals.

Something best not to dwell upon.

At the last station, jobs were assigned.

Vasile exhaled a huge breath when it came to pass that he would be tested for the Warrior Class.

He knew the land and the moon, *and* he knew how to fight. So this was good.

And being a warrior was an honorable profession—only four Moon-Riders were chosen for testing: Vasile, Nicolae, Bujor, and Enric.

"All right," said Toni, startling Vasile back to the present, "the vote is complete. Reese Terrella will be allowed to join the new group of Dragons arriving tomorrow."

Vasile shoved straighter on his long-seat. By the devil in red pants, the council had conducted an entire discussion while he was daydreaming.

A different councilman spoke now—Alex. He was brother to Toni, a man who could make computers sing. Whatever that meant. "I propose we hold off on starting the training for two or three days. A Dragon woman I've been tracking is probably ripe for a change, and I want to ask her again if she'd like to join us." Alex consulted a paper on the table in front of him. "Her name is Catherine Disdale. She's a lawyer."

Roth Mihnea made a harsh, truncated noise. His surly relationship with the present community lawyer, Kimberly Stănescu, was well known. Roth like enough did not care for the idea of another lawyer joining the community.

"What makes her ripe for a change?" asked Toni.

Alex tapped a forefinger on his cellular phone. "Social media has lit up in the past hour about something that happened in a San Diego courtroom." Alex adjusted the fit of his eyeglasses. "Catherine's life pretty much just fell apart."

CHAPTER FOUR

POLLY ALLRED IS A BADASS.

A tiny, silver stud earring glints in her left nostril, she smokes Eves, and she uses words like "cock" and "pussy." She should've been in the seventh grade, not sixth like the rest of us girls at Camp Monarch, but she flunked a grade, so she's a year older, and that makes her Queen-All of Everything That Matters in our entire world.

At night, when it's lights out in our cabin, she holds court on her bottom bunk, the rest of us sitting cross-legged in a semicircle around her, gazing up at her in the moonlight and hardly daring to breathe so we won't miss a word of the Truths she speaks.

"There's nothing worse than being a cocktease." Polly raises her cigarette, inhales hard, then exhales even harder, as if to say, So there! "You start up with a boy, you finish with a boy." She jabs her forefinger at us.

The Word has been spoken.

I exchange glances with Sheila Hobgood, who smells like farts all the time. She eats Junior Mints® a lot. Maybe that's why.

Polly Allred is a goddess to Sheila.

Sheila lives with only her dad, and so Sheila needs Polly as much as I do.

How else will Sheila and I learn about Everything That Matters?

Back home at Mary Sills' Angels, Mama Mary has to spread her love around to five other foster kids, so she's always super busy. I try to help out Mary a lot, and that makes her smile at me.

And anyway, Mama Mary wouldn't teach me about not

being a cocktease.

Polly Allred is all about the Gospel of Sex.

That's what she calls it.

Because of Polly, I know better than to smile at the boy from Camp Yellowtail during the summer camp dance mixer the next night—I should've caught myself.

But I didn't, so when he walks over, I have to wait for him. I smiled, didn't I?

The boy strolls with one hand tucked into his jeans pocket. Only one hand. The other swings free. He stops in front of me and talks about Big Things, and I make myself listen. I smiled at him, and so if I don't listen, I'll be a cocktease.

He's going to be a jet pilot someday. He's going to fly very fast. He uses his free hand to gesture while he talks. His blond bangs keep flopping into his eyes, and when they do he flips them back.

That part is cool.

Surrender spreads wide and warm like sunshine inside my chest.

Together we go around to the back of the dance room—the cafeteria, decorated with silver and white balloons—and we crawl under the wooden deck. Lying on his back next to me, he says, hey, look at the stars. I peek through the cracks in the wood floorboards. I can see a few, like grains of sparkly sand floating down.

He rolls toward me.

A storm builds in my belly. His lips are dry and cracked against mine.

He digs around at the edge of my panties.

Every time I try to say something, he tells me to hush.

So I hush.

He makes blower noises in my ear. Not quite like a whale, but close. He sticks half his finger inside me.

It feels wrong. But I don't want to be a cocktease.

I turn my head aside and watch a row of silver-colored ants crawl over a pinecone.

The song inside changes from C+C Music Factory's "Everybody Dance Now" to Madonna's "Vogue."

I'm 11 years old, and this is the first time a boy has ever touched my privates.

His name is Alan Farley.

10:53 p.m.

CORKY HICCUPPED, THEN BELCHED.

Slouched in one of her living room armchairs, she slurped her Manhattan while the violet shades of dusk settled over the gray chenille couch across from her.

Her blouse was half-untucked, her bun was coming loose with a dozen frizzy strands of hair, and a wet tissue lay crumpled in her lap.

She stared at her feet, propped on the ottoman, her legs spread wide, one shoe on, one shoe off. "Diddle, diddle, dumpling, my son John," she sang. "Went to bed with his trousers on… One shoe off and one shoe on." She hiccup-laughed and took another slurp.

She'd plunked a pretty maraschino cherry into the first two drinks she made for herself, but at this point in the evening, she was now down to base alcohol, no garnish.

Ding.

"Aw, hell!" she yelled, startling a couple of wing flaps from Tweets the parakeet, who was perched in an elevated, freestanding metal birdcage on her right.

Another message on her cell.

Corky had finally set her phone facedown on the armrest of her chair a while back. She did *not* need to read anything else from anyone else about her screwup in court this evening.

When she arrived home a few hours ago, she texted Mary that she wasn't giving up on the case against Rand—she *would* think of something.

Mary texted back K.

Not "okay." Just a short "k" that sounded very disappointed.

Corky gave the K a long, teary-eyed stare. Then started drinking.

She drank more when all her incoming messages sucked big toe rot: colleagues reveling in her demise—*Whoa, heard you got your ass handed to you in court today…* Clients bailing from a sinking ship—*We've decided to go another direction on our case, Ms. Disdale. If you could send a final bill…*

"I don' need 'em." She gave the birdcage a groggy look. "I juss need you, Tits, thass all." She blinked a couple of times. *Tits?* She gurgled a laugh. "Tweets! I mean Tweets."

She sloshed more Manhattan into her mouth and squinted at the back of her phone. Like any red-blooded woman, she was too damned curious about the message to resist taking a peek. She flipped over her phone and checked the screen. The new text was from Nadine, a friend who worked at a local coffee joint, BEANS, THE MAGICAL FRUIT—inasmuch as a woman who Corky chatted with for as long as it took to fill her order could be called a friend.

Hey, what's up with you and Hunter? I saw his post on Instagram and…

Corky slammed her phone back down. "I'm not pathetic!" Wobbling to her feet, she lurched toward Tweets' cage. "You don' think I'm pit-a-billy eager to please others, do ya, Tweets?" She jammed rigid fingers between the bars of his cage and wiggled them.

The parakeet edged away on its perch, eyeing her warily, probably wishing his owner, Sharon, would cut her business trip short so he could go home.

Corky dropped her hand. "You unnerstand me, I know ya do." She angled a drunken leer through the bars, but Tweets didn't offer her a compassionate chirp. "Pah!" Corky swung around and wove her way toward the kitchen, limp-walking on her one shoe.

She knocked her hip into the dining room table on the way past, jarring the furniture hard enough to send a banana toppling out of the centerpiece fruit bowl.

It landed on the tabletop with a dull *thud*.

She pointed her empty Manhattan glass at the banana like she was aiming a pistol. "Can't fuck me up tha ass with a spiked banana, no sirree Bob, not me." That wasn't exactly what Hunter had said, but something like it.

Tears spilled down her face. *Four years, down the drain.*

A nibble on your ear, a flick of your nipple, and I've got you ignoring every attorney-client confidentiality rule in the book just so I'd go clam diving…

"Liar!" she blared. "I juss wann'ed to prove tha my itsy-bitsy law firm s'not a joke, you…you…" She cut herself off and grumbled, "Think yer sucha hotshot, Hunner, you douche hockey puck."

Her phone dinged.

Argh! "Leave me 'lone! Vultures!"

She took two steps toward the kitchen, then stopped. A fifth Manhattan lay that way, but…

Back the way she'd come was another message.

Jutting her jaw, she stomped over to her armchair and snatched up her cell phone, blinking twice as it sank in that she wasn't looking at another nastygram.

It was an email from a research institute.

A new client? She started to perk up, but then didn't. *No way.* Still…the name snagged on a memory.

She opened the message and read it. *Well, hell.* She 'membered these guys, though it'd been a while. What? Like four years ago they emailed her with a job offer to…what was it? Oh, yeah! Executive assistant to one of the town CEOs—apparently their research institute was supported by a self-sustaining community. Underground or a weird something like that.

She'd declined because she was just starting her own practice.

And now they were offering her a job again. The assistant position had long since been filled, they said, but they were interested in hiring a legal consultant.

Corky slitty-eyed the email. Was it weird that they knew she was a lawyer now? Her sloshy brain was having trouble telling if that was, like, normal, or a stalker thing.

"You know wha' is, Tweez?" she asked out loud. "Ittza chance to get outta this stupid city." Where her reputation was now mud. "Escape tha vultures." She tipped her glass up to her lips. *Oh. Yeah. Empty.* She let her arm flop back down. "Nothin' keepin' me here, right?" All her clients had jumped ship. *Buncha babies.*

You broke privilege…

"Or m-maybe," she warbled, "tha problem iz tha I blew it, Tweez. Big time." She hunched her shoulders and wept. All she ever wanted to do was help people. It was why she became a lawyer—to save the little guy. And in the most important case of her life—the one to help Mary—she'd let insecurity ruin everything.

I found an ace in the hole, Hunter! Aren't I the hotshot now?! Case dismissed! Wham!

"Y-you know…you know what…? If I go innew a courtroom right now, Tweez, *I will barf!*" A legal consultant sounded exactly like her current speed. And maybe a little peace and quiet would help her figure out how to fix the mess she'd made of *Mary Sills versus Rand Resources.*

She skimmed down to the bottom of the email, tears dripping off her nose and chin. The Research Institute would like to inform her that a training session was starting in two days. They advised her to pack a bag with enough personal items to last for a week of indoctrination. If the fit was good after her training, she could send for the rest of her things.

Wow. She scrubbed her nose. She'd have to move to their

town. That was a major commitment.

I'm sorry, Catherine, but I can't go out for a drink tonight after all. Something's come up.

"I'm sorry, too, Ria. Sorry tha I smelt too bad with my shitty deod'rant for your delicate sensa-billies!" Corky started to type an acceptance.

Tweets let out a sharp chirp.

"Oh, *now* you speak. Well, too late! Fung it! I don' care! I said I wann'ed outta this stupid city, so I'm gettin' out."

She needed to jump on this opportunity before these people at the Research Institute figured out that Hunter's description of her as a pathetic loser was exactly correct.

Chapter Five

Two days later
The underground community of Țărână
7:00 a.m.

"Welcome, everyone. Thank you for joining us today. My name is Dr. Toni Parthen. I'm one of the directors of this community called Țărână, a town unlike any you'll ever encounter. I'll cut right to the chase and say that I'm going to reveal some strange things to you over the course of the next few hours, so I ask that you try to keep an open mind about what you hear and see. Because as strange as it all seems, this town is going to be the best thing that's ever happened to you—it's where you belong. We wouldn't have invited you if it wasn't.

"One of the most obvious oddities is that our town exists underground, as I'm sure you noticed from the twenty-minute ride you just took in a *down*ward direction on our platform elevator. Living without a sky overhead will be a little uncomfortable at first, but we've found that everyone adjusts within a couple of months. And the charms of this town far outweigh the downsides."

Click—pictures appear on a large PowerPoint screen, showing several storefronts...some with awnings, others with zigzaggedy trim, bright paint, everything immaculate. Click—a pub made of well-worn wood, rugged and Western. Click—a tall, glass-fronted apartment building. Everything surrounded by chunky brown cave rock.

"Another oddity is that we flip the time. So even though

it's currently a little after seven at night in San Diego—the time you four feel in your bodies—it's seven in the morning here in Ţărână. You should be able to make the time switch without a problem too.

"The best way to get a true sense of our quirky town would be, of course, to see it. But before you can leave this building, you'll need to read about this community's special culture and then pass a short test. I'll be handing out study guides in a minute.

"But before that, I need to address a few big deals. The first big deal to clear up is that there is *no* Research Institute. It wasn't our intention to misrepresent ourselves to you—the jobs we've offered you are legitimate—but this town's existence is top secret, so we had to devise a front for it. Research Institute is what we chose. It's merely a security precaution.

"So what is this town really? It's a refuge. We provide a safe haven for people who have faced prejudice in the world above due to their unique genetic makeup. All of *you* fit that mold. Through various means, we've discovered that each of you carries something called Peak 8. This is a marker for an ancestral line of yours going back to an ancient race known as Dragon." *Smiles.* "Sounds like something you might read about in a Harry Potter book, right? That's because main-stream medicine isn't aware of it. I assure you, though, it's very real.

"The Dragon race earned their moniker from the beauti-ful dragon image they have on their backs. See here." *Click—a picture of a blond man's bare, muscular back appears on the screen. A scaly dragon adorns the entire span of his back, the head of the creature stretching over the left scapula, the wings arcing over the right side of his back, the tail curving down to the lower spine, and clawed feet reaching out to the left. The body and wings of the dragon are bright green, the belly, claws and mouth, red.* "As you can see, this dragon is made of shimmering, living scales. No, this picture hasn't been photoshopped. Yes, this is weird. What's going to seem weirder is that all of you have a piece of this dragon on your backs, but as a brown birthmark.

"Focus, if you will, on the arc of the wing, the clawed foot, and the nose of the dragon. Each of you has one of these marks—a nose, a wing, or a foot. Like so." *Click—a picture of three blond women lined up in a row, bare backs aimed at the camera, each with a brown blotch to the left of her spine.* "See how these marks are identical? If you have a dragon foot on your back, your birthmark exactly matches these women's. Doesn't it?" *No one answers.* "I can tell by your expressions that it does.

"And I've just walloped you with big deal number two— you *are* descended from the ancient Dragon line. This birthmark proves it. If you're still skeptical, then take a moment to think back over the life you've lived. Have you ever truly fit in? Ever felt like you were deeply close to anyone? You don't have to say anything. I know you haven't. You've been rejected by the people topside because they sense your Dragon side and pull away from it. I'm sure that sounds crazy to you, but this is where I need you to keep an open mind and please hang in there. There are bigger shocks to come. But after some initial upset, all of this will make amazing sense to you.

"All right. Onward to big deal number three—Dragon people like you are extremely important to another type of human who finds safe harbor in our town. This other race has rare bone marrow. Theirs makes too many white blood cells and not enough red. The extra white gives them heightened powers of healing and other strengths, but the lack of red means they need to supplement their red blood cells from another source.

"Who cares about the biology, right? I'm guessing you don't, but at this point in the explanation I've found that speaking clinically helps to ease you into what I have to tell you next. This other type of human accesses the supplemental red blood they need using fangs.

"Yes, I said *fangs*. That's big deal number four. I'm just going to say it: there are vampires living in this community.

"We call them—okay, hold up, please keep listening. We call them Vârcolac, instead of vampires, to help remove the stigma that goes along with the term vampire. Vârcolac are *people*, as you can see." *Click—men and women appear on the screen doing various normal, everyday activities…click, click, click. In every picture they are happy and smiling—showing fangs.*

"I belong in a rubber room, right? That's what you're thinking. I can and will prove all of my assertions, but for now I think it's better if I don't flash around fangs, super speed, scaly dragon tattoos, and eyes capable of lighting up. Let's allow things to sink in for a bit first. Take a breath." *Dr. Parthen herself inhales.*

"I'd like to circle back to why you're here. The Vârcolac race hovers on the verge of extinction. The study guide will go into detail about the reasons why, but the main takeaway for now is that you four, with your Dragon bloodlines, are the only type of human being who can give the Vârcolac living children.

"You are the Vârcolacs' salvation.

"So here comes big deal number five. The real reason you've been invited here is—yes, to work—but also to get to know the Vârcolac. Date some, enjoy yourselves while making new friends, maybe discover a different hobby or two. Experience the kind of acceptance *here* that you've been denied your entire life, and maybe along the way find someone to love, marry, and create a family with. However, let me pause a moment to emphasize that having children is *not* a requirement of your tenure here. It's only a hope. You are *our* people. This community will always be your home."

Dr. Parthen scans her audience. "Minds are reeling. Understandable. At this point I think the best way for you to fully absorb what I'm describing is to meet and talk to couples in Vârcolac-Dragon relationships—they know exactly what you're feeling right now. So I'm going to turn the floor over to a Q&A panel." *Dr. Parthen moves out from behind a podium and walks to the door. She opens it.*

Four couples file in and head for chairs lined up at the front of the room.

Dr. Parthen introduces the couples. "This is Chelsea and Gábor Pavenic, Marissa and Dev Nichita, Lara and Kardos Izbaşa, and Ty and Daciana Vega."

The four couples sit.

Dr. Parthen gestures toward them. "All the men on this panel are Vârcolac, expect for Ty. He's a Dragon, along with Chelsea, Marissa, and Lara. They all experienced the same level of shock and disbelief when they first heard the word *vampire.* Although actually, when Marissa and Chelsea were invited into our community, we maintained the Research Institute ruse for a good three months. So when the facts came out, they were caught totally off guard. We've since decided it's best to bring in new people with the truth leading the way. Lara joined us in such a manner, and it's worked out much better. This is why we're being up front with you four.

"All right." *Dr. Parthen smiles graciously.* "Who'd like to ask the first question?"

CHAPTER SIX

ALWAYS GO FOR THE MEANEST motherfucker when things turn to shit.

Moving only his eyes, Reese Terrella shifted his attention away from the head blonde—nice set of lungs, body running a little thick in the hips and waist—and combed over the other people in the prissy drawing room…an actual *fainting couch* was set in the corner, for fuck sakes.

He first checked on his fellow recruits, two chicks and one dude, all looking like their brains had been run over by a lawn mower. All three were blonds.

Reese was the only one of the recruits with black hair. 'Course he dyed his.

Of the two chicks, Catherine Disdale had made a stopover at Sexville on the way here—leggy, perfect tits, a full mane of wavy gold hair down to mid-back that Reese would guess always looked styled into just-been-fucked no matter how much she combed it.

The second chick had never even been in the same zip code as Sexville: Coke-bottle glasses, short, putty-colored hair caught in a ponytail that resembled a broccoli stalk, an expression like a whipped dog. Diamond Gibbons was sweating like she'd just stepped out of a Bikram yoga class. Good bet she was also working on a bad case of swamp ass.

Evan Silva, the other male recruit, had muted blond hair down the back of his neck, styled by a hacksaw. He was slender, not much to him at all, guaranteed to be as nonviolent as a gerbil—the type who even refused to swat a mosquito on his leg. Just gently whisked the bug back to freedom.

None of these three were equipped with the means necessary to park one in the mouth of anyone who tried to deny them an immediate adjournment.

That was on Reese.

He shifted back to the panel.

Guy with the goatee and black ear gauge. *Yeah. He's the one to take down.*

When Goatee had first tramped into this prissy room, entering with the other drugged-out townies, all the hairs on Reese's nape rose.

"Dev Nichita," according to introductions made by the head blonde, who'd clearly had her lips wrapped around a crack pipe for the longest.

Nichita was huge. A set of enormous lats cut visible creases into his T-shirt, and he had some serious height going on. To top things off, the guy was no swole juicer who added a healthy jab of steroids to his morning puff of sugar block. Not to say he didn't hit the barbells, but there was enough natural strength in his body to broadcast that he fought for a living.

Good. He was just what—

Then he sat down.

Reese got a better look at his eyes. On top of them being a bizarre bright metallic color, his eyes held a steady calm that broadcast something else: *leader.* It wouldn't be easy to provoke this dude.

Not good.

Reese needed to make some noise. Fuck some shit up. Nothing leveled the playing field better than a sudden, ugly act of violence.

Talk, as the saying went, was cheap—and all discussion came to a halt anyway, as soon as a person spouted off about things like vampires and Dragons. Then it became time to vacate the premises. Immediately. No other option.

Easier said than done when a band of meltbrains had

trapped their victims *underground*. To achieve a rapid exit, it'd be necessary to smack the idea out of anyone's head that weakness was present anywhere on Reese, available to be abused or exploited.

It was just a matter of picking *which* motherfucker to smack.

If not Nichita, *who?*

Movement on the panel brought Reese's attention over to Nichita's wife, the woman called Marissa—multicolored blond hair, bangs catching in her lashes, slender to the point of skinny.

She leaned forward to talk to Chelsea—pregnant belly stuck way out to there on a tiny body. "All I'm seeing is deer-in-the-headlights looks, Chelz." Marissa chuckled. "I think you and I are going to have to kick-start this."

Chelsea nodded. "The good, the bad, and the not-so-ugly of life with a Vârcolac? I'd say we begin with—"

Reese pushed to his feet, uncoiling to his full height. 'Bout six-one, type of body that was lean and wiry. His muscles were like nylon cables. He was stronger than he looked. He was rattlesnake fast.

Chelsea's mouth clacked shut, and her eyes startled wide.

The men on the panel instantly put Reese in their cross-hairs.

Excellent. He had everyone's attention.

Guy seated next to preggo—buzz-cut black hair, a skull tat on his left bicep—didn't mince around with his expression. Right off he looked like he wanted to rip Reese a new asshole and then cram him into it, head first.

Bingo.

He was the meanest motherfucker.

The one introduced as Gábor Pavenic.

Reese hitched his baggy jeans, then started toward the panel, his weight forward, his thick-soled Bates boots making him sound twenty pounds heavier than he was. He locked onto Gábor, openly threatening.

Dude didn't waste time vaulting out of his chair and getting ready to knuckle up. He angled his body into a fighter's stance, also shifting his weight onto the balls of his feet.

"Shit." Nichita was on his feet, too, hustling the women out of the way.

When Reese was one step away from Gábor, he grabbed his own left wrist with his right hand and shoved a rapid-fire arm-bar at the man's throat. No opponent expected to be hit this way right off. Every guy prepared for a *punch*, and the surprise factor never failed to sit a man down, wheezing and gasping.

Except this time.

Gábor got his chin tucked low enough to protect his throat, and Reese's arm slammed into Gábor's forehead.

Even so…a powerful hit like that should've sent Gábor stumbling backwards by yards. Not hopping back with elastic agility by mere inches, still ready to fight.

Reese paused.

He evaluated.

From the side of his vision, he saw the head blonde stroll over to the drawing room door and depress a button with a casual push of her thumb. A yellow light on top of the door began to blink.

Gábor growled, his body tensing up.

"Do *not*," Nichita barked, "hit him."

Knew it. Reese sneered. A pain-in-the-balls leader.

"This fucking asshole hit *me*," Gábor retorted.

"Well, maybe you shouldn't have let him tag you," Nichita lobbied back.

Dude was standing protectively in front of the four panel women and one of the panel guys, Kardos, whose arm was wrapped around his wife, Lara. The man called Ty Vega stood just to the side of that group, sizing up Reese with an exaggerated calm that oozed *cop*—every police officer Reese had ever dealt with possessed the same ability to look super chill even when he was probably nuts deep in adrenaline.

"He's just freaking out," Nichita went on. "Why does crap like this keep surprising you?"

Freaking out? Reese silently repeated the two words. *I sound fine to me.* "Hey, shit-eater." He aimed this at Nichita.

Nichita looked at him. His expression was calm, but muscles all over his body were showing against his skin like knobby tree branches. Maybe this guy *could* be provoked.

"I don't freak out," Reese corrected. "I get things done."

"Yeah? What is it you think needs doing, Terrella? Because as I see it, no one here has done anything to you—*any* of you—even remotely threatening. We've laid some bizarre shit on you, and that's it."

Reese grated out a laugh. "*Bizarre* would be my car running for a month straight without breaking down. Bizarre would be me wanting to have a sleepover with you, big broski, giggle and do your hair and cuddle spoon-style with you, my dick snuggled against your ass." He smoothed his tongue over his front teeth. "Bizarre would be me waking up this morning as a doofus fuck-brain who would believe all the butt fudge you've been shoveling. *Vampires* and *Dragons* aren't even a distant relative of *bizarre*, shit-eater, so the four of us are leaving." Reese turned his head toward his three fellow recruits behind him and snapped, "Get up."

Catherine, Evan, and Diamond scraped hurriedly to their feet.

"You got anything to say against us getting the fuck outta here," Reese continued to Nichita, "I'll beat your ass so hard your mother will feel it."

Nichita let out a dark laugh. "Not exactly a major threat to a man like me."

Reese paused. *Whatever.* He turned toward the door. The head blonde was still by it. "Move out of the way, lady."

Reese lifted his boot to take a step.

Nichita was right in front of him.

Reese hopped back, bumping into Evan.

Fuck! Where the hell did this asshole come from so fast?

"I *hope* you're not thinking of making a move on Dr. Parthen," Nichita said. Pleasant, and not so pleasant. "Because then you and I *will* have a problem."

Reese's pulse throbbed at his temples. His eyeballs vibrated.

Everyone in the room was *breathing*. He could hear them. Dev Nichita…Ty the cop…the four panel-women…his three fellow recruits… *Whoosh*. Like being inside Kim Kardashian's head after someone asked her to recite the Pythagorean Theorem.

Reese's hands heated, and—

He threw a punch. No telegraphing. He just shot his arm straight out from his side.

Nichita still managed to see it coming. He caught Reese's bunched fist in his palm, *thwack*—like a line drive into a baseball glove.

Nichita yanked Reese around, moving to lever his arm up between his shoulder blades.

Reese slithered free and light-footed out of striking range.

Surprise registered.

Nichita had expected to catch Reese.

No one caught Reese.

Bang. The main door swung open, sudden and fast, and a dark-haired man appeared in the jamb, scanning every inch of the room.

Dressed all in black, a knife at his side, forearms covered in tribal tats, he had a solid jaw on him and was built somewhat like Nichita—huge. But also like Nichita, this guy didn't look like a 'roid fiend.

This man looked like he spent more time chewing iron than powerlifting it.

"What's going on?" he demanded, stepping inside.

"Jacken—" the head blonde began.

Always go for the meanest motherfucker when things turn to shit.

Reese put his head down and cannonballed forward.

Chapter Seven

Hurling all his weight into the attack, Reese rammed his skull into Jacken's torso, nearly breaking his own neck on the guy's locked-up, concrete abs.

No grunt or hiss came out of the dude either.

Fuckstick.

Growling, Reese held on tight and drove Jacken backwards until they both hit a wall.

Plaster boomed into a meteor shower of white, and a painting hopped into the air then hit the floor, stiff-walking from one corner to the other before whacking over onto its face.

More herding of the women occurred, Nichita directing them in an urgent tone.

Jacken dropped down over Reese's back, latched his arms around Reese's chest, and squeezed.

Lungs. No. Can. Expand. A hippo sat on Reese's chest. His vision swam with squiggly black things. *Paddles, stat! Myocardial infarction!*

"Grab his legs," Jacken ordered, "before I have to hurt him."

Reese dug in his heels, pain closing his eyes. If this was Jacken going easy on Reese, then the fuck if he wanted to find out this guy's version of hellbent.

He lowered his skull to head-butt Jacken in the acorns, but—

His boots parted company with the floor, stealing his traction.

As his body went horizontal, Jacken grabbed the back of Reese's T-shirt and yanked it over his head, using it to bind him—and giving the entire room an up-close-and-personal view of Reese's tatted-up torso: a graphic Death Valley landscape of snakes and skulls and scorpions and cacti.

Whoever held his feet gave them a hard yank.

Adrenaline surged like acid in Reese's veins, pushing bile into his nose.

No one catches me!

He jerked his body all over in a series of violent convulsions, pumping his thigh muscles in brutal half-kicks.

The grip on one of his boots loosened.

"Watch it!" Nichita shouted. "The guy's slicker than shit through a goose."

Whoever had his feet scrambled to re-grab him, but the guy accidentally seized hold of Reese's pants cuff. When he yanked again, Reese's baggy jeans whipped down his legs to his ankles. His undershorts made a partial trip along with his pants, the elastic waistband catching on the root of his cock, preventing him from being totally exposed. But still. Everyone saw his—

"Fuck," Gábor swore. "This asshole has red pubes."

How many schools had Reese been to in his young life? How many of his nightmares were haunted with images of him showing for the first day of class without clothes on? There he'd be, standing in a hallway of lockers, just hanging hog in front of all the girls in their ponytails—why did they always have ponytails?

This was about as bad, being held against his will and having his pubes gawked at.

Gritting his teeth, Reese twisted his right arm so hard toward escape the ball joint almost burst out of its socket. Pain speared down his arm, but he kept twisting. His flesh burned where his bone jammed against it.

Jacken must've seen what was happening because he spat

out, "Let him go."

Reese was dropped.

He *clomped* down.

He shot to a standing position, hauling his pants up as he went vertical. He took two steps back, and yanked his shirt down.

He assessed.

The occupants were now clumped into an obtuse triangle.

At the ninety-degree angle, Reese was standing in a loose knot with his combatants: Jacken and Gábor, the three of them breathing heavily and keeping each other under wary surveillance.

The western point ended at Nichita and Ty the cop, both looking intense. The panel-women and Kardos were gone—they must've been evacuated during the fight.

The last point of the triangle contained the three other recruits, Catherine, Diamond, and Evan—not a one seeming to know what to say or do—now standing near the door beside the head blonde.

Reese gestured sharply at his co-recruits. "Come over here," he barked. "Stand behind me."

They did as he commanded.

Jacken watched this from beneath lowered brows.

Reese hard-stared the man. Dude's eyes were the blackest Reese had ever seen. "You ever try to get a load of my cock again, anal munch, and you'll end that attempt with your nuts in your pocket."

Jacken's nostrils flexed once, then his focus shifted over to the head blonde.

She offered him a droll expression. "Mr. Terrella appears to have a penchant for scatological insults."

Jacken didn't say anything. Just kept staring at her.

Her lips twisted. "The council notes your objection."

Gábor suddenly lit off. "What the *fuck* is up with all the assholes in our world lately? First Waterson turns out to be

Vârcolac, now this prick"—he directed a curt hand gesture at Reese—"is a Royal."

Sweat trickled down the back of Reese's neck. *A what?*

Jacken looked at Reese again. "What the fuck's your malfunction?"

"Don't got one," Reese returned. "Not if you let us go."

"Who the hell's keeping you?"

"*All* you peckerwoods are."

Jacken checked in with the blonde.

She shook her head.

Gimme a break. Reese made a big show of rolling his eyes. "You fuck-holes have brought the four of us *underground*. We can't just stroll out of here whenever we feel like it and go back to normal, can we?"

The head blonde moved over to the podium and set an elbow on it. "We were up front about our town being subterranean, Mr. Terrella."

"Yeah, I know." The underground part hadn't sketched out Reese when he first read the email sent to him by the "Research Institute." It wasn't an unheard of way of operating—the military used to have an underground installation called NORAD in Colorado Springs, as an example. But on the twenty-minute trip *down*, a hammer started striking his internal gong on repeat.

He should've listened to it.

He wouldn't still be walking this earth in one piece if he hadn't developed a pinpoint accurate instinct for life about to tank into a shit casserole. And now look—he was being served up a steaming plate of it…

Vampires.

"But you weren't up front about the bloodsucker part," Reese accused, "were you?"

"You may refer to the people who live in this community as Vârcolac or vampires." The head blonde could pull off a pretty decent scolding-librarian tone when she wanted to.

"And the vampire part of the explanation needed to be done in person." She scanned the others. "I was hoping all of you would give us more time to explain everything, give yourselves a chance to learn the true depth of what we're offering you. But if you can't do that—if you truly want to leave—then we would be happy to transport you back to San Diego. It is the policy of this community—no, the *law*—never to keep anyone in this town who doesn't wholeheartedly wish to be here."

Reese stayed tight. The head blonde looked and sounded sincere, but the best con artists always did.

"We have some refreshments laid out for you." She gestured at a sideboard on the far side of the prissy drawing room. "Why don't you refuel and think about it before you—"

"No," Reese cut in. "We want out now."

Nichita interjected his unwanted opinion. "Let the others speak for themselves, Terrella."

"No," Reese repeated. These three needed protecting—Whipped Dog Diamond especially looked like she could be talked into anything. "I've elected myself spokesman. If you don't like it, you can—"

"No need to tell me to make a sandwich out of my own butt." Nichita held up a hand. "I get where you're going."

The head blonde nodded firmly. "All right. I'll call a Traveler to—"

Reese came close to jumping out of his own feet when a roaring, snarling, howling cacophony rolled like thunder down the hall outside.

Jacken was already in motion, leaping toward the head blonde, urging her away from the door just as it burst open. The sound of every creature in Jumanji entered…along with two large, black-haired men, moving at a dead run.

A man with long hair was chasing another man with bushy sideburns.

Catherine, Evan, and Diamond scattered.

Reese moved to—

What the *fuck*?

All kinds of shit were spinning on the long-haired dude that shouldn't have been: a grouping of interlocking circular tats on his right arm, rings of tiny black ball bearings surrounding his irises. And then there was—

Sharp. White. Long. Animalistic.

Reese's feet threw down roots.

Both men had glistening canines extended into their mouths.

Fangs.

The real deal.

Reese's brain could tell. Like the difference between movie violence and real violence. No matter how much a movie might try to make violence appear genuine, a part of the mind always knew the difference between fake and real.

Real fangs…

Hockey check to the brain!

Reese's knees actually juddered.

Long Hair flew through the air, catching Sideburns in a tackle. The two men slammed to the floor in a clinch hold and rolled into Reese, sending him stumbling backwards. Tripping over his own feet, he hit the carpet on his ass and somersaulted elbows over canteen, lurching up onto his seat in time to see Long Hair trying to manhandle Sideburns' arms behind his back.

"I'm not fucking going to jail," Sideburns snarled, fighting like hell against the efforts to restrain him.

Nichita plowed toward the fighters, presumably to help.

"All the women *out*," Jacken ordered.

Wide-eyed, Catherine and Diamond hurried past the fighters toward—

Long Hair's head snapped up.

His nostrils flared.

His stare tightened on Catherine, and with a ferocious

bellow, he leapt off Sideburns and charged her.

Catherine screamed and up-shifted to a full run. Her hands reached for the door as if that could somehow increase her speed toward escape.

"Vasile!" Jacken called to Long Hair. "Stop!"

Dude didn't stop.

Long Hair Vasile tackled Catherine in much the same way he had Sideburns, his arms wrapping around her legs a couple of inches above the knees. They *thumped* to the floor.

Whey-faced, Catherine screamed again.

Whipped Dog Diamond staggered away from the jumbled-together couple and screamed too.

Evan propelled her out the door.

Across the room, Nichita, Ty Vega, and Gábor were making a racket with Sideburns. "Knock it off, Vinz!" one of them yelled.

Long Hair Vasile climbed on top of Catherine and straddled her, his muscled thighs gripping her hips.

Panting and choking, Catherine slapped and shoved at her attacker.

Vasile grabbed a fistful of Catherine's hair and angled her head to the side, exposing her throat. His fangs dripped.

"Oh, crap." The head blonde whipped a remote control out of her pocket.

Jacken finally left her side, rushing toward the two on the floor.

"Help!" Catherine shouted.

Reese had been sitting like a dummy through all the rapid-moving fucked-up, but that *help!* got his ass in gear.

Catherine was one of *his* people.

He scrambled to his feet.

The head blonde pointed the remote at the wrestling couple. "Watch out, Jacken!"

Reese shoved Jacken aside, jumped on Vasile's back, and—

Ahhhhh!

An electrical current barbed through him. His limbs locked into a rigid starfish pose. His mouth wrenched into a rictus of pain. His entire body shook, and his brain went gray.

Beneath him Vasile howled and spasmed.

The electricity cut off.

Reese drooped into a boneless heap on top of Vasile.

Vasile collapsed onto Catherine.

Catherine whimpered.

Cursing, Jacken hefted Reese off, letting him flop to the floor on the right side of Catherine's body, then he grabbed Vasile and rolled him left.

The head blonde hustled forward. "Are you okay?"

Reese didn't bother trying to answer. The head blonde wasn't asking him.

Catherine's response was a sob.

Reese stared at the ceiling and listened to Catherine cry. Slobber gathered at the corners of his mouth. Hot pins stabbed through his pupils. He'd lost all command of his limbs.

Gábor appeared above him, his lips curled into a nasty sneer.

Fuck.

The inmates caught him after all.

CHAPTER EIGHT

CORKY'S BEST FRIEND YASMIN BLEEKER left Mary Sills' Angels when they were both five years old. Other friends were adopted and went away, but Yasmin was the hardest to lose. No one was better at building Play-Doh dinners than Yasmin—she rolled perfect, round meatballs when they made spaghetti. And she was a great mommy to her Baby Chrissy doll when they played house.

Corky vomited all over her best sneakers when Mary Sills told her that Mr. and Mrs. Peterson would be taking Yasmin home with them. When the Petersons drove away with her best friend inside, Corky raced after the car, but it never slowed. The car belched exhaust into her face, aimed swiftly for the highway, and disappeared forever.

Corky flung herself down on the driveway and sobbed.

To this day the smell of oil and exhaust could push bile into her throat like nothing else. So here—back in the community garage with Evan, Reese, and Diamond—Corky was practically choking on acid.

The four of them were standing near a wooden work-bench, Reese with one arm wrapped around Corky's shoulders, the other around Diamond's, protecting them—holding himself up, too, Corky would guess.

He'd been walking on rubbery-looking legs a few minutes ago.

Corky wasn't sure what to make of Reese Terrella. He was both heroic and a volatile pain in the ass. When she first met him at their rendezvous point in San Diego, she was silently shocked by his appearance. Not so much over his extreme black hair—which, ahem, they all now knew was dyed—but by his choice of attire.

The waistband of his jeans hung low enough on his lean hips to show off the elastic of his underwear, and one of the knees was ripped out...not fashionably. His gray T-shirt, which said SAN DIEGO CHARGERS in bright blue letters across the front, was wrinkled, probably slept in.

The rest of them had arrived for training in various versions of nice pants and smart shirts, choosing to exhibit a modicum of professionalism.

But now Corky was sort of glad Reese was rough-looking. It felt like he was the only thing standing between her and a lot of scary.

Little Miss Catherine sat by a lantern, eating her curds and whey. Along came a vampire, who flashed his incisors, and frightened Miss Catherine away...

Bile pushed from her throat into her nose at the memory of that...that...*thing* trying to eat her.

"What's the word, Vlad?" Dr. Parthen aimed this question at two dark-haired men with tool belts who were angling out of a three-foot gap in the elevator's double doors—the doors were stuck in that position.

Of the two, the man dressed in engineer boots and thick denim pants walked toward Dr. Parthen, who was standing next to an unsmiling Jacken and a preppily dressed blond guy wearing glasses.

The man in tan cargo pants stayed back, eyeballing Corky and Diamond with a hand pressed over his nose.

"Can you fix the doors?" Dr. Parthen continued to the first guy.

"Yes, ma'am, I can open them," Vlad answered. "But it won't do you much good. The elevator's not going anywhere."

"Is it an electrical problem?"

"Nope." Vlad flipped the screwdriver in his hand so that

he was holding the metal part. He aimed the handle at the preppy blond. "His."

Dr. Parthen arched a brow at Preppy. "This is a programming issue?"

"I don't know…possibly. Heck, probably." Preppy threw his arms out, jostling the backpack on his shoulder. "The entire system has been glitchy ever since the town went into full shutdown."

Dr. Parthen looked dubious. "That was four years ago."

"Yeah, I know, but the system is old and wonky. It was created before my time—even before Cleeve's time, which in computer years is pretty much dinosauric. The only way to fix the main program is to go totally offline long enough for me to rebuild it from the ground up."

"How long would that take?"

"A week to ten days, maybe longer."

"Hah!"

"Exactly," Preppy agreed. "Which is why I've never brought it up. Cleeve and I just fix problems as best we can when they come up."

Dr. Parthen indicated the elevator. "How long will it take to fix this?"

"Two, three days."

"*Days?*"

Wait, what…? Corky fisted her hands together. Did that mean they were *stuck* here?

You assholes have brought the four of us underground. We can't just stroll out of here whenever we feel like it and go back to normal, can we?

Corky cut a glance at Reese.

He moved his jaw like he was working over a piece of Bubble Yum.

Oh, God, Reese was right. The four of them were at the mercy of these community people—their sole means of escape was via *a broken elevator!*

Corky's heart rocked in her chest. *Okay…no, no…don't freak out. Think only good thoughts.*

That's what Mama Mary had told her to do after the Petersons took Yasmin. Mary picked Corky up off the driveway and hugged her close. "I know it's difficult," Mary said. "But you have to try and put away the sadness and think only good thoughts. Yasmin has a mom and dad now. Shouldn't you be happy for her?"

Corky *should* have been happy for her.

She just would've been *more* happy to have her best friend back.

"Buck up, *comoara mea*," Mary went on. "Someday a mom and dad will come for you too."

But none ever did.

Every prospective parent who came to Mary's looked at Corky like she had horns growing out of her head.

But if Mama Mary believed that thinking only good thoughts was the best way to handle upsetting things, then that's what Corky would try to do.

It was what she needed to do now.

Smile nicely for all these community people.

Hide all your panicky thoughts with a pleasant expression.

Corky forced a smile, but her grin felt like a small seizure.

Okay, how about Be Lawyerly.

Remember the case when you represented your client in a vicious dog bite suit? You claimed egregious irresponsibility on the part of the dog owner…then found out mid-trial that your client actually went into his neighbors' back yard to rip off…er, borrow some barbecue equipment, and that's why the dog attacked him…

You kept a straight face when that tidbit came out on the stand, didn't you?

Unfortunately, a non-expression seemed to be way beyond her capabilities right now. Possibly…probably…no, *definitely*…there was too much bad and weird going on for her to white it all out.

Big Deal Number Four: there are vampires living in this community.

La la la la la la la...

She'd been okay with all the Big Deals at first.

Big Deal Number One hadn't been all that much of a big deal to her. So this town didn't serve as a support system for a Research Institute. *So what?* The community was still honoring their job offers.

Big Deal Number Two hadn't thrown her off by much either—at least in the beginning. If the people in this town wanted to believe Corky was descended from something called a Dragon, who was she to say it wasn't true just because it sounded far-fetched? Hadn't scientists back in the 1850s believed the idea of "bacteria" was preposterous? When obstetrician Ignaz Semmelweis told his colleagues they could prevent their patients from becoming ill merely by washing their hands, they ostracized him. *Particles unseen by the naked eye that cause disease?! Are you insane, man?!*

No one could possibly know everything there was to know about the world at any given point in time. So—as Dr. Parthen had requested—Corky kept an open mind.

But...then...you know...

Then she *saw* the identical birthmarks on those three blonde women, and she began to unravel a bit.

Because...yeah...

She had the same birthmark on her back. *Same*, as in same-same. An indisputable duplicate.

Objection as to form, Your Honor! Something cannot be deemed indisputable if I would very much like to dispute it.

She hadn't presented an argument, though—to self or others—because Big Deal Number Three diverted her attention away from the birthmark spookiness to something good.

Corky was destined to be some man's salvation—a woman he would *absolutely require* to have a home and happiness.

That was pretty *wow*. Sounded like a dream.

Sounded too good to be true.

Yeah…because…

It was.

The man she was supposed to save from a life of solitude was a *vampire*, and since vampires didn't exist, well…

That erased that.

Although a part of her would like to go back in time and *not* doubt the existence of vampires. Because the gods of Thou Shalt Have Proof If Thou Hath Desire Of It plucked the thought right out of her head and sent proof hurtling her way.

Indisputable proof.

Can I say indisputable *here?*

Oh, yeah, hahahaha, definitely.

Enter, stage left—a man with drooling fangs bent on eating her.

Rub-a-dub-dub, three men in a tub, and who do you think they were? The toughie, the intimidator, the guy who's a troublemaker…

"Why *days*?" Dr. Parthen demanded of Preppy.

He lifted a helpless hand. "For some asinine reason the dope who programmed the original schematic tied the elevators to the drainage system. I have to proceed carefully if I don't want to cut off our water supply, reprogramming the elevator via a backdoor—and hope I don't make any mistakes along the way. It'll take time."

Dr. Parthen pinched the bridge of her nose, maybe taking a calming three-count time-out. When she straightened, she walked toward their group.

Jacken kept pace with her, his focus on Reese.

"I'm sorry," Dr. Parthen said. "I can't transport you out of here right away."

"Bullshit." Reese dropped his arm from Corky's shoulder and gestured at the elevator. "And I mean total bullshit."

Dr. Parthen eyed Reese coolly. "Mr. Terrella, if you're

insinuating that I might have purposely sabotaged my sole means of bringing food and supplies into this community in order to hold a man here who's been nothing but unkind ever since he opened his mouth, then you would be way off the mark." She included them all when she added, "I apologize for this inconvenience. I will do my best to return you to San Diego as soon as possible. In the interim, you can stay in the luxurious bedrooms we promised you in the email we sent about—"

"Um…" Vlad interjected. "No, ma'am, they can't."

Dr. Parthen leveled a look at Vlad.

"Sorry." He grimaced. "The rooms are being painted."

"During an indoctrination?" Dr. Parthen asked this with exaggerated calm, like she was putting a concerted effort into not exploding.

Vlad gestured defensively at their foursome. "They're two days late."

Dr. Parthen now looked at Preppy.

"Er…" A sheepish expression chased across his face. "I guess the postponement didn't get put on the main schedule."

"Not buying it." Reese shook his head.

Dr. Parthen's expression returned to cold and flat.

Well, at least Reese hadn't said *total bullshit* this time.

"I don't believe this shitshow for one second." Reese raked his gaze up and down Dr. Parthen. "You may be a lot of things, lady, but somebody who'd run a slipshod operation ain't one of them."

"You may call me Dr. Parthen, and if you're about to give me a lecture on how to best manage the complexities of this town, I can't wait to hear it."

Jacken growled. "He should be keeping his trap shut." His growl turned into a low snarl and red lights flashed in his eyes.

Corky straightened her spine. *Red lights…*

Dr. Parthen shot Jacken a startled look.

Jacken inhaled a deep breath, shaking himself, and his

eyes cleared.

Dr. Parthen observed him closely.

He made a short, impatient gesture of *never-mind-that*.

Dr. Parthen cleared her throat, then said to Preppy, "All right, Alex, have some sleeping bags brought down here for—"

"Are you serious?" Alex cut in. "You're going to make these guys camp out in a garage for three days?"

"What other choice do I have?"

"Let them go into town."

Dr. Parthen lifted her gaze to the ceiling.

"Yeah, I know," Alex said. "I remember the disaster with Charlize when she was allowed out before she was ready. So I'm not suggesting they go into town *alone*. Assign them each a community buddy who will never leave their sides. That should keep them out of trouble for the next two or three days."

"Forget it," Reese snapped. "That's just what you want us to do. You fucks are probably a bunch of cannibalistic serial killers who think they've lured their next meal down to the crockpot." Reese pointed at a hallway behind the four of them, steel-colored and too long to see where it ended. "I bet it's a fucking bloodbath out there."

A group of muscles bunched in Jacken's jaw. "You know jack and shit about what's going on, Terrella, so shut it."

Reese narrowed his eyes.

"Hold on," Diamond inserted herself into the tension. "I think we need to… Do you mind if I confer with my…" She paused, as if wondering what Reese, Evan, and Corky were to her. "My friends for a moment in private?"

"Of course not." Dr. Parthen smiled. "Take all the time you need. We'll be right over here." She drifted off with Jacken and Alex, the three again manning a spot in front of the elevator.

CHAPTER NINE

CORKY FORMED INTO A CONFIDENTIAL circle with Evan, Reese, and Diamond near the Lincoln Town car that drove them into the oversized elevator that brought them here. The vehicle was still parked in front of a hash-marked loading zone.

Diamond faced them. "Look, nothing's going to come from us getting upset. All right?"

Corky felt herself nod. *Good…good. True.*

Diamond was probably managing to think only good thoughts.

Like Corky should be doing.

Right.

Corky turned her head to focus on Toni, who had her cell phone to her ear and was murmuring into it.

The doctor was a beautiful woman with shoulder-length strawberry-blonde hair and blue eyes—the same sky-blue shade as Corky's.

Dr. Parthen's *eyes,* yes… *Focus there.* Something about them was calming.

I move for Plaintiff's Exhibit A to be introduced into evidence—Dr. Parthen's reasonable mode of speech, her obvious intelligence, and the kindness of her expression (at least when Mr. Reese Terrella isn't annoying her).

This woman wasn't cruel, and she didn't look especially crazy either.

These people might be odd, but they weren't evil.

Diamond continued. "I think we need to calm down and

be logical about all this. And in that vein, I'd like to first point out that if the goal of these people was to hurt us, they could've done it ten different ways by now." Diamond looked at Reese. "What are they waiting for?"

"Fuck sakes," Reese retorted. "They told us they're *vampires*."

"I know," Diamond replied, "and, frankly, that just strengthens my point. Why call themselves vampires if they were up to something? Wouldn't it be better to lull us into a false sense of security by saying they're recruiting us for a curling team or a quilting bee or something like that?"

Reese didn't respond.

So Corky did. "That *does* make sense."

Reese piffed.

Diamond set her hands on her hips and continued to make her case. "We all saw *real* fangs on those two fighting men. Not to mention that one of them had stuff swirling all over his body." She pointed across the garage at Jacken. "*He* has fangs, too."

"So this *is* real." Reese's forehead folded into exaggerated creases. "Jeepers."

"All right," Diamond said in a biting tone. "What about no one in the world ever accepting us—I sure as hell can relate to that." She swung a look across the others. "Can any of you?"

"I repulse people," Corky admitted in a morose tone.

Evan remained quiet, just observing everything as if he was an innocent bystander and not part of it all.

Reese rolled his eyes so high into his head, it was a wonder he didn't tip over. "These assholes could've simply researched our backgrounds and picked people they thought were easy marks. It's part of public record that I went through the foster care system. I bet you have something in your past too."

Diamond's face reddened.

"See?" Reese turned on Corky. "You?"

"I was raised in a group home."

"Hah! Like I said. The moment these guys found out shit like that, they figured they've got fucked-up outsiders, ripe for manipulation. What about you?" Reese aimed at Evan.

Evan hiked a shoulder. "My parents have been together for thirty years and live in an upper middle-class neighborhood. My older brother is married with two kids. My middle brother goes to MIT. You'll never find a more normal and upstanding family than mine."

Reese paused. "Whatever. So maybe there's *one* normal among us. It doesn't mean—"

"Normal *on paper*," Evan cut back in. "I've always been the black sheep of my family. I've never thought about why I didn't fit in." He stuck his hands in his pockets. "Till now."

Diamond went back on the attack. "So maybe the deal is that all of us really are fucked-up outsiders. It's not a matter a record, but of reality."

"Because we're a bunch of Dragons?" Reese scoffed.

"Do you have one of those birthmarks on your back?" Diamond asked in challenge. "The wing or the foot or the nose?"

After a beat of silence, Evan said, "I've got the wing."

Corky raised her hand. "I have the foot."

"The nose." Diamond met Reese's gaze again. "Are you going to come clean or what?"

"Would you people listen to yourselves?" Reese said instead. "A broken elevator? Rooms being painted? It's all a little too convenient, don't you think?"

"Okay," Diamond played along. "Let's say these people are trying to trick us into doing something. What's their endgame? They're not out to swindle money from us. Just the opposite—they're offering us jobs. They're not trying to convince us to do anything illegal. They're—"

"Do you know what you're doing?" Reese interrupted, wagging a finger at her. "You're glossing over all the wrong shit in front of you because you want to belong so much."

Corky winced. *Shit*, that was a direct hit.

"Maybe I am doing that," Diamond acknowledged. "On the other hand, what if everything these people are offering us is true?"

Date some Vârcolac, enjoy yourselves…experience the acceptance here that you've been denied your entire life…

Sounded like a heckuva lot more than Corky could count on in San Diego.

Diamond exhaled. "We don't want to miss the chance to find out because we were too suspicious. Why not at least check out their town?"

Corky nodded again. Situations didn't come more bizarre than this one did with all its Big Deals, but still, giving this town a shot was starting to seem like a better choice than returning to her old life, where nothing had improved. Her professional reputation was mud, her career in ruins. Her personal life was in a shambles, her breakup with Hunter a social media joke.

"I don't see the harm," Diamond added.

"You don't see the *harm*?" Reese laughed at Diamond. "Are you fucking kidding me?"

Diamond's lips pressed together. "If we don't like it, we only have to endure it for three days."

"So they say. Judas Priest—" Reese rounded on Evan. "Help me out here, man."

Evan shrugged. "I don't want to sleep in a garage for three days."

A woman appeared out of the steel hallway, two golden pigtails trailing down the front of her ruffled white blouse. She wore casual beige slacks and flat brown sandals. She was as hugely pregnant as Chelsea from the Q&A panel.

She strode over to Dr. Parthen, and the two exchanged a few quiet words.

Dr. Parthen rested a hand on the pregnant woman's

shoulder and led her over to their group. "This is Hannah."

A man clomped into the garage from the same hallway. "Hey."

He had on thick work boots and coveralls coated in cave dust. Actually, *all* of him was covered in dust—his clothes and shoes, his hair, and his entire face, except for twin ovals around his eyes where he'd clearly been wearing goggles.

"What's going on?" He lifted his cell phone. "I got a text about buddying up with one of the new humans."

"Hi, Fane," Dr. Parthen said. "Thanks for coming. Just give me a second." She turned back to their foursome and went on with her introduction. "Hannah is our community mama bear. She has a house full of kids, a library stocked with books and movies, and she knows everything there is to know about this community. I think she'd make a great buddy for you, Diamond."

Hannah smiled broadly.

"If you're okay with that," Dr. Parthen checked.

Diamond picked up her suitcase. "I'm okay."

"Jesus," Reese muttered. "Anyone ever hear the saying 'divide and conquer'?"

"Alex," Dr. Parthen said to Preppy. "Before Diamond leaves, can you please issue her temporary funds and some mud?"

"Coming right up." Alex swung his backpack off his shoulder.

Corky blinked. "Mud?"

"Special scent-reducing mud," Dr. Parthen explained. "All of you will need to put some behind your ears whenever you go into town."

Alex extracted a plastic credit card from his backpack and handed it to Diamond, making a note in a pocket binder as he did. He also gave her a small ceramic pot stoppered with a cork.

Diamond opened the pot and smudged some mud behind

each ear, then she and Hannah ambled down the steel hallway, chatting pleasantly.

Dr. Parthen turned to Reese. "Fane is your buddy."

"Is he now?" Reese smirked.

Dr. Parthen said to Fane, "I'm going to need you to take the next few days off work to hang out with Reese. You'll still be paid full wages."

"Really?" Fane smiled, his fangs extra-white against the dust on his face. "Cool."

"Lookie at that—" Reese flung his forefinger in the vicinity of Fane's face. "Sharp thingies in your mouth. I guess that means you're a vampire."

"Ah, yeah." Fane nodded. "That's what they tell me."

Reese dropped his hand.

Fane's eyes crinkled.

Reese scanned Fane from head to toe. "Where the hell did you just come from, man?"

"Oh." Fane patted his dirty coveralls, releasing small puffs of dust. "I'm one of the community miners."

Reese hiked an eyebrow at Dr. Parthen. "So you're assigning me a blue-collar buddy, are you? Plan is for us to become best buds, right?"

Dr. Parthen spoke in a neutral tone. "We'd like for your short-term stay with us to be as comfortable as possible, Mr. Terrella."

Jacken crossed thick arms. "Not that you deserve it."

Reese eyed Fane, sucking his teeth. "I'm a nonbeliever. Just so you know."

"Sure, man. That's your right." Fane pointed at Reese's CHARGERS T-shirt. "So you play ball?"

Reese made a noise in the affirmative. "I was headed for a full ride at UCLA, but then"—he tossed a wink at Dr. Parthen—"I fucked the coach's wife."

Who would've thought black eyes could turn so much blacker? But Jacken's did.

"What position?" Fane asked.

"That I fucked the coach's wife in?"

Fane burst out laughing. It was a robust, gregarious sound, and his smile was engaging. Underneath all the dust he was probably a good-looking man.

One corner of Reese's mouth tugged. "Free safety," he said, addressing the real question.

"A man with some *actual* skills, *yes*." Fane swept a finger over his cell screen. "Lemme call Ninza, tell him to get the guys together for a game."

"So you play too? Stupid question. Of couuuurse you do." Reese cut a glance at Dr. Parthen. "We have *so* much in common."

"Do you like beer?" Fane asked, his attention still on his phone.

"Yep."

"Well, if it makes you feel any better about us, I hate beer. Now tequila. That's—" Fane stopped talking. He winced and fidgeted, as if the bottom half of his coveralls were suddenly too tight.

In the next second a gorgeous blond woman stepped into the garage.

She was about Corky's height, mostly all legs too, and had blue eyes, also like Corky's. The woman's honey-colored hair was cut in a layered style that gave it a sassy, carefree quality. Corky had never been tempted to switch from Team Heterosexual, but even *her* belly did a little flip over how beautiful this woman was.

For the first time today, Reese's composure slipped—he looked utterly shocked by her.

"Grab your shit, okay?" Fane muttered to Reese. "So we can get outta here."

Alex held out a credit card and a small mud pot to Reese.

Reese observed the items for a couple of seconds. "Yeah, all right, I'll check out your creepy little town. But *only* if

Frightmare Homey over there"—he nodded at Jacken—"gives me his knife."

Jacken snorted up both nostrils. But other than that he didn't hesitate. He yanked the knife off his belt, sheath and all, and stalked over to Reese. "Any man in this town lets a guy like you get the drop on him, he deserves his injuries."

Reese's lips pushed out in a pout. "Your face." He took the knife from Jacken and accepted the plastic card and mud pot.

He strode off with Fane, the two men making their way down the steel hallway.

Another man stepped into the garage. Dark blond, he was wearing jeans, a red polo shirt, and slip-on topsiders.

This guy glowered at the back of the gorgeous blonde as he sidled past her.

"Ah, this is Shanelon." Toni introduced the polo shirt. "Your buddy, Evan. And Corky, meet Hadley."

Gorgeous Hadley gave Corky a friendly look, meeting Corky's eyes without any wariness, either subtle or blatant. She didn't recoil over Corky's mysterious *bad odor*. No repulsion whatsoever.

This can't be right.

Any second now the theme song for *The Twilight Zone* would start playing.

Except it didn't feel wrong. When Corky shook Hadley's hand, a shock of pleasure surged up her arm.

Hadley's lips parted. She'd felt it too. "It's nice to meet you, Corky."

"Likewise."

They gazed steadily at each other, both their expressions acknowledging some unnamed thing between them.

Then they smiled into each other's eyes.

It was girlfriend-love at first sight.

Chapter Ten

CORKY ALSO FELL INTO INSTA-LOVE with the town of Țărână.

When she and Hadley exited a four-story mansion decorated with wrought iron balconies, Corky found herself standing at the end of a long road made of cave rock, smoothed to a high shine by years of wear—the town's Main Street.

Her jaw dropped.

She hadn't expected the place to be so charming—the slideshow pictures Dr. Parthen showed them hadn't done it justice. Țărână was…well, the most enchanting place you could imagine. A Christmas village. A Norwegian chalet. An elven hideaway. A vacation postcard.

Do you know what you're doing? You're glossing over all the wrong shit in front of you because you want to belong so much.

She certainly didn't want to do that. Although in her defense, she didn't see a single person being used as a blood bag. But still…thinking *only* good thoughts probably wasn't the best way to proceed, not with all the attendant weirdness.

Go slow. Collect data from my surroundings. Keep on the lookout for bloodbaths going on in back alleys.

"Strange, isn't it?" Hadley said.

"Huh?"

"A town underground."

"Uh. Yes. Pretty strange."

They started down Main Street, Corky silently reading the signs as they strolled. *Town Cinema…The TradeMark*

Clothing Store…Aunt Ælsi's Coffee Shop…Teague Sisters' Dance Studio…

Whoa. There was a *dance studio* inside a cave?

Hadley waved at a woman who was visible through the plate glass window. She had copper-colored hair swirled into a bun and a svelte figure…except for the large mound of her belly. Beyond her, there was a spacious room with wood floors and ballet barres lining the walls.

Corky shifted her suitcase from one hand to the other. "How far back does the town go?"

"Oh, a ways. And the community's constantly expanding. Wait till you see our apartment building—it's brand-new and ten stories tall."

Corky glanced up, checking how high the ceiling went. Large lights were mounted at regular intervals.

"There's where I work." Hadley gestured at a four-story building painted a glaring white with an arched portico at the entrance. "The hospital."

There was a *hospital* inside a cave? Okay…she really needed to stop doing that.

"I used to be an event planner," Hadley went on. "But now I'm a nurse's aide. The community wants me to go back to college and earn my full nursing degree—they recently lost their actual nurse—but I can't go topside right now."

"Oh? Why not?"

"There's a woman that…a…a…my real mother. She might be searching for me."

Corky cast Hadley a swift sidelong glance. "You don't want her to find you?" Corky would walk through fire for the chance to meet anyone who was even remotely related to her.

"She's a… She's not a nice person, from what I understand. Uh…well, it's complicated. So what job were you hired for?"

"Legal consultant."

"Oh! You're the new lawyer! Kimberly's super excited to

meet you."

"She is?" Corky couldn't hide her surprise. There wasn't one data point she could think back to, not even a single memory, where anyone had been *super excited* to meet her.

"Kimberly is the community lawyer, but she's way too busy these days." Hadley smiled. "She really needs your help."

"How…that's nice." *Except that Dr. Parthen said I'm only staying for three days.* "I knew a Kimberly in law school. Well, sort of knew—I met her once after she came back to Loyola as a guest lecturer. What's her last name?"

"Stănescu—but that's her married name. I don't know her maiden name." Hadley stopped at a road angling left off the main path. "This is the turnoff to our apartment building, but Kimberly lives just a little way farther down the road. Do you want to meet her now? The sooner you get up to speed on how the law works around here, the better, right?"

"The law's different?"

"Different culture, different laws," Hadley said with a shrug. "The Vârcolac used to be ruled by a king, but ever since Toni became co-leader, the way of governing is more democratic. Kimberly has been on the ground floor of developing new policies and laws to include *all* races and cultures. I'm sure you'll be involved in that too."

A strange ache rushed into Corky's throat. That sounded just like something she'd love to do.

Hadley checked her watch. "It's eight-thirty. Kimberly should be back from her topside job by now. She works at a San Diego law firm too."

"Oh?" *Damn.* Then Kimberly might've heard about Corky's epic fail in court against Rand Resources.

Hadley aimed straight, leaving Corky no choice but to follow.

They walked into a short tunnel, coming to another fork in the road.

Hadley gestured brusquely toward the left path. "Don't

go down there. It's a bad part of town."

There was a *bad part of town* in a Christmas village?

They headed right.

In a few more feet they exited the tunnel, the cave open-ing up to a high-ceilinged space that'd been transformed into a—

Corky started gawking again. "This place is *impossible*." Talk about a charming postcard. The space had been transformed into a welcoming neighborhood of single-family homes, each house painted a different color—light blue, soft green, mellow yellow, others—but all with a white picket fence enclosing a yard landscaped in a neat and homey way.

"I wasn't expecting to see so many plants," Corky said. "How do they grow down here? Are the ceiling lights sunlamps?"

"All the plants are fake. Vampires are allergic to sunlight."

"Uh, yeah…um, of course…" *Vampires*. "That makes sense."

Hadley smiled. "I'm sure it doesn't right now—you're still in freakout mode. But eventually it will."

More than freakout mode, Corky felt like she was floating through a dream. Maybe she never woke up this morning. Maybe she was still in a haze from her Manhattan binge two nights ago. "It's difficult to imagine a day when vampires and Dragons who live in a quaint town built a half mile below the surface of the earth are the norm."

Hadley laughed. "I know. But that day comes."

"How long did it take you to adjust?"

"Oh…any day now." Hadley chuckled. "Just joking. Although kind of not. I mean, I'm not adjusting to the town. More like I'm just plain *adjusting*."

"To what?"

Hadley hefted a breath. "About five months ago I found out some freaky stuff about my family, and it changed my life. I'm still trying to work it out, and I…I haven't yet."

Corky was about to ask *Freaky, how?* but Hadley turned up the steps of a house painted lime green.

"Here we are." Hadley knocked. "Kimberly's married to a community warrior."

A moment later a tall, blond man opened the door.

His long hair was caught in a man bun, revealing a massive set of shoulders—his white T-shirt was stretched to capacity over large, well-shaped muscles. A blond boy of about five was propped on his hip.

"Hi, Sedge." Hadley reached out and gave the young boy an affectionate pinch on his knee. "Hey, Breuse." Back to Sedge. "This is Corky. She's the new lawyer, and I thought it might be nice to introduce her to Kimberly. Is now a good time?"

"Yeah, no problem. We're just getting the kids breakfast." Sedge smiled at Corky. Fangs again. "Nice to meet you." He shifted his son from his right hip to his left hip so he could shake Corky's hand. "Kimberly's in the kitchen—working, actually."

They stepped into a living room of book-lined walls and light gray, deep pile carpet. There were two armchairs and a sofa, the overstuffed couch taking up most of the space—no doubt big Sedge's roosting spot. Besides a wall-mounted flat screen TV, family pictures made up most of the hanging decorations.

Opposite the front door there was a pass-through between the kitchen and the living room. Corky spotted a woman sitting at a four-seater dinette table. Off her left elbow, a blond girl of about seven months was in a high chair, a bowl of mushy cereal in front of her, although she was currently drinking whatever was in a sippy cup—milk to judge by the runoff.

The woman was writing on a yellow legal pad but paused and glanced up when Corky and Hadley stepped just inside the pass-through and stopped beside a refrigerator, a behemoth appliance—probably necessary to feed big Sedge—which blocked the rest of the kitchen.

The woman's blond hair was fashioned into a smart bob, and—*oh, my God!* "Kimberly Wilson!" Corky exclaimed. "I can't believe it's you!" Although she looked exactly the same.

Kimberly's eyebrows flew up.

"You and I were at Loyola together," Corky reminded her.

Sedge angled into the kitchen, moving to set his son Breuse in a booster seat beside the high chair.

"I mean, we didn't *go* to school together," Corky clarified. "You were long graduated by the time I was a first-year, but you came back in 2010 to give a lecture on the First Amendment—you'd just won a major case on that. I talked to you afterward. I don't know if you remember me. I'm Corky Disdale. Catherine."

Kimberly came to her feet. "I do remember, actually."

"You do?" Corky grinned from ear to ear. Kimberly Wilson was one of Loyola Law School's rock stars.

Sedge opened a cupboard to the left of the sink.

"We talked briefly," Kimberly said, "but you stood out."

"I did?" Tears caught in Corky's throat. An utterly ridiculous reaction, but this was the first happy moment she'd experienced in many hours. *Days.*

"Where's the potato bread Breuse likes?" Sedge asked.

"Right cupboard." Kimberly pointed to it while continuing to Corky, "We didn't talk about anything special, so at the time I wasn't sure why I was drawn to you. Now I can see it's because you're a Dragon. Like I am."

"Oh, ah… Yeah." The smile fell off Corky's face. So much for a happy moment.

A Dragon.

Kimberly Wilson had called Corky a *Dragon.*

Sedge found the potato bread and dropped a slice into a toaster on the counter.

Corky opened her mouth. Nothing came out. Well, air did—in a stream. And maybe the tip of her tongue poked out a bit.

If Loyola's rock star said Corky was a Dragon, then…then…

"Holy crap! This is *real!*" Corky staggered sideways.

"Hadley!" Kimberly made a hurry-up gesture, the pen still in her hand. "Help her sit down."

Hadley took Corky by the elbow and urged her toward a chair at the dinette.

When they stepped past the large refrigerator, a man came into view.

He was leaning against the kitchen sink, a coffee mug in his hand. He had long black hair and circular tattoos on his—

Corky went rigid. It was the *thing* that'd attacked her!

The bread popped up from the toaster with a sharp *tusht!*

Corky gasped.

The baby's sippy cup fell out of her little hands and hit the high chair tray.

Bamp!

Corky clutched her throat.

The long-haired man lifted his coffee mug to her in cautious greeting.

She shrieked.

Chapter Eleven

10 minutes earlier

SEDGE STĂNESCU, A MIXED-BREED VÂRCOLAC with long blond hair—longer, even, than the length Vasile wore his hair—strode up to Vasile and handed him a mug of coffee.

"Here, Lazăr, drink this."

"My thanks to you." Vasile accepted the mug with a hand wracked by tremors from the leftover shock of his pig-ass of an ankle band. His knees also still felt a bit like watery potage. Moving a few steps back, he propped his bum against the washbasin in the Stănescu kitchen.

"Breuse!" called Sedge up the stairwell. "Come down for breakfast, buddy."

"I'm stuck in my shirt!"

Sedge glanced at his mate.

Kimberly Stănescu was a solicitor of law. She had summoned Vasile here to her home to gather facts about the skirmish Vasile engaged in this morning with Vinz Mihnea.

Now Kimberly-Solicitor smiled at Sedge with sentimental warmth. She told him, "Breuse has trouble when the buttons are small."

Sedge shared a moment of affection for their son, holding the gaze of his mate.

Vasile could not recall his father and mother ever looking at each other thusly. The two had not been enemies or acted in a hateful manner toward one another, but Lucien and Cătălina had been little more than civil acquaintances. Now that Vasile was learning about the mated union, it seemed this was a very tragic way to live. So many mated couples in this community were *not* like his father and mother.

"All right, buddy," Sedge called out as he trotted up the stairs. "Hold on, I'm coming."

Kimberly looked at Vasile again. "Continue." She hovered her writing instrument over paper the color of a banana. "At what point did you determine Vinz had gone into a procreation glaze-out?"

Vasile sipped his coffee. It was like brown water compared to the Turkish-style coffee he drank back home in Transylvania. "On-duty Protectors got call at half past the seventh hour."

Kimberly-Solicitor noted this on the yellow paper, her writing instrument making a light scratching noise, like cricket feet on parchment.

While he waited for the next query, Vasile observed the girl-child seated in a chair with a plastic table attached to it. The babe was drinking from a strange cup, also plastic with a lid on it, a protrusion on the lid. The girl-child was sucking on the protrusion, making slurping noises equal to those of a lumber worker.

"What were you told?" asked Kimberly.

Vasile downed more coffee. "Report came that Vinz was trying to have the sexual intercourse with Lidanna."

"Where?"

"In street. In front of—" His spine convulsed, and he slopped coffee onto his hand.

"Kimberly Wilson! I can't believe it's you!"

Vasile ground his teeth together as the clutching sensations began anew—hot, grabby fists in his belly, beneath his man-balls, and up through his arsehole. He lost his next breath.

She was standing in the archway…

The glowing woman.

Flesh as fair as a shiny pearl…eyes the blue of a cornflower…hair like gold-dyed silk. Her body was…her breasts were…her bottom…

Lightning forked along sensitive, vibrant trackways in his mind, making his skull twitch beneath his hair. A throb surged up his pole.

"You and I were at Loyola together," said the glowing woman.

Sedge entered the kitchen and situated his boy-child in a chair with a padded box on it.

"__ mean, ___ didn't *go* to ___ together," continued the glowing woman, but Vasile had lost the capability to translate English. "___ were long ___ by the time ___ was a first-year, ___ ___ came back in 2010 to ___ a ___ on the ___ ___— ___ just won a ___ ___ on that. ___ talked to ___ ___. ___ don't know if ___ remember ___. ___ Corky ___. ___."

Vasile felt his fangs slide down.

"*Sit.*" This command Dev had given to Vasile right after pulling him off the glowing woman in the parlor room.

His fangs were elongated then too.

Dev had rushed Vasile into the room of lockers and forced him to sit on a long-seat with a hand on his shoulder.

"If you damned well don't learn to control yourself," said Dev, a hand still on his shoulder, "you'll never get that fucking shocker band off."

Gábor stood behind Dev, observing everything through narrowed eyelids.

Gábor once told the four Moon-Riders who were selected to audition for the Warrior Class that they would have to travel a long path to earn his acceptance. But since Gábor looked cross most of the time, it was difficult to tell if Vasile, Nicolae, Bujor, and Enric *had* traversed that road over the past five months.

Vasile kept his focus on Dev. "Make stop." The grabbing sensations…the forked lightning…

Dev did not oblige. "*You* make it stop."

Vasile felt his fangs clatter against his bottom teeth. Like a steel bear trap, his mind sprang shut around the image of that Dragon male with false black hair staggering to his feet after being shocked, then putting his arm around the glowing woman. As if *he* was her protector.

Her man.

Vasile lost his vision under a drenching of red.

Dev continued to speak as if from a deep well. "Try doing what ___ from going ___. Focus on different... Hey! Are you ___ to me?"

Vasile gaped his mouth open, thrust his fangs forward, and sent an unholy snarl boiling up his throat.

Only half made it out before Dev squeezed his shoulder—hard. "<Control yourself. Try do what half-demons do to stop from go Rău. Different scents are the focus. Anything but her.>"

Dev was studying the Romanian language along with others in the community, and he must have the old country in his blood because he was taking to the language with great speed.

"She glow." Vasile told Dev this in a voice scratchy as tree bark.

"Not to me she doesn't." Dev glanced over his shoulder at Gábor. "Does she glow to you?"

Gábor exhaled. "Lazăr's in big trouble, man."

The woman did not actually glow to Vasile, either, but such was the only way he could think to describe her. There were no common words available to define what she was like.

"She's special to you," explained Dev. "You're going to have to work hard at controlling yourself around her."

Vasile wiped coffee off the back of his hand on the rear part of his dark jeans pants, then lifted the mug to his mouth and pretended to drink while really taking in the earthy scent of coffee. He inhaled twice, then checked his fangs. They had retracted some, but not all the way.

He kept his lips together as he gazed at the glowing woman—Corky, she had just named herself—and tried to produce the word "hello." This was what a man was supposed to say to a woman he liked. This was what socialization class had taught the Moon-Riders. After "hello," a man should then try to engage the woman he liked in discussion.

What manner of discussion?

Vasile did not know.

For his whole life his dealings with women had consisted of issuing orders. No conversation was exchanged.

Just commands given.

Just feedings taken at the sole will of the man.

This was bad behavior—another thing socialization class had taught the Moon-Riders.

But Vasile *felt* this now too. At a blood level. Deep in his bones.

The changes wrought by sex education class had transformed his view, as if Uriaş, the mythical giant, had reached down a hand and painted all women gold. Not in color.

In value.

It made him care about upsetting females—female upset created more lightning in the brain, but a different kind. Painful, troubling wrongness.

Earlier in that parlor room, Vasile scared Corky, and this sat ill with him. Drives beyond his reckoning ruled him at the time, true, but this was a reasoning he should not use to excuse what he did. Like Dev instructed, Vasile needed to control himself. Although his newly enlivened pole made control difficult—it kept trying to drag him across the room toward Corky. And once he was next to her, he would push his hips forward and press his pole against her.

This was also bad behavior.

After sex education had changed the Moon-Riders into true men, several of them pressed their poles against women in town.

This was not received well.

Socialization class immediately taught the Moon-Riders in the strictest terms that they should not do this. Not unless invited to do so.

A difficult decree to follow for a breed of man accustomed to doing whatever he wanted to women, whenever he wanted.

So further incidents of uninvited pole-pressing occurred.

It was this, plus a couple of near-bite disasters—with Laurenţiu and Tudor forgetting themselves and grabbing women on the street to feed—that earned the Moon-Riders their shocker bands.

Every unmated female, as well as the town leaders and the warriors, carried a device able to stimulate the bands to activation. Toni had enchanted the shockers to react solely to males, so if a Moon-Rider was in any way touching a female when the band went off, the female would not be hurt.

Hatful things, those shockers.

But in all truth, Vasile had no idea what he would have done to Glowing Corky in the parlor room today if not for the firebolt of pain hindering him.

There was, admittedly, another benefit of the shocker bands. As soon as the Moon-Riders donned them, the town females once again were not afraid to talk to them.

Except that Vasile could not think of a single deviled thing to say.

He could not even summon the word "hello" out of his mouth now.

"This is *real!*"

Vasile frowned over the noise of fright Corky made and abruptly pushed off the wash basin when she staggered her footing.

"Hadley!" Kimberly-Solicitor gestured at the Dragon-Witch. "Help her sit down."

The Dragon-Witch urged Corky to move forward, but Corky stopped of a sudden and made large eyes at him.

Since he could not inspire his tongue to produce "hello," he lifted his coffee mug to her.

This generated an astounding reaction.

Corky screamed as loud as a Muma Pădurii, witch of the forest.

This startled the girl-child, and she began to weep.

Vasile squinted against the hectic lightning in his head.

The Dragon-Witch helped Corky to sit at the table while Kimberly hoisted her girl-child up from the chair-and-table and hugged the querulous baby against her breasts, patting the little one on the back.

"What's wrong?" asked Kimberly of Corky.

"That man tried to eat me." Corky pointed a rigid finger at Vasile.

CHAPTER TWELVE

I TRIED TO…? VASILE FROWNED. *What did I attempt to do?* He strained his mind back to the parlor-room episode, but he had been in a predatory fugue and so could not summon a picture that was wholly clear.

"He…he…" Corky kept pointing at him, even though there were only two men in the kitchen, and it seemed obvious to Vasile that there could be little confusion about which of the two of them had manhandled her.

In the end her pointed finger produced the desired re-sult—everyone looked at him.

Heat seared up his nape, and his stomach traveled into his boots. He braced himself for the shunning to come.

But Kimberly-Solicitor addressed the accusation with astonishment, not disapproval. "*Vasile?*" Her tone proclaimed her opinion of him in this matter—Vasile Lazăr was a man who could not even speak to a woman. Why would he attack one?

Except for the need to press his pole against Corky and drink down the ecstasy of her blood.

Kimberly glanced at Sedge. "Do you know anything about this?"

"Yeah." Sedge nodded. "All the warriors received a flash report about this morning's incident. When Vinz Mihnea went into a procreation glaze-out, it took three warriors—and Vasile was one of them—to pull Vinz off Lidanna." Sedge placed a piece of toast slathered with butter and berry jam in front of his boy-child. "Once Mihnea's mind cleared, he ran off. Vasile pursued. The chase brought the two men into the mansion's Garden Parlor where the indoc was going on. Mihnea resisted arrest, and while Vasile was in the middle of an intense fight, his bloodlust up, he lunged at her."

Sedge turned to speak to Corky. "But Vasile wasn't trying to *eat* you. He was trying to bite you, yeah, but that wouldn't have killed you or 'turned' you. I know it seemed scary, but most Vârcolac males can and do control their urges. Lazăr was just caught up in the fight when he reacted to your scent."

"My scent?" Corky jerked forward in her chair. "So I *do* stink."

"Stink? Hell, no. You, uh… Vasile scenting you means…" Sedge cut a swift look at Vasile.

Vasile dropped his focus to his coffee. *It means you are mine.*

She's special to you, Vasile…

Kimberly now addressed the Dragon-Witch Hadley. "Why wouldn't Corky know any of this?"

"Corky's group is being indoctrinated differently," answered Hadley. "None of them have read the manual yet. Instead they're being let out in town with escorts."

Kimberly lifted her eyebrows high. "Well…hmm. Okay. You'll hear more later, Corky. For now I can vouch for Vasile as being a totally nice guy."

It took some moments for Vasile to comprehend Kimberly. He understood her English words well enough. It was the endorsement of his character that required slow gradients of speed to accept. He was too used to being shunned for the taint of humanness in his blood—fearing a shunning was his automatic response.

But here in Ţărână his blood was not considered stained. There were many human beings in this town, as well as half-breed Vârcolac. A man was judged on the quality of his actions, not his ancestry. Vasile had seen this to be true thus far, but it was still taking time for him to acquire the habit of truly believing it.

Kimberly nodded toward him as she explained matters further to Corky. "Vasile is here this morning giving me details about today's incident. Vinz Mihnea—the man taken into custody—was arrested for breaking the community's no-fraternization law."

"No-fraternization…?" Corky paused. "So Lidanna is Vinz's subordinate?"

Kimberly looked confused for several moments, then her expression cleared. "Ah! No. I'm not talking about a boss-versus-underling thing. In this town, Vârcolac are prohibited from associating with other Vârcolac—at least in a romantic sense."

"You're kidding." Corky raised her brows. "Why?"

"Oh, it's complicated—the reasons are tied to a very sad history." Kimberly rocked her girl-child, even though the baby was no longer crying. "As cases go, it would make an interesting first one for you to work on with me."

For some reason, this suggestion made Corky flush a light shade of pink.

"Oops," said Sedge when his boy-child fumbled the jellied toast—it stuck to the chest part of the shirt the boy wore. "New shirt time, buddy." Sedge swept up his son.

"No buttons," said the boy to his father.

"No buttons," agreed Sedge, exiting the kitchen.

Kimberly situated her girl-child back in the chair-and-table, then she also aimed for the archway that led from the kitchen to the living room. "Let me pop upstairs and grab you a legal pad and pen so you can take notes." She called back over her shoulder to the Dragon-Witch, "Hadley, would you mind feeding Chally her cereal?"

"I'd love to." Hadley claimed the chair Kimberly had vacated and angled it toward the baby. Cooing, the Dragon-Witch started to deliver spoonfuls of pap to the mouth of the little one.

Now it was just Vasile and Corky, staring at each other, and Hadley, making absurd noises while failing to install most of the pap into the mouth of the girl-child. The rest went onto her chin. Much food plopped onto the plastic table, and Vasile did not understand the wastefulness of such a feeding process.

Long, unbearable moments of silence passed.

Vasile made sure to sip his coffee with slow and non-threatening lifts of his hand, so as to make himself appear agreeable and thus lend credence to the valued assessment Kimberly gave him as a "totally nice guy."

Corky observed him warily, clearly still unsure of him despite the assurances given.

Now would be a good time to commence a discussion.

While butchering a deer, be careful not to catch your blade on a bone. You could break the haft that way…

He did not tell her this, even though it was sound advice.

The Dragon-Witch glanced at him. "Why don't you get Corky a cup of coffee, Vasile?" Hadley spooned more food. "Take my advice, Corky. Drink lots of coffee today and press straight through this first night. You'll adjust to the time change right away if you do."

Vasile did not wait for Corky to respond in the affirmative about the drink. He crossed to the coffee machine. It was placed next to the machine that toasted slices of bread. Better to serve her coffee than say something foolish. Or say nothing.

He was doing the latter, anyway.

He poured coffee from a glass pot into a ceramic mug, then brought it to Corky.

"Thank you." She stood to accept the mug from him.

She wore pants.

The pants were not exceptionally close-fitting but still showed the area where her woman parts were located—a flat area without pole and man-balls.

Vasile stared there. His gut twisted.

What would her woman parts look like?

He had only seen one woman in a naked state—in sex education class when the town medical man presented moving pictures of sexual intercourse to the Moon-Riders.

The woman Vasile observed up on the film board had a pink, supple-looking hole with fleshy folds around it.

Strange at first…

… Turned mesmerizing after his change into a true man.

Upon first glance, these folds appeared delicate. But when they were called upon to perform the act of sexual intercourse, they became capable, it seemed, of wrapping around a pole with a great degree of strength.

Vasile tightened his hand around the handle of his coffee mug.

Did all woman parts look the same? Since he had only seen the one, he could not be sure if they came with small variances. Did all grasp a pole with an identical level of power? What would it feel like to have Corky grip his pole with her woman parts?

He jerked his chin in, balking at the strange idea. Maybe pain would be involved in the process. For gracious sake, his pole was not made of leather hide. The strong suctioning that woman parts were capable of might—

Corky was standing very still.

He shifted his focus up from the crotch area of her pants to her face.

She wore a composed expression, but he could tell—by something in her eyes—that she knew what he was thinking about, and of course she could tell where he had been staring. He sensed that her unnatural stillness indicated she was merely tolerating his inspection rather than finding pleasure in it.

Did that mean *imagining* pole-pressing a woman was as ill-behaved as *doing* the uninvited pole-pressing itself?

Socialization class had never made a distinction between the two.

Shame nevertheless flooded his neck with heat.

He had behaved badly again.

"I sorry." He set down his mug. "For all." He hurried for the door. "Tell Kimberly I finish give more evidence later."

Chapter Thirteen

Moving with long strides that made his shocker band thump the top of his boot, Vasile entered one of the town dwellings that offered prepared food. This one was named "diner" and was decorated with non-color pictures of people in old-fashioned garb and motor vehicles of a bygone era.

Lining the walls were cushioned bench seats of a brick color set on either side of rectangular tables. On the far side of the establishment a line of steel stool-seats were positioned before a long counter-table. Beyond the counter was a spacious kitchen where food was prepared by a man in grubby white clothing and a comically tall white hat.

Other community establishments that offered prepared food for purchase were the pub of Garwald and the restaurant of Three Friends. Also, the bowling alley provided some basic drinks and "snack grub." Food could also be concocted in a house kitchen, of course.

Whenever his stomach grumbled with hunger, Vasile stopped in place and did not know how to proceed for a moment of time. Having so many choices was a peculiarity and a struggle. Back home, all meals were cooked by the un-women—no, he must not call them that anymore—the *Vârcolac* women, and served in a large dining hall in the Manor House at a designated time. The food was simple but wholesome fare, and no decisions were required as to accompanying "condiments," or if sauces should be on the meal itself or put to the side of it, or whether meat should arrive on the plate bloody or not so bloody.

Sometimes he considered skipping a meal rather than muddling over where to consume it, but his hunger did not allow this.

The diner-facility was very full of patrons, and Vasile had to scan the vicinity twice to find a grouping of warriors. Gábor and Dev sat on one side of a rectangular table, Jacken and Thomal on the other. Remnants of breakfast meals were on plates before them.

Vasile strode toward these four men, mostly interested in discussing his worrisome thoughts with Dev.

Devid Nichita was his best friend and had been since Vasile decided to stay in the community.

Dev was a man of upstanding character.

Proof of such lay in how Dev responded to the abhorrent act the Moon-Riders perpetrated against him five months past.

As payment toward a blood debt for the sins of Grigore Nichita, the father of Dev, the Moon-Riders whipped Dev for two nights straight, lashing him nigh unto death. On the third night a band of community fighters arrived to save Dev, and in the process of rescuing him they killed and wounded many Moon-Riders.

Of the Moon-Riders who survived, Dev insisted that the injured be transported to Țărână to receive medical care. Dev could have walked away and left his enemy to die, but instead he chose the path of forgiveness.

He even demanded that others forgive them.

On the morning after jobs were assigned, the four Moon-Riders who were invited to audition for the Warrior Class reported to a space named "locker room," an enclosure furnished with two rows of tall, narrow metal closets with steel long-seats set before them. This room of lockers smelled strongly of fusty sweat.

In front of some of these metal closets, other fighting men were already present, busily changing from street garb into attire made of stretchy black material.

Dev Nichita was at a metal closet farthest from the main door.

Sedge Stănescu started a conversation among the men with an odd mention of horse fodder. "Hay," said Sedge, donning a shirt as he turned to Thomal, another half-breed, but with blond hair that was short. "Kimberly really ___ the ___ you painted of Toni and Shaw. She wanted ___ to ask ___ if ___ could do ___ of her and Breuse."

Before Thomal could respond, Gábor interjected himself in a drawling tone. "___ have to see if ___ ___ fit it in between ___ and ___ ___ his new pants."

Some men chuckled while Thomal scoffed. "___ going to give ___ shit for ___ when this ___ fuck ___ wine?" Thomal jerked a thumb toward Dev.

Dev laughed low in his throat, hitching his shorts on. "___ not the ___ under the ___ of a woman who doesn't even ___ ___ at a hundred pounds."

Gábor whipped a shirt out of his metal closet. "___ seen my wife when ___ pissed. She's fucking ___."

Breen, his black hair concealing part of one golden eye, slung a hand over the top of his metal closet door. "Would that be ___ ___ your wife is doing ___ ___ to ___ or other times too?"

All the warriors broke into loud laughter.

Vasile, Nicolae, Bujor, and Enric stood in a line and stared at the other men.

Jacken Brun stalked into the room of lockers. He was a man who always seemed to move in the circle of his own ominous power.

He was the man who cut down Vasile on the night the community fighters came to rescue Dev Nichita in the greenwood—at least Vasile was reasonably certain Jacken inflicted the near-fatal injury. The community fighters moved with blurring speed that evening.

Jacken handed Vasile, Nicolae, Bujor, and Enric each a stack of stretchy black clothing. "Find an ___ ___."

Vasile looked at Nicolae.

"<Find an empty locker,>" translated his brother.

Vasile turned his mouth down. "<A what?>"

Nicolae gestured at the metal closets.

Enric asked Nicolae, "<What, by the pits of hell, were these men saying a moment ago?>"

"<Ah. Well, this one>"—Nicolae pointed at Sedge—"<wants that one>"—he shifted his pointer finger to Thomal—"<to paint a portrait of some people named Kimberly and Breuse. And that one>"—he shifted over to Gábor—"<butted in to say Thomal will have to see if he can fit it in between pedicures and blopping about his new pants.>"

"<Blogging,>" corrected Bujor. He understood much of English too.

"<What's blogging?>" asked Nicolae.

"<I do not know,>" admitted Bujor.

The community warriors had gone quiet and were now staring at the four of them.

Enric wanted to know, "<Why did they laugh?>"

"<I'm not sure. But that one>"—Nicolae pointed at Thomal again—"<responded to Gábor by saying 'you're going to give me shit,'—shit is cow dung—'for painting, when this snobby fuck slurps wine?'>" Now Nicolae indicated Dev Nichita.

Gábor scowled.

"<Dev Nichita responded with a comment about not being under the pinky of a woman who doesn't even clock in at a hundred pounds.>" Nicolae frowned. "<I think he said 'clock.' I don't know what weight and timepieces have to do with each other. But he>"—Nicolae pointed at Gábor again, who was now looking murderous—"<defended himself with a comment about his wife being scary when she's pissed.>"

"<Drunk,>" clarified Bujor.

"<No,>" corrected Nicolae. "<In American English *pissed* means angry. Breen then asked, 'Would that be only when she's doing butt stuff to you or other times as well?' And afterward all the men laughed.>"

"<I don't understand,>" said Enric, his face clouded.

Neither did Vasile. "<You must have misheard.>"

Nicolae shrugged. "<Maybe.>" He addressed the group of community fighting men, switching to English. "___ have desire to ___what is butt stuff? Is when—?"

Snarling, Gábor lunged at Nicolae and grabbed him by the throat, slamming him back into the wall.

"Pavenic!" barked Dev.

Gábor glared. "___ the fuck are these ___ ___ here, anyway, after everything ___ ___ in the forest?"

"That's over," said Dev. "___ are one of us now."

"Not to me ___ not," snarled Gábor. "___ have a long ___ to go before I ___ ___."

Dev closed the metal door on his closet and moved toward Gábor.

The other fighting men made way for him.

Nicolae was beginning to turn blue in the face.

Vasile surged forward and seized the arm that restrained his brother, jerking it off.

Gábor rounded on Vasile, his upper lip contorted into a snarl. He cocked back his fist.

Blow oncoming. Battle vision snapped into place, and Vasile now saw Gábor through an array of sharp, concentrated, and defined squares, the image of his opponent centralized.

"Stop!" ordered Dev.

Gábor did not stop. He took an aggressive step forward.

Vasile felt his fangs spring out. He moved forward too.

"I ___ stop it." Dev now spoke in an even sharper tone.

Jacken watched everything with crossed arms and a penetrating stare.

Gábor pointed a rigid finger at Vasile. "___ unsheathed!"

"___ doesn't ___ ___ better," said Dev, then he addressed the other men. "Listen—"

He gave a speech.

Nicolae had to translate it for them later, but this was what Dev Nichita said:

"These men are Vârcolac, *our* people. *We* asked *them* to join us with the promise that they would have equality and acceptance and a fair chance at making a better life for themselves. We need to stand by our word. If any of you have a personal problem with these men, that's one thing. But if you're holding a grudge because of what they did to me in the forest"—Dev regarded Gábor with extra meaning—"*don't.* Ever since I found out it was *my* father who betrayed our breed, I've been… I haven't been right."

Dev breathed in deeply. "But now I've paid a blood debt. I sacrificed a pound of my flesh and then some toward cleansing the Nichita name and myself. No one can say otherwise. I have a back full of scars to prove it." He looked at individual men as he spoke their names. "Thomal, Breen, Gábor, I know what you saw me go through five months ago was fucked up."

Five months past, the Moon-Riders had strung up the men Dev just named and forced them to watch the agonizing whipping.

"But," concluded Dev, "I'm asking you to move past it."

Glances were exchanged around the room of lockers.

Breen shrugged a single shoulder; Thomal exhaled from both nostrils; Gábor maintained a narrow and hot regard for everyone.

Dev shifted over to Vasile and set a strong hand on his shoulder.

Vasile stood stiffly.

"These men freed me." Dev gave Vasile a staunch nod.

No rancor lived in Dev.

The rigidity all over Vasile moved into his throat.

Jacken broke the silence. "Anyone have anything ___ ___ ___before ___ ___ ___to fucking work?"

Breen, a quiet-mannered man in most respects, stepped forward and punched Enric in the face.

Enric lost his feet and toppled over, hitting the hard, cold floor in a way that appeared very bone-jarring.

Nicolae and Bujor gaped down at Enric.

Enric massaged his jaw and blinked up at Breen.

Breen glanced through his hair at the other fighting men. "This is the ___ ___ hit me at the ___ house the night ___ took Dev and ___ to the forest."

Breen offered Enric a hand up.

"Anything ___?" drawled Jacken.

"No. ___ good," said Breen.

It was over.

Because of Dev Nichita.

Because from the start Dev had withstood torture from the Moon-Riders with nothing but forgiveness in his heart.

Such a man merited loyal regard.

It was just such a man of honor that Vasile had sought as a friend and mentor for the last decade, ever since the most worthy man in the world was stolen from him.

Ever since his father was killed by the scurvy witch, Savatina.

On that fateful night, the loathsome witch first struck down Vasile, incapacitating him so he could do naught to save Lucien.

The shame of it was like a canker growing deep in his soul.

After his father was killed, Vasile had no one of strong character to emulate, and he faltered in his life.

But now he had Dev Nichita, a man of noble character, to help motivate him toward his own rightness.

CHAPTER FOURTEEN

VASILE HALTED AT THE DINER table the warriors occupied, and all four men regarded him with expressions of greeting.

"You okay, Lazăr?" asked Jacken.

Vasile lowered his brows. Was the tugging sensation Corky had wrought in his pole obvious? "For why?"

Gábor made a horse-snort. "Because the shock from your ankle band looked like it blew chunks."

To blow chunks was a slang term for *to vomit*. But Vasile did not recall heaving up food following the shock of his band. Had he? "I fine."

Thomal pushed his dirtied plate away. Thomal Costache looked like a jaunty coxcomb, but he was in truth a very dangerous man and, at times, hot-of-blood. "Dev was just telling us what a fucking shart today's panel was."

Vasile looked at Dev. "Sorry to be disturbing of that."

"Nah," said Dev. "The situation was fucked long before you and Vinz showed." He drank some coffee. "So how did it go with Kimberly?"

"We no finish. She came and I left."

"Who came?"

"The glowing woman."

"You mean Corky?"

"Yes."

Jacken finished the last of his coffee. "You can take my place, Lazăr." He stood. "I have a meeting with Toni to—" His eyes flared red and a snarl boiled out of him.

Vasile took a quick step away.

Jacken hissed, then sucked in a long breath. His eyes cleared.

"Whoa, Jacken," exclaimed Dev. "What the fuck?"

"I don't know, dammit." Jacken firmed his lips. "My Rău has been slipping past my control lately and at the most illogical times. I have no idea why."

"That's weird," mused Thomal. "The same thing's been happening to Pandra." Pandra was mate to Thomal, and her bloodlines contained a portion of demon, same as Jacken.

"I don't need weird in my life right now." Jacken checked the timepiece on his wrist. "Shit, now I'm late for my meeting with Toni." He turned and stalked off.

Gábor watched Jacken leave. "Does anyone else think 'meeting with Toni' really means Jacken's gone off to bang his woman?"

To bang was a slang term for *to have sexual intercourse.* As were the terms *screw, boink, bone, pork, get laid, plow, ride, get busy,* and *fuck.* Although *fuck* was also used liberally for many language purposes. Vasile had also heard *bump uglies* and *lay pipe,* but these were too strange to accept.

Dev showed Vasile his mug. "You want some coffee?"

Vasile sat in the vacated seat as offered. "Good."

Dev lifted his mug in the direction of someone behind Vasile, then aimed the mug at Vasile.

Vasile shifted his rear end on the bench seat. "I like."

"You like what?" asked Dev.

"The glowing woman. Corky."

"Ah, yeah." The partial beard Dev wore split with a grin. "That's kind of obvious."

"My pole… It has throbs when she is near."

Thomal ducked his head and smiled into his coffee.

Gábor pushed air out of the sides of his mouth, making his lips move about. "Christ, Lazăr. How many times I gotta tell you not to call it a pole. It's a *cock.*"

"I care not what you instruct, Gábor Pavenic. I will not

name my appendage after a rooster. I know not why you do."

Thomal chuckled.

Dev waved the two to silence. "What else do you like about her?"

"What else?" This was a confusion. "Everything about Corky affects my pole."

"There's more to a woman than what she can do to your pole."

Gábor guffawed.

Vasile glanced over.

"Don't look at me." Gábor showed Vasile a hand palm. "I don't agree."

Dev made a noise from his throat. "Ignore Pavenic. He's crazy about his roly-poly wife."

"Roly-poly?" repeated Vasile. "What means this?"

"Yeah," said Gábor. "I'd like to know that too."

Dev twisted his lips. "Have you seen how pregnant Chelsea is?"

"She's *all* belly," added Thomal in agreement.

"Bah." Gábor blew air forcefully again. "She's tiny. She can't help it."

A waitress dressed in a pink skirt under a white apron that was purfled along the hemline with lace brought a mug of coffee to the table. She set it in front of Vasile.

Vasile nodded to her.

"Thanks, Tillza," said Dev.

"My pleasure." The aproned woman picked up the be-fouled dishes, taking them with her when she left.

Vasile tasted the coffee. It was better here than what Sedge served. "What else is woman to man?"

"She's everything." Dev gave the coffee in his mug a pensive swirl. "She's companionship. She's warmth and understanding. She's the one person who'll know you better than you know yourself. She's connection to...a larger part of yourself, actually."

Gábor lolled his tongue out. "I think I just barfed in my mouth."

Dev ignored Gábor. "And to our breed, she's the second half of you."

Tillza arrived at the table with a pot of coffee. "Can I top you boys off?" She started pouring more drink.

Thomal held up his mug for Tillza. "But you're not going to get anywhere with Corky if you don't ask her out."

Vasile waited for Tillza to depart before speaking. "Ask out?"

"On a date," clarified Thomal.

Thomal was like enough referring to the meal-date Vasile learned about in socialization class. "To consume food?"

"Exactly. Bring her to this diner or to Three Friends Place restaurant. She'll talk more easily with you if she's someplace she likes."

"But what if I ask her and she refuses?" Vasile did not make a habit of seeking out opportunities to be shunned.

"She might refuse, yeah. You risk having your ___ stomped on. But you'll never know unless you try."

Vasile did not know what an *ego* was, but any sort of stomping on any part of him was not desirable.

Thomal said in addition, "You just gotta nut up, Lazăr."

Nut up was a slang term for *to have courage*. And, yes, it would take much nerve to ask Corky on the meal-date, for the likelihood was high she would reject him. "But I too…what is the word? Rough. Rude."

"Says who?" challenged Dev.

"No one to the face, but Nicolae finally gathered courage to ask the Dragon-Witch on the meal-date and she shunned him."

"Hadley did *what?*" Thomal put his mug down with a *thump*. "Damn her, she needs to get over herself already."

Dev wiped his hands on a napkin and tossed the crumpled wad on the table. "Corky saying yes isn't your biggest challenge right now, anyway, Lazăr."

"What is?"

"Convincing her to *stay*."

Chapter Fifteen

"OH, WHAT A NICE PLACE," Corky said as she strode into apartment 4B of the Water Cliffs Apartment complex.

"Thanks." Hadley walked to an open kitchen area and tossed her keys on the counter—gray-speckled granite. "All the apartments in the Water Cliffs complex have the same floor plan." Hadley moved to the center of the room, gesturing as she explained. "Dining area to the left of the front door, open kitchen to the right, then a step-down to the living room with a panoramic view of the Water Cliffs through a plate glass window, plus a balcony off the window. Bedrooms are on either side of the living room, each with a private bath. My last roommate took all her stuff with her when she moved out, so I've had fun redecorating. It's up to everyone to make their apartments unique."

Hadley had achieved that with tasteful choices of tex-tured, flowered wallpaper and hand-knotted rugs on gleaming hardwood floors. Two sofas of sage green faced each other in the center of the living room, accessorized with colorful throw pillows, plus a bird's-eye maple coffee table between. The small dining table was made of the same type of wood. A pear-shaped lamp sat on a side table next to the right-hand sofa.

The apartment was clean without being immaculate, seeming lived-in enough that Corky wouldn't feel like she had to tiptoe around the whole time she was a guest here.

Guest…

Her heart curled in on itself. Two steps inside the door, and the mere thought of leaving was already making a wreck of her emotions.

All her life she'd wanted a real home. Not an overcrowded group home for scraggly orphans. Not an institutional college dorm. Not a small apartment where she lived alone, her sole companion a fly-by-night parakeet, whose real love was for his true owner.

But a place of love and warmth, intimacy and friendship.

This apartment was it.

"That's Charlize's old room." Hadley pointed left, indicating an open door. "Now yours."

"Okay, thanks." Corky crossed to the bedroom and poked her head inside. There were linens on the bed, but the rest of the space was bare. Just waiting for her to *have fun decorating.* A lump of emotion wedged in her throat.

"Why did Charlize leave?" Corky set down her bag, purse, and legal pad just inside the door.

"She got married and moved to the 'burbs." Hadley headed into the kitchen. "It's kind of a common occurrence around here."

Maybe along the way you'll find someone to love, marry, and create a family with…

Corky's lump grew.

She wandered into the living room and peered out the plate glass window at the Water Cliffs below.

A sugar-sand beach fronted a rocky outthrust of cave wall that rose all the way to the ceiling. Pools of every size were at each level, some with slides, others fed by waterfalls, with the largest pool at ground level. This one was lit by a red bulb, and some mechanism was creating small ripples across the surface. The whole picture-perfect scene was decorated with ferns and algae and tropical flowers. "What an amazing view."

"Yes, I love it here." Hadley opened the fridge and peered inside. "You want something to drink?"

"Sure. Just nothing with caffeine." Corky's insides already felt like they were spinning a lot of plates on sticks. "And no water—there must be something in it around here."

Hadley's head popped up. "Why do say that?"

"Practically all the women in this town are pregnant." Chelsea from the Q&A panel, Hannah—Diamond's buddy— then the copper-haired woman at the dance studio.

Hadley laughed. "No need to worry about the water. Back in September the community accidentally brought in a batch of faulty ovulation test sticks, and that's why there're more pregnant women than usual." Hadley entered the living room with a couple of small juice bottles. She handed one to Corky.

It was a Naked Juice, strawberry-banana flavor. Corky stared at the label for longer than necessary. She didn't know what she'd been expecting—not a "normal" brand, evidently.

Hadley sat on one of the couches and set her juice on her lap.

It was green. Probably something with kale or spinach in it.

Corky dropped down on the sofa across from Hadley. "So, have any future baby daddies caught your eye in this town?"

"God, no!" Hadley exclaimed, then sighed. "Unfortunately, I have a special skill for picking the wrong men."

"I know what you mean." Corky raised her juice. "I'm a card-carrying member of that club."

Their gazes met and held.

Corky felt the connection between them growing, and the lump in her throat swelled until it was about to burst.

"My addiction is arm candy." Hadley cracked open her juice. "If a man is good-looking, nothing else matters. You?"

"If a man is big and strong but totally unavailable emotionally, I snap him right up."

Hadley snorted softly, a small laugh of understanding.

Corky laughed too, then stopped.

You couldn't handle anything unless I babied you, Hunter!

It wasn't funny, actually.

"Well, don't give up," Hadley urged her. "You're in Ţărână now, and this is the one place where people like you and I can find a mate."

"Women who fall for the wrong men?" Corky arched her brows. How did that work?

"No." Hadley smiled. "Women who are Dragons."

"Oh, yeah." *I'm a Dragon.* Corky kept trying that on for size but still couldn't make it fit.

"It's why I came back."

"Came back?" Corky tried not to gape. Hadley got out of here and *came back*?

"Yep. My first time here, five years ago, I was dating one of the community warriors, Thomal Costache. You haven't met him yet—flattop blond hair, insanely handsome, perfect ass. He cheated on me, and so I left."

"Oh, I'm sorry."

Hadley took in a slow breath. "Yeah, I was really torn up about it. To make matters worse he tried to excuse his actions by saying that the woman he was with *forced* herself on him." Hadley *tsked* in disdain. "Thomal would've had to bond with her on purpose to screw her, so… I've never seen how that was possible."

"Bond?"

"Oh, right. You don't know about that yet." Hadley made a sweeping gesture with her juice bottle. "Don't worry—you'll learn all about bonding later."

Corky opened her own juice and stared at the strawberry seeds floating in the drink. *Except that I've only been given three days here.* "So what happened after Thomal got together with that woman?"

"Well, *they* are living in happily wedded bliss," Hadley replied bitterly. "Meanwhile, I was so messed up that when I left the community I picked *another* wrong guy. No big surprise it ended in divorce."

Corky sipped her juice. Thank God she'd never *married*

one of her hosed-up man choices.

"I tried dating topside again," Hadley went on. "But nothing felt right. So six months ago, I asked to come back."

"Weren't you worried about running into Thomal all the time? This is such a small town." Corky would hate to be too near one of her exes.

If I'd wanted to stick your head in the toilet while I fucked you up the ass wearing a barbed condom, you would've let me…

Yeesh, what woman wanted daily exposure to a man who thought *that* about her?

Hadley spun the plastic ring left behind by the juice lid. "I was really unhappy topside, back to feeling like I didn't belong, so…I think I was too desperate to return home to Ţărână to feel nervous."

Home.

Corky swallowed.

"And Thomal and I are on polite terms, although we don't talk much. The difficult part is that every time I see him it reminds me of the huge mistake I almost made—Thomal and I came close to bonding *for life*, and that would've been a disaster."

Bonded again.

"It makes me skittish about other men. And there's this guy…" Hadley wet the corner of her mouth with the tip of her tongue. "There's a guy who likes me…Nicolae…and I…I'm not sure if I should go out with him."

"Why not? Is he arm candy?"

Hadley laughed. "Actually, he is *now*. But I think, you know, I should probably figure out my personal life before I date anyone." Hadley gazed out the plate glass window. "And…Nicolae and I didn't get off to the best start. When he first got here he was…how should I put it?" She looked at Corky again. "Behind the times? I didn't treat him so well because of it. Of course I didn't," she added in a self-deprecating tone. "He wasn't arm candy back then."

She exhaled and slouched. "I give the Moon-Rider vampires a lot of credit for coming a long way in the past five months, though. Before arriving here, they lived their entire lives in the Carpathian Mountains having very little contact with the modern world—only a bit through computers and television, from what I understand. So it's not like Nicolae could help it. The Moon-Riders just arrived here without any idea of how the modern world work." Hadley rearranged one of the sofa's throw pillows. "Nicolae is Vasile's younger brother, by the way."

"Vasile?"

"The guy from Kimberly's kitchen."

"The man who attacked me in the parlor?"

Hadley's mouth twisted. "Try not to think of it that way. Vasile's a nice guy, like Kimberly said—both Nicolae and Vasile are."

Corky cleared her throat. "So Vasile is one of the behind-the-times guys?"

"Yep."

"Hmm. Now I think I understand the lengthy crotch-stare."

"The what?"

"At Kimberly's house, I caught Vasile staring at my crotch. It's nothing a hundred other guys haven't done in the past, but when I noticed Vasile doing it, he didn't stop staring." Although at least he had the decency to look embarrassed afterward.

Hadley chuckled ruefully. "You haven't had the best introduction to that man, have you?"

"No, I guess not." Except that Vasile had also looked a little scared when she caught him, and how could Corky stay disgruntled with a man after seeing that?

"Vasile *does* like you, though." Hadley smiled. "If that makes any difference."

"How do you know?"

"Remember how Sedge said Vasile reacted to your scent and that's why he jumped on you? A vampire doesn't do that for no reason. To Vasile you smell like a potential mate."

"A mate? You mean like…like a *wife*?"

"Exactly."

Corky stared. How could he possibly know that already?

A NEW BOY HAS COME to Mary Sills' Angels, and Sheila Hobgood says he stares at me a lot. He likes to run all the time. He likes to throw things, and he likes to catch things. He tells me he can surf big waves. Then he lies belly-down on the large, cracked trunk in the TV room and makes paddle motions with his arms. He jumps up on top of the trunk, shouting woo-ha! and spreads his arms wide, teetering his body this way and that like he's riding a surfboard.

He leaps off and says, You try!

I lie belly-down on the trunk and start to paddle. He climbs on the trunk too, sits on my butt, and moves his hips in a weird way. His privates feel like a bag of gummy bears, the way they smash-smush against my rear end.

I'm not sure how to act polite about that, so I say woo-ha! and paddle faster. A side of the curtains by the TV has come off one of its rings.

He leaps off my butt.

Let's run! he tells me.

Later we meet in the dark hallway when everyone else is asleep. He shares a half-finished granola bar with me that he's swiped from the kitchen. His favorite flavor is cranberry-vanilla. His eyes are very bright in the shadows.

He wasn't supposed to leave. People don't adopt older kids, but a man came to Mary Sills' Angels who had tried to be a famous football player, but he hurt his knee and so couldn't play anymore. Now he wants a son who's super good at sports to live his dreams for him.

I'm good at things too. I'm good at writing in my journal

and hopscotch and being a nice girl. When Mama Mary says "Pick up the living room," I clean up, and when she says "It's quiet time," I read a book.

I was eight years old when the surfboard kid came to live at Mary Sills'. He's the first boy who ever liked me.

His name is Joey Ybarra.

Chapter Sixteen

The next day
10:11 a.m.

"Hey, man, wake up."

Lying facedown on the mattress, Reese's sensory neurons roused at the sound of his roomie's voice. But nothing else happened.

He didn't stir.

His hiked-up T-shirt was bunched uncomfortably under his armpits, and the wrinkled bedspread felt hilly beneath his bare belly.

"Yello. Did you hear me?"

Reese shifted his eyeballs back and forth against his closed lids as a pressure band wrapped around his skull and nausea roiled at the back of his throat.

"Hey!"

"Fuck sakes," Reese croaked. "Don't shout. I heard you the first time, shithead." He just couldn't open his eyes. He tried again and finally managed to pry past the disgusting crust gluing his lids together. He rolled onto his back, feeling too shitty even to demo a nice case of morning wood—lucky for Fane.

His roomie was standing bedside, wearing plaid boxers and a pitted-out white T-shirt. His dishwater blond hair was sticking up like bristles on a push broom, and his eyes looked like they'd come up cherries on a slot machine.

"Jesus," Reese moaned. "If I'm doing as bad as you look, you might as well call the coroner."

Fane scrubbed a hand over his forehead—an act that appeared to be sheer hell to perform.

"What do you want, anyway?" Reese asked.

"You need to get up."

"What the fuck for?"

"Toni wants to see you."

"Why?"

Fane moved his tongue around with a gummy *smack-smack* noise. "The taste in my mouth is heinous."

Reese's stomach bucked. "You keep making those revolting mouth noises, and I'm going to hurl all over your bare feet."

Fane took a step back.

Reese must've looked like he meant it. "What if I send an *I'm-otherwise-engaged* message to Her Majesty."

"You'd be more of a dick-brain than you already are."

Reese grunted. No doubt it *would* be a dick-brain move to do anything that might risk the head blonde sending over some pec-poser minion to haul Reese bodily to her office. He was in no fit physical state to reconfirm the size of his penis with a confrontation. Probably in no fit mental state either.

With painstaking slowness, he made the trip to a sitting position on the edge of his mattress. He immediately clamped both hands around his head. The veins in his brain felt compressed down to fishing line. "What time is it?"

"'Bout ten. Christ, but I need to feed."

Head still bowed, Reese aimed his next sentence at the floor. "How in hell can you think of food at a time like this?"

"*Feed* doesn't mean eat food, dick-brain. It means take in blood. You know, use these fangs that I don't really have in order to act like the vampire I really am not."

Reese slid his fingers down his face low enough to peer at his roommate.

Fane had his cell phone pressed to his ear. "Hey, Ectarina, it's Fane. I gotta feed, so could you—I know I'm not scheduled for today, but I'm hungover as fuck, so could you please fit me in and I'll—If you don't see me now, I *will* die, I'm not fucking kidding you. Okay." He exhaled. "Okay, thanks. I have to take Reese to the hospital, so can you meet me there in, like, ten minutes? Great. Thanks again." He ended the call, letting his phone-hand droop down at his side and his head loll back on his neck. "Not that the taste of your blood won't make me toss my cookies anyway," he muttered.

"Dude, I was only kidding about the coroner." *Half* kidding. Fane split into two images. Reese winked. Ah—now there was one.

Fane straightened. "The hospital is where Toni's office is."

Nausea climbed another inch up Reese's throat. "You and your fucked-up love for tequila." Who knew so many different drinks could be made from that golden liquor of puke-iffery. "Why does Blonde Sahib, Madam of the Night, want to see me?" he asked again.

"Hell if I know." Fane shuffled for the door. "But Toni calling you into her office this early in the morning isn't a good sign. You probably fucked something up royally."

Reese poked at a tooth with his tongue. Sounded about his speed, although for the life of him he couldn't think of anything he'd done in the last twenty-four hours to put sand in the head blonde's vag.

He paused another moment, then faced the inevitable and slowly hoisted himself to his feet. He tugged his CHARGERS T-shirt down, adjusted his dick in his pants, and set off for the door.

MISTRESS DOCTOR TONI PARTHEN'S OFFICE was a gender-neutral space with light-colored wood furniture—good for chicks—but chunky in design—acceptable to dudes. The art was chill watercolor, nothing that would shrink the size of a man's pecker if he was forced to spend too much time surrounded by it.

Reese was ushered into the office by Blonde Sahib's assistant, Donree—cute, petite, black-haired. A little sweetie who Reese might've flirted with if his pores weren't oozing some kind of assified distillery-stink.

Not to mention that his game was off.

He'd flirted his balls off last night at Garwald's Pub but hadn't scored a single hookup. *Weird.* Not that he was the most attractive guy in the whole world, but when he hardcore put his mind toward not going home alone, he generally pulled that off. He had no idea what part of his game was busticated…although if he had to guess he'd say the whole not-believing-in-vampires thing might've worked against him in a crowd full of Draculinas.

Reese stopped beside a desk that was to the left of the door.

Across the room Blonde Sahib herself was standing at a sideboard situated at the far end of a living-room-style setup—couch, chairs, coffee table. She was dressed in black slacks and a blousy white top patterned with streaks of gray that were probably supposed to be fashionably artsy, but to Reese just looked like Gollum had used it to wipe his ass.

Mistress was pouring herself a cup of coffee.

When he entered, she glanced over, went motionless while she looked him over, weighing and measuring, then finished pouring her coffee. "Mr. Terrella," she greeted him in a droll tone, then started toward him. "Usually when people come to my office, they show me the respect of showering beforehand and dressing in appropriate attire."

Yeah, well, those little teacher's pets probably hadn't been totally zombie-headed while dealing with feeling like a boiled turd before they showed up for their summons.

"I wasn't sure why I was bade to appear." He shrugged. "Thought maybe I should keep it casual in case the plan was to pop out to your favorite strip club—the 'Fang & Beaver,' right?—or maybe go catch an adult film, you know, 'Creeps and Creampie,' 'Love at First Bukkake,' and, of course, the ever-popular, 'The Vampire Who Sucked Me.'"

Donree inhaled softly.

Parthen gave him a patient smile and sipped her coffee.

Reese ran his tongue along his fuzzy teeth. "But, hey, no worries, I *do* know how to be a Mister Mannerly if the need arises, so you can count on me to do the right thing." He set his shoulders into a proud line. "I always pass food from the left while breaking wind to the right; I never forget to dab my nose with a frilled hankie after kissing the ass of megalomaniac queens of the blonde sort; and I flush my used condoms down the toilet without fail. Never do I *ever* leave a sticky rubber to languish in the trashcan." He flared his eyes wide. "That would be frank barbarism."

Parthen angled behind her big desk and took a seat. "Donree, could you please fetch Mr. Terrella a cup of coffee? He appears to be in dire need of one." Blonde Sahib waved him into one of the chairs in front of her desk. "Please."

He remained standing, scratching one of his armpits—an act which released a stink on par with camping out inside an elephant's colon. "Why is Mommy upset wid me?"

Donree handed him a mug of coffee and headed for the door.

He watched her leave, then slanted his brows at Parthen. "We're going to have this discussion *alone?*" He purposely leered at her tits—which was no imposition. "You sure you don't want to call in your bodyguard?"

"Who would that be?"

"Inked-up guy in the garage yesterday. A face about as friendly as a claw hammer."

Parthen's eyes warmed. "That's my husband. Shockingly, I somehow manage to conduct meetings without him in the same room." She gestured again to one of her guest chairs. "Please, Mr. Terrella, make yourself comfortable."

He gave up.

If he was going to continue to try and rile a reaction out of someone who refused to be riled, he would first need a couple of Excedrin, some banana-flavored Laffy Taffy, and a testicular massage. *Hello, Donree! Toddle back in here for a moment, wouldya?!*

He plopped down in one of the offered chairs, knuckling an eye. He was also really curious to see how well Mistress could rack ass.

Parthen observed him quietly.

He observed her back. As the silence stretched, he let a slow smile spread across his lips. *Oldest trick in the book, lady.* Disappointed High School Principal Entry Level One: *remain quiet until your squirming victim fesses up, "Er, so what am I in trouble for? Taking a shit in the science lab? Or is it because I jerked off all over the picture of Mr. Cowsom's wife, why that little countrified buttercup, with ears sticking out far enough to create handles for…?"*

"You were given a credit card yesterday," Parthen said.

Reese slurped his coffee. Seemed like a comment out of the boondocks, but whatever. "Yeah?" He slurped more coffee and felt some of the veins in his brain unpinch. Joy almost started him speaking in tongues—in other words, he nearly broke into a Taylor Swift song.

"Those funds were provided for the sole purpose of relieving Fane of any financial burden while acting as your buddy. The card was intended to be used for sundry purchases, *not* to buy round after round of drinks for everyone at Garwald's Pub last night."

A laugh blurted out of him. Was that all? *Jesus.* She had him thinking he sharted himself in front of the President of the United States.

Or worse, in front of Shakira.

Relief relaxed his shoulders but was immediately followed by a ping of disappointment. So, he and Parthen weren't going to take turns sticking the pointy end of crimes and misdemeanors into each other. Sins, faults, crushed dreams, wishful thinking…

I am born; therefore I am loved.

Ha! Total *reductio ad absurdum.*

Smirking, he lounged back. "It was one helluva party." A totally awesome way to round out the day after a game of football with Fane and his buddies.

"I'm glad you enjoyed yourself, Mr. Terrella, but you are now in serious overdraft." Parthen scooted a manila file folder from the side of her desk to a position in front of her. "You're going to have to work off your debt over the days you're here in Ţărână." She opened the file and glanced down at the top page. "I see from your application to us that your last job was with CALTRANS. You were in charge of city planning and roadworks." She regarded him with an even stare. "You were about to be promoted to supervisor, but then you were fired about a week prior to your arrival here."

"Yeah." He drained his coffee. "Boss got all butt hurt over me fucking his wife."

Parthen folded her hands over the top of the paper. "The community is growing to such an extent that we need to incorporate the use of vehicles—golf carts only. But it's complicated transforming a town that's always been exclusively pedestrian, and our engineers are a little stymied."

"Are they? Fascinating stuff. Really and truly. No grass growing here." He tapped his temple. "No drool leaking outta this mouth." He showed her his mug. "Do you mind if I grab a refill?"

"That won't be necessary." She came to her feet. "Our meeting is concluded."

"Rightio." He set down his mug and stood too. "Your meetings are kind of like getting a hand job from one of the Laker Girls, aren't they?" He bobbed his head in approval. "Over before ya know it."

Parthen strode for her office door and set her hand on the

knob. "Two doors down, there's a conference room where the roadworks planning commission will convene today at noon. You'll be lending them your knowledge as part of working off your debt. Please arrive clean and dressed in appropriate attire."

He picked at his teeth with the edge of his thumbnail. "And if I refuse?"

She smiled pleasantly. "I will offer you new accommodations for the remainder of your stay with us, Mr. Terrella, and those will make a sleeping bag on a garage floor seem like a suite at the Waldorf."

He kept his focus trained on her. Man, but he really got off on a woman who could properly lob a threat. And Mistress—

A pulse of energy came off her.

It drubbed through his entire body, wrapping his organs in sausage casing and giving his eyeballs a good bounce. Air seeped out of his nostrils. The power had just been a second's worth, but *holy shit.*

"Full disclosure," he breathed out. "Female authority figures give me serious wood." More than a hard-on, Mistress Chesty here was making his dick sweat.

She was really starting to grow on him, this woman. Only person he'd met in his whole damned life who didn't fold at the first sign of trouble.

Parthen opened the door, her smile still in place. "Don't be late."

CHAPTER SEVENTEEN

WHAT BIG BOSS LADY'S IDEA of *appropriate attire* was, Reese didn't know, but since the best he could put together out of the clothes he'd brought was "upscale casual," that's what he went with—a pair of dark blue jeans not ripped and stained all to shit, plus a brown Henley that likewise wasn't stankified.

All right, maybe it was more like "decent casual."

No need to get judgey.

He wasn't always a slob. He just hadn't bothered bringing a suitcase full of button-downs and khakis because the job he'd applied for was "short-order cook" at the town diner—a job he was totally overqualified for, but a guy had to do what a guy had to do to keep his beer kitty funded. And like Mistress Doctor noted, Reese had recently been canned from CALTRANS.

With an hour to kill before he needed to show at the planning commission meeting, Reese topped off a shower with a shave, then downed a gallon of water, rolled right into a satisfying vomit session, and ended with a trip to the diner that was supposed to have been his new place of employment—before he found out he'd be flipping burgers for those of the nocturnal persuasion and their fangbanging familiars.

Fane, buddying along, wolfed down a bacon-egg-and-cheese sandwich on an English muffin. His roomie's complexion had regained some color after he did that feeding thing.

Reese made dismal work out of a bowl of chicken noodle soup. Mostly he just poked carrots under the broth with his spoon rather than do any actual eating.

"Just ask somebody to text me when you're done," Fane said when he dropped Reese off outside of the conference room, "and I'll come get you."

"No prob." Reese pushed into the meeting room, entering to an argument already in progress.

There were four people inside, three men and a woman, all wearing pants of non-denim material and shirts with collars and buttons, but at least they weren't dressed in jackets and ties. They were gesturing and talking over each other.

"…not enough room over in the…"

"No way. We'd have to knock down too many buildings if we…"

"…too close to the family neighborhood. You want to risk running over a kid with a golf cart or…?"

As Reese moved forward, he saw that the group was huddled around a model of the town. It was decently detailed, even though none of the buildings were painted.

He examined it for a few seconds, then said, "Hey."

The four stopped arguing and looked at him.

A man situated across the table raised a weak hand in hello.

At first Reese didn't recognize the guy—not with the dude dressed in slacks and an oxford instead of workout gear—but then he realized it was Ninza from yesterday's football-game-plus-drink-fest.

The man looked like dogshit that'd been stepped on twice.

Well, *fuck beans*. There was a human being on this planet who hated tequila more than Reese did right now.

Introductions were made.

Ninza Gogean, as it turned out, was an archeologist—any cave-digging that went on in this town was overseen by him.

Vlad Roşu, the engineer from yesterday's Broken Elevator Yeah-Right, was also in attendance.

The third man was an architect named Luken Gigârtu.

The sole chick was Steliana Şofronie, also in possession of a degree in architecture, but with an emphasis on urban planning.

You'll be lending them your knowledge as part of working off your debt…

Reese didn't see how a hungover high-school grad with only a Bachelor of Arts degree in being a twat would have much expertise to add to this group.

But he wasn't in the mood to analyze how sketched out he should feel about it or not.

Instead he let his cock lead the way and stayed focused on the chick—short, white-blonde hair, nice lips, nicer rack.

He normally didn't like uber-short hair on women, but this Steliana was killin' the style. Her cut was very Alecia Beth Moore (the lead singer of the rock band *Pink!* for those keeping up at home).

Despite Steliana's degree in desk-sitting, she had the body of someone who kept active—tight muscles, solid ass, shapely thighs, a neat tuck of a waist, and those nice tits he'd noticed right off. Not big, but high and round. Her skin wasn't blemished by zit, wart, or flea bite, and her brows were thinly arched over uptilted eyes, amber-colored but flecked with green and gold.

She had a lot going on in all realms of bodacious, no denying it, but she was an *architect*. A stiff among stiffs, with her belt and buttons and Bruno Maglis. Not his usual pork-puffer sort.

Except that there was something about her…

An edge.

A coolarity.

Maybe it was the row of stud earrings running the entire length of her right ear—all the way into the cartilage—giving Reese the vibe that underneath all her proper she might be the type of woman who'd grind her stiletto into the webbing between your toes while sucking half your innards out your cock.

Just his type.

His genitals went *yo!*

Luken—who seemed like the chillest of chill dudes—got them back on track discussing how to convert a town built of basically immoveable structures into someplace that could handle a shitload of traffic.

When Reese asked about the *immovable* part, he was told about how pipelines for plumbing and electricity had already been laid, and that was no easy thing to do under cave rock. No one wanted to redo it.

Soon everyone was talking over each other again.

As Reese listened, it hit him—this town was too small for a *shitload* of traffic.

"You guys are thinking too big," he cut in. "Not everyone in town needs to have a car—or golf cart. There's not enough room. So why don't you set up several parking areas around town? Like here, here, and here." He pointed out potential spots on the model. "You can leave three to five carts at each inlet. If someone needs a ride, he grabs a cart at one spot, drives it to another, and leaves it there for the next person."

Luken, Vlad, Steliana, and Ninza just stared at him, all *what-the-fuck?* over hearing words come out of Reese's mouth that didn't sound like a Taylor Swift song—in other words, he just made a suggestion that had merit.

Was it Reese's jeans that had thrown them off? Or his assified distillery-stink?

After a long silence, the four shifted their eyes down to the model and stared at that.

After several more long seconds, Ninza finally said, "Huh."

Which was one of those sounds you can never tell if it's a veto or an agreement.

Vlad was frowning.

Luken glanced up with a smile. "An excellent idea."

Steliana gave Reese a twinkly look of approval.

And wasn't it a face-burner that he started to get all feel-goody over that.

"To go along with Reese's plan," Steliana said. "We could reserve two carts for specialty purposes—one for Toni, for example, and another for the hospital. Those could be designated with colored flags."

Luken nodded. "Yes. Good. We'll always want transport available for our town leader and medical emergencies."

Ninza nodded too. He was fully on board.

"We'll still have to widen some roads," Vlad killjoyed.

They busted brain over that conundrum for a while. The one thing they could all agree on was to keep Main Street pedestrian-only and dub it Old Town. Finally they decided to meet again tomorrow to hash out the best way to create byways around Reese's suggested parking inlets.

As the meeting broke up, Steliana drew up next to Reese, sliding her arm through his. "Great work today." She gazed at him like he was a ten-foot-tall bar of chocolate. "We never would've thought of the parking spot idea without you."

"Yeah. No prob." *Focus on the softness of her tit pressed again your arm, not on the pride in her expression.*

"You want to grab some dinner later?" Steliana smiled at him.

Fangs.

And you know what? They didn't really bother him all that much.

Chapter Eighteen

1:38 p.m.

VASILE WAS SEATED AT THE rectangular-shaped table used for dining in the home of Kimberly-Solicitor—he was kitty-corner from Corky and Kimberly was across from her. A single-wick candle sat in the center of the table. The candle was smooth on all sides except where one thin, knobby line of wax had frozen mid-melt halfway down from the lip. The table was made of cherrywood, the top furbished to a high gloss with something that smelled like rotten chestnuts. Why someone would put an unpleasant odor in a place where meals were consumed was a puzzlement, but helpful to Vasile, nonetheless.

He could focus on the strong scent—as Dev had advised him to do to stay in control of himself—even though endeavoring to ignore the scent of his glowing woman was a task equal to trying to catch the Mares of Diomedes with naught but a length of twine.

Vasile tightened his hand around the mug of brown water—he had accepted the terrible coffee out of courtesy—and shifted his butt in his chair.

"So…" Corky pulled a notepad out of a satchel and set it before her. The pad was of the same banana hue as the paper Kimberly used yesterday. "At our earlier meeting you mentioned something about the Vârcolac having a sad history."

"Yes." Kimberly put some banana-colored paper in front of her too.

Both women seemed to like this type of paper very much. Did using it lend to their powers of understanding?

"Back in the 1980s," began Kimberly with her storytelling, "the Vârcolac stopped being able to produce live offspring. For a lot of years, they suffered ___ after ___."

Vasile swung toward Kimberly. "What is *stillbirth*?"

Kimberly twisted her mouth so that one side was drawn up higher than the other. "When a baby is born dead."

Corky looked at him in a forlorn way, lines appearing along her brow. "That *is* sad. I'm sorry."

He did not know how to respond to that. He had lived with the certainty of never being able to pass on the fruit of his loins for so long, he had nigh forgotten how miserable this happenstance truly was. Looking back now, he saw how it had stripped him of his heart, leaving him nothing but empty days to tread upon—empty but for constant toil and struggles.

Corky went back to speaking to Kimberly. "Dr. Parthen mentioned that the Dragons were the only people Vârcolac could have living children with, but I had no idea they'd been through such heartbreak."

Kimberly nodded. "It's been devastating to them, especially to the generation who lost the most children—aptly named the Lost Generation. Roth Mihnea, who was acting king at the time—Vinz's uncle, incidentally—couldn't stand watching his people endure any more stillbirths, so he forbade breeding among members of the race."

Kimberly tugged the cap off one end of a writing instrument and stuck it on the other end. "Twelve years later, Dr. Jess discovered Dragons, and that changed the game. Now the younger, unbonded generation of Vârcolac do have a chance to mate and breed."

"Well, that's good," said Corky, and her forehead smoothed.

"But Roth has kept the no-fraternization law in place."

"The law Vinz and Lidanna broke?"

"Exactly. Vinz and Lidanna secretly bonded, a 'criminal act' the two of them successfully concealed for years by feeding in hiding and by making sure to stay on opposite sides of town whenever Lidanna was ___."

Corky frowned. "Why did they have to do that?"

"Ah. Another thing you don't know is that a bonded male Vârcolac slips into a dazed, semi-conscious state whenever he scents his mate is ___."

"You spoke word *fertile* two times," said Vasile. "What means that?"

"It means a woman is ovulating—a time when a man can put his child in her."

Vasile turned back to Corky. Was Corky presently in such a state? Letting his eyelids drift low, he tilted his chin up and dilated his nostrils. Her mind-scrambling, delicious scent caught hold of him as usual. With his next inhalation, he took in a deeper breath. No false aromas such as body perfume or skin moistener plagued her naturalness. She exuded a tang of sweet flesh and something sweeter... An elemental fragrance that coated his tongue with the essence of her womanhood.

Saliva flowed into his mouth, and taut ropes wrapped around his belly and groin. His heart pounded a hard drumbeat against the cage of his ribs.

He jerked his chin back down.

A mistake, probing so deep.

His senses were now drenched with the primal need to taste her...not only her blood, but her woman parts, to lick her there in the manner he had seen a man do to a woman in the sex education class movie. In such a way, he would determine the readiness of Corky to receive his pole, like the movie taught—her opening must become very slippery—then he would do the hip-thrusting actions and put his child in her.

The thought expanded his chest with a large feeling.

Be the greatest protector, the most skilled hunter, the strongest in moral character...

These lifelong teachings of his father had left out the importance of being the best father.

There could be no greater accomplishment or honor than having his babe grow within Glowing Corky.

Corky's head came around, and she pinned him with her eyes, as if she had divined his thoughts again.

He tensed. Had he behaved badly? Was imagining licking her woman parts and procreating with her as ill-behaved as envisioning pole-pressing her? He had not been thinking of pole-pressing her.

Except…

Now he *was* thinking about pole-pressing her.

He took a drink of his coffee. He did this out of need for a distraction and out of the habit of having a mug in his hand, forgetting how foul the weak brew was. He swallowed quickly.

"Unfortunately," continued Kimberly, "yesterday morning Vinz and Lidanna misjudged her cycle, and some very startling activity almost occurred at…" Kimberly glanced at Vasile. "Where?"

"In street," he answered. "In front of tavern."

"Garwald's." Kimberly wrote this on her banana paper.

"So what's our defense?" asked Corky.

"We can't defend them," answered Kimberly. "Vinz and Lidanna broke the law, plain and simple. But Vinz wants to use this case to overturn the no-fraternization law. He claims that there's a faction of Vârcolac who don't want children, even if they could get a Dragon—he and Lidanna among them. He contends that this faction shouldn't be made to suffer a life of solitude, waiting for a Dragon who would be wasted on them, anyway."

"I guess that makes sense," said Corky.

"It won't to Roth. He wants every Vârcolac of child-bearing age to remain able to have children. But if a Vârcolac bonds with another Vârcolac, then that puts a stop to that."

"It does?"

Kimberly nodded. "Vârcolac mate for life. It's why the Lost Generation will remain childless forever."

"God…how awful." Corky looked at Vasile again, her forehead lines returning.

There was much kindness and compassion in this woman.

"It can't be *hopeless*." Corky kept her gentle gaze on Vasile, as if he might be able to offer a solution.

He could not.

Shifting his focus to the single-wick candle, he stared at it until it disappeared. Now before his eyes he saw a full moon shining through the knobby branches of a dead oak tree.

Every night when he was young he would stare at that moon, night after night watching it shrink to a half-moon. And each night his soul would die a little with the certainty that his life would never change for the better.

So, no. He knew nothing of solving a hopeless situation.

CHAPTER NINETEEN

The next day
9:25 a.m.

SMACK.

Reese caught the football. "Best quarterback of all time?" He rocketed the football across the living room.

Fane caught it. *Smack.* "Joe Montana." He threw the ball back.

Reese caught it. "Someone who's *not* retired."

"You said best of *all time.*"

Reese fired the football at Fane.

Smack. "All right," Fane said. "How about Tom Brady?"

Brady, yeah. He's been the Super Bowl king for the Patriots. Good choice.

Knock. Knock.

Reese and Fane both glanced over.

Fane crossed the apartment and opened the door.

It was Breen Dalakis, wearing a Lynyrd Skynyrd T-shirt, a picture of the OG lead vocalist Ronnie Van Zant frozen in the act of scream-singing into a standing mic.

Fane spun the football between his palms. "Hey, Breen. 'Sup?"

"Elevator's fixed," Breen said, then directed at Reese, "Grab your shit."

Reese froze.

Fane frowned. "Do what?"

"Elevator's up and running," Breen repeated. "Time to go."

"Go where?" Fane asked.

Breen gestured at Reese. "Terrella's not staying."

Fane rounded on Reese. "What the fuck's he talking about?"

For a weird slip in the space-time continuum, Reese wasn't sure. Because somewhere along the way over the past two days—in between playing ball, making friends, showing off his smarts on the planning commission, and dating Steliana—Reese had forgotten he was planning to leave.

So he just stood in place, drawing a blank on comeback options. Finally he went with something totally lamesauce. "I thought you knew."

Fane said something like *fuu-huuh*.

How big of a dick-brain are you, exactly? A lot of that sentiment was in the glower Fane shot his way.

So Reese went on the defensive. "Why *wouldn't* you know? You've been dogging my every footstep these last two days." Which, weirdly, had been no hardship.

Breen came to Fane's rescue with, "Only the council members knew, and the warriors. I'll meet you in the garage," he aimed at Reese before turning to leave. "I gotta go tell the others." He headed off.

Too many more silent seconds slinked by. All the while an expression of hurt and betrayal built on his roomie's face.

Without another word, Fane spun on his heel and strode into his bedroom.

The door slammed, and Reese flinched.

Shit.

He shifted air from one cheek to the other. What should he do now? He didn't know. He'd never let himself feel bad about leaving someone before.

So he went into his bedroom and packed his duffel.

Going back out, he stood in the middle of the living room. He thought about yelling, *See ya later, shithead*. But he didn't. Just took off for the garage like some mincing coward, the words tight in his throat.

Making his final trek down Main Street, he felt a little like he had on his tenth birthday—like his legs had just been kicked out from under him—after his father didn't show.

Dad had always managed to visit him on his birthdays, no matter what foster family Reese was putrefying in at the time.

Except on his tenth birthday.

And every one thereafter…

THE LINCOLN TOWN CAR WAS parked in front of the hash-marked loading zone again, all the doors open and the trunk lid up.

Dr. Parthen and another woman with her brown hair caught in a ponytail and wearing an avocado-colored jumpsuit were standing at the rear of the car, talking.

Diamond, Evan, and Corky were clustered near the closest open passenger door. Not talking.

Not looking good.

Evan gave the impression of a man who'd accidentally swallowed a mouthful of his own snot, Diamond looked like she hadn't managed a decent bowel movement for the past two days, and Corky's soul had clearly cannibalized itself.

She captured his gaze and held it. Her head moved in an almost imperceptible shake. *We're not really going to do this, are we?*

What, you mean, like, leave the only place where we've ever been the cool kids? Fuck yeah! Let's burn rubber outta here, baby.

Parthen glanced up. "Ah, there you are, Mr. Terrella. We were waiting to load your bag in the car, then we're all set. Ready to go?"

Sure, I'm ready. Just gimme a sec to recover from my holy-fuck-tits reaction over how messed up my heart is right now.

Somewhere on the trip from his apartment to this garage that organ had gone to its final reward. His lungs weren't working at top capacity either.

Parthen strode out from behind the Lincoln and smiled at their group. "Once again, I'd like to thank all of you for your patience while we dealt with the elevator fiasco. I hope—"

"Can we stay?" Diamond gulped out.

Parthen's eyebrows rose slowly.

"If we read your manual, like you said, and take your test, uh…" Diamond licked her lips. "Can we?"

Dr. Parthen swept a look over the rest of them. "Does anyone else want to stay?"

Evan's hands slid into his pockets. "I do."

"Me too," Corky said, then stared down Reese. *Say it! Say you want to stay.*

Problem was he couldn't gather enough air to speak. Maybe he was in the middle of an incorporeal erotic asphyxiation event gone terribly wrong. *That's it.* He was choking telekinetically between the thighs of that chick with the clit piercing he went down on last week…

But Corky wouldn't let him suffocate in peace. "Swallow your pride, Reese, and admit that you want to stay. Fane is already like a brother to you; you feel great about the brilliant work you've done on the commission; you're half in love with Steliana; you—"

"Hell if I am," he plowed in. He might cop to the other two, but the third? No way. *Love is doopid.* So Corky could stop spouting shit right there.

I will not be sworn but love may transform me to an oyster…in other words, into a brainless blob of an idiot.

Not that he'd let any of these yahoos know he could quote the Bard.

Evan told him, "The rest of us won't stay if you don't, Reese." He added a helpless shrug. "We came into this together."

Diamond peered owlishly at him from behind her glasses. "Yes, please stay."

Aw, crap sacks.

The mansion dining room

REESE CLAWED HIS FINGERS AROUND the edges of the community manual and glared at Blonde Sahib, who was seated at the head of the dining table. "What the fuck is this shit?"

Diamond, Evan, and Corky stopped reading and glanced up.

Evan was seated next to Reese, facing Corky and Diamond across the table.

All of them were in a dining room that ran as heavy on the froufrou as the prissy drawing room where they'd started this freaktastic escapade. Reese was beginning to get the sense that whoever had decorated this mansion went through life with a bottle of starch up his or her ass. The tea service was baroque sterling, the tablecloth Chantilly lace, and the basket that held a selection of muffins was probably woven by gypsy peasants in tents where they'd gone blind to serve the whims of capitalist prestige-mongers and Eurotrash.

Or it was Longaberger.

"Is something wrong, Mr. Terrella?" Parthen took a sip of coffee from a china cup—dainty, white, covered in tiny roses. *Gag me.*

"Holy fucking yeah there is." He stabbed a finger at the page open in front of him. "Hooking up with a Vârcolac is for-fucking-ever." He looked at his co-recruits. "Did you catch that? According to this"—now he slapped the backs of his fingers down on the page—"bonding with one of these people creates a *biological attachment.* Like in, you take off, they croak." He threw his hands in the air, really getting his hyperbole on. "Divorce equals death to this crew."

"What page are you on?" Evan squinched his eyes at Reese. "How fast do you read, anyway?"

Fuck sakes. Stay focused on the main point here, dude. "I jumped ahead." He *could* read fast, but mostly he wasn't destined to be the bestie of anyone who insisted on reading a magazine or newspaper page by page from beginning to end.

Corky selected a chocolate chip muffin from the basket. "Then you probably missed the part about them being virgins."

Now Reese squinched his eyes. "Who being what?"

Corky glanced down at the page she was on. "I quote—'a Vârcolac can't have sexual intercourse until he or she is permanently bonded to a mate.'" She looked up. "All the singles in this town are virgins."

"Whoa, whoa, whoa"—Reese lifted a palm—"wait, wait, wait. You're saying…like… Fane has never fucked a chick before?"

Corky peeled the top of her muffin off its base. "If he's single, he hasn't."

Reese rounded on Parthen. *Exsqueeze me?*

"Corky's right," Blonde Doc confirmed.

"Holy fuck-a-moly." Reese slammed back in his chair. "*That's* why I have no game in this town." Even if the women here wanted to screw him, they couldn't.

Blonde Doc wrapped both hands around her dainty teacup. "Yes, Mr. Terrella, and I'm afraid that means your usual method of ruining your life won't be available to you in Țărână."

Reese stared blankly at her. *My usual method…?*

Then his own words echoed back to him.

I was headed for a full ride at UCLA, but then I fucked the coach's wife…

Boss got all butt hurt over me fucking his wife…

Reese threw back his head and roared with laughter. "Nice pull, Dr. Fire Hazard." He eyeballed Parthen up and down. "Man, if you weren't already with a guy who could open up a can of ouchies on me with just a bad case of halitosis, I would *so* go for you."

Parthen gave him one of her patient smiles.

"What's wrong with being a virgin, anyway?"

Reese turned toward Diamond.

She was all mouth-pinched and defensive.

"Because I…I-I happen to be…" Diamond's face flamed.

"There's nothing wrong with it at all," Parthen assured her. "Virginity is normal around here."

Corky set down both halves of her muffin. "What if we're not a virgin? What happens then?"

"Nothing happens. All of you can be exactly who you are in this town. No expectations. No judgement." Parthen set her cup in her lap. "Do you remember Ty Vega from the Q&A panel? He didn't even date for the first six months he lived here. He pursued a new career and hobbies and figured himself out. We understand a forever-commitment is major. No one expects you to make one until you're ready."

Forever… Fuck my motherfucking ass! Reese went back to smothercating. "What if we never hook up with a Vârcolac?" he challenged. "You going to kick us out?"

"Most certainly not. Like I said on the day of your arrival, you're *our* people and this is your home. You each have your own journey to take." Parthen now addressed them all. "And we're here to support you through whatever it is."

"You know," Diamond said to Reese, "there are a lot of good things that go with bonding to a Vârcolac too." She set her palm on the open page of her manual. "Something called fiinţă comes out of a Vârcolac's fangs during feeding. Regular doses of this elixir will increase your health and longevity, *and* fiinţă gives an immense amount of pleasure…kind of like a drug." She smiled archly. "You should like that part."

"Excuse you, ethnic profiler, but I don't do drugs." Ink yourself up with a dozen or so tats and the straights assume the worst.

"Let's just keep reading, okay?" Corky picked up her muffin top. "I have a meeting with Kimberly this afternoon to go over our case, so I want to take the test as soon as possible."

Yeah, yeah, me too. I wanna get back to frolicking with all the nice, supportive virgins.

Evan and Diamond returned to their manuals.

Reese dropped his focus to the page and read, "You'll need to prepare yourself for the first bite of a Vârcolac. It is very painful…"

Well, hallelujah, praise Jesus. At least something in this town wasn't all rainbowy love ballads and cozy dick mittens.

Chapter Twenty

Reese strode into his community apartment, swinging the door wide on a smiling Fane.

"Hey!" Fane brandished his cell phone. "Just got the text about you staying."

Reese banged the door shut.

He was a colossal idiot to have entered this roommate sitch without first issuing Fane a solid punch to the jaw—set things straight from the outset about how it was going to be between them.

No brotherly love for you, dickhead, and wipe that fool smile off your face.

Reese now slammed his duffel down.

Fane glanced at the bag, blopped over from the abuse, and lowered his arm. "'Sup, bro?"

"You've never fucked a chick."

"Ah." Fane tucked his cell into his back pocket. "All up to speed on Vârcolac culture now, are ya?" He grinned. "I'm actually going to miss following you around."

I'm going to miss that too. Reese glowered. "Shut the fuck up."

Fane laughed. "Why are you so pissed that I've never been laid?"

"Because," Reese growled. *Because you're like a brother to me, and so I have to make sure you're good.* "Because it's *sex.*"

"You want to get yourself really in a junk bunch?" Fane smirked. "Consider that I can't even jack off."

Whaaaaaat?! Reese reeled back a step. "That's horracious.

We've got to find you a girl, man—like, now."

"It doesn't work that way." Fane picked up Reese's duffel and tossed it on the couch. "I have to be in love with the girl first and then bond with her—well, *marry* her, to put it in terms your pea-brain can understand."

"Gah." Reese tipped his head back. "You really are a town of saps, aren't you?"

All of you can be exactly who you are in this blah, blah, blah. *You each have your own journey to take and* yadda, yadda. What did any of that *mean*, anyway?

Reese straightened and gusted a huge breath. "What am I gonna do with you?"

"Hey, don't worry about me, bro. My time will come. Just look at this face." Fane pointed at his chin and smiled. "What woman could resist?"

Someone knocked on the door.

Reese just kept staring at his roomie. Fane *would* find a chick someday…because he just so happened to be *the best damned guy on the planet.*

"You gonna answer that?" Fane drawled. "You're kinda closer."

Reese spun around and jerked open the door.

"Reese!" Steliana threw herself against him, wrapping her arms around his neck in a strangle hold and crushing her breasts against his chest. "You're staying," she breathed happily into his ear.

After a beat of hesitation, he hugged her back—and it was about as wrong and as right as anything could get in one fucked-up bundle.

Steliana leaned back in his arms, her eyes twinkling up at him with adoration.

We understand a forever-commitment is major. No one expects you to make one until you're ready…

Hey. Yo. Did anyone bother to give Steliana that memo? *'Cause it looks like kinda not.*

"You want to go out and celebrate?" she asked.

"Can't." He stepped out of her hold. "I already told Diamond, Evan, and Corky I'd go out with them for a drink."

Yeah, so what? It wasn't the first lie he'd ever told and wouldn't be the last.

"Oh." Steliana's smile flagged for a second, then returned to full chuffed-to-fuck brightness. "Okay, how about tomorrow we—"

Pfff-whump!

Steliana visibly startled.

Reese glanced up at the ceiling. "What the hell was that?"

✧ ✧ ✧

6:28 p.m.

THE PUB OF GARWALD POSSESSED a strange rectangular box that winked with bright lights and spewed music. At present, a male voice was singing about liking big butts.

Vasile had once been rammed in the seat by a billy goat, so he could not agree with that sentiment.

Looking for Dev, Vasile found him at a table with Gabor, Thomal, and Arc. Thomal and Arc Costache were brothers, Arc being the eldest.

Vasile did not know all the happenstances that had put a divide between the two, but an old event had done so. They shared a deep regard for one another, yes, but also bore a certain distance between them.

Although not so much anymore.

Five months past, Thomal and Arc discovered the existence of a secret sister. She was related to them by half-blood, conceived by their father and a Regular Human during a full moon on Beltane night—a time when Vârcolac could mate freely, bonded or no.

In Vârcolac lore this type of moon was known as Luna Zânǎ.

Thomal and Arc had gotten close while pursuing their mutual goal of finding their wayward sibling.

Vasile made his way toward the four men, feeling unbalanced, like he held a sack of grain on one shoulder but not on the other.

His warrior comrades were seated at a rectangular table that'd been fashioned by pushing two square tables together. In the middle of the table was a jug of beer. Clear glass tankards with some amount of beer in them were set before each man.

"Hey, Vasile," said Dev to him upon his arrival. "Grab a seat."

Nodding his thanks for the welcome, Vasile sat.

Dev set a tankard before Vasile and poured beer into it. "I heard about Corky staying."

"Yes, I heard that news too. But I am of a divided mind over it. It has making me feel unbalanced."

"Really?" Dev arched his eyebrows. "You're not ___ about her staying?"

"Am I what?" Vasile frowned. *Stoked* was something a person did to a fire.

"Happy."

"I am happy, but I deem that both good parts and bad parts go with this news—so I divided, as I say." Vasile would have to remember that *stoked* was a slang term for *to be happy*. "Good part is that I can undertake to win Corky with her in Țărână. Bad part is I must summon courage to ask her on the meal-date in order to win her, and the likelihood is strong she will deny me."

"Oh, I don't know about that, Lazăr. She might surprise you." Dev smiled, clearly thinking he had presented heartening news, when in truth, if Corky did agree, it would introduce other difficulties.

"More bad," stated Vasile. "I lack knowledge of what man and woman do on the meal-date. I struggle still with creating a discussion." He picked up his beer, then set it right back down. "Images of pole-pressing Corky invade my thoughts, and this is no aid to my endeavors."

Thomal raised his tankard to his mouth and made a snuffle noise into his beer.

Arc glanced at Thomal, then looked at the other community fighting men. "What?"

"Sex thoughts," said Dev to clarify.

"Ah." Arc made a nod gesture of understanding. "But that's good, right? Lazăr didn't have those when he first got here."

Vasile sat forward. "So these thoughts come from me be true man now? I am not ill-behaved?"

"Nah," said Dev. "Don't worry about it. Most men think about sex 24/7. We can't really stop ourselves. It's normal."

"But don't tell the woman what you're thinking," jumped in Arc to advise.

Vasile turned his mouth down. "Why, if is not ill-behaved?"

Arc looked at Dev.

"You might as well keep explaining."

Arc screwed his lips into an expression of reluctance and glanced at Thomal and Gábor.

"Don't look at them," admonished Dev. "Thomal can't keep a straight face during these convos, and do you really trust Pavenic to handle anything like this?"

"Shit, all right, um…" Arc paused as if to search his mind. "It's like the idea that you don't have sex in the middle of the grocery store, right? You have sex in your bedroom. Sex is private and so are sex thoughts."

Gábor made a gagging sound. "Jay-sus. I might never fuck again after hearing that."

Arc narrowed his eyes.

Dev made a perfunctory gesture at Gábor and Thomal. "You see what I'm dealing with?"

Vasile considered both Dev and Arc. "So desiring a woman is offense to her?"

"No." Arc rubbed his jawline. "She likes to be desired. It's, um…crap. Just tell your woman your sex thoughts after you've bonded to her, all right? Before that, there are a lot of ___ to talking to a woman you don't know."

"What is *nuances*?"

"Small shit." Arc moved his hand in a general way. "The kind of stuff the rest of us learned by fucking up and saying the wrong things."

Wrong thing…right thing… Little wonder Vasile felt off-balance. "I am bootless to even say *one* thing." Vasile turned to Dev. "<How do I talk to Corky? What do I say to her?>"

"<What topics of conversation have you attempted? Have you asked about—>"

"Would you two *not* speak in Romanian?" interrupted Gábor in a grumpy tone.

Dev picked up the jug of beer and poured more libation into his tankard. "You need to study more, Pavenic."

"Yeah, Nichita, because I just scream book learning."

Vasile stayed focused on Dev. "I no understand what to say during the discussion."

Dev glanced at someone across the room, then pointed at the clear jug, now empty of beer. "You want to find out if you like Corky, right? So ask her about herself—her likes and dislikes. What are her hobbies? What's her job like? Find out about her childhood. Where did she grow up? Did she have any pets?"

Pets. Yet another bafflement. Animals were for putting to work or eating. "If it comes to pass Corky owned a fish in a bowl, I think she will be silly."

Dev shook his head. "Lesson number one going into this, Vasile—no woman is perfect. If you expect her to be, you'll never end up with one. Accept her flaws. Love her for them. In fact, her flaws make her more interesting. And if she's the right woman for you, she'll accept your flaws too."

"Quick!" Gábor pushed forward in his seat. "Somebody check under the table. Nichita's balls have fallen off."

Thomal rumbled out a chuckle.

Arc half-smiled.

Dev grabbed Gábor at the back of the neck with a strong hand. The muscles in his forearm bulged.

Gábor made slits out of his eyelids. "Ow."

The bar owner, Luvera, arrived at the table with another jug of beer. She was sister to Dev, black-haired and very amiable. "Here you go, fellas." She set the jug on the table.

Gábor bashed off the forearm restraining him.

Dev just smiled. "Thanks, Luvera."

Vasile sat in thought, trying to plan a selection of discussion topics.

Out of the large music box came a female voice now, singing about paving paradise to put up a parking lot. Vasile paused to try and imagine this process but could not. Such a thing seemed—

Pfff-whump.

Vasile nigh left his chair at the sudden noise.

The other warriors froze.

The sound had been somewhat muffled, but loud enough for them to detect the strangeness of it.

Another came, more pronounced—*pfff-whump!*

Now everyone in the bar went quiet, a wave of unease passing through the gathering.

Expressions tight, all the warriors looked at the ceiling. The sound was coming from the earth above.

PFFF-whump! Noisier still!

Dev leapt to his feet. "Everyone, get under your tables! Now!"

The occupants scrambled to comply while Vasile sat stiffly in his chair, the hairs on his nape electrifying. A current was riding the air…something familiar…something he had felt before…

PFFF-WHUMP!

Direct hit! Right above them! Windows shuddered and dust misted down. Several patrons cried out.

Vasile hissed.

Dev snapped his focus over to him, his pupils lit. "What is it?"

Vasile snarled through clenched teeth and clutched his waist as heated pain forked through the scar on his side, the evil magic finding the spot where the witch once stabbed him with her sword.

The witch who tried to kill him.

The witch who murdered his father.

Fangs unsheathing, Vasile staggered to his feet and threw back his head. "Savatina!" he bellowed.

Chapter Twenty-One

Corky's attention flew to the ceiling.

Hadley looked up too. "What was that?"

"You're asking *me*?"

They sat in silence at the bird's-eye maple dining table, eyes still glued to the ceiling, two vodka-lemonades set between them. They'd just been celebrating Corky's decision to stay.

"You've never heard it before?" Corky asked, in the quiet way people usually reserved for words like *cancer* and *divorce*.

"No."

Pfff-whump!

Corky gasped and startled.

Hadley made a face. "Crap, I hope the Om Rău aren't up to something."

"The who?" *Oh, wait.* Hadn't the manual mentioned something about a neighboring demon race. "Maybe it's bad plumbing," Corky suggested.

Pfff-whump!

"Shit! You know what it probably is?" Hadley leapt up. "An earthquake!"

Corky jumped to her feet too. "You're kidding."

"No. These caves are naturally created along a fault line between—" *Pfff-whump!* "Hurry! Stand in your bedroom doorway."

Corky raced to her door and braced her hands on either side of the frame. "Does this happen a lot?" If it did, she might have to rethink her decision to stay.

"Never."

They waited, attention pinned on the ceiling.

And waited.

Corky's palms were damp. Her heartbeat didn't feel right. Any second the roof would cave in.

Outside, the Water Cliffs' waterfalls splashed and played.

Corky studied every inch of the ceiling but couldn't find any cracks in the plaster. "Nothing is quaking," she pointed out softly.

"True. Maybe it—"

The door crashed to the floor.

They both yelped, even though an earthquake hadn't caused it—not unless you defined one very large male vampire charging into their apartment as a similar force of nature.

Long hair flowing behind him, Vasile's eyes were doing that spinning thing again. He focused solely on Corky, staring at her with such intensity that now the earth *did* quake beneath her feet.

She tightened her grip on the doorjamb. Was it a trick of the light, or pure imagination, making his pupils look so black? All pupils were black, but Vasile's were so black right now, they seemed endless.

"How be you?" Vasile clipped out the question, grim and tense.

Before she could answer, Hadley butted in. "What the hell was that noise?"

Vasile swung on her. "You hear?"

"Yes!"

Three more men poured through the gaping hole where the door had been.

Corky recognized two of the men from the Q&A panel: Dev Nichita—who had a knife in his hand—and Gábor Pavenic. She'd never met the third man, but she'd bet he was Hadley's ex, Thomal. He had flattop blond hair and a face that made her ovaries ache.

Vasile looked between Hadley and Corky. "Do you feel evil magic when the noise go?"

"I…" Hadley checked gazes with Corky. "I don't know what that feels like."

Vasile thought about it for a second. "Like you touch electricity, then need vomit."

"No." Hadley shook her head. "I didn't feel that."

Vasile looked at Corky. The rings around his irises were no longer spinning.

She dropped her hands to her sides. "I didn't feel that either."

Some of the rigidity left Vasile's shoulders.

Dev holstered his blade.

Vasile stepped closer to Corky.

Her pulse thundered, but she didn't move. Either because she couldn't, or because she was too curious about what he was going to do. Funny how she couldn't tell.

"Are you of a certain mind?" Vasile took her by the upper arms. "You are not unwell?"

Corky didn't speak. She was fine, just…beyond words. This man was genuinely concerned about her. He barely knew her, yet here he was. He'd rushed to her rescue when he thought she might be in danger.

Hunter Scott would've saved his laptop and Rolex before he lifted a finger to help her.

"Well, uh…" She gave Vasile an awkward smile, guilt shrinking her stomach over having thought of this man as a *thing*. "I think my heart fell out of my chest at one point."

Vasile's brow furrowed. He glanced at Dev.

"She means she was frightened," Dev explained.

Vasile turned back to her. "Do not be affright," he told her in a severe tone. "I protect."

Okay, soooo… This guy was making up for their inauspicious beginnings by leaps and bounds. "I'm okay now, thanks."

Vasile's hands put pressure on her arms, as if he was about to pull her into an embrace, then the sides of his eyes tightened, like he was considering what her response might be to a hug. He released her.

"All right, Lazăr." Dev's hand still rested on the hilt of his knife. "We've confirmed the women are safe. Now you need to explain what the fuck that noise was because you clearly know."

Vasile stepped back from Corky and angled toward Dev. "Noise is of daughters of Zalina dropping seeking-orbs to earth above us."

"Zalina!" Hadley's eyes went wide. "Oh, no!"

Corky watched the color drain from her friend's face. So the noise *had* been bad. Not earthquake-bad, but still bad.

"Who's Zalina?" Corky asked.

"Chieftess of Warrior Witches," Vasile told her plainly, as if calling someone a witch was no biggie.

Vasile pointed at Hadley. "Her mother."

Hadley moaned. "Please don't call her that."

Vasile now pointed at the ceiling. "Magic in orbs burrows into ground to hunt Hadley."

Hadley clasped her cheeks with both palms. "Oh, no! She found me!"

"No." Vasile shook his head. "You no feel evil magic."

"But…" Corky began.

Everyone looked at her.

She blurted out the one syllable again—"But"—then stopped. A strange panic was unraveling up her throat. *The itsy bitsy spider climbed up the waterspout. Down came weird things and washed her sanity out…*

She swallowed twice. "Could, um, someone please clarify what you mean by witches?" *You're talking about a club of women who practice Wiccan rituals, right?* "Because, er…" *Other kinds of witches don't exist.*

The one called Gábor snorted. "You believe in vampires

now, and you're going to question the reality of witches?"

Corky paused, blinking. She supposed there was a valid point in there somewhere.

"Wait a minute," Dev bit out. "How the hell would Zalina's witches know where to search for Hadley? The location of our town is secret."

"I know not for certain," Vasile answered, "but I make conjecture. When chief of Moon-Riders, Octav Rázóczi, is here in Ţărână five months past, he most likely sense this area. After he return to warded lands in Transylvania, Octav seek to preserve wellbeing of the Vârcolac lands by make deal with Zalina—in the war between Warrior Witches and Vârcolac, vampires suffer many losses. It is my estimation that Octav present Zalina with suspicioned location of Dragon-Witch"— he gestured at Hadley—"in exchange for some advantage."

Silent tears slipped down Hadley's cheeks.

Dev's cell trilled. He pulled his phone out of his back pocket and checked the screen. "Arc just confirmed the security of the rest of the town. Looks like the witches have bugged out for now." He shoved his phone away, looking at Hadley as he added, "Keep it together, Had, okay? Vasile said Zalina's daughters didn't find you."

"That is correct," Vasile confirmed. "But to our misfortune, witches find *me*." Vasile pointed at himself. "I feel bad magic from Savatina."

Dev set his brows into a straight line. "The witch who tried to kill you?"

"Yes. That how she find me." Vasile patted the left side of his belly. "Connection to wound she bestow."

"So Zalina's daughters know they're hunting in the right area?"

Vasile nodded gravely. "They know."

"Shit," Dev cursed. "We need to brief Toni about this. Let's go."

Chapter Twenty-Two

Corky poured extra vodka into the second round of vodka-and-lemonade cocktails while eyeing Hadley from beneath her lashes.

Her friend was pacing in front of the dining room table with big, stomping strides.

Corky set down the bottle of Grey Goose. Well, now she knew the answer to the question *freaky, how?* when it came to Hadley's family. "I'm so sorry to hear about your mother."

"Mother?" Hadley jerked to a stop and threw her hands up. "What's a mother?! I don't even know who that is anymore."

Corky screwed the lid back on the vodka and scrunched her forehead in wordless sympathy. She knew the feeling.

"My whole life I assumed the woman who *raised* me was my mother, only to find out that I was stolen at birth from my real mother—who just so happens to be a queen witch—and secretly given to this other woman who isn't my mother. Except she *is* my mother, right? Because she raised me."

Corky blinked. That *was* pretty convoluted.

A timer *dinged*.

Hadley marched into the kitchen. "I just don't... Ugh." She snatched a potholder off a hook and yanked a cookie sheet of TGIFridays' potato skins out of the oven. "How am I supposed to think about this?"

Corky didn't have an answer. Mary Sills had raised her, and so, yes, she felt a special love for the woman, but that didn't completely fill the void inside her—Mary wasn't her real mother. Corky had jumped through every imaginable hoop—including trying to save Mary's foster home—to get Mary to love her like a real daughter, but nothing Corky ever did created the kind of primal bond she craved.

Tossing aside the potholder, Hadley seized a spatula and transferred the potato skins from the cookie sheet onto a serving plate. "Not knowing who my true family is has left me feeling so…so rudderless."

Rudderless…so that's how I've been feeling my whole life.

Hadley crossed back to the dining table and plopped the serving plate in the center—one potato skin flipped over. "I'm not making sense, am I?"

"You're making perfect sense. At least to me." Corky pulled out the chair she'd been sitting in before all the not-really-an-earthquake drama began. "I was left on the doorstep of a group home when I was a baby." She sat. "I know *nothing* about my parents." And she would never know anything either. If she'd been part of a secret adoption, then maybe she would've had a place to start digging. But an abandonment left her nowhere.

"God, that's worse." Hadley sank heavily into the chair across from her.

"Oh, I'd say each of our situations has its own level of horrible." Although in her secret heart, if Corky had to choose between not knowing her parents at all versus knowing them—but knowing they were bad—she'd pick the latter.

"I suppose so." Hadley's eyes rimmed red. She kneaded one with the heel of her hand. "Let's talk about something else, okay?"

"Sure." Corky grabbed an appetizer plate.

"I…I'm so glad you're staying." Hadley's smile was both forced and genuine. "I never got the chance to tell you."

They'd just been sitting down for celebratory cocktails when the weird *pfff-whumping* noise started…and, no, Corky wasn't a big fan of earthquakes, but she almost would've preferred that the noise *was* due to a natural disaster instead of magic search-orbs being dropped by a band of witches.

Her brain was beginning to hurt from trying to take in all the bizarre.

The existence of vampires…in an idyllic town built underground…a woman who Corky hadn't seen since law school mysteriously appearing in the same strange town, claiming to be a sister Dragon…no-fraternization laws and life-bonds and a populace of virgins…and now witches…the queen baddie turning out to be her best friend's mother…

"I didn't even know you weren't going to stay," Hadley said.

"Um, yeah…" Corky reached for a potato skin and dropped it quickly onto her plate. *Ouch.* It was still really hot from the oven. "Sorry. It was the whole vampire thing."

"Totally understandable." Hadley took the other appetizer plate. "How are you doing with all that now?"

"There's still a lot of information to absorb."

Hadley nodded. "Vârcolac culture is complex." Reaching for the serving plate, Hadley turned the upside down potato skin right-side up. "What's been the most surprising thing for you?"

"I guess the virgin part." How many times had Corky caught Vasile staring at her like he wanted to fuck her brains out? Stares like that didn't come from a man who'd never fucked a single brain out, ever.

Did they?

Then again, maybe *wanting* to finally fuck a brain out was why he looked at her like that.

"I was in the dark about that with Thomal too." Hadley spun the potato skin she'd righted but didn't take it. "When he still hadn't tried to sleep with me after three months of dating, I started to get a complex."

"*Three* months." Corky gaped. "My God, that's—wait. Dr. Parthen mentioned that Marissa and Chelsea weren't told the truth for three months. Were you part of that group?"

"Yes." Hadley slouched back in her seat, suddenly sullen. "Except I got the cheating louse of the group, and those two ended up with great guys."

"I'm so sorry, Hadley."

Hadley snatched up her glass and gulped down half her cocktail. When she came up from her drink, she was smiling again—although it was another one of forced gaiety. "So speaking of great guys… Now that you're staying, we need to fix you up with someone."

We? "Um…maybe I'll just chill for a bit." Corky eyed the skins, trying to remember which one Hadley had messed with so much.

"C'mon." The idea had already perked Hadley up. "Let me play matchmaker for you. It'll be a good distraction."

But, see, a woman who'd confessed to choosing the wrong men all the time putting her head together with another woman who'd confessed to the same problem didn't seem like the smartest plan.

Hadley drank more of her cocktail. "Does anyone stand out?"

"Not yet." Corky poked a forefinger at her potato skin, testing its temperature. "I've only had run-ins with Vasile."

Hadley *hmmed.* "Vasile's really severe. In the five months since the Moon-Riders arrived in Ţărână, I don't think I've ever seen him smile. It makes him a hard guy to read."

That was a definite negative. If Corky couldn't read a man, how was she supposed to properly negotiate a conversation? She needed to know the right things to say.

"Are you attracted to him?" Hadley asked.

How odd, but Corky wasn't sure.

She squinted back at the times she'd seen Vasile but still couldn't decide if he was handsome or not.

His mane of black hair was luxurious, she could say that much, and his body fit her big-and-strong requirements—he was tall, broad-shouldered, and flat-bellied, looking powerful enough to lift the Lincoln Town car she'd arrived in. His big-boned frame carried a great deal of muscle but without the usual awkwardness or clumsiness of most large men. He moved with…with something darker than simple masculine grace…something that gave the impression of night and silence and a sort of raw, feral vitality.

Corky sat blinking in her chair, the pulse at the side of her throat suddenly quickening.

"You should go out with him," Hadley said. "Find out if you like him."

Corky gave one last hard blink, then picked up the salt shaker. "Uh…I don't know, Hadley. Between the language barrier and our cultural differences, the two of us are probably worlds apart." She salted her potato skin.

Hadley wobbled her highball glass back and forth, clanking the ice. "Vasile will be a bit of a project, yeah, but you'll never know if he's worth the effort if you don't give him a chance."

A project? Another negative. Every man Corky had ever dated was a major project, always requiring so much effort and self-sacrifice.

But then you never complain, do you? Ever. You're pathetic.

She grimaced. "I think I need to figure out my personal life before I date anyone, just like you're doing."

"Oh, no, don't say that! You don't know what you're missing until you've dated a vampire." Hadley finished off her drink. "And the cultural gap will lessen as Vasile continues to adjust to life here, don't you think?"

Maybe. And she could always brush up on her Romanian. She'd once been fluent, thanks to Mary Sills, née Zugravescu, speaking the language to all her foster kids.

On top of that, Kimberly had vouched for him…and so had Hadley.

Despite Hadley calling him *severe* and a *project* now, back on Corky's first night in the apartment, Hadley described him as nice.

Vasile's a nice guy—both Nicolae and Vasile are…

Hmm. Taking a drink, Corky looked over her cocktail glass at Hadley. "How about this—I'll go out with Vasile if it's on a double date with you and Nicolae."

Hadley's smile fell away. "I don't know about that, Corky. I rejected Nicolae when he was scruffy and grimy, but after his makeover turned him into smokin'-hot yum, *now* I'm willing to go out with him. That doesn't seem fair. Not only that, but if I date Nicolae because he's hot, then I'm still the same arm-candy addict I've always been, aren't I?"

"I suppose," Corky admitted. "But when you think about it, the same applies to me with Vasile."

"How?"

"You called Vasile *really severe.* That sounds a lot like 'emotionally unavailable' to me."

"Oh." Hadley stared down at her empty glass in a defeated way.

Corky ate her potato skin and sighed.

Chapter Twenty-Three

Three days later
7:25 p.m.

VASILE APPROACHED THE HIGH, WOODEN long-table and chose the jug containing an orange potation—not simply the juice of an orange but rather a mixture of many fruits and vegetables. This jug was different from the ones found at the bar of Garwald. This one was made of crystal glass and carved with an elegant pattern of swirls.

The entire room—named "Main Parlor"—was comely and cultured, outfitted for the noblest of guests. Dark brown draperies of a thick and heavy fabric were drawn back with ropes of gold from windows that soared taller than a man. Two walls were painted a deep green, the other two lined with shelves containing Old World, leather-bound volumes of books. Lamps on the walls resembled nineteenth-century design.

Odd, how this community sought to be modern in so many respects, yet this room appeared out-of-date. There was even a chute into which dirty laundry could be deposited—to be used by domestic staff, such as maids and footmen and the like, who existed no more.

Vasile knew not how the room was furnished before the arrival of the Moon-Riders, but now it was equipped with numerous straight-backed wooden chairs clustered into tight circles—an arrangement meant to facilitate conversation.

Main Parlor was the location assigned for Romanian Conversation Class.

Once the attendees refreshed themselves with the offered provender, all would take seats in their assigned conversation circle and discuss a topic chosen by Bujor, the language schoolman.

Conversation Class met two times per week.

The one on Monday evening was organized for intermediate to advanced students and lasted sixty minutes. The one on Wednesday—this evening—was for students of all levels and lasted thirty minutes. Bujor explained that a beginning student oft became overly taxed while trying to speak a foreign language for a full hour.

This dilemma Vasile understood very well.

The people gathered tonight consisted of a great many Moon-Riders—for Romanian Conversation Class was a place where they could feel like leaders and experts—plus most of the warriors—whom Vasile had already greeted—plus many council members. There were also a few other interested parties, including two new students.

A student wishing to attend Conversation Class had to first graduate from classroom work with a sufficient understanding of Romanian vocabulary and sentence structure, and tonight one of the new students was Rachel, mate to warrior Kasson. She was a new mother to his baby son.

The other new student was Corky.

Vasile had not seen Corky in three days, and being near to her now made his heart thump. He could not entirely tell if this reaction was due to fear or gladness. In all likelihood it was both, the fear being born from not knowing whether Corky had not seen him due to life busyness or because she had avoided him purposefully from motivations of mislike. The gladness sprang from a reason most evident—she was *his*, and she was fair, and kind, and in so many ways a comfort to him.

He had missed her.

Vasile poured himself a glass full of the orange-colored

juice and drank it with a hand that was of a sudden slightly unsteady—Bujor was leading Corky toward him now.

"<Vasile,>" said Bujor. "<Corky will join your group tonight. Ælsi can't make it, so it'll be you, Roth, and her. Okay?>"

"<That is fine.>" Vasile nodded a greeting to Corky.

She offered him a smile.

The thumping in his chest accelerated. Her proffered expression was, in most respects, a polite one, but her smile still showed her soul, and it was most beautiful. Even better, her eyes were no longer full of fright or hesitancy toward him. She must have determined that he was not a man bent on hurting her.

This was a glad tiding to discover.

As Bujor left to join his own group, Vasile told Corky, "<I am sore astonished to see you here. How did you graduate from classroom work with the necessary language skills in just three days' time?>"

She paused before answering, her expression altering to one of inquisitiveness.

He had no inkling what he had said, however, that was such a curiosity.

"<I learn when a small child,>" responded Corky.

Hearing her, he was *very* impressed. As basic and unpracticed as her Romanian was, she spoke with very little accent. This was an unexpected and welcome boon. This woman he had liking for spoke his language. This would help him discuss subjects with her if they should ever go on the meal-date.

"<Come. Please.>" Vasile gestured at his grouping of chairs, set in the corner of Main Parlor at a farthest distance from the door and near to a window. "<We will be situated over here.>"

Vasile led Corky to the circle of chairs he had indicated.

Roth Mihnea, co-leader of the community, was already there and seated.

Roth was a man of quality, black-haired, and always dressed in fashionable attire made of expensive material. Tonight was no exception.

Roth came to his feet when they arrived.

"I'm not sure if you remember me," said Roth to Corky, holding a hand out to her. "I was in the garage to greet you on the day you arrived."

"Of course." Corky shook the hand Roth had extended to her and accorded him a smile—polite again. "It's nice to see you."

Bujor called out to the class. "<All right, everyone. Let's get started.>"

They all sat.

"<Tonight we're going to discuss holidays specific to our culture,>" instructed Bujor. "<Community members might have something different to say from Moon-Riders. This is another way for us to learn about each other.>" Bujor joined his group.

Roth turned to Vasile. "I'm sorry, but I didn't quite understand everything Bujor said. What's tonight's subject?"

"<Days of celebration,>" clarified Vasile.

Roth remained hesitant. He glanced at Corky.

"Holidays," offered Corky. "Christmas, Easter, New Year's Eve, and the like."

"Aha," said Roth in indication of his understanding, adding a nod too.

"<Try to speak in Romanian,>" urged Vasile.

People in each circle commenced their discussions, and soon the room was abuzz with overlapping voices.

"<Of which holiday do you have a mind to discuss?>" asked Corky of Roth. "<Christmas, Easter, the Eve of New Year?>"

"Wow," said Roth—this was a common exclamation of awe or surprise. "How do you already speak Romanian so well?"

Corky made the same explanation to Roth as she had to Vasile. "<I learn when a small child. From my...>" She paused to consult with Vasile in English. "How do you say foster mother?"

"<I do not know this term in Romanian.>"

Corky thought about it for a moment. "<This type of mother is a substitute mother. Mary Sills is from Romania, and she speaks Romanian to me when I am a child. The language remains in certain areas of my mind.>"

Roth crossed his legs, the expensive material of his trousers making a *swish* sound. "That'll be helpful."

"*Da,*" agreed Vasile. "<Now let us discuss days of celebration.>"

"Right," said Roth. "Do you already know about Christmas, Easter, and New Year's Eve?"

"<Yes,>" answered Vasile.

Roth paused, then looked at Corky. "How about Valentine's Day?"

Corky checked with Vasile. "<Have you heard of the Day of Lovers on a previous occasion?>"

"<No. What is it?>"

Corky gestured for Roth to begin.

"Uh..." hesitated Roth. "<It is a day for bonded mates to celebrate love of theirs...um, their love.>"

"<But,>" added Corky, "<the lovers celebrate the *romantic* side of love.>"

"<What do you mean by romantic?>" The moment Vasile asked this question, spots of heat sprayed up his nape.

Lovers was a term used to refer to people who engaged in sexual intercourse. So if Corky was about to make an explanation of *romantic* that contained descriptors similar to those used in sex education class, Vasile did not see how he would prevent himself from imagining pole-pressing her.

He squeezed the muscles in his thighs.

Chapter Twenty-Four

Sitting with tensed muscles, Vasile waited in apprehensive silence for the explanation to come.

Corky conferred with Roth. "<How explain you to him this idea of romance?>"

"Hmm," ruminated Roth. "<How about it is showing love with actions and things rather than with talking speech?>"

Corky looked at Vasile again. "<Roth is saying that on the Day of Lovers a man brings flowers to his special woman or candies of chocolate.>"

"<These are considered *gifts*?>" Vasile felt it important to verify this, for he did not see how such impractical items would be well-received.

"<Yes,>" confirmed Corky.

Vasile frowned. "<Not a brace of rabbits for the kettle?>"

"<Not in general.>" Corky smiled. "<Flowers or candy.>"

Picking flowers from a field did not seem like something his hands were designed to do. He had always imagined building a house for Corky in order to communicate his intention to win her, or slaying any creature—man or beast—that should threaten her, or stoking the hearth fire to the perfect degree so she would never be cold, and likewise keeping the larder well-stocked so she would never be hungry. But...*very well.* If he must pick flowers to show her how he felt about her, then he would do so.

"<The lovers,>" continued Corky, "<may also share a meal together in a private way. Or in a setting that is...>" She switched to English. "How do you say *intimate*?"

"<Intimate,>" provided Vasile.

"<Yes. The two lovers are the only people present at the table—no one else. Candles light the space. Soft music plays. This is what an intimate setting is.>"

"<And women like this?>"

She smiled again. "<Well, I do.>"

He would memorize all those things then. "<But I don't understand something. If mates share a great affection for each other at all times, why must they have a special Day of Lovers?>"

Corky paused, that expression of inquisitiveness again passing over her face, as if she was trying to fathom certain things inside his mind.

Why did she not ask him directly? He would tell her of his own free will, if only he knew what her questions were.

He frowned internally. If these things were not bad things.

Put your best foot forward with a woman was something socialization class had taught the Moon-Riders. This was not an instruction on how to properly ambulate, but rather it meant not to be uncouth and rude: to chew with the mouth closed, to wash the stink from the armpits, to not speak in an unflattering manner. But most of all, to listen with interest to the words she says.

Nowhere in all these stratagems was it mentioned that a man should confess all the ways he had failed to achieve certain expectations of himself. *This* Vasile understood. It was the same as his father had taught him throughout life.

Be the best.

Be the greatest protector, the most skilled hunter, the strongest in moral character.

This recitation came often in his mind as a ready remind-er that the Lazăr men confronted the lifelong burden of their heritage. They would never progress through their days with ease. There would always be people who sought to shun them, so they must never give anyone reason to do so—they must always be the best.

Vasile was not the best.

And winning a Dragon woman was already such a complex and confusing undertaking that he did not see how presenting a list of his shortcomings would help his exertions.

Roth noticed the extended silence and inquired, "Is something the matter?"

"No." Corky chuckled. "<I'm just unused to Vasile's style of speech.>" She looked at Vasile. "<You don't speak Romanian in the manner of Mary Sills. The Romanian you speak is of a much more old-fashioned kind than hers. I thought it was only your English that was an older style, but it is your native speech too.>"

Vasile sat very still, not at first able to deem if this was a criticism of him or not. After some thought, it seemed to be solely an observation. So he admitted, "<Yes. I learned my language in the ancient tongue. My brother is ever scolding me for not modernizing.>"

Roth leaned toward Corky. "His brother does what?"

"Gives him a hard time," translated Corky. She crossed her legs, and the new position exposed a long length of her leg at the side of her skirt.

Vasile observed this part of her body with fascination. Her leg was slim and lovely, the flesh soft-looking but firm-looking. Her shoe had a pointed stilt at the heel that formed her foot into a pleasing arch.

Grabbing sensations built in his belly, and he forced himself to stop staring. "<I try to better my understanding of English. I watch more television now.>" Although many times this was as much a confusion as a revelation. He could not discern what was so comical about *Schitt's Creek*, for instance. "<I also study your common words. For instance, I have learned many slang terms for the male appendage.>"

He recited them in English. "Dick, wiener, member, unit, shaft, pecker—which makes me think of a bird—rod, pud, dong, ding-dong, cock—another bird—schlong, third leg"—*an absurd anatomical construction to imagine*—"tallywhacker, staff, and then some very odd permutations I do not think I have correct: skin flute, love muscle, main vein, pork sword, and meat popsicle. Are these latter ones accurate?"

Corky did not speak, even though her mouth was open very wide.

"Skin flute?" asked Roth, his forehead knitting.

Corky swung toward Roth. Her mouth opened even wider, so wide that Vasile could see clear through to the back of her tongue.

"That can't be correct," stated Roth.

"Verily," agreed Vasile. "These last ones all seem like abominations."

Roth addressed Corky. "*Is* skin flute correct?"

Her lips moved about in what looked like uncontrollable twitching. She still made no sound, though.

Maybe she was disturbed because Vasile had failed to recite words for her woman parts. So he said to her in assurance, "I will learn slang terms for the female appendage next." She should not be made to think that these terms were unimportant to him.

Her eyes grew watery and bright. "Oh, no, no, haha, that won't be necessary for you to…uh, uh…" Her chest lurched and she laughed.

It was a joyful, harmonious sound, and many heads in other groups pivoted toward their circle.

Vasile did not know what he had done to inspire Corky to make this sound, but whatever it was, he was most glad he did it.

"<All right, everyone,>" announced Bujor. "<Class is over for the evening.>"

People in the other circles began to come to their feet.

Toni wandered over to their group. "Sounds like you're having a great time over here. What was so funny?"

Corky looked at Toni with eyes still sparkly with her good humor. "Oh, nothing. Vasile is just a fabulous group leader."

Toni turned a smile on him. "I might have to join your group next class. If that's okay?"

He nodded to Toni in acceptance of her suggestion, then nodded more deeply to Corky, indicating his thanks for her compliment. Her praise was putting a monstrous swelling in his chest, the likes of which he had never felt before.

He did not know what would come of such a feeling, so he ducked his head and made hurried strides through Main Parlor, departing the room before Corky should bear witness to a strange happenstance.

Chapter Twenty-Five

CORKY JOGGED OUT OF THE mansion's front door after Vasile, spotting him as he exited the gate that was built into the iron fence surrounding the building.

"Vasile!" she called out, still jogging. "May I talk to you?"

Vasile stopped and turned. "I am here."

He said the words simply enough, but she caught a glimpse of uncertainty in him—the same as she'd seen right before he recited penis slang terms.

Tenderness welled in her. Beneath the stern expressions and the hard strength of his body, there was an endearing, lost quality to Vasile, maybe even a bit of innocence and vulnerability. She'd bet there was even more. She just needed to learn how to find it.

You'll never know if he's worth the effort if you don't give him a chance…

"I was wondering," she said, "if you'd like to go out for a drink with me at Garwald's."

"Go out?" he repeated.

"Yes. On a date." *Innocent* and *vulnerable* were about as far away from her typical man choices as she could get, but now that she was in Ţărână, maybe it was time to change things up. And wouldn't a non-petulant-and-selfish man be refreshing?

"You would like an appointment to consume a drink together and discuss ourselves. Correct?"

She started to chuckle but cleared it from her throat. The way he put things was such fun. "Yes. Correct."

"Is this permitted?"

"Um…" *Isn't it?* "You don't think we're allowed to date?"

"No, my question is otherwise—is it permitted for *you* to ask *me* on the drink-date?"

"Why wouldn't it be?"

"I thought it man duty to ask the woman?"

"Oh, no." She brought up a smile. "It's permitted for the woman to ask the man too."

A micro-twitch of an eyebrow. "Very well. When is good hour for you?"

"How about now?"

Garwald's Pub was decorated with an eclectic jumble of western- and fishing-themed décor—sawdust on the floor, an old wooden boat hanging from the ceiling with a fishing net draped over the side, a life preserver on the wall—along with typical bar advertisements, like lit-up *Coors* and *Budweiser* signs.

Directly across from the main door was a large oval-shaped bar with a brass footrail set in the middle of the room. It was surrounded by barstools, except where there was a pass-through for waitstaff. Off to the right of the bar was a dance floor plus a curtained stage for live music. Square four-top tables and chairs took up the left side. Lining the walls were booths lit by shaded lamps hanging from the ceiling. A pool room way in the back was quasi-separated from the main bar by a line of upright wood poles, kind of like open framing. A huge deer head with big, intricate horns hung on one of the pool room walls.

Corky and Vasile sat in a booth next to the jukebox.

Michael Jackson's *Wanna Be Startin' Somethin'* was playing, but not too loudly. The bar was less than a quarter full. It was eight o'clock on a Wednesday, so the happy hour crowd was long gone, and since it was a weeknight, nothing too boisterous would be happening later in the night.

For drinks, Corky chose a glass of white wine. Vasile

ordered a draft beer.

He didn't talk to her while they waited for their drinks to arrive.

He might not have anything to say, but Corky also got the sense that Vasile was the type who did one thing at a time.

Now was the time to wait for the waitress.

Later was for talking.

Corky sat with her hands folded and observed him.

He had the most immobile, unexpressive face she'd ever seen…and maybe this was why she couldn't figure out if he was handsome. His face gave away nothing about the man he was—and how could anyone be either good-looking or bad-looking with no personality attached? His eyes were extraordinary, though, a unique gray-on-gray color—thunder gray near the black seed pearls surrounding his irises, a lighter gray near the pupils.

The waitress dropped off their drinks.

Vasile still didn't speak, and it was then Corky realized he didn't know what to say.

She needed to come to the poor guy's rescue.

"Yeah, so…" She gestured in a vague way behind Vasile at the pool room. "I've never been able to figure out why a bar would put a deer head on the wall." For starters, a dead animal probably stank to high heaven.

Vasile glanced over his shoulder. "It is elk."

She squinted at the animal. "How can you tell?"

"Head bigger than deer. Antlers bigger."

Antlers…oh, yeah, that's right. Not horns.

"Males make loud, roaring noise during rut."

"Do they?" She laughed a weird laugh. Something about the rawness of the word *rut* made her mouth go dry. *Wow.* That was a new level of hard-up-ness to sink to, wasn't it? "Maybe that's where the term 'randy buck' comes from, eh?"

Vasile stared down at his beer, the corners of his eyes tightening.

Corky observed the top of his head. His hair was such a deep, rich black, it glinted almost blue in the dim light.

The silence from him continued.

She moved her lips around. *Hickory dickory dock. The mouse went up the clock. The clock struck one. The mouse went down…*but, you know, not in the *good* way of going down, not like "going down *on…*"

Really? That's where she was going with this?

Tick tock, tick tock.

"Did I say something wrong?" she asked.

One of Vasile's shoulders edged up an inch. "Male elk called bull, not buck."

"Oh." Now she needed to peel the mask off Vasile's face and find out who he actually was. Because what guy on God's green earth ever hesitated to mansplain when given the chance? "Why are males called bulls?"

Vasile lifted his head and looked at her for a long moment. "Because he make roaring sound during rut."

"Oh, hah. Yeah, duh."

A couple of creases appeared between Vasile's eyebrows. "What means *duh*?"

"It means I *should* know my deer from my elk. I grew up in the middle of the woods, after all." She just hadn't paid a whole lot of attention to the wildlife, preferring to pretend she didn't live where she lived.

"Truly? You live in woods?"

She seemed to have caught his attention with that—he was now sitting up straighter. "Yep. A place called Pine Hills. It's about an hour and a half from here."

A bit of the tension eased from the corners of his eyes. "I, as well, live in mountains."

She drank some wine, nodding. "Hadley mentioned that to me. In the Carpathians, right?"

"Correct," he said. "Where in Romania does substitute mother hail from?"

"Mary Sills? I'm not sure from where, exactly. Sighişoara, I think."

Vasile rumbled in approval. "Medieval town in Transylvania. Very beautiful."

The medieval part made sense. "Mary was always telling us kids old-fashioned fables from back home." It was one of Corky's favorite memories of her life at the group home, Mary Sills sitting in her big, lumpy armchair, spinning her yarns. "The Bălaur dragon and the Căpcăun ogre and others."

"I know these," he said, and there was something different about his face now.

Maybe it was the tautness around his eyes. It seemed completely gone.

"Mary also recited American nursery rhymes to us." Corky drank more wine. "When I'm nervous or scared, I tend to repeat them inside my head. Crazy, huh?"

Vasile observed her intently.

She'd meant the question to be rhetorical, but he seemed to be giving it serious consideration.

"Haha. Well, don't lock me up or anything."

"Mircea from back home stick pickles in ears. *He* crazy. You, no." Vasile paused. "Unless you put strange items in ears."

"I don't," she assured him, laughing again.

"What things make nervous?"

"Witches and vampires," she tossed out as a joke—well, a half-joke—but then she cut off her chuckle.

The tautness in Vasile's face was back. "*Me.*"

Chapter Twenty-Six

"Oh, no, haha, you don't make me nervous—I mean, not anymore." God, how Corky hated to blow a conversation. She finished her wine in a single gulp, then gestured at her goblet. "May I have another?"

Vasile stared fixedly at her glass. "Another," he repeated. "You want second cup?"

"Please."

He aimed his focus out to the bar and searched the premises. After a moment, he stood, strode to the bar, slipped a wine goblet out of its notch in the overhead hanger, then strode back.

The dark-haired woman behind the bar studied him with surprise.

Vasile set the empty glass in front of Corky.

Corky bit her bottom lip, sitting quietly amused. *Well, that's never happened before.* She twisted around and wiggled her fingers at the bartender.

The dark-haired woman came over.

"May I have another glass of white wine, please?" Corky said to her.

"Sure thing." The dark-haired woman took notice of Vasile's untouched beer. "Your draft okay, Vasile?"

He nodded. "Good."

"Okay. Be right back."

"You want more *wine*," Vasile told Corky as the dark-haired woman walked off. "Not second cup."

"Ah, yes. I should've been more clear."

Vasile finally took a sip of his beer.

Lionel Richie began to sing about being able to go *All Night Long*.

Dancing…he was referring to *dancing*.

Corky tapped her fingernails against the bowl of her goblet.

Vasile set his mug down.

"So, uh…" Corky spun her wine goblet by the stem. "Do you miss the woods?"

"*Da*. Very much. The smell of tree. The air of a certain cleanness. The moon."

The musical chirp of crickets…the hoot of an owl… The memories brought a twinge of nostalgia to Corky. Funny how a person didn't appreciate certain things until after they were gone.

"You miss?" he asked.

"Thinking about it now, I guess I do miss some of those things."

The dark-haired woman brought Corky a new white wine.

"Thanks," Corky said.

Nodding, the bartender took Corky's empty when she left.

"Although I do have one bad memory about the forest," Corky told Vasile.

Vasile watched her in an oddly still way. "What is?"

"A boy I liked went off in the woods with someone else when he was supposed to be with me."

"This bad, why?"

She laughed in a burst of air. "Well, Vasile, how would you like it if during our date I went off with another man and made out with him?"

"What means *made out*?"

"Kiss and…" Maybe she'd just leave it at *kiss*— "…things."

He scowled. "I no like."

Now they were communicating. "I didn't like it either. The boy used the forest to sneak around and hide, and…and it hurt my feelings. So it's a bad memory."

"I sorry to be hearing that."

"Thank you."

The song changed. Madonna warbled about getting her groove on and how her man needed to prove his love to her.

Did the jukebox not have *any* songs from the past ten years?

"The forest is good place to hide." Vasile curled his hand around his beer mug. "But not for motivation of hurting."

She started to take a sip of wine, then set her goblet back down. "Did you ever hide in the forest?"

"Betimes."

There was a hint of something in his eyes again. "From what?"

"Endless quarreling. Insults. Ill-bred people."

"Who?"

"Other Moon-Riders." The skin beside his eyes clenched. He picked up his beer. "I no talk about."

But…the conversation had finally started going deeper.

"It is no-good discussion."

"Um…okay." Turning aside, Corky heaved a sigh and gazed out at the bar.

She spotted Thomal at one of the tables, sitting with a striking blond woman. Probably his wife, and although Corky hated to be disloyal to Hadley, there was something about the woman that Corky immediately liked.

Norah Jones' *Don't Know Why* started to play.

Corky covertly searched for a clock. *Vasile will be a bit of a project…* No kidding. Could she leave already without being rude?

"You have pet?"

She startled back around. "I'm sorry?"

"Animal in house you no eat," he clarified. "Only for show."

An animal I…? She hid a smile. "Sort of. I look after a parakeet on a regular basis."

"A what?"

"<A parakeet.>"

"Ah. I know this type of bird. Very tiny bird."

Not good eating was sort of an implied hanger-on to that sentence. "He's called 'Tweets.'"

"You name this bird?"

"His owner did, yes."

Small muscles contracted all over his face, like he was absorbing that information in gradual increments. "And you like this bird?"

"Um…" If she was being honest with herself, she bird-sat more out of a need to encourage Tweets' owner, Sharon, to like her rather than out of an undying love for parakeets. "Sure…you know." She rearranged the ketchup and mustard bottles, switching places with the salt and pepper shakers. "He's a good boy. And what about you? Did you have any pets?"

"We have dovecote for birds back home. But…" One of his shoulders rose a little. "We consume those birds."

"You never had a dog?"

"For hunting?"

"For friendship."

His eyebrows knotted. "No."

The concept seemed so utterly foreign to him, it was kind of sad. "Well…um…" She searched for something to say. "Were those dovecote birds tasty?"

"Ah, yes. Very delicious." He hooked a thumb behind him. "Elk good eating too."

A laugh bubbled out of her. "You seem to know a lot about meat."

"<I'm a fine hunter, Glowing Corky.>"

She popped up her brows at the odd endearment.

"<You will never go hungry with me as your man.>"

She lowered her lashes, heat creeping into her cheeks. "It's a little early to be talking about being my man, isn't it?"

"<No. You are mine.>"

She dropped her hands into her lap and pinched up a piece of her skirt. He seemed remarkably sure of himself.

To Vasile you smell like a potential mate…

"<It is a veritable moil having to win you before I can make you mine,>" he said. "<The process gives me tension in places all over my body. Not that such a nuisance has bearing. I will work to win you, Glowing Corky, no matter.>"

She blinked at him, her jaw loosening.

"<I will pick the flowers and light the candles and tend the cows and patch the roof and kill any threat to your being. I will do whatever the task. Because every moment I am near to you, my senses grow more awake. I cannot have true happiness in this life without you. Nor can you without me. I am sure of this.>"

A swallow worked its way slowly down her throat. He might've just broken a major rule of first date etiquette—don't overshare—but who cared?

He'd knocked her heart out of the park with that speech.

"Why, Vasile Lazăr," she said in a soft voice. "I do believe you've figured out what *romantic* is."

✧　✧　✧

VASILE STRODE WITH PURPOSE UP the stairsteps to the house where Dev bided. Stopping at the door, he knocked and waited.

The house was painted a pale blue color and not to his liking. It was a shade contrary to what would be needed to blend into a forest well. But then, seeing as this community did not have to hide from the Patru Puternic—the Otherworldly enemy factions in the warded lands back home—what mattered a non-obscuring color?

The door to the house swung open, and Dev appeared. He was dressed in loose pants of a cotton material and a simple T-shirt. His right hand was wrapped with bandage tape, for he cut himself earlier today while installing the last of the "deflectors" on the cave roof.

These devices were enchanted by Toni to do what the name indicated—deflect the magic of the seeking-orbs the daughters of Zalina were using to find the Dragon-Witch. Over these three days past, Vasile and the other warriors had been climbing long ropes that dangled from the ceiling in order to place these deflectors. This was strenuous work, demanding much brute strength. His muscles ached, and other warriors had sustained slight injuries from the hard labor, same as Dev.

Dev smiled. "Hey, Vasile. How goes it?"

Dev always greeted Vasile with enthusiasm, and this was a pleasure.

Vasile spoke without preamble. "<I went on a drink-date with Corky after Conversation Class tonight, and it was good.>" He had talked very well with her.

Dev grinned wider. "Yeah?"

"Yes." It was almost too much to fathom. "<We didn't discuss hunting or fishing or woodworking, but I still found interest in her. I still like her.>" He liked her very much. "<It's how you told me—there is more to a woman than what she can do to your pole.>"

"That's great, man." Dev switched to Romanian. "<Invite her to depart with you on another date. This time take her to have dinner at the restaurant of Three Friends.>"

"<Yes. I will.> Now that Vasile knew Corky liked him, he could ask her on the meal-date without too much agonizing thought.

"You want to come in?" Dev started to step aside to let Vasile pass into his dwelling.

"No. My thanks, but the hour be late. Enjoy your family. I will see you at the room of lockers on the morrow."

"Sounds good." Dev held out his hand.

Vasile studied the outstretched palm for a moment. It appeared Dev wanted him to shake it. He did so.

"Nice job." Dev gave his hand a solid squeeze.

Needles of sensation peppered his cheeks. A compliment from a man of upstanding character was an extreme honor.

Vasile nodded once. "May the Zâne look upon you well this night." He stepped back.

He would not wish the luck of the fairies on just any man.

But this was Dev.

CHAPTER TWENTY-SEVEN

HER NAME IS ELIZABETH SAVOY, which becomes Miss Lizzy, which becomes Sissy. I give everyone nicknames because Mary Sills likes that—it helps her keep track of all the kids. I'm a senior in high school, and Sissy and I room together at the group home. She and I are the same age and in a lot of the same classes. She says a boy in her physics class wants to date me.

She calls him Leather because of the jacket he wears.

Leather says that I don't have any zits. Why don't I ever have zits?

I don't know. But I never do.

Leather has a nice car.

No zits and a nice car—why can't those things be the start of something between a boy and a girl?

Leather roars up to the front of Mary Sills' Angels in his Camaro on December twenty-fourth to take me to a Christmas party at his parents' house.

I think it's strange that he wants me to meet his parents on our first date, but Mary Sills calls ahead to make sure everything is okay, and she says it is.

His car smells like his suede jacket.

Suede, not leather.

I buckle my seatbelt, and he glances over my shoulder at where I live. Run-down building. Overstuffed with people.

So you live there?

I work there.

It isn't entirely a lie.

I tell him I'm going to college next year. I'm going to major in English and attend law school. I'm going to help people.

He says lawyers are a buncha prima donnas, then he shoots down the street with a screech of tires.

Rockin' Around the Christmas Tree *is playing in the brightly lit living room of his parents' house. Not the Brenda Lee version. Connie Francis. People are drinking and laughing. There are a lot of red Christmas balls hanging around as decoration.*

Leather puts his hand low on my back and urges me toward his parents. His hand is tender and nice, but distant. I don't know how it can be all those things at once, but it is.

This is Catherine, *Leather tells his parents.*

His parents smile widely. They seem very relieved to see me. Look how pretty!

She's going to be a lawyer.

Oh, how wonderful!

Leather checks out the party over my head. Hey, the Jergensons are here.

Leather tells me that we should go over and say hello to the Jergensons' son. He is eighteen years old, i-dent-ti-cal to us.

An unusual skip separates Leather's syllables. I don't know what it means for him to talk this way.

The Jergensons' son is very attractive. His hands are soft and white, and he wears a fancy ring on his pinkie finger. His parents are elderly and want to leave the party early. They ask if Leather and I can take their son home when the party is over.

Leather answers for me, saying we'll be glad to do it.

I smile.

The Jergensons leave, and their son talks to the girl with a poinsettia pinned to her blouse.

Leather's eyebrows are down when he insists that I dance with him. His tone is urgent, and this makes my stomach sloshy. He holds me close with his tender, distracted hands, and my stomach gets slushier. Bing Crosby sings White Christmas, *and I don't even care that it's not Frank Sinatra.*

The Jergensons' son is suddenly standing beside us, asking if we're ready to go.

The music has stopped.

Yes, we're ready.

It takes a long time to return to Mary Sills' Angels that night. The streets are lined with twinkling Christmas lights, and on the way home Leather pulls his Camaro down Shantyback Road. He parks next to a stand of trees.

I stare at the forest with the window halfway down, my heart a brick, watching Leather take the Jergensons' son by the hand and lead him deep into the dark woods.

This is the first time I understand the importance of a man's hands—that they tell the truth when words don't.

Leather's hands are tender, but that tenderness was never meant for me.

Leather's real name is Jacob. Not Jake, but Jacob.

Jacob Sassabo.

CORKY SHOULD'VE PAID BETTER ATTENTION to Hunter's hands.

How his fingernails were always so immaculately, *obsessively* clipped, warning of the kind of man he was on the inside. The kind of man who kept his hands so neat because even the appearance of a mere hangnail would send him into an emotional tailspin.

Or what about the boyfriend before Hunter? Dillon. His fingers were short and stubby—pretty much exactly how emotionally stunted he was.

Exhibit one is received into evidence…

Just ignored.

Corky surreptitiously checked out one of Vasile's hands.

He was sitting across from her in Three Friends Restaurant, and the hand under surveillance was wrapped around a water glass.

Battered knuckles. Squared fingernails. Wide palms.

Corky shivered.

Strong, productive, protective hands.

Hands that had never—unfortunately—touched her.

Not once. Not in four consecutive dates.

Vasile's hand had never even made a play for her hand, just to hold.

She couldn't begin to guess where *kissing* lay in their future. Although, according to Hadley, there wouldn't be *any* action if it wasn't Corky who busted a move.

"The Moon-Riders only discovered their sex drives a few months ago," Hadley explained last night. "And when they did come into their sexuality, they were too aggressive with women at first, which landed them with their shocker anklets. So now they're nervous about starting things."

Corky had gone to bed scratching her head over what to do. What kind of broad hint could she give to a man who didn't understand even the rudiments of flirtation?

Maybe a *hint*, no matter how broad, wasn't enough. Maybe a virgin with a brand-new sex drive required a blunt approach.

Kiss me!—direct, to the point, and unlikely to be misinterpreted.

Although the blunt approach wasn't the most romantic, was it?

Maybe Nature would take its course if Corky got the ball rolling, like...what if she pulled an age-old trip-and-fall maneuver? Do a little *oops* over an uneven part of the cave road and end up in Vasile's arms.

Two bodies pressed close could be very inspiring...although if Vasile still didn't know what to do from there, she could fall back on *Kiss me!*

The waitress glided by and collected their dirty plates, jerking Corky out of her daydream. "Um, so..." she began, searching for a subject to discuss.

Over the course of their dates, they'd pretty much covered all everyday topics, discussing daily life in Romania, daily life in the community, daily life at Mary Sills' Angels, her work as a lawyer, his work as a warrior, favorite food—they agreed on pizza, favorite drink—his, water, hers, coffee (really Manhattans, but she didn't think that sounded appropriate), favorite movie—she preferred films where an underdog prevailed, he didn't watch movies, favorite television show—Romanian TV was now piped into the community, so for him it was *Umbre*, a Romanian drama with a lot of fighting (even though he was supposed to be concentrating on English language shows now…although a case could also be made for him needing to modernize his Romanian), for her, *Schitt's Creek*, which earned a frown from Vasile for some reason, favorite books— he wasn't a big fan of reading, but had recently tried out some Romanian comic books Hannah ordered into the library, and Corky didn't read for pleasure anymore because she read so much at work.

Subjects they had not discussed included his childhood— he refused, his friends beyond the warriors—she suspected he didn't have many, his family—except for a limited amount about Nicolae, and the whole *what-do-you-have-on-your-bucket-list?* question received a confused stare.

Basically, whenever she tried to introduce a personal topic, he clammed up.

"So what do you…" She trailed off again and stared down at the tablecloth.

If she asked him about his ambitions, she got the sense he would just give her another blank stare.

And she was sick of idle chitchat, anyway.

"Is all well with you?" Vasile asked.

She brought her head up. "Yes. Why?"

"You keep begin speak, then stop."

"Oh, uh, I was just admiring the restaurant again. I like it here."

Three Friends was decorated in classic minimalist style, with etched glass fronting the restaurant and a few hanging plants in macramé holders clustered in each corner. The white-clothed tables were set with white china decorated by a simple, but elegant, silver rim.

Lara Izbaşa from the Q&A panel was the one cooking in an open kitchen just inside the main door.

Corky and Vasile had decided to meet for Sunday brunch today, instead of dinner, because they both had to work later—Vasile was on guard duty, and she was still honing an argument with Kimberly to overturn the no-fraternization law.

Corky had also asked her fellow attorney for help with strategizing ways to stop Rand Resources from harassing Mary Sills.

Yesterday Corky received an email from Mary, complaining that not only was she still receiving late-night hang-ups, but just a few days ago a sewer main along the edge of her property "mysteriously" burst and flooded the west side of her land with wastewater.

Fuming, Corky shook her head at the email. *Sewage*, spilled to contaminate a home for *foster children*… Did these corporate monsters have no morals at all?

Typing a response with fast, clumsy fingers, Corky assured Mary that she was still working on her case, although she neglected to add that she and Kimberly had yet to come up with any ideas about how to stop the harassment.

Not without rock-solid proof—and Mary still didn't have that.

Vasile pointed to the two lit votives in the center of their table. "This restaurant has intimate candles you favor. Like for Day of Lovers."

She glanced down at the candles, then giggled. "So it does." He'd remembered that.

"You like meal?"

"Yes. It was very tasty." She'd ordered a vegetarian omelet, Vasile, the steak and eggs. He was a big meat eater.

The waitress returned. "Can I interest you two in dessert?"

"I think we're fine." Corky set her napkin on the table.

Vasile gave his money card to the waitress.

Corky stared at Vasile's hand. "Um…do you want to go for a walk?"

"Good."

Chapter Twenty-Eight

Walking at a footpace of leisure and with no exact purpose or destination was a strange use of time—or waste of time—but humans seemed to enjoy this pursuit, so Vasile kept his strides to a stroll. In between nodding greetings to the occasional passerby on the main byway of Ţărână, he took special care not to collide with Corky.

This was difficult.

Her strides were especially unsteady this day—she oft wandered very close to his person and bumped shoulders with him. He did not understand this. She had not drunk any alcohol beverage with her brunch-meal, so she should have firm command of her footsteps.

If he were to speculate on a reason for her difficulties, he would guess her silly shoes were like enough to blame. There was hardly anything to them, merely a stilt at the heels with crisscrossed leather straps over the top of her feet held in place near to the ankles with a metal latchet.

Such footwear could not be stable. Clearly not—her shoulder just rubbed against his again.

He politely moved over.

She gestured down an offshoot road. "Let's go check out the Water Cliffs park. It's pretty."

"Good."

They aimed down the pathway, but even though they now had a planned destination in mind, they still ambled. There was, of course, a beneficial side to this senseless rate of speed—Corky was the person he most enjoyed being near.

When he was with her, time progressed with ease, not difficulty, and she made him feel like a different person, like a man who *could* be the best someday, if he would but put his utmost effort into the task.

So why hurry to end his time with her?

The Water Park gate was closed. A sign was strung across the front, proclaiming there was no one on duty to guard the life of swimmers, but Corky ignored this warning and entered, urging him to follow.

Empty of people, the aquatic arena was quiet. The *shush-shush* of water flowing against the shore was the primary noise. Birds did not carol, and this lack of song was one of the most difficult adjustments for Vasile—along with the absence of the moon—about living under the earth.

Directly in front of them was the largest manmade pond. Colorful lights shifted from one shade to another at a set interval. This was a spectacle Vasile had never seen before, but of course there were no manmade ponds back home, only real ones.

Corky stepped out of her footwear and trekked onto the sandy ground, evidently wanting to have a closer inspection of this light display.

He followed, watching her toes sink beneath the white sand with each step she took. Heat raced up his spine.

Her toenails were dyed red, and this contrast of bright color next to flesh tones somehow made her toes appear pinker and more feminal. These were *toes*, and he could not fathom what he possibly desired about them, but he did desire them nonetheless. Perchance this was a sign that he desired *all* of her, from the top of her head down to the tips of—

"Oh!" Corky gasped as her foot disappeared into an especially deep pile of sand. Her balance was put out of order, and she lurched forward.

Vasile snapped his vision into focus on her—his woman was falling!—and leapt after her, seizing her upper arm to steady her. *Fir-ar să fie!* he cursed to himself. She had almost—

She swung around to face him and flung her arms around his neck.

He acted quickly to step back from her, as he must do as a gentleman, but she tightened her hold. He went very still, breathing shallow breaths as he tried to ascertain why she was grasping him thusly. She had regained purchase of her feet— she was standing with good balance now. She had no need to keep hold of him.

"Thank you." She peered at him from beneath the lowered fan of her lashes. Her lips were apart by a slight degree.

Her mouth appeared exceptionally soft in that pose. A shudder tumbled through him. He made himself pull his eyes away from—

"Kiss me, Vasile."

He slammed his focus back to her. Had he misheard? It would be a terrible error if he mistook her true desires.

She ran her fingers into his hair, and he nigh vaulted out of his pants. *Dumnezeule!* The feel of her touch upon him was a pleasure beyond any imaginable pale. Heat exploded in the deepest regions of his belly, and a sudden flood of saliva drenched his mouth.

She murmured, "Your hair's so soft."

Her observation served to douse some of the flames in his belly. *Soft?* This was not a complimentary descriptor for him to receive. Yet…the amorous manner in which she gazed upon him now implied that this was not an insult.

She tugged on his nape.

By the glade, what now?

"I give you permission to kiss me."

He blinked twice. And twice more. *Permission.* According to socialization class, this was the voucher he needed to forge ahead. Unfortunately, obtaining permission did nothing to augment his knowledge of what to do. The movie in sex education class had shown a man and woman engaged in the act of kissing, true, but Vasile could not fully deem correct what he had seen. The two lovers had mashed their lips together in a way that looked a mite…unsavory.

Corky stepped into his body. Her chest pressed his.

His stomach muscles quivered. Her closeness added more credence to her sincere desire to kiss him, but he still stood stiffly in her embrace, unable to proceed. He dared not lip-mash his beloved.

"Just *try* kissing me," whispered Corky. "You'll like it, I promise." She tugged again, and even though a herd of centipedes ran amok in his belly, this time he let her draw him down to her mouth, careful not to let his hips touch hers.

She had not invited him to pole-press, only to kiss.

Their mouths touched, and a startled noise flew up his throat. The feel of her lips on his was every sensation he had never known. Warmth and tenderness…softness and sweetness. *Astounding.* This was not an unsavory mashup at all.

After a mere second of hesitation, he swept his arms around her waist. Upon his soul, she was an amazing and pleasing armful. Her breasts were a cushiony, soaring endowment of everything that was *woman*. The feel of them pushed up tight against his chest was sending his new drives lashing through the true male part of his brain—now so open and so hungry.

His fangs throbbed in the sheath of his gums.

Corky took a gentle grip on his hair and angled her head to one side, finding a better placement for their mouths. His heart hummed like a beehive. Everything fit better.

His flesh on his body…his muscles on his bones…

A woman is the second half of you…

All these years—his whole life—he never realized that such a deep want hid inside him. But here it was, coming to life from the tempting kiss of this precious woman.

Corky Disdale *was* his other half. Her scent stoked his hunger as much as a fire in his soul.

When she pulled away too soon, bringing their kiss to a distressing conclusion, he pressed his fingers into her back. "Did I mistake?" He sounded oddly hoarse.

"Not at all." Her eyes appeared sleepy. "I just want you to open your mouth to me."

"I no understand." Was it required that she examine his back teeth at this point in the kissing process?

She took his cheeks between her hands. "Relax your jaw a bit, Vasile, and then let your lips drift apart."

"For why?"

She smoothed both her thumbs over his lips. "<It is feeling of goodness to taste the tongues of one another.>"

He could hardly countenance that to be correct. In truth, to smush one tongue against another sounded wet and sloppy. But then…he had been wrong about the lip-mashing.

"Trust me," urged Corky, her voice softening to a husky rasp.

He had trusted her at the start of this kiss, and so he did again. When she strove to coax his lips apart with her thumbs, he let her, and when she lifted her body onto her toe tips and rubbed her partially open mouth against his, he sucked in a sharpened breath.

He was right to have trusted her to know better—her lips felt even softer kissing in this manner.

Tunneling her fingers through his hair again, she held him in place while she set her lips fully on his, mouth open and wet, but *good* wet—he could not believe how good. There was so much more to taste of her like this.

His blood thundered.

Her tongue found his.

He flashed his eyes open, then shut them. Moist flesh stroking over moist flesh… Not in a thousand moons would he have fathomed how sensitive a tongue was…or how stroking one against the other could send flashes of pleasure through his stomach and groin.

A deep moan broke from him. He tried caressing his own tongue over hers in return.

She sighed into his open mouth.

Pressure built near his pole. He curled his fingers into her shirt.

Corky pushed her hips into his.

His man-balls tugged in tight to his body, and he rolled his eyes high into his head. His balls had never done that before! He choked on the air in his throat and shot away from her, his boots kicking up sand.

"Vasile…?" gasped Corky, a hand flying to her chest. "Are you all right?"

He was not sure how to answer her query conclusively. He had very much liked kissing her, but the peculiar congestion near his male appendage was now painful, and his ability to think, cloudy. He was breathing with more exertion than usual, and everything was strange and powerful and outside of his control. It was, in some respects, alarming.

He gulped and said, "You pole-press." He had not meant to sound accusatory, but he was in an extreme state of bedazzlement.

"I—what?"

He watched the rapid rise and fall of her breasts. A steamy musk came off her and burrowed into his nose. Inside his brain, a whip cracked, and his fangs pounded down.

She stared round-eyed at his long incisors.

His body forced him toward her a perilous step, his fangs aching. He pointed a rigid finger at her purse. "Have mechanism to make ankle shocker function?"

"What?"

He pointed again. "In bag?"

"What?"

Did her repetition of *what?* signify an inability to hear? Or was her mind awhirl, same as his? "You need shock me." He told her this in a firm tone. "You pole-press, and now I want bite."

She took in several large lungfuls of air and in this manner calmed herself. "I don't entirely know what you're talking about, but I'm not going to *shock* you. I would never hurt you."

He absorbed her words, forcing himself to re-hear them in his head several times to be sure of their meaning. He then swallowed with care. No one had ever made such a declaration to him before. For his whole life, people had been more of a mind to hurt him on purpose, not to avoid doing so.

"I—" He could not continue. Her generous promise wholly deserved a response, but he did not have words to explain the depth of what was in his heart.

She gazed at him with radiance in her eyes. "I liked kissing you, by the way. Very much."

Her comment did not help to settle the havoc in his mind. He tried her method of calming himself by drawing in several large breaths, but he did not have as much success as she did.

The glow in her eyes changed from orange to yellow according to the shift of the pond lights. "I want you to feel free to kiss me again whenever you want. Okay?"

It was simple enough to say *yes*—this was not a complicated word-construction—but he could not produce the single syllable.

So he nodded.

"All right." She smiled. "I guess we'd better go now."

Yes, it was time for him to report to work. But he first escorted Corky back to her abode, seeing her safely settled inside, as socialization class had taught him a gentleman must do for his lady.

Chapter Twenty-Nine

C ORKY DROPPED HER PURSE AND keys on the small table beside the door and called out, "Hadley!"

Her roommate shouted, "I'm here!" then appeared in her bedroom doorway. She was wrapped in a bath towel, her wet hair slicked back from her brow. A few droplets of water still pebbled her shoulders. "Is everything okay?"

"Oh, yeah, haha. Sorry, I didn't mean to startle you. It's…well…" Moving farther inside, Corky propped a hip against the kitchen counter and crossed her arms. "I kissed Vasile."

"Oh, wow!" Hadley sailed toward her. "How was it?"

"He kisses like a total virgin." Close-mouthed and uncertain and a little bit awkward.

"Oh, no. Bad?"

She giggled. "Sweet, actually. And when I upped the passion he was totally able to handle it." She still felt a bit scorched from being in his embrace, his powerful arms wrapped around her, his body—all those muscles—pressed intimately against her. "And, by the way, to answer your question: yes, I am most definitely attracted to him. You may have missed this, but"—she raised a finger—"he's extremely hot."

Hadley laughed. "Oh, I've checked out his bod a time or two. Next time you go out with him, try to get his shirt off. I'm curious to know how inked-up he is." She bobbed her eyebrows. "I can't see how far his arm tats go up—"

A knock interrupted her.

Corky turned to answer, but before she could even take a step, the door flew open with a loud bang and Thomal stalked inside.

"Thomal!" Hadley gasped. "What the hell are you doing!? We just got our door fixed from the last time you busted in here."

Thomal roared over to Hadley. "You couldn't say yes to a date with Nicolae, could you? One fucking date, that's all. Would it've killed you?"

Hadley's chin jerked in, her hands tightening where she gripped her bath towel.

"Nicolae just got in a fight at the diner. Tried to pulverize a bunch of Moon-Riders? Does that sound like something Nice Guy Nicolae would do?" Thomal didn't let her answer, just spat out, "*No*. He hasn't been right in the head ever since you rejected him."

Color bled into Hadley's cheeks.

"You're a fucking snob," Thomal hurled at her.

"Shut up! You don't know anything about anything!"

"The fuck I don't," Thomal shot back. "I met your mother while we were going out, and I saw how she was. The snooty former soap opera queen. She didn't give two shits about who I was as a person. She only cared that I'm good-looking. And she raised you and your sisters to be just as shallow."

Tears sprang into Hadley's eyes.

"*Quit* caring so much about what other people think, Hadley. It's ruining your chances for happiness. Get the fuck over yourself and—"

"I'm not listening to this!" Hadley whirled around and dashed for her bedroom.

Or she *tried* to dash—Thomal grabbed her shoulder.

But with her skin still wet, his palm slipped down her back and his fingers accidentally snagged on the edge of her towel...and since he was already in mid-pull, his hand just kept pulling…

…and Hadley's towel got yanked off.

She shrieked and clutched her arms across her naked body. "Holy crap! You monster!"

Thomal gave Hadley's body an indifferent once-over, the towel dangling from his fingertips. "Leave it to you to say the one word you know all Vârcolac hate."

"Get out!" Hadley screamed. "I mean it!"

Thomal slapped the towel down on the floor, did an abrupt turn, and stalked back out.

The door slammed shut, and Hadley ran crying into her bedroom.

Corky gaped at the space where the two combatants had just been.

Had those two really been a couple at one time?

✧　✧　✧

REESE COLLAPSED BACK ON THE couch, watching Steliana exit her kitchen carrying a bag of frozen peas.

"Here—" She handed Reese the bag. "Put this on your bruise."

Grunting, Reese shoved the frozen peas against his left eye.

He'd been doinked in the face by an unidentified fist during the throwdown at the diner—a wreck *he* hadn't started, *oh, mylanta*, if you can believe it.

One Moon-Rider began bumping titties with some other Moon-Riders—weren't those peeps all supposed to be kinfolk?—and before you knew it, a cylindrical sugar caddy was hurling across the restaurant at Steliana's head.

Reese jumped up in time to knock the projectile aside. He then followed that dance move with a flying leap into the fray. *No one* threw shit at his girlfriend—even a girlfriend he was currently chapped at—and escaped a fonging.

Pain…lotsa pain…

He slumped back on the couch.

Girlfriend…

Wadafuck? He'd been dating Steliana for less than a week, and now everyone was bandying about the word *girlfriend.*

Natural assumptions being made.

Inevitable conclusions being drawn.

Excuse the fuck out of him, but shouldn't he be consulted before being committed? Yeah, and feel free to assume he also meant going to the Funny Farm.

Because things were getting waaaay too serious waaaay too fast.

Proof lay in the parental ambuscade he'd endured at the diner just before the fight broke out—and, by the by, rolling around in that brawl was the first time he'd felt like himself since he decided to stay in Schmaltz Town.

Other Reese—who'd been gallivanting around Țărână in his place—was some anomalous successful Man About Town, a guy who contributed towering brilliance to the planning committee and basked daily in the adoration of a smart, beautiful, caring woman.

That fucking wiener dude didn't make trouble or fight or trash talk at all.

"Thanks for what you did for me at the diner." Steliana settled next to him.

Her *How-Low-Can-You-Go* Bridgewater sofa had way more bounce in it than the couch in his apartment—and parenthetically, no way did Fane and he keep peas in their freezer. Other than those conveniences, Steliana's apartment was no place Reese liked to be.

The curtains in the living room were ruched chiffon, the walls a nauseating pale pink, the end tables porcelain-topped with curlicue wooden legs, and three corner shelves were weighed down with fragile glass knickknacks of birds and owls, a peacock at full plume erection, and Cinderella's glass slipper decorated with a dainty, glass-blown bow.

Being in an apartment this frilly put Reese's penis in serious jeopardy of withering.

He'd have happily dealt with—or marginally accepted—all the girlie shit if there was a chance he could've made it into the next room and played a little hide the salami.

No chance of that.

Not unless he bonded forever and ever and ever and ever—*continue ad nauseam*—with the little Draculette.

Steliana touched his knee. "I appreciated you looking out for me, honey."

Honey. Next she'd be calling him poopface, and he'd have to stick a gun in his ear. That'd prolly be a huge favor to everyone, actually.

Reese grunted.

She took her hand back.

In his peripheral vision, he saw her scrape her teeth across her bottom lip.

"Uh…" she said. "I'm so sorry my parents waylaid you at the diner. I swear I didn't know they were going to show up during our date. They've just been really eager to meet you."

He jerked the bag of peas off his face. "We've been dating for, like, four fucking days, Steliana." That didn't even add up to an entire workweek. He couldn't get a package of grunge clothing from *Affliction* delivered that fast, and now suddenly he was *meeting her parents.*

"I know, I know. They just see how crazy I am about you, and they couldn't wait."

How tight-butthole for them. What would they think about Reese never being able to return the favor and introduce them to *his* parents? Like in, *ever, ever, ever.*

Ad fucking nauseam.

Mr. and Mrs. Şofronie, hate to break up the love fest here, but Mom's dead and Dad signed my life away. Gosh, no, Mr. and Mrs. Şofronie, Dad wasn't supposed to do that…

Whenever Dad found a job, he was *supposed* to come back

and rescue Reese from whatever foster home he was festering in. But eventually, inevitably—inescapably, inexorably, blah, blah, blah—the old man would lose his job again. Reese would be bounced back into the system, soaking his pillow every night with a river of stupid fucking tears while he waited for Pops to get his shit together and pull Reese back out. The wait was interminable, but it always ended.

Until Reese turned ten.

"And I *am* crazy about you." Steliana ran her fingers through his hair, angling several strands up to examine them. "I never see any red roots. How do you keep your hair so dark?"

Reese pushed her hand away. Every morning he touched up the dye-job, but he wouldn't tell her that. Fuck if he was allowing her the kind of subject change that would save her ass from a well-deserved ream-out.

'Course *ass* and *ream-out* made him think of sex.

Of which he was having none, thank you.

Steliana rested her hands in her lap and went back to chewing her lip. "You should let your hair go back to its natural color."

So he could spend his days getting twatted? "People harass redheads." Funny, how much less he'd been janked once his hair was black.

"Not here, they don't."

Great. More mushpot. He bounded to his feet. "Why?"

She blinked up at him, her lips parting. "Why what?"

"Why are you crazy about me, Steliana?"

Wrong question. Her expression turned all gooey.

"First off," she said, "you're smart."

"No, I'm not," he lied.

Her head tilted. "Why don't you want people to think that about you?"

Because when people underestimate you, they assume you're not worth the hassle.

"Secondly—"

"Never mind," he cut her off. "Forget I asked." He tossed the frozen peas on the couch and made for the door. "I've got a thing going on tomorrow night, so I can't see you." He didn't, but he'd drum something up.

He grabbed the doorknob.

"Reese." Her voice was a pained whisper behind him. "I'm *really* sorry about my parents, okay? Please don't be angry."

He turned slowly around to face her. There were a lot of things he could forgive—or not many, depending on your perspective—but his bae was skirting dangerously close to the ultimate in unforgiveable.

"Steliana," he said in a cool and precise tone. "You need to quit being so damned nice to me."

CHAPTER THIRTY

The next evening

CORKY SET HER PURSE AND soft briefcase by her apartment door, then trudged into the living room and sank down onto one of the sofas. "Weeeeell…" she said to no one in particular.

Hadley was working the night shift at the hospital, so the apartment was empty.

Which was a total bummer. Corky could've used a friend to unleash her woes on.

"Lost another case in court," she said out loud, anyway.

She supposed she could call Vasile and vent to him, but…

She made a *brrrrrm* sound with her lips.

Conversations with him generally required a lot of explaining, and she didn't have the energy to put in the necessary effort right now.

"So I've extended my losing streak," she told the vacant, echoing room, sagging into the sofa.

She hadn't been entirely sure about the wisdom of overturning the no-fraternization law in the first place, but she still didn't like to lose.

And she had.

Again.

Someone knocked.

She hefted herself off the sofa, strode across the living room, and opened the front door on Reese.

He was dressed in baggy jeans and a gray T-shirt frayed along the sleeves and hemline. He was lounging one shoulder against the doorjamb, his tatted-up arms crossed. "Go change," he told her, raking his eyes over her clothing as if she was a cover model for Office Dweeb.

"Why?"

"So you can come out and be bad with me."

"Be bad? With Reese Terrella?" She spluttered a laugh. "I shudder to think what that might entail."

He grinned.

Uh oh. "I'm not really the bad girl type, Reese."

"I bet you are. Deep down."

Think only good thoughts…

She wrinkled her nose. "No."

He didn't budge. Just stared at her with gleaming eyes.

He looked like he was in league with the devil.

"Even my worst version of bad would be too vanilla for the likes of you." She held up a palm. "Not that I'm profiling."

He exhaled in a dramatic burst. "Would you just get a drink with me, Corky." He shoved off the jamb. "I need to hang out with someone I can relate to for once."

"Oh, I-I…" *Reese relates to me.* She flushed. "All right."

He was only asking her out for a drink—that didn't sound so bad. And hadn't she just been pining for someone to talk to? Reese would be a good person for that. He could understand how much even the simplest failure could make a person feel worthless. He'd been brought up in the system, same as her, where self-esteem-building wasn't exactly the highest priority.

She could unload on him with *no lengthy translations required.*

"I could stand a drink myself," she added. "Give me five minutes."

It took her that long to exchange her skirt for a pair of jeans, her heels for flats, and to sling her blazer over a hanger and leave it behind in the closet.

Another five minutes later, she and Reese were heading

into the tunnel that passed from the residential neighborhood to Main Street. When Reese angled for the left-hand passageway, Corky took hold of his arm to stop him.

"Don't go there," she warned. "Hadley told me it leads to the bad part of town."

Reese gave her a droll look. "Where else do you think people are *bad*?"

She made a face. "That's not exactly a selling point for me." She peered down the tunnel. It was dark and drippy, and she couldn't see where it ended. *Ugh.* "Have you ever been to Stânga Town before?"

"Nope."

"Then you don't know how bad it is."

Reese's mouth curved up at the corners. Clearly he relished the idea of finding out.

"I vote for a drink at Garwald's."

Reese looked like she'd just suggested he fish a turd out of a toilet. "Fuck sakes, Corky. If we go to Garwald's it'll be more of the same we're-so-glad-you're-part-of-the-gang backslaps and slobbers I've been dealing with for the past week. And all that *affection* is like a pig dick in my throat right now."

"But—" she tried again.

"Act like a yellowbelly quakebuttock if you want to, but I'm going."

She exhaled. Then she'd better go too and keep an eye on him. Last time he'd *been bad*, he got into a fight with town security, been pantsed, then was electro-shocked through Vasile's anklet. So even though she wasn't feeling especially adventuresome after her shitty night in court, Reese *was* her friend.

If she left him alone while he was in such an edgy mood, God knew what he'd do to himself.

"All right," she conceded. "Let's go."

"Good God." It was worse than Corky had imagined.

They'd just popped out on the other side of the low-slung, eerie tunnel and come to a stop at the edge of a U-shaped, high-ceilinged, dim cavern. In front of them was a conglomeration of buildings shoved next to each other, everything out of alignment—roofs slanted, walls warped, latches rusted and dangling, and windowsills crooked or loose.

The place reeked of decaying sweat, urine, dirty clothes, and some sort of sulfurous stink. The latter appeared to be emanating from the quagmire of sludge next to them. Corky watched bubbles percolate to the surface and shivered. It was just the sort of sinkhole where something reptilian and prehistoric would live.

"I've changed my mind," she said. "Let's get out of here." The whole place exuded a general *fuck off!* vibe she was eager to obey.

But Reese was already fixated on a building off to the right where a red neon light glowed around the edges of drawn, tattered curtains. He read the sign posted on the front door out loud, "The Shank Tooth," then busted out laughing. "Classic. This is too much, really. *That's* what these people call their dive bar. Who the hell writes the script for this crew, anyway?"

"Let's go," she repeated.

"Are you kidding me? We are so heading inside there to—" He broke off and squinted at her. "Something's happened to your hair."

"What?"

"You look like the comedian Carrot Top, only blond."

"Oh, shit!" She swiped her hands down both sides of her hair, frantically smoothing. The damper cave air over here was making her naturally curly hair frizz.

"Come on, Corkster, don't worry. I'll protect you." Reese took her arm and led her toward the bar.

Corky stumbled along beside him. Yeah, but protect her

from what?

✧   ✧   ✧

REESE KEPT UP A STEADY scan of Stânga Town as he urged Corky along, all the while scouring for trouble.

As dumps went, this neighborhood was right up his alley. It was the type of place where a guy could find all kinds of hidden corners to do stuff in and not get caught.

Wonder how many bodies are buried here…?

Ah, more bitchin' ahead.

Just past The Shank Tooth—Reese hummed with glee over the name again—there was a barred gate stretching across a boarded-up opening in the cave wall.

If he remembered his hit-the-books sesh with the community manual correctly, that was the Outer Edge—an old entrance into something called the Hell Tunnels, mega-hot passageways leading in a serpentine route to a demon town called Oțărât.

Demons…hmm. Hanging out with those of the hellhound ilk sounded like it'd be a nice change from all the bright 'n shiny faces he was dealing with in Slaphappy Țărână.

Reese just wasn't a fan of roasting his nuts like so much shrimp on the barbie in order to get there.

Still…

He grinned at the gate. Anything that screamed *Keep Out!* pretty much guaranteed he'd *Get In!*

Nobody told him where he could and couldn't go.

When they arrived at The Shank Tooth, Reese had to physically drag Corky through the door. She was being a real potato butt about this.

Inside, it was even darker.

Light came only from a red neon sign advertising *The Shank Tooth* on the right-hand wall and a few ceiling bulbs barely hanging on for dear life by naked electrical wires.

The main part of the bar stretched out in front of them,

as dive-y as Reese had ever seen. The floor was nothing but pitted concrete, the walls plastered in cheap drywall that was bombed out in spots like someplace out of postwar Bosnia.

At the far end of the joint, past a dozen or so beaten-up wooden tables with chairs, there was a stage with a drum set, amps, and speakers—though no musicians. To the left was a long bar in the shape of an L, a few more tables off the short end of the L, which was closest to the door.

Three-quarters of all the tables in the joint were full.

Every occupant stopped drinking and talking to stare at Reese and Corky.

Reese leaned over to drawl next to her ear, "Whaddya think of my dyed hair now?"

She stiffened.

In her current stick-up-the-rear state, she clearly didn't appreciate him pointing out that she was the only blonde for miles. All the other customers had black hair and wore dark, ragged clothing. And every last one of them was a real sourpuss.

"Sit." Reese gestured at an empty table off the short L.

Corky hesitated. He could practically see the wheels of her mind chugging as she ran through alternatives.

So he proposed one for her. "Or you could head back down that dark, creepy tunnel all by yourself."

She sat.

Reese tugged out his wallet. "What do you want to drink?"

Wheels cranked again: *in a place like this?* "A beer's fine."

Reese approached the bartender who was working their side of the bar—another younger guy was at the far end.

The older guy had beady pebbles for eyes, and what Reese would guess was a permanently cheesed-off expression.

"What do you have on draft?" Reese asked him.

"Take a flying hike, maggot-sack."

Glorioski! Reese slashed a look of barely suppressed joy at

Corky. *We've come to the right place, my sweet Willow.*

Corky scooted her butt to the edge of the chair and kept her purse on her lap.

"Nah," Reese told the bartender. "We're gonna stay. Two drafts."

Dude gave Reese a double sneer. *Doppio, doppelt, le dou-blé*…as in, both sides of his upper lip lifted. "I mean it, shitbagger, get outta here."

Reese smiled. A slow smile. An oh-so-meaningful smile. "Bend over when you say that."

The bartender's eyes slitted.

"No? All right, anything you have on tap will do."

The double-sneer grew, upper lip touching lower nostrils. "We don't serve your kind here."

"Yeah? What kind's that?"

"Dragons." The bartender jabbed a forefinger in Corky's direction. "Especially not *her.*"

Reese pulled his money card out of his wallet and set it on the bar. "Tonight you do."

"Look, pustule-face, you don't like the way things are, take it up with the town uppity-ups. It's them that don't want their precious Dragons getting all stanky in our part of town." The bartender smashed a forefinger down on Reese's money card and shoved it back in his direction.

"Sure, man. I'll do that. First thing tomorrow morning after I bash one out. Two *full* drafts, now. No wimpy half-pints."

The bartender crossed his arms and jutted his whiskered jaw—a mule couldn't have pulled off obstinacy better.

Everyone in the bar was quiet and watching.

Reese blinked with faux innocence. "Do you like hospital food?"

Several people stirred in the main bar. Someone exhaled a coarse breath.

Corky clutched her purse in tight fists.

Adrenaline pumped through Reese. *Neato Cheeto!* This night was about to go cray-cray.

The bartender's eyes caromed around. He was probably pre-calculating all the damage a gangland bar fight would cost him. "You know what? Do I give a fark? No. It's your damned funeral." He grumpily drew two beers, slapped them down on the bar, and ran Reese's money card.

"Thanks, pal. It's been a slice of heaven." Reese brought the beers over to Corky, set them down, and sat.

She looked across the table at him. "Dare I hope you got your need for trouble out of your system with that?"

"*Gawd*, no, Cork." Reese smirked. "We're just getting started."

CHAPTER THIRTY-ONE

THE MUDDY PEN—NOW *THAT* was one shit-shack of a booze joint.

Cigarette-scarred teak bar, awful smell, cramped room that was barely lit enough to see who was about to kneecap you. The clientele was strictly criminal, all of them one strike away from their momentous third.

Reese lost a tooth the one night he hung out there.

The front left one got stuck in the knuckle of the unibrow hairy bastard who'd punched him with a fist resembling something you might find on a Caterpillar Evacuator arm.

While Reese went spinning to the floor, Unibrow plucked Reese's tooth out of the skin on his knuckle and growled out a string of obscenities. *Uncouth charlatan! What utter and complete cheek to wedge your tooth in my fist!*

Funny.

Well, funny *now*, since Reese wasn't bleeding profusely from the mouth and fumbling to find his dentist in his contacts list.

Compared to The Muddy Pen, The Shank Tooth wasn't so bad.

Besides the fuckdiculous name.

And the male barflies who could bench-press a small condo.

Sigh…*life with vampires. Never a dull moment.*

Reese took a sip of beer, raised his brows, then gulped down a larger mouthful. It was good. He hadn't expected that.

Corky was inspecting her foam…probably for telltale

signs of phlegm.

"I didn't hear the snit bartender make a hawk-a-loogie sound," he told her.

She glanced up.

"And cyanide is colorless and odorless. You won't find it just by looking."

Her smile was tight. "Why am I not surprised you know that?"

"I *do* have a way with people." He slugged down more beer and licked foam off his upper lip. "So why did you need to come out for a drink tonight?"

"Oh." Corky took a sip, then smacked her lips—clearly she was also pleased with the beer. "I lost my case in court this evening."

"That sucks. What case?"

"Kimberly and I argued to overturn the no-fraternization law."

Reese again ran through the card catalog he had in his brain of the community manual. "You mean the law preventing Vârcolac from hooking up with each other because they can't reproduce anymore?"

"Yes. Well, no. Well, sort of. They *can* reproduce now. With Dragons. But they're still being kept apart because Roth wants every Vârcolac who *can* breed *to* breed."

"Ah. Kind of an all-hands-on-deck thing, eh?" If it wasn't for the forever-bond stupidness holding everyone back, it'd be a regular fuck-fest around here.

"Exactly, and that's why Kimberly and I couldn't overturn the law—there's too much at stake."

"Like?"

"Like the existence of the entire race," she answered with an emphasis on the unspoken *duh*. "Vârcolac aren't off the endangered species list yet. So even though I hated losing, I could understand the court's decision."

"Because the need of repopulating a dying race takes

precedence over the individual freedom of one Vârcolac to choose another for a life partner?" That statement didn't sound *duh* at all, did it? Very much A Seer of All Important—If Not Asinine—Truths.

Corky clonked her beer down. "Don't put it that way."

"Why not? It's what it is, isn't it?"

"You need to think of the big picture," Corky argued. "The long-term consequences."

"Like?"

"*Like* what if the single, unbonded Vârcolac only think they don't want children because they're lonely. But if they'd been made to wait, then they could've had a family."

Jesus Harry Christ. Ol' Cork here must've been raised by a different Governmental Man than he had—someone who dressed all his wards in hemp, gathered them in a love circle, and urged everyone to *share your feelings.*

How many psychologists does it take to change a light bulb?

It depends on whether the light bulb wants to change. Ha-yuk, ha-yuk, ha-yuk.

Reese sat back. "I've lived under some pretty heavy-handed rule myself. Can't say I'm a fan of being *made* to do anything either."

"No one wants that, of course. But sometimes people need laws in place to ensure their own protection and well-being."

"We're not talking about the fucking seatbelt law here," he shot back. "The people in this community are being told who they can and can't *love.*"

She tilted her head. "Don't tell me Reese Terrella has a sentimental side. Wouldn't hell have to freeze, pigs fly, and all that jazz for you to speak of love?"

Ah, yes, Reese Terrella, he hath no heart...he hath no soul...

He moved his beer mug around in its wet circle. Why even exist as such a Tin Man Icecunt? He should commit his own version of hara-kiri and pierce the barren hole where his heart should be, do everyone a massive favor and step off this mortal coil.

Reese raised his mug. "*Nos morituri, te salutamus!*"

Corky squinted at him.

We who are about to die salute you! "I'm supporting *free will.*"

"I'm for free will too."

He scoffed. "Just words, Cork. You'd change your tune real quick if the wonks around here tried to tell you who you could or couldn't love."

"Aren't they doing that? I mean, I've been invited into this community with that in mind, haven't I?" She picked up her beer again. "I get the sense that if I told Dr. Parthen I wanted to get together with *you*, instead of a Vârcolac, it wouldn't go over so well."

Reese laughed. *For more reasons than one.* "Land o' Go-shen! Please let me be in the room when you tell Blonde Sahib that."

Corky *tsked* and rolled her eyes and shook her head—the full-tilt boogie.

"But, hey," he went on, adding a leer. "Because of the virginity pact going on in this place, you and I might want to consider the occasional stress-release meetup."

"Oh, barf."

It was difficult not to laugh again. "Thank you."

She flapped a hand. "I need to be done with drama in relationships, Reese. You're *all* drama."

"I wasn't offering a *relationship.*" He smirked.

A guy across the bar twisted his upper body around to give Reese a very stinky stink-eye.

Dude was wearing a Mötley Crüe T-shirt with the faces of the band warped out of round by the muscles beneath the shirt.

Maybe Reese should've kept his dentist on speed dial after all.

"Anyway." Reese got back on topic. "Sounds to me like you should've fought for the other side."

Corky sobered. "Maybe you're right. I've always fought on the side of hope."

"Ah. Okay. *Now* it's time to barf." *Hep me! Ms. I'm-not-really-a-bad-girl Disdale is a gigantic goose dropping of sappy on top of goody-goody, and*—A laugh burst out of him. "Oh, hell. You're one of *them*, aren't you?"

"One of who?"

One of whom, *but who's keeping score?* "A caretaker." He gave his head a doleful shake. "There was one in every foster home I lived in."

"I am not."

"You are *so* hardcore blushing right now, Corkster."

She blushed some more. "I don't think…I mean…I-I…"

"You become everybody's second mother, don't you?"

Her posture got all prim. "I suppose, yes, at some point I knew I wasn't ever going to be adopted, so…so I became Mary's *helper*."

"Finally! Your relationship with Vasile makes sense."

"What's that supposed to mean?" Indignant and prim—now she was an 1860s schoolmarm right out of *Bonanza*.

"C'mon, Corky. You're a smart, beautiful lawyer, and he's a fucking knuckle-dragger. Doesn't that light off any warning bells in your head? You two are as far apart as the proverbial Mars and Venus." He sucked on a tooth as he considered her. "I bet he's your little pet project, isn't he? You see the poor guy lost in his Brave New World, and you swoop in to save him."

"It's not like that," she insisted, tendons showing in her neck.

He gave his shoulders a blasé, *whatevs* shrug, letting her know what a tremendous pile of bulldoodle he found that to be.

"Well, what's wrong with taking care of people, anyway?"

she defended herself, her voice a little shaky. "You make it sound like it's bad to be a loving person."

"It's not bad if you have boundaries. But I've never seen a caretaker who did." Reese thought about it—for, oh, a millisecond—before jumping on the schadenfreude bandwagon. "I bet you let people walk all over you. A total doormat."

The color drained from her face, making her eyes look dark and sunken. Her lips trembled.

Okay, so maybe he was being a bit too hard on her. But this was *her bad*. She was the one who'd called him heartless.

"So I was the caretaker in the house," she snapped. "So what? We all had our roles to play to survive—you of all people know that."

Ho, yeah! You go, Hollaback Girl! Rally some spine.

"You think you're so much better than me because you were the house *spokesman*?" Corky leaned forward, her tone strong and biting. "The superhero whose fists flew whenever the weak needed protecting from all the heavy-handed treatment?" She shoved her beer aside. "Well, you can pull that crown off your head, Reese, because I've got your number. You're the guy who fucks everything up for himself the moment life gets too good."

Reese offered Corky a benign stare but felt a muscle in his jaw pulse.

"Why did you want to come out and be bad tonight, Reese? Huh? Are you on the verge of a job promotion? Does Fane make you feel like you can always be yourself around him, no matter what? Did Steliana slip up and utter the L-word?"

Reese's throat filled.

"That's it, isn't it?"

Score! He almost lauded her with a golf clap.

"Steliana's flipping for you, and you can't handle it. So you're going to do your usual and start wrecking shit. No—" Corky shoved to her feet. "You already *have* wrecked shit because you just fucked this friendship away."

Whoa! Multiple direct hits! Reese pouted up at her. *You sunk my battleship, smexy.*

Corky gripped her purse at her side. "I came out with you tonight to feel better, not to have you point out what a pathetic loser I am."

Behind her, the bar door swung open.

"Keep doing your usual," she ground out. "I could care less, you asshole."

Dev Nichita and Goof Gorilla Vasile stepped inside The Shank Tooth.

"Except I don't plan to be anywhere near you when you do a full self-destruct." Corky took a halting step back. "My life doesn't need the fallout."

The crowd quieted, and for some reason the young bartender at the far end of the room darted out the back door.

Reese flung an insolent arm over the back of his chair. "Glory be, it's the po-po. Ain't nuttin better for a full self-destruct than mixing it up with some boys in blue."

Corky turned stiffly around.

Dev and Vasile started toward them.

The snitty bartender did his cheesed-off bit. "Don't get on *my* case about these two bein' here. I told 'em to fuck off."

That little nark ratted on us.

Blasting out of his chair, Reese grabbed the bartender by the front of his shirt and yanked down, slamming the man's forehead onto the bar. "You fucking snitch!"

The bartender yowled.

Nichita leapt at Reese and pulled him off. "Cool it, Terrella."

The bartender stumbled backwards, his forehead red from the abuse. "Get the hell outta my bar!" he bellowed, pressing a hand to his brow.

Reese pointed a finger at the rat fink. "*Shitbagger.* That was a good one, buddy. I'm going to use it."

"OUT!"

"Let's go." Nichita gestured at the door.

CHAPTER THIRTY-TWO

VASILE WAITED FOR THE OTHERS to depart The Shank Took, then he himself exited and strode to join the three in the street that fronted the shabby building. His stride was not wholly steady.

His flesh was fevered, his stomach swatted at flies, and his throat was clogged with a roiling gorge. If he had not woken this morning feeling hale, he would fear he had contracted the ague.

It took him some moments to conclude that he was afflicted with strong emotions over seeing Corky cavorting with the Dragon male of the false black hair.

Why had she been on the drink-date with that boor?

Dev turned to the knave now, his hands on his hips. "Just so you know, Terrella, when you paid for your drinks with your money card, it popped in our system. *That's* how we knew where you were."

"What the *fuck*?" The knave curled his upper lip. "Is this some kind of police state?"

"You're new here," countered Dev, "so you don't understand all the—"

"I'm going home." Corky spun around and marched for the foul-smelling tunnel.

Vasile watched her retreat, then looked at Dev. "I follow."

Dev gestured. "Yeah. Go."

Vasile hurried after Corky, calling her name.

She halted and waited for him, pinched of lip and shoulders set at a firm angle.

Something was amiss with her. And now concern became his foremost emotion.

He waited until Dev and the unlikable male disappeared down the dank tunnel before inquiring, "<Are you all right?>"

"Please don't…don't speak to me in Romanian right now. I'm too…I can't understand you."

This feeling, Vasile knew well—he could not translate either when he was very distressed. His stomach dropped. So she was indeed in a bad way. "Do you be all right?"

"Yes."

He did not believe her. Her words were brusque and her lips still inflexible. Perhaps the magic-deflectors had failed. "You feel evil magic?"

"No. Why do you ask?"

"You look like you touch electricity." He pointed to her hair. It was fuzzed around her head like a dandelion flower.

She gasped and slapped her hands down on her hair. "God! It's nothing!" She stomped for the tunnel again.

He kept pace with her. "Why go you on the drink-date with that man?"

She stopped.

He stopped.

"It wasn't a *date*." Her words were so curt now, she sounded hot-tempered. "Reese and I are just friends. Or *were*."

"You no be friends anymore?" This would be prosperous news to hear.

Her chin quivered. "He was a dick to me tonight."

Vasile tensed his spine. *Dick* was a slang term for the male appendage. "That knave tried to use his pole on you?" A thrumming began in his fangs.

"His what?"

"His dick. He tried to—"

"No! I mean he was a douche."

Vasile stared at her. He did not know this word.

"An ass."

He had to give this descriptor a deep consideration as well. What must a man do to be likened to a donkey...?

"Oh, for Christ's sake. I'm trying to tell you Reese was *rude* to me."

Ah. This, he understood, and it was no surprise to hear it about the odious man.

Vasile drew himself up. A male had acted in an ill-bred fashion toward his woman. It was upon him to issue the douche-man a proper dressing-down for her.

Corky went on with her harangue. "I didn't need a bunch of Reese's attitude. I had a bad day, and I was upset, and I just wanted someone to talk to. Someone to listen to me and understand and be nice."

Vasile drew his eyebrows together. But...that someone should have been him, should it not? As her man, did it not lie within his purview to grant her an understanding ear? "For why you no come to me?" He would have done all those things she just mentioned. With all his heart.

"Because I..." She angled her face aside and pressed her thumb to her nose bridge.

He heard the musical string of a guitar being plucked repeatedly, as if someone was trying to find the correct note for it. The sound was coming from inside the slummy bar.

"I'm sorry," said Corky, turning back to him. "But I didn't think you'd understand what I was going through, and I didn't want to explain it. I totally ___ in court today."

"What means *flopped*?"

"Jesus!" She belted out the word with a snap. "This is exactly what I'm talking about."

The flesh across his cheeks constricted in reaction to her critical tone. It appeared Corky was not only upset with the actions of the douche-man and the difficulties of her day, but she was dismayed with *him*. And he did not know what to do to placate her. Socialization class had taught him how to avoid upsetting a woman, but not how to undo her agitation once she was in such a state.

Corky continued to speak in clipped syllables. "Flop means fail."

After astonished seconds of silence, he uttered, "You think I no comprehend what it be like to *fail?*"

"How the hell would I know if you do or you don't?" Her retort was still fervid. "You've never told me anything about yourself."

The volume of her voice was spiraling into higher and higher notes. His stomach churned the same as it did right before a shunning. He stood without motion, fighting panic, and thought hard about how to address this current accusation. But it was another confusion.

Had he not told her more about himself than any other person in the world?

He reminded her in a careful way, "We have discussed ourselves very well over four meal-dates."

"We've discussed ourselves *reasonably* well, and that's because *I* made it that way."

Heat began to rise from the roots of his hair.

She exhaled a tumultuous breath. "And even after all of my hard work, you've still only told me about the television shows you like and your favorite foods and…and…For God's sake, Vasile, I don't care how you brush your teeth."

Gracious sakes, she has lost her memory. "I no tell you how I—"

"Stop it!"

Vasile could not help but move back a pace in reaction to her shouting volume. The air would not leave his body all the way. It sank low and made his chest heavy.

"I'm sorry." She apologized to him in a scratchy voice. "I didn't mean to yell at you."

He was not consoled. Tears were welling in her eyes, and this was a bad omen.

"I can't..." Her eyelids pressed shut. "I can't do this anymore."

Do what? He did not ask this. He did not want to know.

She opened her eyes—they were still wet. "I need to back off from our relationship for a while."

"Back off." He formed the repeated words into a statement instead of a question, since his queries seemed to be upsetting her. He did not altogether know what she meant by *back off,* but it did not sound favorable.

She re-said it in Romanian. "<I need to discontinue going on dates with you for a time.>"

Panic tightened the coils of his innards. *No.* He shook his head. "Tell me what I mistake. I repair it."

"It's not... I don't know if I can make you understand this, Vasile. It's just not a good idea for me to be in a relationship with you right now."

He stared at her.

"I..." She pressed her fists to her brow. "Reese pointed out some character flaws in me that...that..."

Vasile clamped his teeth. *Filthy douche-man, I will choke you.*

She dropped her hands. "The things Reese said reminded me of how much I always take care of everyone else when I'm in a relationship, and I never take care of me. So I need to take care of myself."

"And you think by leave me that you take care of you?"

"Yes. Well, maybe." Her throat moved with a swallow. "I'm not sure. Honestly, I don't trust my decision-making right now, and that's part of the problem."

His pulse beat furiously at his temples. If she was not sure, he had to make her feel sure. "I am right man for you. I tell you so already."

"I know you're sure about us, Vasile, but I'm not. I think...I don't think the timing is right for us. You're struggling with a lot of your own challenges. There's nothing wrong with that, but it's lighting off a caretaker instinct in me."

It felt like his cheeks were swelling, the onrush of heat into his face-flesh was so intense. She thought he was too weak for her. "You *no* take care of me. *I* take care of you. *I* be man."

"I know you're the man. And you're a good man—I don't mean to insult you. I..." She inhaled a deep breath. "Every relationship I've ever been in has taken an unending toll on me. And now our relationship...us...it's very demanding, and I don't...I-I..." Her lips whitened. "You deserve someone who will work hard to make things good, Vasile, and me..." A tear overbrimmed one eye. "I'm just *so damned tired.*"

His stomach churned with rougher waves. How was he to stop her from making this terrible error? He knew he could help her to slay any problem she faced, if she would let him, but it seemed that every word he uttered only served to push her further away. "I must needs explain you...but I no have right words...the nuances...to say you..." He clenched his hands in preparation to rip his tongue out. *Useless slab!*

She gave him a despairing look. "There's nothing you *can* say."

The finality in her tone twisted his innards with a worse feeling. She was truly leaving him. "You promise you never hurt me." His nose burned. "After our kiss, you say you no hurt me. And now you do."

Her cheeks pinkened. "I'm sorry. I don't mean to hurt you. I know I sound selfish right now, but *for once* I need to have the courage to think of myself." She drew the back of her wrist across her face. "For my whole life my foster mother told me to always think good thoughts. Buck up, she said. But after a lifetime of this, I'd like to know when it's time for *my* pain."

He did not speak. It was beyond his ability to understand her purposeful desire for pain. He only knew that his Glowing Corky was leaving him, leaving him bereft of her—she, who was his other half. His throat went very taut. Like claws of anguish clutched it, tearing him raw. He tried to swallow but could not.

Two on-duty warriors, Breen and Jeddin, wandered out of the foul tunnel.

Vasile stepped back from Corky. "I would rather you activate my shocker band than do this to me, Corky Disdale."

Another tear dripped down her cheek.

He looked at the on-duty warriors and chopped a hand at Corky to indicate her. "Escort Corky safely back to abode."

With no other words to say, he walked away, his boots making a heavy sound on the cave rock.

✧   ✧   ✧

NAH, I'M GOOD, REESE TEXTED Fane.

It was a lie, but, hey, what was another lie added to the mountainous pile he'd been working on ever since he could utter his first word—*Da-Da* (for Dad), incidentally, if we're going to build another pile here…like…how about Things That Ought To Be Bleached From My Mind For Their Irrelevance To Happiness?

Lolling back against the couch cushion, Reese typed, *Have fun with the guys. See u tomorrow.*

Fane was out with their sports buddies tonight, but Reese couldn't join them because drinking margaritas and playing fantasy football weren't ideal activities for a man who was bound and dead set on a wreckage bender.

You're the guy who fucks up everything for himself the moment life gets too good, so you're going to do your usual and start wrecking shit…

Reese tossed his cell aside on the couch and gazed up at all the whiteness of the ceiling.

Ah, wise and sensible Cork. You do indeed have my number. And I will not—I cannot!—offer insult to your spot-on judgment by belly-laughing the night away with my bros. That would un-

paint your sparkling character assassination of me. No! I must get busy doing all the things that will erase Successful Man About Town Reese from the earth.

First up?

He'd say take a dump in Steliana's *I'm-crazy-about-you* Cheerios by cheating on her.

He'd met more than a few hot babes in this town who'd be down to party, maybe even indulge in a little RPG sex— *you play Nadja, I play Jason Stackhouse* (hey, if you can mix metaphors, why can't you mix vampire pop culture?). But willingness meant diddly when the hot babes were biologically lacking in follow-through capability.

I'm afraid that means your usual method of ruining your life won't be available to you in Țărână...

Hear that, Cork? Would've been nice if you'd helped a buddy out, gone around the back of The Shank Tooth and let me give you a nice, Steliana-ruining screw.

He sprawled his legs out in front of him.

So what now?

You already are *wrecking shit because you've fucked this friendship away...*

Aw, well, there's always that. Thank you, Cork. It gives me a great deal of comfort. One friend down. A few more to go!

He heard a knock.

Getting up from the couch, he made for the door, opening it on—

Bam! A fist plowed into his mouth.

The next thing he knew he was skidding across the hardwood floor on his back, thunking down the short step, then striking the couch—which brought him to a stop in a spread-eagle position. A hailstorm of needles hit his lips, then they went numb. Tasting blood, he peered blearily at the door.

Goof Gorilla Vasile was hulked in the jamb, his eyebrows veed into a thunderous scowl.

Reese struggled to a sitting position, took hold of his left front tooth, and tried to wiggle it. Solid. "Good ol' Dr. Willard." He smiled around his hand. "His implant held."

"Corky leave me because of what you say her," Vasile growled. "Everything you touch become stained and ugly. You befoul everyone."

Wow. Who knew the knuckle-dragger had the third-eye capability to see into the dark wasteland of Reese's heart.

Except I hath no heart…

Reese lurched to his feet.

"I no like you." Vasile pointed a finger at him. "You no-good man." He turned and stalked away.

Reese gazed at the open doorway. *Hats off to Goof for getting it right!* Everyone else in Schmaltz Town was all about trying to save the people here. But sometimes a guy needed to be called out for the befouled stink-turd he was.

Stamped *Un-Save-Able.*

I came out with you tonight to feel better, not to have you point out what a pathetic loser I am…

I'm sorry, Reese, but your dad isn't coming back, and since, uh, you know, we don't want to keep you, a social worker will be by later to pick you up…

Reese's stomach knotted.

You no-good man.

He glanced down at the floor.

What to do…what to do…?

He headed into the kitchen, grabbed an ice cube out of the freezer, and held it to his mouth.

Keep doing your usual. I could care less, you asshole. Except I don't plan to be anywhere near you when you do a full self-destruct…

Right, Cork. Good idea. I need to stick to the original plan of a wreckage bender.

But setting off on a roll of fuckery *here* would be just about impossible. The moment he spent a dime the principle principals would know what he was up to. Plus all the pussy was bond-impounded.

First off, you're smart.

Aw, thanks, Steliana, you honey bunny, you. You're right. I'm a creative guy. I can find some way to piss you off.

He tossed the ice cube in the sink, then strode into his bedroom and opened the bottom drawer of his dresser, digging through his socks. He shoved aside a knife—hell, he'd forgotten Frightmare Homey gave him that—and found the sock where his lockpicks were hidden.

Yeah, baby.

He dumped the cluster of thin metal instruments into his palm.

Time to *get in* where he wasn't allowed.

CHAPTER THIRTY-THREE

The next day
11:17 a.m.

CORKY HADN'T BEEN IN ANY rush to go back into a courtroom after losing her case yesterday, but here she was. *Back.*

And for a shitty reason.

She'd been called in as a material witness in the "assault" charge Hadley filed against Thomal for ripping her towel off.

The three of them—Corky, Hadley, and Thomal—were currently standing in front of Roth and Toni, who were seated at the head of the U-shaped council table.

Thomal was on Corky's right, arms crossed and scowling.

Hadley was on Corky's left, arms crossed and scowling.

Scowls were also low on Corky's list of things she was in the mood for—yesterday's mega-scowl was still haunting her.

You say you never hurt me…

Talk about slapping a girl right where she lives. Catherine Disdale was *not* a woman who hurt people. She was the one who fixed people, comforted them until they felt better, even if it meant…

I bet you let people walk all over you. A total doormat.

She squeezed her eyes in a tight blink, holding back tears. She had *never* experienced an equal exchange of giving in a relationship. Her boyfriend choices pretty much guaranteed she would be let down in an emotional sense…

Would you just shut up and let me sleep, Catherine. I've got to be in court first thing in the morning.

Her nostrils fluttered. So why should she think Vasile would be any different?

He wasn't—*I no talk about. It is no-good discussion.*

Although to be fair, she got the sense that Vasile *wanted* to give to her, and that was more than she'd ever gotten from any other boyfriend…

I will pick the flowers and light the candles and tend the cows and patch the roof and kill any threat to your being. I will do whatever the task…

…except talk to her with any degree of depth.

She exhaled. And in Ţărână, that lack had to be a deal-breaker. Because in this town if she blew it, there was no going back on her Man Mistake.

Hooking up with a Vârcolac is for-fucking-ever—

"Ms. Disdale?"

Corky snapped her chin up. "Pardon?"

Roth was addressing her. "*Did* Thomal strip Hadley naked?"

"Oh…um…" In a literal sense, *yes*, Thomal had torn off Hadley's towel, and, yes, Thomal had acted like a total jerk. But it seemed to Corky that what happened between ex-boyfriend and ex-girlfriend amounted more to a shouting match than an *assault*—and for Hadley to bring charges against Thomal felt a lot like unresolved bitterness coming to the surface than anything else.

But Corky said, "Yes."

"It was an *accident*," Thomal defended himself.

Roth fingered the handle of his gavel, his focus still on Corky. "Would you agree that this part of the altercation appeared to be unintentional?"

"Yes." From her peripheral, Corky saw Hadley stiffen. "But Mr. Costache," she rushed to add, "barged into our apartment without being invited, which was wrong to do."

"I *entered*," Thomal cut back in, "with the intention of *helping* Hadley." He leaned forward to peer around Corky at the woman in question. "Help you pull your head out of your ass."

Hadley's expression tautened. "How I live my life is none of your damned business." She faced Roth and Toni again. "And his intentions don't matter—his behavior was inexcusable."

"I agree—it's a right shame."

This comment came from the back of the courtroom—in a British accent no less.

Roth and Toni shifted their attention there, and the rest of them turned around.

Thomal's wife, Pandra, was standing at the end of the center aisle.

She was wearing snug blue jeans and a T-shirt with the three *Rugrats* on it—baby Tommy, bossy, blond Angelica, and redheaded Chuckie—which seemed *really* not to match the Uma-Thurman-*Kill-Bill* quality she also exuded.

"Thomal needs to pay," Pandra went on. "And it would be my extreme pleasure to dole out the necessary castigation." She lifted her right hand.

A pair of boxing gloves dangled from her outstretched forefinger by a couple of strings.

"Aw, buzz off, Pandra," Thomal growled. "You've got the wrong fucking idea going on in your head about this."

Pandra ignored him. "If the court allows Mr. Costache's actions to go unpunished, then it would be tantamount to saying that a woman should get with a mate simply because some bloke"—she flicked her left hand at Thomal—"demanded it."

Corky blinked, then slid her gaze over to her friend.

Hadley's lips were parted.

Toni tapped her forefinger on the table. "This community wouldn't want to send that message, certainly not." Toni looked between Thomal and Pandra, and something seemed to register on her face. She leaned over and whispered something to Roth.

Roth nodded.

"It is hereby ruled," Toni said in a resounding voice, "that Thomal Costache's actions warrant consequences. The court decrees that he will spend twenty minutes in the community boxing ring with Pandra."

Pandra inclined her head at Toni, then smiled with acid sweetness at Thomal. "I'll go clear the gym, snookums. Meet you there in ten minutes." She cocked a single brow. "Unless you scarper."

Thomal rolled his eyes. "You know what? Fuck it. You want to throw down with me, snuggle-bunny, I'll be there."

"Brilliant."

Now Hadley looked between Thomal and Pandra, and the same something registered on her face as Toni's—an understanding that maybe a beatdown wouldn't be such a big punishment between this particular couple.

Hadley's features tautened again.

Pandra left.

Roth *whacked* down his gavel, then he and Dr. Parthen exited.

Corky started to leave with Hadley, but Thomal stopped her. "Can I talk to you for a second, Corky?"

Corky bit back a sigh. She'd rather get out of here. But— "Okay." Then she told Hadley, "See you back at the apartment."

"Sure." Hadley left.

Thomal waited until Hadley was gone before speaking. "I realize you and Hadley are becoming good friends, so I don't want to get between that, but..." He shoved his fingers through his hair. "I just want to make sure Hadley's not filling your head with a bunch of poison about the Moon-Riders."

"Why would she be doing that?" Corky asked with a hint of ice in her tone, bristling in defense of her friend.

"I heard you broke up with Vasile."

"Yes. So?"

Thomal's brows arched.

Her cheeks prickled with heat. She hadn't meant to sound so unfeeling. "Not that I have to explain myself, but for the sake of stopping any rumors before they get started, I'll tell you this—I broke up with Vasile in part because of *you*."

"Me? What did I do?"

Corky pointed at the courtroom door where Hadley had exited. "Do you realize how horrible you were to Hadley the other night? If you were truly trying to help her, like you said, you could've been nice about it."

Thomal shook his head. "Hadley has a stubborn streak a mile long. She wouldn't have listened if I didn't knock some—"

"Sounds like a rationalization to me." Corky was betting Thomal had as much unresolved bitterness as Hadley. She gave him a probing stare. "Did you ever even love Hadley?"

It was a huge question.

Thomal glanced aside. "I don't know anymore."

Great. "*Now* do you see why I broke up with Vasile?"

"No."

Corky's next breath was measured. "If you and Hadley had bonded, would it have been a total disaster? Because that's what Hadley said about it."

"Yeah. It would have."

Corky crossed her arms. "And how close did you and Hadley come to bonding?"

Now he saw where this was going.

He moved his jaw around. "If Hadley didn't suffer from a needle phobia, we would've bonded."

"For *life*," Corky emphasized. "So can you see why I might be scared? We're talking about a forever-commitment here, Thomal, and I don't want to end up with my own version of an eternal disaster."

"Lazăr's not a disaster."

"I know—I don't mean to insult Vasile. He's a wonderful man in a lot of ways, but he just might turn out to be a disaster for *me*." Corky stared off into the distance. "I've made a lot of mistakes with the men I've chosen over the years, and right now Vasile is fitting right into that mold."

"How?"

"It's hard to explain without sounding judgmental. He's just so…taciturn. I have no idea who he really is. He's not letting me see anything deep, and that's exactly what all my former boyfriends did. None of them ever connected with me emotionally." She paused. "I was really unhappy."

"Vasile *can* connect with you, Corky. Okay? Lazăr's got a lot of heart. He just doesn't know how to talk to you yet. Give him a chance."

"I did. I have. He's not out of the running. He…he…" *Argh, I'm caving.* "Do you really think it's all that unreasonable for me to want to be sure about Vasile before I settle down with him for *the rest of my entire life*? Come on, Thomal. Think of you and Hadley."

"No, I guess not. Not when you put it that way."

"Okay then."

An awkward silence fell between them.

"I just…" She exhaled. "I have a lot to figure out."

You're one of them, aren't you? A fucking caretaker. Her chest squeezed.

"All right, I'll trust that you know what you're doing." Thomal checked the wall clock. "I've gotta go." He strode for the door.

"And, by the way, just so you know…"

Thomal turned to face her again.

"Hadley has been very supportive of me dating Vasile."

"That…that surprises me."

"I'm sure it does." Corky picked up her purse and brushed past him on the way out. "You really don't know Hadley at all."

I'M EIGHTEEN YEARS OLD WHEN I lose my virginity.

It's a hot afternoon in August, and the food pantry at Mary Sills' Angels is barely large enough for two people. It should've been larger. Then maybe Mary wouldn't have to go grocery shopping so often. She's always so busy. Shopping is just another thing to take her away from us.

The shelves are stocked with as many cans as they can hold. Chef Boyardee—Beefaroni, Ravioli, Cheesy Burger Macaroni— and Del Monte—Fruit Cocktail, Apricot Halves, and Sliced Peaches.

There's a small window near the ceiling, and sunlight slices through it, cutting across the peaches.

I watch the can rock back and forth while I grip the edge of the shelf, my chin coming close to hitting the board with every inward thrust.

My teeth are gritted and I'm fighting back tears.

Because sex hurts.

Nancy Loobaker warned me about the first time. She lost her virginity to Nick Stoppard last week when her parents were in the Poconos. But Nancy did it in her bed with the Cars playing in the background ("My Best Friend's Girl").

Having sex with a boy standing behind me doesn't seem like a good position for a first time. It makes it worse somehow. His penis is going in really deep. We're also rushing so we won't get caught.

That probably makes it worse too.

Nancy Loobaker warned me about another thing—boys are cold. Once they "jack a load" into you, they're done. That's it. You have all the power in the world over them when they want you. None at all the moment after they come.

One thing Nancy forgot to tell me is how much icky stuff runs out of you when the boy is done. A bunch of goop splatters onto the concrete floor when he pulls out, and I have to hurry to press my thighs together, then yank up my panties.

I rake the toe of my sneaker through the stuff on the floor to smudge it away. It smells funny.

And that's when I see the pantry door is half-open.

Andrew Freidmont is staring at me.

His face is red, his eyes wet, and snot is shining around the indents beside his nostrils.

He's the boy I play Monopoly with at the group home.

He's the boy I should have lost my virginity to—Andrew Freidmont likes me.

Instead I've given myself to a guy on my ultimate Frisbee team. We're both leaving for college next week, and we talked about wanting to show up with some experience.

It's a stupid reason to have sex. I see that now.

I didn't see it when we talked about needing experience.

So I picked the wrong boy.

I chose Phillip Beedman.

CHAPTER THIRTY-FOUR

The next day
9:01 a.m.

VASILE OPENED HIS METAL LOCKER-CLOSET and looked at Thomal, who was standing in front of the locker-closet next door. The left side of his mouth was a vivid red and puffed by swelling, and his left eye socket was darkened by a bruise. A cut lay near the border of his hair, but this was partially obscured beneath two narrow strips of bandage tape.

"Ignore what Costache does." Dev gestured toward the man he had just named. "Never hit a woman."

Vasile set his shoulders. "Of a certain I will not. It is a barbarism." He pulled a black stretchy shirt out of his metal locker-closet, then directed at Thomal, "I know not even how you hurt mate. Do you not feel bad lightning in your head?"

"Not this time." Thomal donned his own stretchy shirt. "Because Pandra wanted it."

Vasile glanced at Dev. How could this be so?

Dev made a brush-aside gesture. "Costache and his wife have a strange history."

Thomal snorted. "*Strange* is putting it mildly." He retrieved his workout shoes from his locker-closet. "Back when Pandra and I were struggling to become a couple, I swore to her that I'd never fight her. But the thing is, on the night we bonded I *agreed* to go along with everything she wanted. I didn't fight her then, so I never knew if I could beat her, and…I guess it's always bothered me. Pandra must've known."

This explanation still made little sense to Vasile. Why would a man want to fight his woman on the night he bonded to her?

Even when Vasile was at his most upset with Corky for her decision to leave him, he had not imagined doing her harm.

He could never hurt her. No matter that her hurting of him had relegated him to spending much of last night sitting stiff on the couch-seat in his abode, his stomach sour and small, his pain trebling every time he pictured himself progressing through his days without her.

The enormous depth of his pain was unexpected. For back when he and Nicolae had first decided to stay in Ţărână, Nicolae expressed excitement about the chance to find a mate, but Vasile said *Who cares?*

Women were a trial, naught but scolds.

This was no longer his opinion.

Nowadays he very much wanted Corky by his side. Being near to her lifted his spirits like nothing else could.

"And now I know," added Thomal with a grin. "I *can* beat her."

"Not by the look of your face," drawled Dev.

Thomal chuckled. "Oh, she got in some awesome shots." His eyes gleamed. "And afterward we had the best sex we've ever had."

Dev *clanged* shut his locker-closet. "I'll never understand you, man."

Thomal laughed.

The door to the room of lockers swung open, and Jacken strode inside. "Training's canceled. I need every swinging dick on a manhunt."

Dev hiked up his eyebrows. "Who the hell's missing?"

"Terrella."

✧　✧　✧

REESE LAY STRETCHED OUT ON the mattress with his hands stacked behind his head, silently singing the "Rubber Tree Ant" song while he traced a line of rust running across the expanse of roof—which was no more than a thin slab of corrugated tin.

He's got hiiiiigh hopes…

The line began at the corner of the roof behind the bed, snaked along for about two feet, then dove into a rust-flaky hole about the size of his thumb.

Hiiiiiigh hopes!

Man, was he stuck in the Shitsburgs or what?

Nonexistent plumbing, barely functioning electricity, furniture on its last legs, and walls of mere plywood. If he and Havel—the hot demon chick he was imprisoned with—ever *did* get this house a-rockin', the entire town would hear them.

And speaking of towns…

Did I mention this place is a complete pile of shit? Oţărât made your garden-variety ghetto look like the love child of Beverly Hills and Sausalito.

Inside this one-room house there were signs of recent improvements: low-pile carpet, hanging pictures, books, and some art supplies that appeared new. But those things hardly made up for the rest.

All of which Reese had been introduced to last night after he picked the lock on the gate into the Neutral Zone—a long passageway that started at the west end of Stânga Town and went along for the length of about three city blocks.

*Temperatures sitting in the high sixties, ladies and gentlemen…*so Reese had managed to avoid the Hell Tunnels.

At the end of the Neutral Zone tunnel, he stepped out onto a ledge of rock that curved for several hundred yards around an open, flat space—like a semi-circular amphitheater bordering an area the size of two basketball courts. This curving ledge rose about ten feet off the ground, with a set of steps carved into the cave rock off to the left.

Beyond the amphitheater was a whole lot of wouldn't-believe-it-if-I-wasn't-seeing it.

Extending back on the right side was a jumbled wreckage of a neighborhood—a scattered mishmash of architecture that looked like God had just dropped the buildings around and about on the seventh day of Creation (because He was all, like, *never mind! I'm tired and need to rest!*).

Sounds echoed hollowly, and an arid, barren musk draped everything.

On the left side were additional buildings, these larger and more purposeful.

The first one he saw was an open-fronted, three-sided structure that was…what?

A Dæmon Gymboree?

If yeah, then it was a play area that'd been funded by the Lehman Brothers in the golden 2007-2008 era. There was nothing much to it but square, boxy TVs, square, boxy computers, couches with no heyday to hark back to, and a threadbare pool table.

Toward the back of the structure, five men had helped themselves to beers at a self-service bar and were hanging out, drinking and bullshitting.

No chicks were around.

Which was a mark against Reese's mission to splode his relationship with Steliana by getting laid. But a mark *for* his plans to stir up trouble and go back to being Regular Reese. Because those a-partyin' big boys were clearly capable of a lotta mean. In fact, they made the clientele at The Shank Tooth look like Piglet and Eeyore's bitches.

Reese almost laughed. Day-um, he was on fire with the metaphors, right?

Ah, well…such were the foibles of an inactive mind…

Anyway.

He'd climbed down the ledge's stairway and sauntered over to the five lounge lizards.

I-wouldn't-have-believed-it-if-I-hadn't-experienced-it happened next. The men surrounded him and starting sniffing, like a pack of coyotes.

Finally one guy bolted off.

Turns out this guy was some sort of stoolie, because next thing you know, a man arrived who looked like…

Hmm, metaphor…metaphor…?

Like Popocatépetl.

You don't think that sounds badass enough? Think again.

Popocatépetl's a big motherfucking volcano in Mexico—one of the most active in the world—and this dude *was* a volcano.

First, he was gigantic (eight feet tall at least, I shit you not). Second, he currently had lava spilling out the top of his head in the form of a shit-ton of long red hair. Third, his power and ferocity were off the charts.

That was the real, fucked-up, holy-shit part about the bastard. 'Cept explaining his power with accurate adjectives would be about as easy as describing Vegemite as "tasty." Because no way had any topside Mr. and Mrs. Peabody ever felt something like it. Power like this guy's was exclusive to the type of creature who lived in the *down-there* regions of the Earth.

Yeah, I'm referring to Hell.

The big dude was shirtless, wearing only black boots with spikes driving up from the toecaps, and black leather pants. His shirtless condition exposed lots and lots of scars—both of his nipples and his navel had extra-gnarly ones—and showed off *all* of what he was packing in the way of muscles.

Lots and lots.

How many burpees per day did it take to build a body like that? Because…*shiiiit.*

Women always gushed about men with "iron" muscles. This dude's were the real deal in that department—although Reese couldn't see any woman gushing over a Volcano Burpee (hey, I could've nicknamed him Popocatépetl. *You're welcome*).

Volcano Burpee joined their little soiree at the Dæmon Gymboree, looked over Reese, then did something with his mouth.

His lips pulled back.

His teeth showed.

In some circles the expression might've been called a smile, but Reese figured anything that made his balls want to crawl away and hide couldn't be called that.

Next thing Reese had to do was lock down all his muscles to keep from jumping out of his shorts because Volcano Burpee bellowed, "Gwyn!"

Dude's voice was a damned eruption (yes, yes, I'm sticking with the volcano metaphors).

One Mississippi. Two Mississippi.

A woman in her late thirties appeared—short, mannish hair, straight posture, not unattractive except she was hardship-aged, two deep lines carved next to both sides of her mouth.

When she saw Reese, her eyebrows soared in a *where-the-hell-did-you-come-from?* expression.

"What females are ripe now?" Volcano Burpee demanded of her.

Without a word, Gwyn turned and disappeared into the misfortune of a building next to the Dæmon Gymboree. There was a red cross painted on the door, so apparently it was the medieval torture chamber that doled out medical care in the Shitsburgs.

After a few seconds Gwyn returned with a clipboard. She consulted it and said, "Havel and Siofranna should be ripe right now." She looked up. "But Siofranna recently bonded to Olacar."

"HAVEL!"

Reese wasn't prepared for Volcano Burpee's bellow this

time and rocketed out of his skin. Jesus Harry Christ on crutches. This man had a voice that started at the foundation of his diaphragm and gathered rubble all the way up before making its voluble exit.

A woman about Reese's age now showed up. She was wearing black cargo pants and a black tank top that displayed rock-hard arms and part of a tribal tattoo on the left side of her chest—he spotted a long, swooping tusk or tooth, similar to Jacken's ink, although most of her tat was hidden beneath her top. Black hair hung in dreads down to her waist.

Then the situation became a *say what?*

Volcano Burpee ordered Reese to impregnate this "ripe" Havel woman.

Reese proceeded to just about pee himself laughing over *that* mandate. In between hysterics, he did his best to clarify his position on the matter.

No laying, no knocking up.

Regarding point, the first—Yes, he *did* want to get laid, but, sorry, he had a zany rule against schtupping any woman who'd been *ordered* into his bed.

Point, the second—No on spermatizing any woman.

Just no.

Despite all the fun and games they were having (What? Was he the only one laughing?), Volcano Burpee was not amused. He sent Havel and Reese off to Havel's Hovel (thank you, yes, I thought of that all by my lonesome), and put them under strict orders not to emerge until the impregnation was complete.

Which brings us to our current difficulties.

Namely, with Reese cooling his heels in the Love Shack while waiting for Team Community to come rescue him, nothing better to do than laze about in his underwear and sing the Rubber Tree Ant song.

Because the only place he was planting his seed was in the reservoir tip of a condom, so no sex was going on.

No sex had been going on for the past twelve hours or so.

I'm so bored with being bored because being bored is really boring.

He turned his head to watch Havel. "What are you doing?"

She was seated at a spindly wooden desk shoved against the wall opposite the twin bed, her back to him. She was dressed the same as yesterday—black cargo pants, black tank.

He ran his tongue along his bottom lip. Her ass looked *awfully* tight in those pants. Her ass *was* tight—he knew this from actual contact with her gluteal wonders. Last night, he hadn't done the gallant thing and offered to sleep on the floor.

Mainly because he wanted to see what Havel would do.

Without batting an eyelash, she climbed into bed next to him and sacked out—although he was going to make a huge leap here and guess that eyelash-batting wasn't one of Havel's go-to moves on any occasion.

The bed was a tiny single, built for one adult body, not two, and so this morning he'd woken to her derriere tucked neatly against his hips—him with a serious case of slumber lumber poked into one of her marvey glutes, her glancing over her shoulder at him with a *you-going-to-use-that-thing-or-what?* look.

Nope.

Funny, wasn't it, how he'd gone out last night on a mission to get laid, and now here he was with rough-as-fuck Havel—his perfect lay—gifted to him for that express purpose, and he couldn't lay her.

Well, *funny* if you have a deep and abiding appreciation for irony of the painful, blue-balls variety.

"Studying for a vocabulary test," Havel answered.

She had a husky voice. *Total hot sauce.*

"Now that Gwyn's able to get school supplies from Ţărână," Havel went on, "she's been able to help us improve our reading and stuff."

"You never went to school?"

Havel tossed a disdainful *tch* over her shoulder, then went back to studying.

A totally unfair slap on the wrist, that disdain. How the hell was he supposed to know what her life was like in the Shitsburgs? Even kids in bad neighborhoods topside went to school.

He fidgeted on her bed. "You got a deck of cards around here? Game of Parcheesi?" *Are you as bored as I am? Hey! Read that backwards and it still makes sense.* "A Slinky? *Anything* we can do while we're pretending to have sex?"

"No." She flipped a page in her vocab book.

He eyeballed her ass again. "Just simple curiosity here. But would you fuck me if I would fuck you? And would a woodchuck chuck wood if a woodchuck could chuck wood?"

Havel turned around in her chair and stared at him.

She had black eyes that somehow looked like they went deep, when, you know, how could solid black do that?

Reese sat up. A man did not face down black eyes while supine. "Well, the saying really goes 'how much wood would a woodchuck chuck if a woodchuck could chuck wood'—and would you?"

She lifted one shoulder in a lackadaisical shrug. "Sure."

CHAPTER THIRTY-FIVE

WOULD YOU HAVE SEX WITH this flesh-eating virus? Sure. How about this newly discovered species of slime mold? Sure. How about a booger? Sure.

"Your enthusiasm just gave me a massive boner," Reese said.

"Hey, you're not bad-looking," Havel offered.

He grinned, sat up straighter, and puffed out his chest.

"And I want a baby," she continued. "One that's *not* a full-Rău."

He jerked his eyebrows up. "To raise in *this* shithole."

She hooked an arm over the back of her chair.

Her bicep was clearly defined from her tricep, not overly big, but…oh, lawks, the handjob this woman could probably give…

"You feel sorry for yourself a lot, don't you?"

He fluttered his lashes at her in mock dismay. "I do?"

"You got a shitty story to tell. I know you do—you wouldn't have ended up in Ţărână if you didn't. Alcoholic parents, maybe. Smacked around, maybe. Neglected, a solid *yeah*, I'm betting. Possibly abandoned."

He kept smiling at her, stretching his lips, putting pressure on his gums.

"But it's all relative. At any given point in time, there's someone better off than you and someone worse off than you."

He bobbed his head. "Deep."

She crossed her legs. "I was eleven years old the first time I was raped. So?"

Reese set his hands on his knees and stared at her legs. He was oddly struck by her decision to cross them when she told him that sex was forced on her while she was probably still pre-pubescent.

Her posture was casual.

"So," he repeated back in a monotone.

Log this: Reese Terrella is without a ready riposte. *Note the time and date, please.*

"I've been raped twelve times total. Up top, that would be bad, right? Down here it's whatever." She shrugged.

Apropos to the moment, a woman outside screamed.

"Fuck off!" a male voice snarled and *smack!*

Reese's heart changed its rhythm for a few beats. "It's not *whatever*," he pointed out, "if you've counted."

Some kind of emotion jumped through Havel's eyes. A red light flickered in their black depths.

Which was, uh, really spooky.

She blinked hard, then did something odd—she pressed the heel of her palm to one ear and picked up what appeared to be a small pincushion with the other hand and held it to her nose.

Reese sat still and watched her, his feet cast in a circle of lamplight, his palms damp on his legs.

She set down the mini pillow. "The *whatever* part is that I'm not going to focus on the shitty. I'm going to educate myself. I'm going to help Gwyn make things better around here. Someday I'll be a mother, and I'll be a good one. I'm not going to be scared. Like you are."

"Me?" He did the classic head-tilt. "What am I a-scared of?"

She skimmed her eyes over his torso, inspecting his tats as if she couldn't believe he'd done that to himself. Weird reaction, since she had ink too, and it wasn't like anyone forced it on her.

Wait. Had they?

It was rapidly becoming a truth universally acknowledged that any and all kinds of shit went down in this place.

Havel's gaze returned to his, a vibe of absolute knowing coming off her. "Do you really want me to tell you?"

No. I don't. He gently curled his fingers toward his palms. *Because I'm too a-scared.*

Sometimes people don't want to hear the truth because they don't want their illusions destroyed…

Goodness me. What a moment to be bludgeoned on the head by Nietzsche.

A fist banged on the door.

"Yeah," Havel called out.

A woman wearing a black do-rag stuck her head inside.

Havel introduced the woman as her sister, Fade.

"Hey," Reese said to her. *Come in, come in. Put on some hemp and join our love circle. We're sharing our feelings.*

Fade didn't acknowledge him. "Some Ţărână muscle showed up, and they want to check on their little lost Dragon. Josnic says to send him out."

"All right," Havel said.

Fade left.

Reese got to his feet and began to pull on his clothes. *Halle-fuckin'-lujah.* Never thought he'd be glad to see some boys in blue, but he was more than ready to have his ass rescued outta this place.

He stomped into his boots and walked over to Havel. Picking up the pincushion, he took a deep whiff of it. It wasn't the newest in inhalation drugs, nor was it the answer to life's mysteries. Just a strong scent of lavender and oregano.

"Bizarre," he said. Which was his way of saying he didn't get it.

He tossed the pincushion back on the desk. "Nice knowing ya, Havel. You make a good bed buddy." *'Cept for the constant knob I had to fight all night.*

She spun around and went back to her book, running a finger down the page to find where she'd left off. "You'll be back."

Nah. No one catches Reese Terrella.

Although in some insane corner of his mind, he almost wished they could.

CHAPTER THIRTY-SIX

THE FIRST INKLING THAT REESE might-just-might be in big trouble hit him when he arrived at the amphitheater.

It was Roth Mihnea—flanked by Nichita and Brun—positioned on the ledge overlooking the Shitsburgs.

Not Blonde Sahib.

Roth appeared commanding enough, standing with his hands tucked behind his back and his legs braced wide. But this leader of the community—according to rumor—wasn't much more than an empty suit.

Jacken and Dev weren't a couple of cocknoggins, but neither of them had the final say on matters.

Should Reese equate Blonde Doc's absence with a lack of affection for the *man who's been nothing but unkind ever since he opened his mouth?* Or was it because of her preggers status?

Reese was going to go with the latter.

Not only for reasons of advanced hubris, but because Vârcolac males became psycho-overprotective of their knocked-up mates—according to what Reese read in the manual—so Jacken had probably gotten all spastic over the idea of Doc taking a jaunt into demon town.

Understandable.

But still.

Reese would've much preferred having the health and well-being of his nuts entrusted to Mistress.

He stopped at the edge of the large open area, which put the Dæmon Gymboree off his right shoulder.

Volcano Burpee—*Josnic*—stood in front of the structure,

mannish Gwyn at his side, and an audience of ruffians gathered behind the two.

"You okay?" Jacken directed this question at Reese along with a piercing stare.

"More or less." *Less* if you counted how fed up he was with booooooredom.

"All right." Volcano Josnic waved off the visitors, indicating they should go bye-bye now. "You've seen your boy. He's not hurt. Now go."

"I'm afraid we cannot leave without Mr. Terrella," Roth informed Josnic in a tone of extreme hauteur.

Whoa, the empty suit comes out swinging! Take that, Volcano Burpee!

Amaaaazingly, Josnic wasn't deterred. "You can't have him."

"That would be an unacceptable breach of our truce." Roth made a dilatory gesture, the height of insouciance.

Yeah! Go get 'em, boss! Threaten to pull out Volcano Burpee's needlework next.

Josnic crossed his iron arms over his massive chest and shook his lava head. "We promised never to steal Dragons from *Ţărână*. We never agreed on what to do with someone who came to us."

Jacken growled. "Plenty of your Om Răo assholes have ended up in Ţărână over the years. We sent them back."

Josnic boomed out a laugh. "That's because you don't want us. I want your man."

"Be that as it may," Roth began—*oh, get ready, get fucking ready for the big guns!* "We invited Mr. Terrella into our town with assurances of our protection."

"Not my problem."

"It is." Roth's eyes chilled to such an ooky-skeery degree that Reese slapped his own smart mouth shut. "Because we will fight for him."

Reese mentally bowed his head and scuffed the cave floor

with his toe. *Gosh, really?*

"All right, you can have him back…" Josnic's teeth glinted; he was doing that thing with his mouth again. "*After* I pass him around to every fertile woman in Oţărât."

Reese's penis screeched out an *eeek*, then tried to skedaddle into a tuck-back. Now he was actually really skeered.

Nichita joined the party with, "You don't want this Dragon, Josnic. He's a pigheaded pain in the ass who never does what he's told. It's how he ended up here."

Reese breathed out a silent *whew. Thanks, man. Owe you a beer later.*

"He'll do what he's told here or suffer," Josnic promised in the kind of voice that…that…

Reese was without metaphor. His brain was too busy imagining all the ways Volcano Burpee and his iron muscles could *encourage* Reese to toe the company line.

Roth Mihnea stepped back in, addressing Gwyn. "I would think you in particular, Ms. Billaud, can understand why we can't leave Mr. Terrella here when we promised him safety."

"I do appreciate that you're trying to do right by him," Gwyn said, a bit white-faced. "But what I don't want is another war. In fact, it would be a breach of the truce if you Vârcolac initiated a fight with us."

Roth's chin stiffened. "What do you suggest, then? Because I will *not* leave Mr. Terrella here. So if you have terms to propose that will give us back our man, I'm all ears. Otherwise—"

"*One* baby," Gwyn said. "With our girl, Havel."

Reese Terrella and Josnic No-Last-Name-Known both whipped their heads in Gwyn's direction.

Josnic let out a low snarl, but Gwyn briefly touched his thigh. "And plumbing."

Roth regarded her with a bland stare.

"We're still dealing with water in canisters here," Gwyn went on. "It would be helpful to us if you could run a pipeline down the length of the Neutral Zone to the end of the ledge, maybe put an on/off faucet on it. Maybe build a shower stall."

One of Roth's eyebrows angled up. "A shower would require a drainage system. That's a lot to ask."

"And it's a lot to ask Josnic to give up your man after only one baby. Reese is a Royal."

Again with the Royal dillyfuck? "People keep referring to me that way," Reese said. "What the hell does it mean?"

"It means," Gwyn answered, "that you have powerful bloodlines that Josnic wants bred into his Om Ră
u stock."

"Ah. Thanks so much for the clarification." *Not.*

Roth pursed his lips. "So would Mr. Terrella have to remain in Oţărât during the entire time of Havel's...fecundity? Or would he return here for conjugal visits?"

Man, if Reese wasn't cross-eyed with panic he'd be writing this shit down.

"Actually," Gwyn said, "the deed might already be done—Reese spent last night with Havel." Gwyn shifted her gaze to a spot over Reese's shoulder. "Did you and Reese have sex?"

Reese turned around.

Havel was leaning against one of the crapshacks, one shoulder propping up the building, her thick arms crossed. She flicked a look at Reese, then half-shrugged. "No."

"Then the Dragon stays," Josnic pronounced.

"Look, I'm not impregnating anyone," Reese finally interceded on his own behalf. "So keeping me here would be pointless."

"All right," Josnic said. "I can suggest an alternative—I'll take a baby off the daughter of Yavell in exchange for the pighead Royal."

Roth looked perplexed. "Who?"

"Pandra," Dev said out of the side of his mouth.

Josnic's eyes glinted like oily asphalt. "She and I have unfinished business."

"No exchanges." Roth sounded quite firm on the matter.

Big bully. "Which brings us right back to where we started."

Josnic shrugged his mighty shoulders. *Do I care?*

Fuck sakes. This was long past ridonkulous. "Answer," Reese said. "A kid of mine plus this shithole of a town. Question: what are two things you'll never find together?"

Gwyn's lips tightened. "You'd rather people die fighting for you?" Her eyes narrowed. "Is *one* child really too much to ask to save countless lives?"

Too much to ask…? It wasn't even in the hemisphere of a question. *Impossible* was where that concept hung out. Other people might be able to flex on the matter. Humans were generally changeable beings, made fluid by ambition and desires and fears, bonds and strictures and the breaking thereof, but there was one immutable truth about him.

He would *never* abandon a kid of his.

But point, the next: he was also pretty un-budge-able on the matter of people dying for him.

Fane, Ninza, Jacken, Nichita…

Reese couldn't stomach any of those guys corking it over his Daddy Screaming Meemies issues.

Talk about your world-class stalemates.

"You know what? I think I'll go ahead and stay." Reese gave Roth Mihnea a solid nod, doing his best impression of an all-sacrificing politician.

Friends, Romans, countrymen, never in the field of human conflict have we asked not what our country can do for us, but rather can we take one small step for mankind, and by doing so know that where there is error, we may bring truth, and at the end of the march, we will wait far too long for our freedom.

Reese turned around.

Havel was gone.

He strode past the crapshack where she'd been leaning, aiming for their hovel, the whole way an inkling hovering above his head, like a thorny halo.

Blonde Sahib might-just-might have found a way to haul his sorry ass outta here.

CHAPTER THIRTY-SEVEN

June
Six days later
6:22 p.m.

A WEEK OF NOT SEEING Corky had dragged Vasile down—his mood was low and his energy depleted.

He was not managing himself as well as he would have liked. But, truth be told, he would have been worse if not for his warrior comrades—upstanding, loyal men all—keeping him very busy with outings and doings as a means to distract him from thinking too many morose thoughts.

For this he was grateful.

So tonight he had accepted with a glad heart an invitation from Dev, Thomal, and Gábor to frequent the Pub of Garwald for the kind of early evening libation named happy hour. The four of them were celebrating Thomal becoming a father for a second time, ten months from now.

Thomal had but yesterday awoken from the three-day dormancy a male Vârcolac falls into after he inseminates his woman—*inseminate* was not the correct term, but at the moment Vasile could only recall the descriptor used for cows. So it appeared Thomal and Pandra had indeed achieved a deeper level of affection since their time of enacting violence upon one another.

Like Dev, Vasile did not claim to understand this. But no matter.

Their group of four entered the drinking establishment to the noise of people talking and a male voice singing from the music box. The singer was bragging about having passion in his pants, and that he was not afraid to show it.

This was an odd condition to sing about, for it did not seem like a matter worthy of conceit, but rather something in need of a curative to—

Vasile came to a jarring halt.

Corky was in the pub.

She was sitting in a booth long-seat across from Fane Vasilichi, a mixed-breed Vârcolac with a shade of hair color that could not decide if it was yellow or brown.

Alcohol beverages were set before them. Corky was enjoying the dark drink with a cherry in it she favored, and Fane was sipping a lime-colored concoction of some sort. The glass had not been washed properly—the rim was covered with sand.

Vasile rumbled low in his chest. "Does Corky be on the drink-date with that man?"

Perchance not. Perchance Corky was "just friends" with Fane, the same as she had been with the douche-man Reese.

"Um, yeah." Dev moved closer. "Looks like it."

Vasile turned on him. "That is not permitted. Corky is my woman."

"Sorry, man," said Dev, somber of tone, "but she's not. Not anymore. Corky broke up with you, and that means she can go out with other men."

A strange, dark acid stung Vasile in his belly. He swiveled his head back around to watch Corky and this *other* man.

Fane was smiling at Corky.

Fane was talking with speed to Corky.

Fane was using all manner of gestures when he spoke to Corky.

Fane laughed at something Corky said.

Vasile made tight fists of his hands.

Fane was doing all the things Vasile had never been able to do with her.

Vasile felt the hairs on the back of his neck bristle. Fane Vasilichi was known to have a jovial manner—this assessment was clearly true—and to be a hardworking and reliable man. He was not a bad person by any definition. But Vasile would gladly embed his blade in him all the same.

Now it was Corky who laughed at something Fane said.

Vasile curled his upper lip, his fangs beginning to throb. This was more than he should be made to bear. Her laugh belonged to *him*. Like the joyful, harmonious sound she had made when he recited slang words for the male appendage. Or when he told her about elks…or about how Mircea used to stick pickles in ears. And many other times she had made this special sound of laughter, filling his chest with pride that he was able to give her happiness.

What next would she give to Fane Vasilichi that was not his due?

A *kiss*? Would she dare to bestow one of those on the toff?

Vasile deepened his sneer, his fangs making a pulsing journey into his mouth. Fire scorched a path through his head—a place where no violence had ever burned before. He launched into an explosive charge for—

He was jerked back by a powerful palm on his shoulder.

Dev.

Vasile seethed a breath at his friend. "Unhand me." He surged forward again.

Dev did not release him. Instead he muscled Vasile around and pushed him out of the pub door with stern force.

When Vasile and Dev reached the street fronting the pub—Thomal and Gábor following—Vasile put a great deal of his strength into freeing himself.

This time he wrenched away. "<You are my friend and an honorable man, Dev Nichita, but if you take measures to hinder me again, I will do you harm.>" He gnashed his fangs.

Community males took easy offense at this kind of demonstration, but, by a rotted moon, the kissing of another man could not be allowed!

Dev held up both hands in an aspect of peacekeeping. "<In my head I cannot have possible pictures of what you go through seeing your woman with a man, not you. But as your friend I ask you to permit me to talk to you for some moments. If you still have desire to hurt Fane after the discussion, I myself will help you bring him here into street. Yes?>"

Vasile felt his flesh crawl and jump over the idea of leaving Corky alone with Fane for any longer than necessary. But Dev had made a reasonable request.

"<Speak,>" said Vasile shortly.

"I have to tell you in English, so if there's anything you don't understand, let me know." Dev inhaled a heavy breath. "Look, I have a pretty good idea about what you're going through right now. Marissa and I had a rough start, same as you and Corky are having, and I didn't handle it well. So I'm going to tell you what I did, then maybe you can avoid making the same mistakes."

Several pedestrians strode for the door into the pub, and so their group moved farther away.

Dev renewed his speech. "When Marissa found out that hooking up with me meant forever, she freaked out. Her reaction was understandable—she had goals that didn't exactly mesh with being stuck underground with a vampire for the rest of her life—but I took offense anyway. So instead of being patient and understanding—which would've earned me massive points toward winning her back—I was a total jerk and drove her away. I almost lost her forever, Vasile, and I see you about to do the same thing with Corky."

Dev pointed at the door to the pub. "If you go into Garwald's and beat the shit out of her date, you'll be disrespecting what she told you she needs."

"She no tell me she needs go on meal- and drink-dates with other men."

"No, but she told you she needs some time and space away from you to figure her shit out. And if part of figuring her shit out means that she wants to see other men, then you have to let her do that. If you don't, you might drive her away, same as I did with Marissa."

Vasile expelled a lengthy breath. "I have gratitude that you try give sound advice, Dev Nichita, but you no understand all the things. Corky tell me she no trust her decisions anymore. So I decide for her. Otherelse she make grave error with that Fane toff."

Dev shook his head. "It doesn't work that way. She has to figure out her own problems."

"But she must needs figure out that *I* am proper man for her," said Vasile through a raging fire in his throat. He *could* and *would* take care of her. "How does seeing other men help her to know this about me? Such actions have no sound logic."

"It doesn't matter. It's clearly what she needs."

"No," he snarled. "She be *mine*."

"I know she is, man, but she doesn't know it yet. You have to remember she's human—she can't scent a mate like we can. It takes longer for humans to be sure."

"How long?"

Dev spread his hands. "Everyone's different."

Vasile exhaled a growl. "The longer it goes, the worse is for me. The more Corky compares me to other males, the more I lose my chance." Comparisons never worked well for him. Corky would only end up shunning him for his lack.

"That's not true."

"It is." Vasile chopped a hand down and spoke in a sharp tone, his frustration boiling over. "Why you community people put me through agony of make me true male, if you only have plan to deprive me of woman."

Dev frowned. "Agony?"

Thomal raised his eyebrows at Dev. "You didn't hear

about what happened in their sex ed class?"

"Me either," said Gábor. "What happened—and how do you know and we don't?"

"Arc told me—he was there. Apparently, the Moon-Riders fell apart when they watched Dr. Jess's sex movies."

Dev turned to aim a grimace at Vasile. "Those movies are difficult for any unbonded male to watch."

Vasile shook his head. Dev did not understand. "It no be difficult for us Moon-Riders to watch at first. That is problem."

Dev frowned again. "What do you mean?"

"Doctor Jess try to use moving pictures to open true-male side of Moon-Rider mind, but watching the moving pictures was not strong enough."

The town medical man had once explained to the Moon-Riders that a Vârcolac male needed the scent of something called "female hormones" to achieve his full development. Since the Moon-Riders were raised around women without hormones, they never acquired the drive to spawn offspring or to protect their women.

The goal of sex education class had been to repair that deficiency.

"When Moon-Riders see images of naked woman," continued Vasile, "they laugh. Horia call female breasts blubber bags, and they laugh more. Moving pictures show male appendage entering female hole with power, and this is cause for much hilarity."

"You *laughed* at that?" Gábor sounded incredulous.

"Yes, and Doctor Jess no like this reaction. So he call in many unmated womens from town to come to our sex education classroom. He instruct them first remove mud from behind ears, then do exercise to become very sweaty. They come to our classroom in such a state and commence jogging hither and yon to spread their scent everywhere."

"Oh, shit," said Dev.

"Yes, it be torture," confirmed Vasile, then he pointed at his temple. "My brain twitch and stretch and jab me. Then the medical man recommence moving pictures, and the penetration of man to woman is no longer nothing. Those images now very much be something. My brain nigh explode." Vasile grasped his head, then threw his hands out to demonstrate the horrendous feeling. "And my pole clog with utmost pain. Same go for other Moon-Riders. In all parts of classroom, the men collapse from chairs; they writhe on floor; they call out in confusion and agony."

"Jesus F'n Christ." Gábor scrunched his facial features. "I'm not sure I can listen to much more of this."

Vasile continued at any rate. "We become true men in this moment, yes, but we know not how to be true men. We gain sudden drives we no understand how to control. So many Moon-Riders jump on sweaty womens in sex education classroom and try to have the sexual intercourse with them right there."

Dev exchanged a swift glance with Thomal.

"Yes. Is bad. Two warriors nearby, Jacken and Arc, hear commotion and rush into room and drag men off. Soon thereafter, Moon-Riders must wear shocker bands on ankles." Vasile stalked several paces away from his comrades. "When I live in Romania, it is not altogether happy time, no, but at least I am not unhappy with females. Now I am true man, and all is changed. Corky is no longer silly, useless creature to me, but someone I desire to be with, someone I must needs protect and care for. Her breasts are no longer blubber bags, but..." He could not find a word to describe his desire to touch her breasts.

"Why you community people do this to me?" He repeated the question with force. "For *why* you make me want something and then say I cannot have?"

"No one's saying you can't have Corky someday," said Dev. "She just needs some time."

Vasile gritted his teeth. "But you no tell me how long."

Thomal spoke again. "Listen, brother, you might not be as bad off as you think you are. I talked to Corky in court the day after she broke up with you, and she told me you're still in the running, okay?"

"What means this…?" Vasile scowled. "I must run now?"

"No, it means that you still have a chance with Corky," corrected Thomal. "She still likes you."

That made no sense. "If she like me, then for why she say she must discontinue going on meal-dates with me for a time?"

Dev stopped further discussion with a raised hand. "Hold on. Are those Corky's exact words—that she didn't want to go out with you *for a time?*"

"Yes," verified Vasile. "She say she need to back off for a while."

"Well, all right then." Dev now spoke in a hopeful tone. "Then maybe enough time has passed. She's had a week of space, right? And *back off* doesn't have to mean *back out* completely, especially if she's still interested in you, like Costache said. So ask her out. And every time you go on a date with her, it gives you the chance to win her back—and *that* needs to be your game plan, Vasile. To lure her, exactly what I should've done with Marissa."

"*But* if you want to win her," advised Thomal, "you've got to talk to her about more than just ___ crap."

Mundane?

"Because another thing Corky told me after you two broke up is that she's afraid she's making a mistake by being with you because…I don't remember exactly how she put it, but something about you seeming too closed off."

"I no understand *closed off.*"

"It means you're not telling her the bad shit about yourself along with the good."

What is this? "But socialization class teach Moon-Riders to always be best self with woman."

Dev put his opinion back in. "That's a good idea at first, yeah, but then you have to show her all sides of yourself. No woman wants to be with a man she thinks is perfect. It'll make her feel like she can't be imperfect around him…and remember how I told you that you need to accept a woman for her flaws?"

"Yes."

"Well, she needs to *know* you're going to do that."

"And she will know that by me tell her bad things about self?"

"Yeah," said Dev. "I mean, don't tell her anything *too* bad, but yeah."

Vasile stood still, going back in his memory to the horrible evening when Corky had set him aside. *You've never told me anything about yourself. We've discussed the television shows you like and your favorite foods and…and I don't care how you brush your teeth, Vasile.*

"*Fir-ar să fie,*" he swore. Now these words made sense. "You are correct. I mistaked with her."

"It's all right, man," said Dev. "Don't sweat it. Just fix it."

Gábor grunted. "You can start by inviting her to go topside with us tomorrow morning—nighttime topside."

"Hey, that's a great idea." Dev grinned.

"What happens on the morrow?" asked Vasile.

"Six of us are going to see a play." Gábor named the participants—"Jacken and Toni, Dev and Marissa, and me and Chelsea."

Vasile glanced at Thomal. "You no go?"

Thomal shook his head. "Pandra already has morning sickness."

Vasile had never heard of this disease, but it was his hope that Pandra would not feel too poorly with it. "What is *play*?"

"Like a television show," explained Gábor, "but with real people on a stage. Women love plays. My wife wants to go see one as a last, big outing before she has the baby in the next few weeks. I'm telling you, Lazăr, if you ask Corky to a play topside, she won't be able to say no. It'll kick things off, and you can go from there."

Vasile liked this idea very much. He especially liked the going-topside part of the proposal. He had not seen a glimmer of the moon for nigh six months. "This is sage advice, Gábor. My thanks to you."

"Yeah, no prob. I'll ask Chelsea to buy two more tickets."

"And I will ask Corky to accompany me to the play as soon as she returns to her dwelling this evening."

"Now that we've got that settled," said Gábor, "can we *please* head to Nichita's for a beer. I need a drink after hearing Lazăr's coming-to-manhood story." Gábor made a strange noise in his throat, like a sewer pipe struggling with a clog.

Thomal and Dev laughed but nodded their agreement.

The four of them turned and started for the family neighborhood.

Vasile walked with a lighter step than usual, and his heart beat with more vigor than it had in six long days.

He now had a solid plan to win back his beloved.

CHAPTER THIRTY-EIGHT

The next night
Topside
10:07 p.m.

BALBOA PARK WAS ONE OF Corky's favorite places to visit, particularly at night, when the crowds were thinned out and the sharper daytime scents of pollution and human life were no longer in competition with nature, leaving behind the pungent perfume of eucalyptus trees and ripe earth.

Home to the world-renowned San Diego Zoo, the park was a sprawling mecca of nature-meets-culture, covering over twelve hundred acres of prime downtown real estate. There were museums galore, venues for dance, music, and theatre, and the surrounding grounds provided an oasis of gardens, trails, fountains, and Spanish architecture.

A tree-lined promenade lined with Victorian-style wrought iron lamps connected the Old Globe Theatre—where the four couples had just seen a play—to a huge, geyser-like fountain in front of the Fleet Science Center.

The eight of them were meandering down the promenade now, enjoying some post-theatre private time—Dev and Marissa were several yards ahead of Corky and Vasile, Jacken and Toni behind, and Gábor and Chelsea even farther back.

Stars peeked out from remnants of patchy June gloom clouds, although the temperature sat at a comfortable sixty-five.

Corky draped her shawl over one arm—she wore a flowered sundress with spaghetti straps—it being too warm to cover her bare shoulders.

She strolled at an easy pace next to Vasile, feeling loose-limbed and relaxed.

God, but it was so great to be doing something fun. She'd just spent a week holed up with her likewise dateless roommate, and she hadn't realized how much she missed going out, especially to a big city.

On rocky emotional ground right after her breakup with Vasile, Corky had focused totally on work, poring over Ţărână's new and evolving laws with Kimberly and the town Soothsayer, Alex Parthen, and reviewing community customs and history in the manual.

She also turned her attention back to her Rand Resources case.

Those corporate monsters were now resorting to outright acts of vandalism.

According to a recent email from Mary Sills, several windows in the group home had turned up broken, and then "someone" drove a tractor over Mary's vegetable garden in the middle of the night, chewing it to smithereens—destroying food Mary depended on to make ends meet.

Now that Mary's finances were being affected by Rand's harassment, she was desperate to have this resolved. She'd pleaded with Corky to fix it.

I will, Corky had promised while feeling an ulcer building over *how*.

She reviewed everything about the case over and over and kept coming back to something Mary had said the evening in Night Court when Corky lost.

Reuben would never resort to foul play. He and I have been friends and neighbors for too many years.

Corky's first thought back then was, *Except that everyone can be bought.*

She still believed that. But if she was right, then what had Rand Resources offered Reuben to get him to sell out a good friend?

The answer to that question had been niggling at her all along.

So finally Corky went right to the source and wrote a carefully worded email to Reuben. After a few back-and-forths, she got him to admit that Rand Resources had paid off his mortgage in exchange for him buying that one-eighth of an acre of Mary Sills' land.

Whoa.

Mary's land was rich in coal, yes, but was it *so* rich that Rand would go to the expense of paying off someone's mortgage? Seemed a bit fishy to her.

All week she'd ruminated about it to Hadley…until her beleaguered roommate finally insisted that Corky get her butt out the door and go on a date. When Corky still hesitated, Hadley pointed out that Corky couldn't learn how to quit being a doormat with men if she avoided men. Right?

That had made sort-of sense.

And since Corky was also restless and lonely, she decided her roomie was right.

So she chose Fane as her guinea pig. Because underneath all the cave dust he *was* a good-looking man. But mainly he was easygoing and uncomplicated—so he wouldn't become her "pet project"—and he seemed independent and self-reliant—so he wouldn't automatically trigger her caretaker instincts.

Going for a low-maintenance guy might not be the truest test of her anti-doormat capabilities, but, hey, baby steps.

Turned out Fane *was* easy, and also very nice. Last night at Garwald's they'd shared some good laughs. But he was also, you know…a typical guy. Not bad. Just an everyday-Joe type. Super-fine, she'd bet, for women who hadn't grown used to Vasile's unique way of seeing the world.

During Corky's conversations with Fane, she found herself drifting a bit while wondering what Vasile would've said to this or that.

So when Vasile showed up on her doorstep yesterday with some convincing arguments for her to go out with him again—reasoning that *back off* doesn't have to mean *back out completely*—she wasn't able to come up with a good counter-argument. And when he invited her to a play at the Old Globe Theatre in Balboa Park, well…that sealed the deal. She couldn't say no to a night out at the theater.

Seeing a play would just be too much fun.

It *had* been fun.

"Did you enjoy the show?" she asked Vasile, turning to look at him.

He was gazing up at the moon, his long hair falling back from his face, exposing his bold profile.

She'd come to really like his face—it was masculine and actually showed a lot of character.

"I did, yes," he answered, dropping his gaze. "Much American humor with words I no understand, but this was humor with actions, so I understand very well."

The play they'd seen was *Noises Off*, a zany physical comedy.

Vasile had never laughed out loud, like the rest of them, but Corky had sensed the relaxed state of his body.

"You like?" he asked.

"Oh, yes. Thank you so much for inviting me."

He inclined his head. "You do me honor by coming."

She smiled. Innocent and vulnerable *and* gallant—the mix was turning out to be one of her favorite combinations.

They arrived in front of Balboa's famous lily pond. It stretched out in an expansive rectangle from the Botanical Building, a structure built almost entirely of dark lath wood.

"There be pond here?" Vasile's voice rang with surprise.

"Yep. Do you want to take a closer look?"

"Good."

They strolled toward it.

"Although you might not like it," Corky warned.

"Because is man-made?"

"Because the fish in it are only for show, not for eating."

He cast her a sideways glance.

She gave him a sparkling smile.

"You make joke with me?"

"I did."

He paused. "But not for insult?"

"Correct. I wasn't insulting you."

They stopped at the edge of the pond.

She watched an orange-and-white koi swim languidly through the water. "A big fish," she commented.

Vasile studied the koi. "It make good meal. I catch with bare hand if you desire it."

She giggled. "You could do that?"

"Of a certain."

"I don't know, *hmm*, that fish looks awfully slippery."

"I may have numerous flaws, *comoara mea*, but the catching of fish is not one."

She flashed her eyes up. Vasile had just called her by the same endearment Mary Sills so often used. *Comoara mea.*

My treasure.

"Ah, well…" She faltered.

"You have flaws too. Yes?"

"I…" *Huh?* "I guess…of course, but…"

He faced her. "Dev Nichita once advise me that no woman is perfect. He tell me a man must needs accept her flaws. Love her for them. I tell you, Corky—this I do with you."

She blinked several times. *Love…?*

"I see that you no understand how to skin a rabbit or build a level shelf. You sometimes clink ice against teeth while drinking a cold beverage, and when you peel a sticky tag off some item you ofttimes put tag on shirt instead of depositing directly into waste bin. These traits surely must be considered flaws."

She blinked more rapidly, then fought back a laugh. *Those were her flaws?*

"But you are my beloved nonetheless." Vasile's voice lowered. "One smile, one laugh, one glimpse at all that resides in the deepest parts of your eyes, and naught else matters."

Corky clutched her shawl to her chest. What the heck? This danged guy wasn't supposed to be speaking of love yet. What was she supposed to do with all this frank honesty?

He turned and hunkered down at the edge of the pond, dipping his fingers in the water. "I impress you now."

"Oh, I think you already—"

Lightning quick, he snatched the koi out of the pond and stood, holding it out to her.

The fish flapped and wriggled, spraying water droplets in all directions.

She yelped, holding her shawl in front of her face.

The other couples glanced over.

"You're right, Vasile." She laughed. "A woman will never go hungry with you around."

The corners of his eyes softened.

She loved it when that happened—the one small gesture said so much.

"Best moments for me are when I make laugh come from you." He crouched down and gently slid the koi back in the pond.

The *whop-whop* of a helicopter passing overhead pulled her eyes up.

Vasile stood, watching it too.

When the helicopter had flown by, he kept his face turned to the sky.

"You stare at the moon a lot," she said.

"This is a truth. I have missed it these many months. Vârcolac have powerful companionship with moon."

Tonight the moon hung in the sky like a gigantic pearl. "It's beautiful."

"Indeed. My father once tell me how a full moon provide strongest power to Vârcolac. True, but not altogether true. A misfortune that his words cause a confusion in me when I was of a young age."

"What kind of confusion?"

"It is silliness. The folly of a child."

"Oh." She stared out at the pond, disappointment sinking like a stone into her stomach. After the wonderful moments they'd just shared, she thought he might finally open up to her. "Okay. Never mind."

Several mosquitos plunked down on the surface of the water, creating star-shaped dimples where they landed.

"But…" Vasile's feet shifted. "But I tell you tale, if you be truly interested."

She held her breath. "I am," she said on a soft exhale.

He nodded once. "<I was perhaps five or six years of age when I came into full understanding of the attitude my people had for us Lazărs: hatred and ____.>"

"What does the second word mean?"

"Prejudice."

She absorbed that. "Why did the other Moon-Riders feel that way about your family?"

"<We are half-breeds, us Lazăr men—part-human through my father, Vârcolac through my mother.>"

"What's wrong with being part-human?" A lot of part-humans lived in the community, and no one seemed to mind.

"<That, I have never understood. I only wanted to be away from feeling bad.>" The eucalyptus branches shuffled behind him in a gentle breeze, and the moonlight shone in his hair with an ethereal glow.

Did you ever hide in the forest?

Betimes.

From what?

Endless quarreling. Insults. Ill-bred people.

"<So every night when I stood beneath the moon,>" he

went on, "<I said to it: if you remain full, I will have the utmost power and I will be strong. I can better my life. I can make sure no one will shun me. I can grow to be an honorable man.>"

"You wanted to be an honorable man at *five years old*?"

"<Very much.>" His shoulders moved in a slight lift. "<There is no other way for the Lazăr men to be—we must be the best.>"

She raised her brows. "A heavy burden."

"<Indeed.>" He gazed at the moon again. "<Every night I would stand beneath the moon and observe it, and night by night it shrank…every night until it was but a half-moon. The next month I tried again. I begged the moon to stay large—to give me power—but again it shrank. It became small, and so I did too. I became weak. I became a half-man.>"

Corky stared at him, brow furrowed, and just listened.

"<My father finally saw what I was about, and so he sat me on his knee and explained that the moon was not insulting me or disobeying me, but rather following its natural course. He assured me that Vârcolac obtain power from a crescent moon almost as much as a full moon—maybe marginally less—but most important, a man must control his own destiny. Nothing outside of him can do so. He told me I could not command the moon, but I could make my own character, and thus I should be beholden only to that. It was a buoying speech, but unfortunately it was spoken too late.>" His attention dropped to the pond.

Corky stared at his averted profile. His features were set in a stone. "Too late for what?"

"<Too late to give me hope.>" He looked up, and the moonlight caught a sudden shine in his eyes. "<I knew my life would never improve.>"

A thick knot shoved into her throat. "Don't say that."

"<Why not? It is true.> He turned his attention back to the pond.

Some of the white lilies were as big as cauliflowers.

"<As I grew to manhood, I did my best to be the greatest protector, the most skilled hunter, and the strongest in moral character—these were the edicts my father taught me. After much hard work, I finally became lead Protector of my people. I thought my life had improved—my status as a man of upstanding character finally accepted. But…>" A tic flashed in his jaw. "<Then my brother and I refused to whip the Son of Nichita in the forest, and my people shunned us. Easily. With hardly any thought at all. It forced me to realize that they had no regard for me whatsoever. I had earned nothing. They cared for me not at all.>" He glanced up. "<So, you see, what I tell you *is* true.>"

A tremble stole across her lips. She knew exactly how painful it was to feel like no one cared. "Who gives a damn what those jerks think, huh?" She took hold of his arm. "The only thing that matters is what *you* think." She squeezed his arm as if she could pass her hope into him. "Don't give up, Vasile. You live in Ţărână now, where you can make a happy future for yourself."

He turned toward her fully. He looked deeply into her eyes…and didn't say a thing.

CHAPTER THIRTY-NINE

THE CORNER DRAFTHOUSE WAS A topside drinking establishment near to Balboa Park, with an interior similar to the pub of Garwald, insofar as both places were constructed out of much wood. It must be a common opinion among proprietors that putting patrons among timber would entice them to feel at ease.

This was a way of thinking Vasile could not dispute.

There were wooden tables of various sizes scattered throughout the room, half full with patrons at present.

Their group of eight chose a round table large enough to accommodate their number.

Since Chelsea and Toni were both with young, neither partook of alcohol drinks. Chelsea ordered orange juice and Toni a tea of herbs. Marissa and Corky selected wine of a red color, both joking that it was really ten-thirty in the morning for them, and so when they returned to Ţărână they would be silly.

The four men ordered beer from the tap. A single beer would of a certainty not make any of them silly.

Vasile sat close to Corky and heard the wellbeing in her voice when she spoke to her women friends. She was content and enjoying herself.

Indeed, she had laughed with pleasure when he impressed her with his fish-capturing skills.

If someone had ever told him that giving a woman pleasure and joy was a more heady power than being able to wield an axe with skill or birth a calf stuck inside its mother, he would have told the malapert to go milk a pig.

But it was indeed the truth.

Corky had also spoken to him of the possibility of a happy future, and he took this as a good omen, daring to believe that her statement was a sign that he was making fine progress with her tonight.

With gusto, he downed a large swallow of his beer when the serving lady settled their eight with their ordered beverages.

Their group made merry, conversing and supping in a lively manner…until Gábor interrupted their convivial mood with an exclamation of "Whoa!"

He was aiming an astonished stare at the main door of the establishment. "Is ___ in town?" inquired Gábor.

Vasile did not know what *Comic-Con* was, but in the next instant a bitter scent sliced into his senses, and he *did* recognize that.

Cursing a foul word, he turned with an abrupt motion to observe what Gábor was seeing at the main door.

Two very tall women were now approaching their table of eight.

Vasile snarled.

Dev snapped his attention over. "Who are they?"

"Bugiana and Muşate," gritted Vasile.

"Witches?" snapped out Jacken.

"*Da.*"

The Warrior Witches stood well over six feet in height, had bodies sculpted of sheer muscle, and were marked with individualistic, interlocking geometric tattoos. These were the same warding tattoos Vasile wore, symbols that were the sole province of the Solomonori to give—wizards from back home.

For armaments, each witch wore a sword strapped across her back, leather arm bracers on her forearms, and a knife in a holder on one hip.

Other than the weaponry, they were scantily clad.

Muşate, the blonde, wore a garment that consisted of no more than many leather straps crisscrossed all over her body, her nipples and pubis barely concealed. Her light-colored hair was barbered off at the sides into prickles while the rest of it was held together by a metal clip decorated with an intricate, whorling design. This transformed her hair into a mighty plume that swept back from her brow and fell all the way down her back. Her lips were red as blood. Tall boots encased her legs from foot to knee.

Bugiana wore boots of a similar height, but her brown hair was caught in a tangled nest of a topknot on the crown of her head. Her woman parts were covered by naught but a leather belt hung with wide strips of polished leather. Hiding her breasts was a bra-like garment, the cups formed of molded metal.

"These chicks are a freak show." Gábor sneered. "How come no one in the bar is staring?"

"<They have invested us in a temporary ward,>" explained Vasile, never taking is eyes off the vile creatures. "<Everyone else in this establishment sees a false image at this table—us drinking our libations over and over in the same way. At some point someone may note the strange repetition.>"

"<Not to worry, vampire.>" Muşate curved her red lips in a carnal smile. "<We won't take too much of your time.>"

Bugiana hooked a thumb into her belt-skirt. "<Once you hand over our dear sister, we'll be on our way.>"

Jacken rose, moving in a lethal and menacing way that did not escape the notice of the witches.

Muşate hoisted her blond brows high in a speculative expression.

Bugiana moved her hand over to the hilt of her hip-knife.

Now Dev stood.

"<My, my.>" Bugiana raked both Jacken and Dev with a speculative stare. "<What fine male specimens. We should take you two with us and put you in our breeding colony.>"

Toni seamed her lips.

"Vasile," said Jacken, his tone honed to steel, "inform these women that their sister is safely protected in our town and that's where she'll stay."

Muşate tossed her head back and laughed with noise and vigor, making her long blond hair sway.

Bugiana tut-tutted at Jacken. "You're an idiot."

Jacken hardened his jaw—a process that seemed to defy the laws of nature, since his jaw was already like rock. "Now that I know you two can understand English, I'll make this really clear. *Fuck off.*"

Still smiling, Muşate regarded Jacken with a maniacal gleam in her eyes.

"Gábor," instructed Jacken, "take the women out back."

Gábor rose.

Marissa, Toni, and Chelsea got to their feet.

Vasile stood, helping Corky to rise.

Gábor ushered the four women toward the back of the pub, but they had traveled no more than a few feet when their bodies pressed into an invisible barrier. They were thrust backwards, stumbling.

Muşate laughed again, even louder.

Vasile cursed under his breath. So the ward was an entrapping one as well.

Dev glanced sharply at Vasile. "How do we escape?"

Vasile shook his head. *We cannot.*

Bugiana cocked her hip. "You want to be set free? Then hand over our sister."

Jacken fixed the witch with a black stare. "We can't go get her if you don't release us."

Muşate huffed. "We're not referring to our sister, Izme, the one you secret away in your lair." The blond witch made a toss-aside motion, leaving her hand to lie sideways on her wrist for a moment before she flipped it forward and pointed a finger at Corky. "*That* sister."

"Wh-what…?" Corky blanched white as the belly of a calf. "What is she talking about?"

Vasile was quick to reassure her. "<Do not concern yourself. These two nithings spew drivel.>" Vasile looked again at Muşate and Bugiana. "<This woman does not carry the scent of a Nature Spirit, nor does she bear the mark of Zalina. So you have erred.>" He paused and frowned, suddenly unsure. Truth be told, he had not seen Corky in a naked state to know this for certain. "<Do you carry the mark?>"

"What mark?" asked Corky.

It was Toni who answered. "It's a Z, but written in the Cyrillic alphabet, so it resembles a 3. Hadley has the mark on her left hip."

A long breath escaped Corky. "No." She spoke with all manner of relief. "I don't."

Bugiana rolled her eyes, as if she was being pressed upon to deal with the worst possible dullards. "Trandafira here doesn't bear the mark *yet* because she isn't born of Zalina and a Solomonori. Zalina begot her off a pure Fey male."

A strange stillness overtook Toni.

Jacken glanced at her.

Two more patrons entered the establishment. They strode right by Bugiana and Muşate without seeing them, heading to claim a corner table.

In a tone of extreme intensity, Toni asked the witches, "Which pure Fey male?"

"A man with blue eyes and"—Bugiana gestured in the direction of her topknot—"silver-blond hair."

Toni closed her eyes in a slow way, as if she was in pain.

"Chrissake," growled Jacken. "Is there *any* powerful woman your father won't fuck?"

CHAPTER FORTY

"ENOUGH OF THIS IDLE TALK," ordered Muşate, then she wiggled her fingers at Corky. "Time to come home to Mommy, Trandafira." Muşate smiled, her teeth very white compared to her red lips. "May I call you Fira, dear sister?"

Corky went paler still and flashed a desperate look around the circle of community people.

"I repeat," said Jacken. "*Fuck* off."

Muşate sighed. "Stupid."

Bugiana reached for the hilt sticking straight up her back and freed her blade with a metallic *whisk*. "I weep over having to slice up such a fine male specimen."

Jacken observed Bugiana with cold and dangerous eyes, his hand slipping to the back waistband of his pants where a knife resided, hidden beneath his lightweight coat.

The warding tattoos Muşate and Bugiana wore began to spin, the shielding properties activating—but only against bullets.

Dev and Gábor now also reached for their hidden blades.

"Stop!" yelled Vasile as the warding tattoos the witches bore flared an incandescent red. *Spell guard!* "Draw not your weapons!"

Too late.

Dev, Jacken, and Gábor already held knives in their hands…and stood frozen in place as if naught but statues.

Toni cried out, "Jacken!" and rushed forward, grabbing her mate by the shoulder and shaking him. He did not rouse to movement.

He could not. He was enspelled.

Muşate and Bugiana stalked toward Corky.

Corky let out a choked cry.

Heart hammering, Vasile quickly scoured the area for a non-weapon to use as a weapon. Sweeping an appetizer-sized plate off the table, he hurled it at Muşate with a wrist-snap motion, sending the thin edge of it spinning toward her throat.

Muşate lifted her arm to block it, and the plate shattered into small bits of porcelain against her forearm bracer.

Bugiana now whirled on him, her longsword braced before her, her eyes bright.

Taking a step back, Vasile picked up his chair and crashed the rear two legs to the floor. The chair exploded into chunks of timber. He chose two of the largest pieces and faced his enemy.

Chelsea, Marissa, and Corky pressed themselves back against the constraints of the ward as far as they could.

Toni remained beside her immobilized mate, watching the witches with a blackness Vasile had never seen in her eyes before.

Bugiana flexed her fingers around her sword hilt, and Vasile heard her knuckles crack.

He prepared himself, likewise tightening his grip around his wooden clubs.

The door to The Corner Drafthouse swung open, and Vasile froze—though not from a spell.

From seeing the witch who haunted his every nightmare walk in.

Savatina.

She was accoutered in a similar manner to Muşate and Bugiana but was differently clothed. She wore gladiator sandals, the strapping crisscrossed up to her knees, and short-pants made of boiled bullhide and studded with metal grommets—the shorts were preposterously short through the buttocks region to display the power of her mighty thighs. Her breasts were bare, and her prominent pink nipples were pierced through with about a dozen thin metal straight-pins to create a star-shaped design. Her hair was the color of pumpkin flesh—the closest to the shade Zalina had—and flowed straight as sheet metal down her back to her waist.

Savatina melted past the ward barrier and came to a halt next to her sisters. "<Why, look,>" purred the witch. "<If it isn't little Vasile Lazăr.>"

Vasile pared his lips back from his teeth but could not even utter her name—it was too abhorrent.

"<I wondered where you'd run off to, baby boy.>"

"<I do not run.>" His pulse ran up and down his throat. He glared at her evil countenance. "<I *fight*.>"

"<You don't fight,>" taunted Savatina. "<You lie down beside your father and let him die.>"

Vasile narrowed his eyes, his heart clenching down to the size of an acorn. "<Silence, you stinking sow!>" A murderous choler stained his vision red, blurring away the image of the witch he so despised.

He could only see his father, Lucien, lying on the ground, bleeding his life into the earth.

Vasile felt his fangs tear down from his gums. He bared the killing teeth, hissing between the lethal points as guilt and shame propelled him forward. Hatred powered the arm that swung a club at Savatina.

With unreal speed, the hated witch ducked the blow, spinning out of range. She cackled at him.

He surged forward again, striking out with another—

His hand juddered in an odd way around the club. For an unreal moment he stared at his fist in stupefaction. Then he felt it—a piercing pain in his lower back.

Behind him, Bugiana kicked him off the end of her sword.

Corky shrieked.

A warm, sticky wetness cascaded from his waist and flowed down to his butt. The floor flew out from under his feet. He crashed to the ground, the clubs tumbling out of his loose-fingered hands. A cloying agony encased his entire body. Air turned to rocks in his lungs.

Gasping for breath, he watched Bugiana flip her sword, now holding the hilt two-fisted above him, the blade pointed at his chest. "<Sleep well in hell, vampire.>"

The witch would now plunge the steel into his heart and kill him.

He tried to move, but his muscles were slack and beyond his command. His lids sagged.

A mighty bellow roared out.

Bugiana bolted her eyes up from her murderous task, and shock spread across her face like an ink spill.

Through squinted lids, Vasile searched for the source of the bellow. Pain glazed his vision as though he peered through melted beeswax, but he still saw what there was to see.

It was *Toni* who had cried out with such ferocity. Her hands were currently outstretched, both palms aimed at the witches. Her pupils were thinned to vertical slits—the eyes of a dragon!

She bellowed again, and a percussive quake boomed off her and slammed into the three evil women. With incredible force and violence, Savatina, Bugiana, and Muşate flew across the room, their bodies tearing through the ward.

The magic was broken.

Jacken, Dev, and Gábor staggered free, and a roomful of flabbergasted patrons gawked at the scene that suddenly materialized before them: a broken chair, a bloody man on the floor, a clump of women piled against the far wall, dressed as no city woman would ever dress, Muşate sprawled with her legs uppermost—quite a *by Jupiter!* sight.

Jacken slashed his arm out and metal streaked across the room. His knife thunked dead-center into Bugiana.

Howling, the witch clutched her chest and popped apart, disappearing into a mist.

Dev and Gábor followed this example and dispatched Savatina and Muşate in the same manner.

This incredible sight woke the roomful of patrons from their shock.

Everyone began to scream.

"___ ___!" Jacken thundered words that inspired the community people to move toward a rapid departure.

Vasile could no longer tell what those words were. He was unable to think or to move or even to groan in pain, the agony was so severe now. Sounds warbled in his ears. Cobwebs stretched across his vision. He was lying in the wetness of his own blood.

Dev suddenly appeared in a crouch beside him, his expression fierce and—

Wild with dread, Corky also appeared above him. "He's bleeding so much!" Falling onto her knees, she clasped his hand. "Please, Vasile—hang on!"

Vasile did his best to do as she begged, but it seemed the task was too great.

Blackness enclosed him.

CHAPTER FORTY-ONE

Six hours later
The community of Țărână
4:27 p.m.

YOU'RE A GIFT FROM THE angels.

That was the answer Mary Sills always gave Corky when she was a very young girl and asked who her parents were. Mary's goal had been to make Corky feel better about being an orphan, but the response only confused her.

Did she have parents or not?

Now she was a thirty-year-old woman, and she wasn't any less confused.

Were a bunch of witches really her *sisters*? Because that would mean her parents were…uh…uh…

Her mind always stopped here, blocked from accepting anything further.

"Tea?"

Corky looked up.

On the other side of the kitchen island in the Brun house, Toni was dipping a teabag into a mug of hot water. She was still wearing scrubs from being in surgery for the past three hours, working desperately alongside Dr. Jess to save Vasile— who was now in recovery but in critical condition. Both his liver and one kidney had been punctured.

Corky had spent those eternal hours in a fetal ball on her sofa, reliving the sight of Vasile being stabbed while also trying to wrap her flustered brain around the possibility that she was sister to such horrible women.

She couldn't be.

Could she be?

Baa, baa, black sheep, can you give me any counsel? No, ma'am, no, ma'am, your head's too full of tinsel.

Corky smiled at Toni with jumpy lips. "Got anything stronger?" It wasn't even five o'clock yet, but how did the saying go…?

It must be Happy Hour somewhere in the world.

Toni didn't seem surprised by the request. "I make a mean vodka martini."

"That'll work."

Toni opened a cupboard and pulled out a cocktail shaker and a jar of pimento-stuffed olives.

"So, um," Corky began. "What Bugiana and Muşate said about me being their…uh…"

"Why don't we wait until everyone else arrives before digging too deeply into that?" Toni sounded weary—from having spent the last three hours on her feet while pregnant or from…everything?

Probably the whole schlemiel.

"Everyone?" Corky asked.

"Hadley, Pandra, and Alex." Toni plunked a couple of ice cubes into the cocktail shaker.

"Why them?"

Toni glugged a healthy portion of vodka into the shaker. "You'll see."

Hadley arrived first, also wearing scrubs—she'd assisted the two doctors in the operating room. She reported *no change* in Vasile.

She caught Corky's eye. *What's up?*

Corky answered with a subtle shrug.

A moment later Pandra strode into the kitchen, entering to the distinctive sound of a cocktail shaker *rattling*.

From beneath her brows, Pandra watched Toni pour the clear contents of the shaker into a martini glass. "It's a mite early for cocktails, isn't it?"

Toni plunked a toothpick speared through two olives into the drink. "You're going to wish you could have one of these in a few seconds."

Pandra's face went still in a way that suggested a long habit of keeping her emotions hidden.

Hadley, on the other hand, knitted her brow.

"And?" Pandra prompted.

"We're waiting for Alex." Toni handed the martini to Corky.

She took a sip. It *was* good.

Hadley let out a huff of air. "Can you please just tell us what's going on now? You've got me really anxious here."

Toni checked her watch. "All right. Alex is running late, so I'll go ahead." She picked up her tea mug. "We"—she made a roundabout gesture with her cup—"are sisters. Well, half-sisters."

Silence.

After a long beat, Hadley barked, "What?"

Pandra gave Toni a droll look. "I agree with that sentiment. What the corking shit are you talking about?"

"Tonight, at a topside bar, three of Zalina's daughters tried to—"

"*Zalina!*" Hadley gasped.

"Yes. Three witches tried to steal Corky, claiming that she's their sister."

Hadley's mouth fell open.

Toni lifted the teabag out of her mug and set it, dripping, onto a small plate.

"I-is it true?" Hadley stuttered, casting a quick glance at Corky. "How can we be sure?"

"Well," Toni said. "I doubt the witches would've gone to the trouble of trying to take Corky if it wasn't."

Corky's second intake of martini was a large gulp. *Oh, dear God.*

"So that means…" Hadley's gaze flew back to Corky. "You and I are sisters, really and truly *sisters*!"

Corky stared back. No words. Just…none.

"Not only that," Toni went on, "but Corky is *our* half-sister." She pointed from herself to Pandra.

Pandra's eyebrows soared.

Corky clattered her martini glass onto the kitchen island. Her heart was beating so fast she was probably in danger of rupturing her aorta.

Hadley frowned. "How's that possible?"

Toni blew on her tea. "While your father is a Solomonori, Corky's father is Raymond."

Pandra made a harsh noise in her throat. "You're having a laugh?"

"Nope."

Corky clapped a hand over her mouth, her eye sockets feeling the strain from her ongoing rabbity expression of shock. She'd just gone from having no family at all to having three sisters!

Dropping her hand, she whirled on Toni. "I *knew* there was something about you. When I first arrived in the community and was so freaked out about vampires, something about you calmed me." Now she rounded on Pandra. "And you. The first time I saw you in Garwald's, I was drawn to you for no explicable reason."

Pandra stared at Corky for a beat, then her mouth lifted up at one corner.

"And *you*"—Corky faced Hadley again—"I've loved you from the instant I met you!"

"I loved you instantly too!" Hadley's eyes filled with tears. "Ever since we met I've wished we were sisters, and now it turns out we really are!" Hadley launched herself at Corky and hugged her.

Corky hugged Hadley back and started to cry.

Hadley cried too.

"Tea?"

Corky heard Pandra snort. "Bleeding hell. I'm trapped in Days of Our Fucking Lives."

"It feels a bit like a soap opera, yes." Toni sighed. "But also, when you think about it, the Otherworldly population is small, so it makes sense that we would run into more of each other at some point."

Stepping back from Hadley, Corky swiped at her tears. "I'm sorry, I don't mean to be a sap. It's just that I've gone from having no family at all to having three sisters."

"And a brother," Toni reminded her.

"What?"

"Alex."

"Oh, yes, I forgot about Alex!"

"What did you forget about me?" Alex asked, trudging into the kitchen.

Toni frowned at the way he dragged himself in the room. "What's wrong? You look weird."

"Yeah, I'm bummed," Alex admitted. "I thought I'd tracked down the Costaches' sister, but then I lost her again—but don't tell Arc and Thomal. They're already freaked out about her enough." Because the woman was on the verge of dying.

From what Corky understood, the Costaches' sister didn't know she was half-Vârcolac. So she was in desperate need of blood but clueless about why she would be feeling so bad.

"Sorry," Toni said.

"Yeah." Alex sighed. "Then I got caught up in a strange vision. It's why I'm late."

"Strange how?"

"I'm not sure how to describe it." Alex massaged his forehead. "It felt like a prophecy."

"Uh-oh. A good prophecy or a bad one?"

"*Really* bad. But I'm not sure why, yet—the vision was unclear and confusing. Except I did sense that someone born of your line will be able to prevent it."

"One of *my* children?"

"Seemed like it, yeah."

"How?"

"I don't know. Look, sorry. I shouldn't have brought it up until I'd seen more. If I have the vision again, I'll let know. Anyway, why did you want me to come over?"

Toni set a fresh teabag into another mug of hot water, placed it in front of her brother, then gave Alex the genealogical lowdown.

When Toni was done explaining, Alex smiled at Corky. "Wow, that's cool. Welcome to the family."

Corky startled, then blushed. *Family!*

"I wonder when Raymond got together with Zalina?" Alex sipped his tea, looking at Corky. "How old are you?"

"Thirty."

Alex glanced at Toni. "A year after he left our mom."

"Who is Raymond, anyway?" Corky asked. "I know that Zalina is a queen witch, but what is Raymond?"

"A sod," Pandra provided in a dry tone.

Corky drooped. She'd been so hoping at least one of her parents was nice. "Is he really? Am I going to have to hide from him too?"

"I don't think so," Toni said. "Not yet, anyway. Raymond probably doesn't even know you exist." Toni set her used teabag back into her mug and poured more hot water over it. "And he also hasn't bothered the community in more than four years now, so he might've moved on from us."

"I wouldn't count on it," Pandra warned. "He's just been in Ireland all this time."

Toni looked over at Pandra with a jerk of her head. "How do you know that?"

"I used to keep in touch with Murk—my older brother through my mother, Yavell," Pandra added for Corky's benefit. "Four years ago, Murk told me in an email that

Raymond was taking the brood to Ireland to hunt down Dragon lads and lasses there—breeders with ancestry similar to your mum's."

Before Toni could comment, Jacken stalked into the kitchen.

Stopping at the outer edge of their group, he set his hands on his belt and scowled at Toni. "How long have you been able to hurl people across a room with just your mind?"

Toni made a face at him in answer and drank her tea.

Jacken muttered an expletive, then crossed to the refrigerator, opened it, and grabbed a can of beer. He popped the tab.

Corky half expected him to pour out the beer and eat the can, but he took a large swallow. "Nice to know you can kick my ass."

"I can't," Toni replied quickly. "I have to access emotions that are…" She cut off the sentence. "Just trust me, I can't."

Jacken held her gaze, then apparently decided to let the argument go. "Do you mind if I watch the game in the living room? I'll keep the volume down."

"Of course not. Go ahead." Toni opened the cupboard behind her and pulled out a bag of Rold Gold® Braided Honey Wheat Pretzels. She held it out to Jacken while tossing a smile at the women. "His favorite."

Jacken's upper lip curled. "Don't tell them that." He walked up to Toni, kissed her on the cheek—although he also rolled his eyes at her—then took the bag.

Toni plucked his sleeve. "Hey, I was so busy caring for Vasile on the ride back to Ţărână, I never got the chance to ask if you're experiencing any aftereffects."

"From what?"

"From the immobility spell you were under."

He waved that off and headed for the living room, growling back at her, "Get off your damned feet."

Corky watched Jacken leave the kitchen. "He's got a sweet side to him, doesn't he?"

Toni chuckled. "Don't let *him* know that."

Toni's cell phone beeped.

She checked the message, and her face fell. "Dammit. I have to go back to the hospital. Vasile's taken a turn for the worse."

The muted sounds of cheers floated into the kitchen, and a sports announcer calling a play-by-play.

CHAPTER FORTY-TWO

The next day
3:01 p.m.

CORKY'S STOMACH SLOSHED WHEN SHE presented herself to Donree, Toni's assistant.

Corky drank way too much yesterday—between celebrating her sisterhood with Hadley and tranquilizing her jangled nerves over Vasile's downturn—and she'd ended up oversleeping.

So she spent the morning frazzled and rushing around, not getting much done—was it already three o'clock in the afternoon?—except for checking on Vasile's status every hour.

He was still in intensive care.

And not improving.

Then ten minutes ago Corky received a message to meet Toni at her office, and whatever the reason for the summons, it was for something bad.

The message was *urgent*.

But dealing with *bad* didn't sit within her current range of capabilities…which mostly consisted of curling up on a sofa and watching *Terms of Endearment* and *The Notebook*, and then indulging in a back-to-back gala of blubbering. She also might be able to assume the position before a toilet and heave up all her guts. After which she would down a combo of two parts acetaminophen, one part ibuprofen and lie in the dark with a wet cloth on her brow…maybe a pillow over her head.

She might've also managed a nonsensical conversation with Tweets if he'd been around, but he wasn't.

Donree showed Corky right into Toni's office. Corky's armpits were already soaked.

Toni was seated at her desk, leafing through a medical chart.

Across the room, standing before a frosted glass door, was a dark-haired man. He had his back to the main door, but when Corky entered he turned around.

His expression was weighted with sorrow, and when Toni introduced him as Nicolae Lazăr, Corky had a heart attack.

Vasile's *brother* was here, looking grief-stricken.

"Oh, God." Corky collapsed onto the couch. "Vasile's died."

"No, no," Toni hastened to assure her. "But—" She paused to exhale. "He's in very bad shape."

"Sorry to scare you," Nicolae said, speaking English with *way* less of an accent than his brother. He strode toward her, holding out his hand. "It's nice to finally meet you, even though it's at a sad time."

Shaking his hand, Corky gave Nicolae a good once-over now that her heart attack had downgraded to angina.

He was shorter than Vasile, although still tall by any standard, with leaner muscles, trim hips, and long, tapered legs. He had the same gray-on-gray eyes as Vasile, and the same black hair, although Nicolae's was cut short all over, except at the front, where it stuck up in a clean line—helped along by some hair product, no doubt. The style added a boyish appeal to his otherwise chiseled face.

He was, actually, drop-dead gorgeous.

No wonder Hadley was noodle over the guy.

Toni stood, moved out from behind her desk, then walked into the sitting area, taking a seat in one of the chairs across from Corky.

Nicolae sat in the other chair.

Corky twisted her fingers into the front of her shirt. The bad news was about to come now. People always sat when it was time to either crush or be crushed.

Toni folded her hands in her lap. "I'm going to cut straight to the point, Corky—Vasile's condition is dire."

A tremor of cold trickled down her spine.

"His injuries were grave enough by themselves," Toni went on. "But he has hemophilia, and that has complicated our ability to treat him effectively."

Corky sat for a moment. "You can't give him medication to help?"

"We have." Toni nodded. "We've treated his wound with a fibrin sealant and have him on a regime of clotting factors, but he's Vârcolac. To truly heal from injuries this severe he needs blood—*strong* blood. He's been feeding on his donor, but—"

"He woke up?" Why didn't anyone tell her? Corky had left strict instructions to be notified if that happened.

"No, Vasile's still unconscious. A Vârcolac can feed through reflex. So he's been feeding, but donor blood just isn't cutting it. This leads me to believe…" Toni's focus dipped to her folded hands for a long second. "It is my belief, as well as Dr. Jess's, that the only way Vasile will recover is if he takes in the kind of strong blood that only comes from a mate." Toni cleared her throat. "This is where you come in."

"Me? I don't…" Wait, *did* she understand? Was Toni suggesting she…?

Toni drew in a deep breath. "It looks like you've guessed where I'm heading. Yes, I called you here to ask if you'd be willing to bond with Vasile."

Corky's mouth went dry. "Like a…uh, a regular bond? The one that lasts forever?"

"Yes," Toni confirmed softly. "There isn't any other type."

"But I-I…" She couldn't bond with Vasile. She barely knew him. "There has to be another way."

Toni made a helpless gesture. "Dr. Jess and I have exhausted every medical option available to us. And there's no one else in the community we can turn to. You're the only woman Vasile's ever dated."

"*Dated*, yes, but just a handful of times."

"I know," Toni said. "I realize this is a huge ask. You should one-hundred-percent feel like you can say no."

Except that if I do, it sounds like Vasile will go down the crapper.

"But you will not be unhappy with my brother." Nicolae shoved forward in his seat. "Vasile is a good man. At his heart. At his core. I know he can seem stern, and he is old-fashioned in many ways, but he is still learning how to be with a woman. He will do right by you, Corky. It is impossible for Vasile to be other than honorable."

Which meant that she'd be a total shit if she didn't get with him. Corky kneaded her thighs, anxiety knotting her stomach. "So that's why you're here—to lay on the guilt extra thick?"

"No," Toni contradicted quickly. "Nicolae wanted to be here to answer any questions you might have about his brother."

Questions. Right. "Except I wouldn't have any questions if I *knew* him, would I?"

Nicolae went on in a rushed way, "Even if you don't love him right now, you will grow to love him. I swear this to you."

Corky tightened her hands into fists on her thighs, all the oxygen leaving her lungs. She didn't have room to breathe in here…no one was giving her time to think… This was all happening so fast.

"You care a lot for him." Nicolae kept at her. "I saw how upset you were when you thought Vasile had died."

Corky's throat lurched. "I'm not an unfeeling monster, for God's sake."

"Of course you're not," Toni assured her.

"But I will be if I let such a sterling example of a man die."

Toni shook her head. "Your life isn't any less valuable than Vasile's. No one would ever want you to live the rest of it in misery."

My life for his… That's what this really comes down to.

Corky pressed both hands over her face. No way could she make a decision like this. "How long do I have to think about it?"

"An hour. At most."

Corky brought her face out of hiding with a jerk. "An *hour*?" To make the biggest decision of her life?

"I'm sorry. But I didn't want to come to you until I knew it was absolutely necessary."

Absolutely necessary…

So Vasile would absolutely, *definitely* die if Corky didn't do this.

Corky's temples pounded. "You have no idea what you're asking of me. I can't… I'm trying not to be a caretaker anymore, and you come to me with *this*—bond with Vasile forever or he'll die? It's the worst possible thing you could do to someone like me." She shot to her feet. "Look, I can't make a decision like this. It's too much." The volume of her voice was rising. "I-I…"

I'm a card-carrying member of that club… If a man is big and strong but totally unavailable emotionally, I snap him right up…

Corky shook her head wildly. "I've *never* gotten a relationship right, okay? My whole life, I've…"

I've made a lot of mistakes with the men I've chosen over the years, and right now Vasile is fitting right into that mold… So can you see why I might be scared? We're talking about a forever-commitment here, and I don't want to end up with my own version of an eternal disaster…

She burst into tears.

Toni stood. "Corky…"

Corky bent over, clutching her middle, and wept harder.

Toni set a palm on her back. "Corky, honey…it's okay."

You're a smart, beautiful lawyer, and he's a fucking knuckle-dragger. Doesn't that light off any warning bells in your head…?

Corky hugged herself as tightly as she could and sobbed until she choked. She couldn't breathe. The walls whirled. She staggered.

"Corky, please—sit back down." Toni urged her onto the couch. "Put your head between your knees."

She stayed folded in half and continued to weep.

"Corky, listen to me."

"N-no," she sputtered.

He's just so taciturn. I have no idea who he really is…

Toni crouched at her side. A tissue appeared in front of her.

"Wh-what am I going to do?" Corky lurched upright and snatched the tissue from Toni. "I don't know what I'm going to do."

Toni glanced once at Nicolae, then rested a hand on her knee. "Let's go someplace else and discuss it, all right? Away from this office. We'll talk as sisters."

Sisters. Corky snuffled into the tissue. That was rapidly becoming one of her favorite words.

"How does a hot fudge sundae sound?" Toni asked.

"We don't have time."

"We can spare ten or fifteen minutes for something this important." Toni patted Corky's knee. "Come on. Let's go."

CHAPTER FORTY-THREE

THE COMMUNITY DINER WAS ALL but empty at this time of day. Only two men in miner's coveralls sat at the counter, drinking coffee. The cook was taking advantage of the lull between the lunch rush and the dinner crowd to give his grill a good scrub-down, but he happily paused his grunt work to whip up a couple of single-scoop hot fudge sundaes.

Corky ordered basic vanilla ice cream, Toni, mint chocolate chip.

They chose a booth far from the counter and sat across from each other.

Sammy Davis, Jr. was singing the blues in the background.

Toni took a bite of her sundae and made a *yum* noise. "I swore I'd watch my weight with this baby, but sometimes a little indulgence is necessary."

Corky tugged a napkin out of the table dispenser. Her nose was still running from her most recent blubber-gala.

Toni took another bite. More *yum*. "So tell me about being a caretaker."

Corky wiped her nose. Jeez, nothing like jumping straight into someone's guts with both feet…but then they didn't have a lot of time, did they?

"I never knew I was one until Reese pointed it out to me—and pretty much ripped my identity to shreds." She crumpled the napkin and tucked it in her purse. "I went from being a kind woman to a doormat, someone with a loving heart to a gullible chump."

Toni scooped up another bite. "Who says Reese is right?"

"Well, it fits. I look back at my relationships, and what I see is a long history of letting men walk all over me. It's my own fault for choosing nothing but emotionally damaged men who required me to constantly pick up the pieces of their wrecked egos. To give and to give and to give—which I did—and never get back. I never *asked* them to give back."

Toni paused mid-bite. "Are you saying that you think Vasile is emotionally damaged?"

"He's… No," Corky conceded. "To be fair, I guess he's not. *Emotionally unavailable* would be the better way of putting it. He never opens up to me—and I can't be with a man who's like *that* either."

Toni sighed. "It's difficult with fighting men. I had a hard time with Jacken at first, too."

Corky sniffed. "What did you do?"

"Nothing, actually. Love just happened. Well, I guess not *just*. Little things started adding up to the big things that really mattered." Toni plucked the maraschino cherry off her mound of whipped cream. "Like, the first time Jacken smiled at me at Garwald's—and it wasn't even a nice smile—and when he brought me a thermos of juice after I'd been attacked by one of the Underground Om Rău." Toni ate her cherry. "You've probably experienced small but special moments with Vasile over these three weeks, haven't you? I bet you can come up with some."

"Maybe." Corky turned aside and looked across the diner.

The two men in coveralls were paying their bill.

"Try not to get too bogged down by your past when you think about Vasile, okay? Those other men you dated don't count."

Corky looked at Toni again. "What do you mean? How can they not count?"

"Because those other guys were *topside* men, spring-loaded to reject you. And to complicate matters further, you weren't really who you were meant to be while you were up there." Toni stirred her sundae. "Back in my single days topside, I used to pick men who thought I was perfect. I'm not, of course—no one is—so their inevitable disappointment in me reaffirmed my disappointment in myself, which of course did wonders for my self-esteem."

Corky blinked. *Really?* That seemed... "That doesn't seem possible, Toni. You're so confident."

She smiled. She was even prettier when she smiled. "I am *now*. Because I've found my footing. I wasn't where I belonged topside, so nothing of who I was then applied. It's the same for you."

"I just...I don't see how I can separate my past from who I am. It *is* who I am."

"Is it? Then tell me who you are."

Corky thought about that for a second, then offered up a sickly smile. "Okay, you've stumped me."

Toni kept stirring—her small mound of whipped cream was a smushed mess. "A Dragon, a sister, a Nature Spirit...you didn't know you were any of those things before. But you *are* those things—here in this community. So maybe who you really are *here* is a kind and loving woman who just needs a man who won't abuse those qualities. A strong man. Like Vasile."

"Do you really think he is?"

"I do. And let's not forget the part about Vasile struggling with a new culture and an unfamiliar language. Those challenges could make him seem more emotionally unavailable than he really is."

Corky gazed down at her sundae. The scoop of ice cream was sitting in a puddle of its own vanilla.

I begged the moon to stay large—to give me power—but again it shrank. It became small, and so I did too. I became weak. I became a half-man.

Corky looked up, tears prickling her eyes. "Thinking back

now, I realize that he did open up to me once. Last night, after the play." *Vasile told me his half-moon story and gave me a glimpse of his pain.*

Toni's head tilted slightly. "And can't once be enough?"

"For a lifetime?"

"To assure you that he's capable of depth? To promise you that there's more where that came from?"

Corky *so* much wanted that to be true.

Toni set down her spoon. "Beneath Vasile's lost confusion, he's a giving, kindhearted man, and I believe that the last thing he would ever want would be for you to caretake him." She gestured. "The point of me saying all this is that I want you to be sure you're making your decision based on who Vasile is as a man, not on saving his life."

Who Vasile is as a man...

Corky sat back and thought about him, remembering how he'd rushed to check on her after Zalina's daughters dropped magic orbs on the community, even though he'd just met her. And how he tried to impress her with his knowledge of penis slang. She smiled a little—*what a trip*. And how he caught a fish for her at Balboa Park with his bare hands.

Vasile is a good man. At his heart. At his core...

Corky inhaled a shaky sigh.

My father told me I could not command the moon, but I could make my own character, and thus I should be beholden only to that. It was a buoying speech, but unfortunately it was spoken too late.

Too late for what?

Too late to give me hope. I knew my life would never improve...

A single tear rolled down Corky's cheek. "Hope," she whispered.

"Pardon?"

"I'm the woman who never gives up hope. That's who I've always been." Corky fumbled in her purse, pulling out the crumpled napkin. "And do you know what? There *have* been some small, special moments between us."

Toni's lips curved into a gentle smile. "So maybe it's the little things that really matter between you and Vasile too."

Corky dabbed at her eyes. "Okay, I'll do it. I'll bond with Vasile."

CHAPTER FORTY-FOUR

"DEAR GOD," CORKY GASPED. "IS that really Vasile?"

Where did all of him *go*? The body lying on the hospital bed was practically emaciated, the skin shrunken around the bones of the face, ribs showing against the hospital gown on each labored breath.

How had Vasile wasted to such a degree in so short a time? "He looks starved."

"He is starving," Toni said sadly. "For blood."

"He's not…he can't feel pain, can he?"

"He might when he comes closer to consciousness, but we have him on pain meds." Toni moved to a cabinet and pulled out something long and thin wrapped in plastic. "Here." She held it out to Corky. "This is an ovulation stick. First I'll need you to pop into the bathroom and see if you're fertile."

Corky studied Vasile again. Other than the shallow movement of his lungs, he wasn't moving at all. "Is that really important right now?"

"It's crucial, actually. We can't proceed if you're ovulating. Vasile couldn't handle going into a glaze-out and having intercourse with you for hours on end."

"Oh." She hadn't thought of that.

Corky took the ovulation stick and went into the bathroom. When she was done, she emerged to see Jacken standing in the middle of the room.

His jaw was set in a rigid line, as if his teeth were clenched behind his closed lips, giving Corky the sense that he was less than thrilled to be here.

Why *was* he here?

"Are you ovulating?" Toni asked her.

"Uh, no."

"Good. Let's get started." Toni plucked a white lab coat off a wall hook and shrugged it on. *Doctor Toni Parthen* was embroidered across the left breast pocket in royal blue. "Before we begin, I need to remind you that the first bite hurts. You read about that in the manual, remember?"

"Yes. I remember."

"In normal circumstances, Vasile would be able embrace you to prevent you from pulling away from the pain—if the feeding stops before his fiinţă can come out of his fangs that would be a very bad thing between you two. But Vasile's unconscious, so I've asked Jacken here to assist."

Corky cut another look at him. "Assist how?"

"Jacken will be in charge of holding you in place."

"Um…" *I need to be held in place?* "How painful are we talking, exactly?"

"It's pretty bad," Toni admitted. "But once Vasile's fangs release his fiinţă, you'll feel great. Better than great."

Corky didn't comment. She was still focused on the *pretty bad.*

"The tricky part is the time between the pain and the pleasure."

She glanced at Jacken again. He was, um…no offense, but the guy was really scary. "I won't pull away," she promised.

Toni smiled in a way that said she'd heard this many times before and knew it to be total bull hockey. "I know you won't intend to, but your survival instincts will kick in and you won't be able to stop yourself." Toni looped a stethoscope around her neck. "We can't proceed unless you give Jacken your express permission to physically hold you in place. And you must be fully aware that no matter what you do— struggle, scream, cry, or beg—he won't let you go."

Jacken offered up more I'm-less-than-thrilled-to-be-here,

clearly wanting to hold Corky in place about as much as she wanted him to do that.

A *beep* rang out, and Toni glanced sharply at the monitor tracking Vasile's vitals.

Corky looked over too. Had Vasile's face grown more skeletal in the past few minutes? "Okay, yes, I give my permission."

"All right." Toni moved to stand next to Vasile's bed. "Come over here and give me your finger."

Corky joined Toni at Vasile's bedside and held out her hand. Toni pricked Corky's forefinger with a small needle.

Blood appeared at the tip in a neat, red pebble, and Toni smudged this across Vasile's upper lip, right under his nose.

Vasile inhaled a quick, harsh breath, then his fangs stretched down from his gums.

Corky stared at the pointy tips, and her stomach cramped. She'd seen Vasile's fangs elongated several times, but his gigantic vampire canines had never looked more capable of doling out pain than they did now.

It's pretty bad.

"Are you ready?" Toni asked.

The question held Corky up for a long moment. Once Vasile bit her, there'd be no going back. "Am I ready to change my life forever?" Corky gave Toni a droll look. How could anyone ever be truly ready for that?

Toni's smile was sympathetic.

"I suppose I am," Corky said. "As much as I can be."

"We can't ask for more than that." Toni offered another smile, then nodded at Jacken.

He came up behind Corky. She inhaled a deep breath as he grabbed her left shoulder with his left hand and palmed the back of her skull with his right. He bent her over Vasile, using his hand on her head to angle her throat against Vasile's mouth.

Vasile rumbled out a low, warlike growl, and Corky nearly went racing out of her underwear—as half-dead as he was, she hadn't expected such a hellacious sound to come out of him.

Shivers shrieked down her spine and a case of nerves overtook—

Chomp!

She screamed—Vasile's strike was hard, fast, and deep. The pain locked her muscles in place.

Holy...holy...

Holy shit that hurts!

The pain got worse...the lancing of her skin...the invasion of her vein...a profound, suctioning force vacuuming up all her blood...

She screamed again against the sheer horror of what was happening to her.

Tangling her fingers in Vasile's hospital gown, she tried to shove off him, but the hand gripping the back of her skull tightened.

Her head swam. Her flesh went clammy. Nausea rose. "Something's wrong," she said in a squeaky voice. "Let go of me!"

Jacken didn't let go.

Gulping noises filled Corky's ears.

Her life was slipping away!

She flailed her legs behind her to try and kick Jacken, but he easily avoided her blows. *Jerk!*

"Stop!" she shouted. "You don't understand!" A Moon-Rider had never bonded to anyone in the community before. Jacken and Toni wouldn't realize just how horrendous it was.

Corky's eyes watered and leaked. "Please," she wept. "*Please.*" Her neck was on fire, burning...burning...

Burning down through her chest and into her breasts.

Her nipples sprang taut.

She blurted out an "Ah!" in surprise. *Oh, my God. Ohmigod.*

"Something…" She panted… *Something else is happening.* Her tongue went soft in her mouth.

She tried again, drunkenly, "Sunthung is…"

Supercharged heat flowed downward, flooding her torso, her pelvis, her privates, her legs—everything came alive with impossible pleasure.

She tingled. Her whole body hummed. Her mouth sagged open. *Oooooooo.*

Ecstasy clutched her belly, quaked through her butt, and then rippled along her privates. She throbbed. She pulsed. The pulses grew into strong contractions, and she spasmed through the most amazing climax of her life.

She moaned out loud now, "Ooooooooo."

Vasile's fangs slid out of her throat.

Her orgasm throbbed a couple of more times before releasing her. She wilted into a spent heap on top of Vasile, panting.

Jacken let go.

At length, Toni asked, "Are you okay?"

Corky didn't answer. She didn't move to rise. Her mushy legs wouldn't hold her.

Someone's cell phone *burrrred.*

Corky finally managed to heft herself off Vasile. Stumbling around, she slapped a palm over the bite spot on her neck. "Dear God. I just had the most amazing—" She cut herself off.

Toni's smile was a bit awkward.

Jacken was standing in the middle of the room again, this time with his hands on his hips and his eyes pinned on the ceiling.

"Oh." Corky blushed. "I guess you guys already know what I just had."

Toni tucked her hands in the pockets of her lab coat. "Happens all the time."

Yeah, but probably in the privacy of a bedroom.

"Can I go now?" Jacken snapped out.

"Yes," Toni said. "Thank you."

Jacken spun around and stalked out.

Toni's eyes danced. "Sometimes it's not easy being my husband. All righty—you know what to do next, so I'll leave you to it." She stepped backwards toward the door. "I'll be at the nurse's station if—"

"I'm sorry, what do I do next?"

Toni stopped. "You have to make love to Vasile."

Corky shifted her palm to her brow and swiped off the perspiration. "Oh, yes." Sex was part two of forming a bond. "Do you want me to sit here and wait for him to wake up or should I come back?"

Toni's features froze. "Um…I thought you understood. You have to make love to him now."

Corky stared at Toni. "What? You mean while he's *unconscious*?"

"Vasile might not wake for days. If you don't have sex with him right away, he'll go into a half-bond."

"What's a half-bond?" The manual had probably explained it, but Corky couldn't remember right now, and, dammit, a person needed to practically memorize the whole stupid book to survive in this place. "Never mind. It doesn't matter. I can't have sex with an unconscious man."

"Corky, you—"

"I'm a lawyer, Toni. I need consent."

"I appreciate your dilemma, but you're citing a *topside* issue. Here in our world, if you don't complete this bond the consequences could be grave. I've seen Vârcolac in their prime taken out by a half-bond. In his current state Vasile might be killed."

"For crying out loud!" Corky exploded. "Does everything have to be life or death with you people?"

Toni's chest moved deeply. "Why don't you think of it this way—if Vasile could give his consent, don't you think he would?"

"You mean do I think he'd be A-okay with me mounting him up and riding him to the finish line all while he's completely unaware of what I'm doing?"

A tense moment dragged by.

"How about," Toni suggested, "we safely assume that Vasile would be grateful to you for saving his life?"

So they were back to that.

Corky crushed her eyes shut. "This really takes the cake," she muttered. "You know that?"

"It's not optimal."

"Fine," Corky said with the enthusiasm of someone heading off to an IRS audit. "What do I have to do? I mean, I know what I have to do. Just…is there anything special?"

"No. Post-feeding, Vasile will have an erection, and you…you're prepared, so…" Toni waved at Vasile's lap.

Right. Mount up and giddy up.

"There's a call button on the right side of Vasile's bed." Toni pointed to it. "Feel free to buzz me for any reason. I'll be at the nurse's station." Toni gave her a wan smile and left.

The door shut behind her with a soft *whoosh*.

CHAPTER FORTY-FIVE

Corky returned to Vasile's bedside and set her hands on the raised metal rail.

How long would she have to classify herself as a total perv for screwing a half-corpse?

How long would it take for the gossip to spread throughout the tiny town of Ţărână about her ravishing an unconscious Vasile?

She squeezed the bar, then blew out her cheeks. Questions like those weren't helpful.

Think only good thoughts…

Right. C'mon. Find something positive here.

She leaned forward and peered closely at Vasile's face. Well, hey, more color was in his cheeks since he'd fed on her. So he was already improving.

Okay, see? You're doing good here.

She lowered the bed rail. "I know this is weird, Vasile, but we've just gotta press ahead. And don't worry. It won't hurt a bit."

Wait…would it? She didn't know anything about vampire virginity. What if there was something wonky about a Vârcolac's first time. Wouldn't the manual have mentioned it? Probably. But then her memory was kind of shot right now.

Stress.

Stress will do that to you.

She glanced at the bedside call button. Should she check with Toni about it?

You're stalling.

Gee, why would I be doing that?

Exhaling broadly, she climbed onto the bed, careful not to jostle him, and studied his gaunt, inanimate face. He really did look like a half-corpse. *Crap.* She plopped down on the edge of the mattress.

Hooking her shoes on the foot rail, she set her elbows on her knees and propped her chin in her hands.

With the court's permission, I move for a sidebar.

What's your issue, counselor?

Your Honor, I would like very much to be served a Manhattan in the middle of these proceedings…

"I need to find a way to make this memorable." She choked out a laugh. "I mean *nice* memorable. Not sex offender memorable." She scrunched her toes in her shoes. "What should I do?"

The hospital walls didn't answer.

Skip, skip, skip to my Lou, and get right outta here, my darlin'…

Maybe she should ask for candles, soft music, and—

Vasile's whole body jerked violently, jarring the bed so hard Corky almost tumbled off.

She swung toward him.

Sweat was pouring off his brow, and his fingers were clawing at the bedsheets.

If you don't complete this bond, the consequences could be grave…

"Shit! Okay, okay…it's okay." She leaned toward him and cupped his cheeks. "I'm here."

Beneath her palms, she could feel muscles twitching all over his face.

"We're going to do this—that's it. Just *do it*." She slid off the bed and undid her jeans, dropping them to the floor, then she pushed her underwear and shoes off. "No more talk. No more stalling." She peeled the sheet down Vasile's body, then grabbed his hospital gown and pushed it up to his waist to expose—

She froze—well, first she widened her eyes, then she froze.

It hit her, in this bizarre moment, that the whole time she'd been thinking about everything she needed to think about in order to decide whether or not to bond with Vasile, she forgot to consider what it would be like to commit forever to a man she'd never seen naked before—much less had sex with.

What if it'd turned out his penis was a strange shade of purple or shaped like a boomerang or smelled like spoiled cheese or was microscopic.

She swallowed slowly. *No worries on any of those points, but especially the last.*

Stretching straight up Vasile's lower belly, reaching from his groin to just above his navel, was one hell of an enormous erection.

Corky rubbed her cheek. She'd never faced down one quite so big. How was she to—

Vasile's body jolted again, and short, pained grunts began to spew from his lips.

Yikes! No time to gawk. Climbing on the bed again, she swung a leg over his hips to straddle him.

Her nearness quieted Vasile's grunts, but his breathing remained uneven.

She reached down and wrapped her hand around his erection.

His nostrils pinched and released.

She set the rounded head of him at her entrance and—shock.

She wasn't just wet, but *super* wet.

You're prepared, so…

No freaking kidding. "All right. We good to go, Vasile?"

His lashes flickered against his cheeks.

She slowly began to work her way down his length, and—*oof.* The first few inches were a bit of a chore. She had to flex her hip muscles and strain in a downward direction. But her super-wetness from her earlier feeding-climax soon made it so his organ was entering her on a smooth glide.

Some of the tension in her body loosened.

She gazed at his face the whole way down—his eyes were darting back and forth beneath his lids—but when she seated herself completely on his lap, his length fully and deeply inside her, she closed her own eyes. Pleasure was radiating in steady waves out from her privates. *Wow.* When it came to penis size, she'd never known what she was missing.

She had to fight like hell not to moan—she wasn't sure if it would make her more of a perv if she enjoyed this.

Bracing her hands on the bed above Vasile's shoulders, she lifted herself off him, still moving slowly, then sank back down, her sheath encasing him in a tight glove. Stronger bolts of pleasure shot through her.

Vasile's head moved back and forth on the pillow once.

"The votes are in," she breathed. "I can happily live the rest of my life with this dick of yours."

That became truer when she really got moving, rocking her hips, arching her neck back and clutching his shoulders, losing herself to the feel of—

A nasty snarl boiled out of Vasile.

She came to an abrupt halt and blinked down at him.

Several tics in his upper lip were quivering toward a sneer. There was something savage about his face, and a tingle of fear touched her nerves.

It hit her now, in this *sorry-it's-too-late* moment, that the whole time she'd been thinking about everything she needed to think about in order to decide whether or not to bond with Vasile, she forgot to consider what it would be like to commit forever to a man who had once lost his mind so much to his predatory side that he had attacked her.

Indecision and fear froze her in place on his lap.

The wall clock didn't so much go *tick* as it did *snip! snip!*

snip!

Vasile's dick pulsed rhythmically inside her several times.

Licking her lips, she tried moving up and down again.

Again the dark noise came out of him.

She stopped, pressing her fingertips into his shoulder muscles, then she stretched forward and pushed the call button.

Waiting for Toni, she tucked the sheet securely around her waist.

About five seconds later, Toni's head stole around the jamb. Her eyebrows shot up when she saw Corky was seated on top of Vasile.

Hi, sis! Yes, I'm presently impaled.

Toni slipped inside. "Is everything okay?"

"I'm not sure. Vasile's…um…he's making a strange noise."

"You mean like he's in pain?"

"It's not a pain-noise. It sounds like…uh, like he's either pissed at me or about to eat me for dinner."

"Hmm, okay." Toni's calm was remarkable, considering. "Why don't I turn around and you do whatever you do to make the noise come out of him, and we'll see."

Why was Corky surprised things were getting even more weird and uncomfortable? "All right."

Toni turned around.

Planting her palms on the mattress again, Corky slid up and down Vasile's cock, the power of his male flesh once again building a throbbing pressure in her clit. She wrapped her hands around fistfuls of bedsheet. *Please don't let me make my orgasm groan in front of Toni again.*

About six or seven strokes in, Vasile started snarling. "That's it!"

"Ah," Toni said. "You can stop now. I know what it is."

"Just a second." Corky rechecked the security of the sheet around her waist. "Okay."

Toni turned around. "That noise is vampire pleasure."

"What, really? Are you sure?"

"Oh, yes." Toni smiled. "I know it sounds strange at first, but you'll get used to it. In fact, you'll grow to love it."

Seemed farfetched to love a noise that made a woman want to hide behind a rock, but then…what wasn't wacky about this arrangement? "I'll take your word for it."

Toni gave her an encouraging nod. "Vasile has more color. You're doing great." She set her hand on the door handle. "And it's no sin to enjoy yourself, Corky. Make as good of a memory out of this as you can."

"Sure…" Corky smiled crookedly. "Someday we'll laugh about this over drinks, right?"

Toni's return smile was faint. "Someday. Oh, and by the way, don't leave Vasile's side after you're done. He'll need to scent you. You can use those tissues beside the bed to clean up."

"Okay."

Toni nodded and left.

Corky looked down at the unconscious man beneath her. "Oh, Vasile," she breathed. "If only I had some idea what you're going to say about all this when you wake up…"

Chapter Forty-Six

Three days later
8:26 a.m.

THE UNFAMILIAR VOICE OF A man speaking Romanian brought Vasile into wakefulness with a large measure of confusion—the voice was talking about the weather in Transylvania.

"<A low pressure system is heading toward Braşov...>"

What is this? I am back in Romania within the Vârcolac warded lands...?

This was an alarming discovery, and Vasile stirred with the intention of investigating further—but then stopped moving when the right side of his lower back throbbed mightily. He grunted and immediately thereafter the voice of the newsman diminished.

"Vasile?"

That was the voice of his beloved.

Relief was a flood of warmth in his chest. The sound of Corky speaking could only signify that he was not, in fact, in his homeland. He was still in Ţărână. And lying on a bed, if the soft mattress cushioning his backside was to be trusted.

He worked his eyelids open, and—

Corky's face was directly above him.

Her hair was caught in a puffy collection of curls on the crown of her head, and she was wearing a top with no sleeves, just strings curving over each shoulder to keep the garment from sagging down.

He was indeed lying on a bed. The bed was located in the

community hospital—a place he knew far too well.

At the end of the bed by his feet there was the type of portable computer he had heard called a lap-board, or some such. On the screen was a moving picture of a newsman making announcements—now muted.

"Oh, thank God," Corky breathed. "You're awake."

The surprised lilt of her voice over his wakefulness suggested that he had been asleep for an unwonted period of time. The extreme groggy nature of his mind added credence to this conjecture.

"What—" His mouth was parched and unused, and he could not fashion a question to ask her what had happened to put him in need of medical care—this need he based on his current location—and of so much sleep.

He would also like an explanation for the oddness of his present positioning with Corky.

She was *not* standing at his bedside, as would be meet, but instead was on the mattress *with* him, tucked between his body and the wall.

"Let me call Toni." Corky extended her body across his to press a button near the—

Her scent punched him in the brain, and he sucked in a great inhalation. *By the purest light of the Zâne.* She smelled incredible now.

It was a certain truth that Corky always smelled good to him, and that he always felt good when he was near to her. But his reaction to her now was different from his usual pole-throbs or his enjoyment of any conversation he had with her. At this moment, he felt invigorated while also dizzied, like having a head full of wine…although his present feeling was much more than simply a drug in his blood.

This feeling went into the deepest parts of him.

Why was he reacting to her this way?

Toni entered the room with a hurried stride.

"He just woke up," Corky told her, her voice breathless in

the manner of someone imparting exciting news.

Toni arrived at his bedside, smiling. "It's good to see you doing better, Vasile." She selected from off the wall a black armband that took readings of blood pressure. "How do you feel?"

As he had noted earlier, his right-side back was sore, but now he took a moment to attend to the condition of his whole body. He discovered that he was weak—not counting the strange invigoration—however he did not care to admit to the weakness. His mouth was too much in need of moisture at any rate.

He moved his thick tongue around without speech, and Toni understood his dilemma.

She reached aside to a table next to his bed. A moment later she presented before him a plastic cup with a thin suction tube in it.

He set his lips upon this tube and drew in several gulps of water. That was indeed better. "What happen?" Despite the recent influx of water into his mouth, his voice still sounded croaky, as if he was the most primitive of ogres.

Toni returned the cup to its place. "You don't remember the fight at The Corner Drafthouse?"

The name of the topside drinking establishment brought memories of the episode into his mind. Muşate and Bugiana arriving…the two witches naming Corky as their sister…his warrior comrades becoming immobilized in a spell guard, and then…

Vasile shut his eyes.

And then Savatina entered the pub, and he charged at her in the kind of foolhardy and thoughtless way that left his back undefended…and thus ripe for a blade thrust.

"I have memory of it now." He opened his eyes. "The foul witch Bugiana stab me."

Toni nodded in confirmation. "The wound you received was severe. You've been ____ for five days."

"*Unconscious?*"

"Asleep."

"For *five* days?" That was an unwonted period of time, indeed!

Toni looked upon him with concern. "Your hemophilia complicated your treatment—you gave us quite a scare."

Hemophilia was yet another disadvantage of being part-human. He had learned upon his diagnosis of such that it was a medical condition notable for the excessive bleeding of wounds. Even the smallest injury was slow to close and difficult to heal, and indeed he well recalled what ghastly straits he had been in six months past, following the severe blade injury he received from Jacken—on the night the community fighters came to rescue Dev Nichita in the greenwood.

Vasile had no doubt that healing him this time had been a similar plague. "My apologies for the trouble I cause you, but my thanks."

"Actually, you'll want to thank Corky." Toni nodded at her. "It was her love and care that saved you."

Her *love and care*…? He gave Corky a befuddled frown. How did love cure a stab wound? Perhaps this was a normal thing, and his mind was still partially abed. "I no understand."

Toni sliced a look at Corky. Her voice lowered. "Do you want me here for this next part?"

Corky shook her head. "No, thanks. I've got it."

Vasile experienced a strange reaction of snakes-in-the-belly over this exchange between the two—it seemed portentous. Something was awry.

"Okay." Toni patted Vasile on the forearm. "I'm going to order a liquid meal for you—getting some food in your system will help bring your energy back." She returned the black armband to the wall. "I'll take your vitals later." Toni left.

Vasile turned again to Corky and observed her.

Now that he was peering closer, he noted that she did not

altogether seem her normal self. She appeared fatigued and not as clean as usual, as if she had not been able to take a proper shower for some time. "Is something amiss?"

Corky pressed her lap-board shut.

This seemed like an unnecessary action to take to answer his question. More peculiar. More snakes. He did not like silence for answers.

Corky finally expelled a great breath of air. "<This will be difficult for me to explain to you, Vasile, because you're going to think I did what I did *only* to save your life, and then you might doubt us as a couple. But it's like Toni said—I did what I did because I care for you. Very much.>"

His jaw loosened as if suddenly slathered in goose grease. Her manner of speech was impeccable! "<Just heaven, how do you speak Romanian so well now?>"

A small smile tilted her lips. "<The whole time you were asleep, I watched Romanian television.>" She set a hand atop her lap-board. "<Almost constantly. Your brother also came by every day to stand in the doorway and practice speaking with me.>"

Nicolae…? Why would he have to remain in the doorway?

"<I worked hard to become fluent in Romanian again,>" added Corky, "<so I can communicate well with my new husband.>"

Husband?! Vasile clamped his jaw. A crushing weight pressed down on his chest. *Fane Vasilichi!*

But then he thought, *no.* That toff did not speak Romanian. "<Who?>"

Corky smiled at him again, but lines of strain grooved creases into the sides of her mouth. This was not her usual smile. It hinted at troubled thoughts.

<You,> said Corky.

Chapter Forty-Seven

Vasile lowered his brows and labored with great effort to determine the veracity of her statement.

In response to his silence and, no doubt, to his worried expression, Corky repeated, but with emphasis, "<*You* are my husband, Vasile.>"

How could that be so? "<But I have no memory of biting your throat or of having the sexual intercourse with you.>"

"<You wouldn't remember,>" agreed Corky. "<Because you were…>" She made a slight cough. "<You were asleep the whole time.>"

He exhaled a short breath. She might as well be sitting beside him with pickles in her ears for all the sense she was making. "<I cannot accomplish bonding tasks while asleep.>

"<You can. And you did. You bit me by reflex and…>"

For truth? He did not know such was possible.

"<…the second part…>" Her cheeks pinkened. "<I…uh…I made the sex happen between us.>"

"<*You* did?>"

Corky made an expression of discomfort, as if she suddenly suffered a digestive complaint.

"<Verily, you must be mistaken about what occurred. In the sex education moving pictures I watched, the male is required to move his hips with much vigor during the act of sexual intercourse. I could not have done so if I slept."

"<Okay, you know what? I'm just going to say what happened straight out: after you fed on me, your penis became erect. I climbed onto your lap and inserted your erection into

my vagina from that position. Then *I* moved my hips with vigor, rousing you to ejaculate inside me. This is how we completed the bond.>"

He stared at her, utterly taken aback. He tried to create in his mind a picture of what she just described, but he could not. In his experience, the bull always mounted the cow, not the other way around. And in the moving pictures Dr. Jess showed the Moon-Riders, the male was always on top of the female.

Corky knitted her brows at him. "<I'm so sorry. I know it must be awful for you to have no memory of your first time having sex with a woman.>"

He startled. He had not thought of that part. Now a creeping heat slid up his neck into his face.

Corky observed his expression, and her distress grew. "<I didn't want it to be that way between us, but I had no choice. Toni told me you'd go into a half-bond if I didn't have sex with you, and that would've killed you.>"

His stomach wrenched—from the arrival of hunger in that moment, yes, but from a strong emotion too.

It was her love and care that saved you…

With painstaking pronunciation, he asked, "<Would I have likewise died if you hadn't bonded with me?>"

She paused—too long.

"*Fir-ar să fie.*" He hissed the curse and closed his eyes. He had needed to be *saved* by her, like he was little more than a puppy caught in a drain. Corky already considered him too weak to care for her properly—it was why she had set him aside—and now…*this.*

Sand coated his throat. His heart shifted into the wrong place inside his chest. For all of his life he thought shunning was the worst thing a man could endure. He was mistaken.

It was pity.

Corky said, "<Now you're thinking what I asked you not to think.>"

He opened his eyes.

"<I asked you not to think that I bonded with you *only* to save your life.>"

"<There can be no other reason.>" He fought to keep the corners of his mouth still.

"<I told you that I also did it because I care for you.>"

He repeated her absurd statement in a flat tone. "<You care for me. Twelve days past you set me aside and today I awake to find that you *care* for me.>"

Corky deepened the troubled knit of her brows. "<I always cared for you. I just…I needed to work some things out for myself before I could be with you.>"

"<And you accomplished this?>"

She hesitated. "<Yes.>"

"<You paused before you spoke. That is a truer answer than your words.>"

"<Well, hell, Vasile, the answer is as true as I can make it. Life is growth, and I'm sure I'll never be completely done working on myself. You either.>"

If this was indeed the case, she would know better than he would. He spent his time thinking about woodworking and hunting and protecting others and the like, not about *working on himself.*

"<Perhaps this is so,>" admitted Vasile. "<But I would also know how you can trust your decision-making on this. For when you set me aside, you confessed that you didn't believe in this aspect of yourself anymore. How do you now?>"

"<Because…>" Her eyelashes fanned at him for several moments. "<I don't know. I just do.>"

He shook his head against the pillow. "<That is no-good answer.>"

"<Maybe so, but it's the best one I have.>"

"<Then I want no more of this discussion.>" He turned his head aside and stared at the plastic cup with its suction tube. The cup was set next to a box of the gossamer-type paper named "tissues."

Corky set her hand on his arm with a light touch. "<Vasile, will you please listen to me?>" She continued to speak absent his permission to carry on. "<I took the decision to bond with you very seriously. Okay? I thought about it a lot. I reflected on what a good man you are, and I made the choice with all the honesty in my heart. Do I wish things happened differently between us? Of course. But I firmly believe that you and I would've ended up together, eventually. Your injury just speeded up the process.>"

He looked at her again. "<*Now* you say I am a good man—now that you are laden with me, no escape at hand. But earlier you alleged that I am too much of a buffoon to correctly manage myself in my new culture.>"

Corky took her hand back. "<I-I…I didn't mean—>"

"<And a buffoon requires hard work, does he not? Yet by your own admission you are too exhausted to work hard anymore.>"

She flushed, her cheeks turning a shade far deeper than pink.

"<Or maybe it is just *me*. Maybe *I* am not worthy of your best efforts.>" He swallowed, his Adam's apple feeling hard as a wood knot. "<Because if I had been worth your care and effort, Corky Disdale, then you would not have set me aside in the first place.>"

She swallowed. "<You're right, I should've never left you. And…>" Her next words came out with a rasp in her throat. "<And there are a lot of things I said to you the evening we broke up that I regret.>"

He saw sincerity in her eyes. But there was a pained and broken part inside him that would not let him believe her. "<Regretting your words does not make them untrue.>"

Her lips trembled.

He could stand no more of this horror. On this day that

should have been the happiest in his existence—he was bonded to his beloved—he instead felt like his entire person was unbalanced.

It no longer felt good to be near to Corky.

"<I grow tired now.>" He turned his head aside again, toward the window this time.

The part of cave wall visible in the rectangle of windowpane shone bright yellow under the glow of the ceiling lights—still so strange a sight for a breed of man who had spent his life prowling the night.

From the side of his vision, he saw Corky draw up her knees, then fold her arms across the tops and hide her face against her arms.

She began to weep.

He stared out the window with a sickness inside him.

Chapter Forty-Eight

Two weeks later
10:11 a.m.

BE THE BEST.

Be the greatest protector, the most skilled hunter, the strongest in moral character...

Vasile was not the best.

He was not a man who had acted to win his woman when the situation warranted it.

He was a man who, in fact, had made his woman cry.

Gritting his teeth at the memory, he stomped across the room of lockers, jamming his wet towel and sweat-soaked stretchy workout clothing into a mesh receptacle designed for the purpose of collecting dirty laundry.

Around him other fighting men were removing their training outfits and dressing in their everyday clothing.

Jacken was still washing off sweat in the shower area.

Six men had just finished morning drills, Vasile among them—he had at last regained the full physical and mental capacity he possessed prior to when Bugiana stabbed him.

Not that the return of his faculties had done him any good.

Be the best...

Stomping back to his metal locker-closet, he shoved a secondary pair of supple workout shoes into his nylon carrier bag—he could not decide which of two sizes fit him best— then zippered shut the bag...and now his hands became unsteady by a small amount.

Not from an impotence of the body.

But of the soul.

He could not think of any solution to change his marriage from a strained one to a happy one.

It was two weeks now since he had left the hospital, departing on unstable legs one day after awakening to discover that Corky was his bonded mate.

Moving directly into the neighborhood reserved for wedded couples, he and Corky claimed the house alongside the home of Dev and Marissa. As luck would have it, Hannah and Willen Crişan had recently transferred to a larger abode to accommodate their burgeoning family, and their relocation vacated this perfectly positioned house.

The color of the former Crişan house was green. Not the green of a woodland, but still much better than loathly pink or blue. But the color and the location of the house were the only glad tidings to come of his new domestic situation with Corky.

Their life as a bonded couple had been most unhappy, and for this, he blamed himself.

He failed to show Corky the patience and understanding she required two weeks past.

In the time since, he had reviewed in his mind many times the reasons why Corky would have bonded with him, and he came to the conclusion that her selfless act had indeed been honest and heartfelt, as she proclaimed.

He concluded this through a sound system of reasoning, starting at his familiarity with her character. She was a kind and compassionate woman—he knew this going clear back to the time they sat together at the dining table of Kimberly Stănescu, discussing the no-fraternization law.

On the night Corky set him aside, he should have viewed her behavior through this lens of knowledge. If he had done so—if he had taken the time to think about her actions in more depth—he would have remembered that the douche-man Reese had wrought an emotional upset in her while the two were in The Shank Tooth. So when she exited the slummy pub, this troubled state of being would have subsequently led her to say things to Vasile that were not her normal wont to say. Or mean.

Had he not done the same thing himself in times past? What person, in life, had not said something he or she did not mean?

Knowing this, Vasile should have been patient and understanding with Corky.

But unfortunately the accusation she had made against him earlier—that he could not care for her properly—already planted a seed of uselessness in him. So when she told him that she bonded with him to save his life, it made him feel small, inept, and weak.

A curse on vain sensibilities! If he had not been racked with these, he would have been able to harken back to her once telling him—after he caught a fish for her at Balboa Park— that she knew she would never go hungry with him as her man. And then he would have been able to quash any self-doubts when they arose.

But instead he did exactly what Dev advised him not to do—he let hurt pride make his decisions for him.

The consequences of that had been dreadful—he could no longer talk well with Corky, like in the prime of their relationship, for every time he drew near to her he suffered a profound embarrassment. And so when they sat at their family table to consume a meal together, his tongue would produce only stiff and uneventful words. And on those occasions when he needed blood, he fed from her wrist in secret while she slumbered, like a larcener in the night.

And day by day he watched more melancholy and regret consume the blue of her eyes.

This gouged his very soul, a part of him that had been in tatters for all of these two weeks of strained marriage. He had become, once again, that most loathsome of creatures—a man who did not act to fix his problems, like so many other times in his past…

Had he chosen to stay in Ţărână to better his life? No, Nicolae did so, and he followed.

Had he commanded the impulses of his body when he became a true male? No, he did not, and thus earned a shocker band around his ankle.

Had he entered into a bond with his beloved of his own volition? No, she alone had been encumbered with saving him from the folly of leaving himself exposed to a sword blade.

You don't fight. You lie down beside your father and let him die…

A savage burning sensation hurt his eyes.

From the locker-closet next door, Thomal growled a complaint to Dev, "Fucking Alex. The damned dweeb let my sister slip through his fingers."

Dev cast Thomal a surprised glance. "You knew about that?"

Thomal rounded on Dev. "*You* knew about that?"

"Uh, yeah." Dev grabbed two sneaker shoes out of his locker closet and dropped them at his feet with a *thump*. "Alex told Luvera, and Luvera told me."

Thomal scowled. "Fuck, Nichita. Why didn't you say anything?"

Dev pushed one foot, then the next, into his sneaker shoes. "Because I knew you'd flip your lid—exactly like you're doing." He bent over to tie his shoes. "No one should be telling you and Arc anything until your sister is actually found."

Flinging his nylon carrier bag over his shoulder, Vasile closed the door of his locker-closet and started with long strides for the door.

Dev called to him. "Hang back a second, Lazăr."

Vasile turned toward his friend and frowned. "Hang?"

"*Wait*," clarified Dev. "I want to talk to you."

"Very well." He set his carrier bag on a long-seat and waited. He would need to remember that *hang back* was a slang term for *to wait*.

Jeddin—a mixed-breed with hair the color of snow—clattered out of the room with Breen, the two men talking about something called an ex-box on their way to exiting.

Only Dev and Thomal now remained—and Jacken in the shower area.

Dev and Thomal strode toward Vasile, Dev saying, "You know that we're here to help you. Right?"

An odd way to commence a conversation. But Vasile said, "Yes."

"Any questions or issues that come up, you should bring them to us."

"And I have done so."

"True." Dev moved his head in a way that complimented Vasile for this habit. "You've been good about it." Dev paused.

It was a *waiting* pause, as though Dev expected Vasile to ask a question or speak of an issue.

Vasile did not speak, even though he of course had an issue—his domestic affairs were in shambles. But if he admitted to this, he would have to make too many uncomplimentary confessions about himself.

The patter of the shower filled the silence.

"So…" Dev pushed his fingers through his wet hair. "Do you have something you'd like to talk about?"

"No."

Dev gave Vasile a look that said he suspicioned this was false. "You're stomping around like a wounded bear, Lazăr. Something's wrong."

Vasile still did not speak.

Dev glanced at Thomal, then hefted a breath. "Look, man, our wives talk, okay? I've heard through Marissa that you and Corky aren't doing well."

Vasile felt his stomach dive down low, same as when his father was teaching him how to hunt with a bow and arrow and he missed the kill. His father, ever supportive—like Dev—told him it was all right. But it was not all right. No venison adorned the supper table that night.

"We fine," insisted Vasile, his tongue aching from the lie.

It was wasted effort, at any rate. Dev just naysaid him. "No, man, you're not. Corky's not happy."

"Of this," said Vasile through the barrier of his teeth, "I am very aware. If I could undo our bond for her, I would." This would tear him limb from limb, but no sacrifice was too great for his beloved.

"She doesn't want to undo the bond. She just wants you to stop acting like a fucking stranger and be her husband."

Be her husband!? Vasile ground his jaw. By a blessed moon, was it not evident that he did not know how to properly don that role? Otherelse he would have done so afore now.

Jacken came from the shower area into the room of lockers. His hair was wet and untidy and a towel wrapped his waist.

"Do you remember what Costache told you right after Corky broke up with you?" asked Dev. "That she was afraid it was a mistake picking you because you're too closed off?"

Dev did not provide Vasile with the necessary time to answer.

"Well, shit, Vasile…" Dev blew out a hard breath. "You've sort of become her worst nightmare in that regard."

Vasile glared down at his carrier bag and so strongly wanted to leave, the muscles in his legs twitched.

"You're not, um…" Dev quieted his tone. "I've heard that you're not having sex with Corky."

Vasile felt his jaw thicken—he jutted it. They were now treading upon exactly why he did not want to have this discussion.

"You need to start having sex with your wife."

Vasile fell sick with a roiling gorge in his stomach—a sensation of being scolded again. And like every other time in his life when he had been rebuked for committing a wrong, he had no recourse for reparation. Because he *was* wrong.

He was a half-breed. He was half.

Jacken combed his hair and applied the sticky product to his armpits that prevented body stink.

The room of lockers suddenly felt too crowded, shrouded in a sense of overwhelming confinement. Strangely frightening. "No." Vasile spat the single word with taut and rising emotion.

"No?" Dev sounded unsure. "You're not going to have sex with your wife?"

"That is correct."

Dev exchanged another glance with Thomal.

Jacken removed his towel and started to change into his everyday clothing.

Dev cleared his throat. "Vasile…listen, man, part of the problem might be that you slept through a lot of your bonding time with Corky. I mean, you scented her, yeah, but you were unconscious for days. You have to reignite your connection with her."

"I no have sex with Corky until I can be man with her."

A silence laden with astonishment followed.

"Uh…what do you think you are," asked Dev, "if you're not a man?"

"I weak. I am pollard."

"I don't know what the second thing is, but—"

"It is animal that has lost horns. That is me—like cow, not bull."

Dev shook his head. "You're not."

"<A lifetime of failing to act says otherwise.>"

"Vasile—"

"<All the time I was a Protector in the Vârcolac warded lands, I was no defender at all. I treated the un-women of our culture little better than slaves—I let others do the same. No real man acts thusly. And when my own mother was consigned to the role of un-woman, I made no attempt to rescue her from her plight, feeling too helpless against our chief. And what of you, Dev Nichita? Did I stand firm in opposition to our chief to save you from torture in the woods? No.>" He snarled the negation. "<I did not.>"

"<You were not among those who struck a whip upon me,>" protested Dev.

"<Because of *Nicolae*.>" The uncertainty of what Vasile would have done absent this intervention by his brother was his most profound shame. "<And what of my recent stabbing injury? I fought unwisely because of my fury at Savatina. Weak again! And now I have done what you precisely cautioned me not to do—I have pushed away my woman out of hurt pride. I have done everything wrong.>" A hollowness carved a hole into his stomach. He was mortally afraid it was the feeling that preceded total and utter loss. "<And so, no, I cannot have the intercourse with Corky. I *will* not until I can be an honorable man with her!>"

Dev did not reply. He stood with his hands on his hips, his eyes dark.

Thomal was running a palm along the line of his jaw.

A *plip, plip* signified that remnants of water were still finding their way down the drainage pipe in the shower area. It was an oddly unnerving noise.

Bam.

Jacken closed his metal closet with force, then strode over to Vasile and halted directly in front him. "Chrissake, Lazăr, you're killing me with all your fucking overthinking. Stop analyzing this. There's only one thing you need to do, and it'll solve everything."

Vasile waited, his heart running at a thunderous gallop.

What great feat was Jacken about to lay upon him?

"Get your woman naked," said Jacken, then he stalked from the room.

Vasile stood in place. Surely there was more he must do.

"You've got it all wrong," said Dev softly, "you know that? About what your problem is."

Vasile turned.

"I know you." Dev still spoke in a somber voice. "You spent your youth following your dad, who was your hero, yeah, so it's understandable. But at some point, every son needs to break free of his father's shadow. Unfortunately, your dad died before he could help you do that, and so now…you're following me." Dev glanced down and moved his feet. "I've been honored by that, man, really, but Vasile…it's time for you to again be the leader that I know you are."

Vasile felt his lungs compress.

"I don't mean you have to go it *alone*," assured Dev. "Thomal and I—all the warriors—are always around. You can ask our opinion on shit anytime…just like I know you'll give me advice whenever I need it." Dev set a hand on his shoulder. "As equals."

Vasile felt the muscles in his throat go taut. He could not speak. It was not possible to find words that would describe how it felt to be likened to this man of honor.

"It's tough," inserted Thomal, "what Dev's asking you to do. I know, because I lived in my brother's shadow for years. I'm an artist, so, you know, my dad and Arc didn't think I'd be a good fighter. Their doubts about me…they stung. I had to struggle past them and learn to be okay with who I am— the warrior who paints." Thomal crossed his arms and leaned one shoulder against his closed locker-closet. "So you see, brother, your problem ain't that you're not a man. Or that you're not an honorable man. It's that you need to be *your own* man."

Vasile blinked two times.

Dev nodded. "Figure out how to connect with Corky your own way, Vasile, and it'll be right. Don't look at me and Marissa or Costache and Pandra or anybody else. Whatever your gut ends up telling you to do, do it. You understand?"

Vasile took in a breath. A strange, weightless feeling was magnifying outward from the center of his chest to all parts of his being, as if his body was acknowledging this insightful reimagining of who he was—or could be—even before his mind could fully comprehend it.

"Yes." He swallowed hard. "I understand."

CHAPTER FORTY-NINE

7:23 p.m.

CORKY SLAMMED THE COMPUTER MOUSE down on the desk.

The small plastic body cracked open, spewing forth a miniature motherboard and the *on* light on top blinked out.

Broken.

"Argh!" Corky buried her face in her hands. *Dammit!*

And damn you, Rand Resources.

Those corporate monsters were behind all her bad luck lately, starting back when she lost her stupid case against them, got flattened by her boyfriend in the process, and tarnished her rep as a lawyer among her peers. Oh, and let's not forget she also lost a stellar job opportunity with Ria Mendoza.

Did she face down the consequences? *No.* She took the coward's path and ran away.

That move landed her in an underground town of vampires, where a bunch of unbelievable revelations ripped her identity to shreds. But, hey, at least she would have the opportunity to create a better life for herself.

Hah! She botched her chance at success again.

She lost her first court case in Țărână—she could only guess what Kimberly thought of her as a lawyer—then let one of her so-called friends light a fire under her self-doubts with his "caretaker" accusations. Her newfound insecurities drove her to commit her worst act of stupidity yet—she broke up with the one man who'd ever treated her well.

Who *loved* her.

Dev Nichita once advise me that no woman is perfect. He tell me a man must needs accept her flaws. Love her for them. I tell you, Corky—this I do with you.

Her heart pushed into her throat.

Here was a man infinitely worth saving, but she'd blown saving Vasile's life along with everything else—instead of feeling loved by what she'd done, he felt hurt.

Regretting your words does not make them untrue…

"Argh!" she exasperated again. How was she supposed to make him understand that the things she'd said to him the night they broke up didn't come from her heart but from a place of pain—the place inside where she'd been shoving all her pain for her whole life.

A place with no release valve…at least not since she decided to be Mary Sills' Good Girl and *think only good thoughts*.

Until Reese Terrella came along and uncapped it.

I went from being a kind woman to a doormat, someone with a loving heart to a gullible chump…

Corky hitched in her next breath, grief rolling over her in scalding waves.

Worst thing she could've done while in the throes of her identity shakeup was push Vasile away. She should've thrown herself into his arms and nurtured her wounds within the comfort of his embrace.

But she *did* push. And too hard. Because now here she was, stuck in a sexless marriage with an emotionally shut down husband. *And this all-inclusive package is for a lifetime, folks!*

Move to strike!

On what grounds?

On the grounds that I don't want to think about it!

"God!" She was such a screwup!

And speaking of screwups…

She glanced again at today's email from Mary, still open on her computer screen.

…heard from Child Protective Services…accusations of…you know I would never…going to take my children away, Corky, if you don't do something… Please help!

Through a blur of rising tears, Corky stared at the computer keyboard, the response she needed to type waiting among those letters… *Do you have proof of the false allegation, Mary? No? Then I can't do anything.*

So they were back to that. Mired there. Cemented.

If additional evidence comes to light at a later time, you may refile. Otherwise this case is dismissed…

Corky dropped her gaze to her lap, looking down at her hands lying limp on her thighs. Such soft, helpless hands…

"Argh!" She was so sick of feeling stuck!

She needed to get the hell out of here, quit reading and rereading the email from Mary. Thinking about all her screwups just made her feel more alone and unloved.

Shoving up from her desk chair, she clomped from her home office and headed for the stairs.

When she arrived at the top, she saw Vasile making his way up.

He stopped and looked up at her. "<Is all well with you? I keep hearing you call out.>"

"<Everything's fine.>" She continued at a hurried pace down the stairs.

He didn't move out of the way.

She pulled up.

"<You don't look like you're fine,>" he said. "<You look upset.>"

She fought to keep her chin from quivering. "<All right. Yes. I am upset.>"

"<Then why do you leave?>"

"<I want to go see Hadley.>"

Because about the only thing going well in her life right now was on the family front—she'd struck gold and found some long-lost relatives…although one side of her family was so supernaturally dysfunctional that they took some of the shine off the discovery. But *whatever.*

"<Why?>" he asked.

"<*Why?*>" She planted her hands on her hips. "<Have you a pickle fork stowed over there and let me tell it!>"

He squinted at her.

Shit. She gritted her teeth and slowed the Romanian in her head. "<Because I need to talk to my sister, that's why.>" She tried to edge around him.

He still didn't let her pass.

"<Do you mind?>" she snapped.

"<I would have you talk to me about your upset feelings.>"

"<Oh, yeah?>" She crossed her arms under her breasts. "<Since when?>"

He examined her face for an uneasy moment. "<This is one of those times when I think you become upset with me when I ask questions, so I am loath to question you about this, but I'm also not sure how to answer your since-when query.>" He hesitated. "<Is it not evident I want to talk to you *now?*>"

"*Futu-I,*" she bit out, laying the F-bomb on him in Romanian.

He blinked.

"<I mean *since when* do you talk to me, Vasile? You stopped after we bonded.>"

Mottled patches of red appeared on his neck. "<Yes, this is true, and I apologize for doing so. I know…I realize this has made me into your nightmare. But during these two weeks past, I have struggled to know how to be a proper man with you.>"

"<What do you mean by proper?>"

The tautness beside his eyes intensified and spread to other areas of his face. "<I have lived with a certain anxiety that I am too weak of a man for you.>"

Corky's heart twisted. "<Is this because of the things I said

to you the night we broke up?>"

"<Yes.>"

She bowed her head. She was a horrible, horrible person for making him doubt himself. "<I'm sorry, Vasile. If I could take back everything I said to you, I would. I'll never forgive myself for giving you a potato dance with…>" She drew in a swift breath, her Romanian falling apart again. "<…for making you feel like you aren't worth working for. Because that's not true. You are. So much.>"

She scrubbed a fist over her stinging nose. "<I've been going over it in my mind, and I think the work you and I do is… It's healthy. You know? It's not like how I was in my past relationships, doing everything myself, taking all the hits. What we do is…we work at getting to know each other, both of us trying equally, and that's good.>" She pressed her fingertips to her eyes to push back a rush of tears. "<And I don't think you're weak. Okay? I never have. I swear it.>" She dropped her hands and gazed at him in earnest.

He rubbed his lips together. "<That…all of that is an incredible boon to hear, and I thank you for saying it. But I must know that I am a strong man for myself, not just from your assurances. And I have not known how to know this.>"

He peered down at the floor, smoothing one hand over the back of the other. "<My whole life whenever I felt wrong I believed there was nothing I could do—because I *was* wrong. So I followed others to find my way.>" He looked up. "<But what happens those times when I don't know what to do and there is no one nearby to ask or imitate? What do I do then?>"

His throat moved. "<I tell you what—I cease to act. I do nothing. This is what happened with you—and so I became your nightmare. I did not do this because I want to be a bad husband or because I don't care. But because…I don't know how to repair us.>"

She blinked back another rush of tears.

"<Except I might know now. Dev and Thomal advised

me to find a way to be my own man, and I think this is what I must do to feel honorable and thus be able to talk well with you again.>"

"<I would like that.>"

"<As of yet I know not the path I must take, but I do know I cannot find my way to being my own man by doing nothing. I must try. So even though I worry about making mistakes with you, I must *do* something. Yes?>"

She gave him a shaky nod.

"<Then I ask that you let me listen to you, Corky, and I will do my utmost to offer you guidance…if I have anything of value to give.>"

She swallowed convulsively. No man had ever *wanted* to listen to her before.

He held her gaze. "<Will you let me?>"

"<Yes.>"

"<Good.>" He took her gently by the arm. "<Then come hither downstairs to our kitchen and let us talk.>"

Chapter Fifty

Corky let Vasile lead her to their kitchen table, a borrowed piece that showed the many owners it'd gone through over the years, its top pocked and scratched. The chair she settled into was also nicked in places and sat a bit off-kilter.

She was still waiting for her own furniture to arrive from topside.

Vasile poured her some water from a pitcher in the refrigerator, set the glass in front of her, then sat across from her. "<All right. Now tell me what upsets you.>"

"<*Everything.*>" Which wasn't a particularly fair response—it didn't give him anything specific to work with.

Still, he tried, nodding. "<Okay. Yes. Tell me the worst upset.>"

"<I guess that would be my court case for Mary Sills.>"

"<Your substitute mother?>"

"<Yes.>"

"<What is the case?>"

"<Right before coming to Țărână, I filed a lawsuit against a corporation that was using nasty tactics to try and force Mary to sell her land to them. I was supposed to stop their harassment, but…but I blew it.>"

He paused. "<You mean you made a mistake?>"

"<Yes.>" She glanced down at her thumbnail. "<And I made the mistake because I was insecure about myself—that's the worst part.>" She looked up. "<I'd found a statute that would discourage Rand Resources—that's the corporation I'm

up against—from—>"

"<What is a statute?>" he interrupted. "<Sorry to be asking questions.>"

"<It's okay. A statute is basically a law—one that prohibits something. The statute I found prohibited a commercial business from operating on any Pine Hills land with a waterway on it.>"

"<Pine Hills? The woods where you grew up?>"

"<Yes.>" *Wow, he remembered that.*

"<And there is a waterway on this land?>"

"<Eagle Peak River,>" she said, nodding. "<So if Rand Resources couldn't operate on the land, then they wouldn't want it. And then they would stop doing nasty stuff to try and force Mary Sills off it. Do you understand?>"

"<No. I mean, yes, I understand all that you said, I just don't see your mistake.>"

"<Well, uh…>" Her tongue grew heavy—it was so painful talking about this. "<This is the part where I let my insecurities get in the way. I bragged to my ex-boyfriend about the statute I found because I wanted him to think I'm a good lawyer. The next day he showed up in court as the lawyer representing my competition and used my idea against me. You see, he had arranged for Mary's neighbor to buy the land with Eagle Peak River on it. It was only an eighth of an acre, but it was enough to nullify the statute.>"

Corky slumped back in her chair. "<So now that there's no law to stop Rand from operating on Mary's land, they're still up to their evil tricks to try and get their hands on it. In fact, those monsters have upped the severity of their tactics. Mary just wrote to me in desperation because someone has accused her of being an alcoholic. *No way.*>"

Corky straightened. "<That is absolutely false. I was raised in that house, and I know Mary never touched a drop. But now she's under investigation for neglect and maltreatment due to her 'alcohol abuse,' and Child Protective Services is

threatening to take away her children until the matter is resolved. God, I want to fix this for Mary so much, but I don't see how. Rand has just been too sneaky. I *know* they're behind the false allegations, but I can't prove it. Ugh.>" Plunking her elbows on the table, Corky cradled her brow on the heels of her palms. "<I feel like I can't win a case to save my life right now.>"

Vasile sat in thought for a long moment. "<An eighth of an acre is only about five hundred square meters. Not much at all. Are you sure of this small size?>"

"<Yes.>" She dropped her hands and frowned. What did that have to do with the case?

"<I would like to view a topographic map of this area you speak of. Do you know where I may find one?>"

"<Why do you want to look at a map?>"

"<I want to see the structure of Eagle Peak River.>"

She still didn't see the relevance, but she got up anyway. "<I can maybe show you something on my computer.>"

They headed upstairs and went into her home office.

She sat at her desk, started to grab the computer mouse, then—*shit*. She'd forgotten it was broken. And she didn't have a replacement on hand. "<Um…hold on, I need to get my laptop.>" She found her briefcase by the door and tugged her laptop out. Returning to her desk, she shoved her PC's keyboard aside, then set her laptop on the desk and booted it up.

Opening Google Maps, she zeroed in on Mary's land in Pine Hills.

Vasile leaned over her shoulder and squinted at the screen. "<That is not a real map. It is like a cartoon.>"

"<Oh, sorry.>" She changed the image to earth mode, then pointed out where Eagle Peak River ran along the edge of Mary's land.

Vasile leaned closer. "<Can you make a bigger image, by chance?>

She zoomed in with several clicks of the mouse, then she rose. "Here—you sit."

Vasile took her place and scanned the picture with rapt attention for a few seconds. "<Okay.>" He stood. "<I will fix this for you.>"

She startled. "You'll…what?"

"<But I must enlist the help of my Protector comrades.>" He headed for the door. "<I will go speak to them now.>"

She gawked after her husband's retreating form. "Vasile—"

He left her office.

"Hey!" She chased him downstairs. "<Where are you going? What are you doing?>"

He opened the coat closet and grabbed his windbreaker. "<I'm not sure yet precisely what I can do. But it would still be best if you could send a cellular message to your substitute mother, alerting her that I will be at her property when the sun goes down.>"

He was going to *Mary's*? "But—" Or was he going to talk to Mary's next-door neighbor? Corky shook her head. "<Making an offer to Reuben Meyerston won't work. I already tried that via email, but Reuben has no reason to sell back the land now that his mortgage has been paid in full.>"

Vasile looked at her as if she'd spoken in Swahili. "<I don't know what a mortgage is, and I don't know this person you speak of. But it is of no consequence.>"

But that was the problem—he didn't know what *was* of consequence and what wasn't. "<Vasile, you don't know topside law. You can't fix this.>"

"<I don't need to know the law.>"

"<Then what—>" She cut herself off with a gasp.

Vasile was *touching* her.

He'd just lifted his hand, and now the backs of his knuckles were softly caressing her cheek. "<I want to see happiness in your eyes again, Glowing Corky. Much melancholy has weighed upon you of late, and that has been my doing. So if it

is within my power to fix this for you, I will do so.>"

Her heart toppled into her stomach while at the same time it still managed to gush out her chest. Vasile had never initiated contact with her before, and now he…he…

Her lashes fluttered toward shutting.

She hadn't been touched in so long, she'd forgotten how wonderful it was…how necessary even the most basic of caresses was to her contentment. She stood perfectly still, gazing up at her husband as a yearning so strong it was almost painful gripped her. Her lips trembled, and *more, dammit, more!* quivered up her throat.

He dropped his hand and stepped back. "<When I go topside, I will be gone for many hours. I warn you of this so that you will not fret after me.>"

He opened the front door and walked out.

Chapter Fifty-One

Vasile trudged into his home, the muscles across his shoulders and back burning from so many long hours of hard physical labor. He and his warrior comrades had worked topside from sundown until the point when the sun was on the verge of rising—it was now six at night in Ţărână, which put the time at six in the morning above.

His mind was as tired as his body, and so it took him some moments to note the cluttered circumstance of his living room. There were many cardboard boxes stacked one on top of the other, set around and about, all with English words hand-written upon them.

His ability to read English was still very poor, a happenstance that might have made him feel like a dimwit if not for his good skills at reading Romanian—he understood many complicated words about husbandry that his brethren did not.

"Vasile!?" Corky called his name as she raced into the living room from the kitchen.

Her expression was harried in a way that conveyed she had been fretting after him all the hours of his absence, even though he had told her not to do so.

Stopping with a suddenness that made her feet skid on the carpeted floor, she gaped at his appearance.

He was covered with mud, and *covered* was no embellishment. There was not a single patch of actual man showing upon his person.

"Holy shit!" exclaimed Corky. "What in God's name happened to you?"

"<I have just returned from many hours of strenuous labor.>" He moved forward a few leaden steps. "<I fixed Eagle Peak River for you.>"

"You…?" She gave him a blank stare. "I'm sorry… What?"

"<I made it so Eagle Peak River runs across the land of your substitute mother. You can now put your statute back in place and win your case.>"

"I can…? It…it…the river runs…?"

Had her long hours of fretting left her mind excessively tired too? She could not seem to form a proper sentence. She was likewise not speaking Romanian to him.

Corky shook her head. "It couldn't."

"<It does. I changed the course of it.>"

She stood frozen for a long moment. "But how?"

"<On the computer map you showed me, I noted striations along the riverbank that made me suspect a certain weakness—lines where a man could put a strong pickaxe to sap the earth. So I guided my warrior friends toward where to dig, and the weakness I suspected proved to be true. The soil crumbled away. We were able to alter the path of the riverbed and thus the direction of the river itself.>"

She set a hand to her breasts. "You really did that?" Her next inhale swelled her chest beneath her palm. "I can't believe you really did that."

"<I know the land.>" He opened the closet nearest to the living room but did not re-hang his muddy lightweight coat. He set it over the top of the jamb. "<On the way home here, I stopped to talk to Kimberly-Solicitor. She will send an inspector to do a land survey later today. Since I did not use a bulldoze machine or the like, the new path of the riverbed appears to have been created by natural erosion. She believes, and I believe, that it will pass inspection. She will then apply for a court date for you to put your statute back in place. She wanted me to ask you to come to her home on the morrow to

discuss this matter with her.>"

"Oh, my God." Corky stared at him with an expression of utter awe.

An intense pride surged through him. This expression was just as fulfilling as the happiness he had striven to create in her, if not more so.

"But what about Mary's foster children?" asked Corky, her expression changing to one of concern. "Will they still be taken?"

"<That, I do not know. But as soon as the corporation you revile cannot operate on their desired land, perhaps you can convince them to retract their false allegation.>"

"That's a good thought, but…" She set her hands on her hips and peered down at the floor in as aspect of deep thought. "It's Hunter who I really need to stop. He'll find a way to undo my success again if I don't come up with something ironclad."

Hunter? Vasile did not know what a huntsman had to do with any of this, but he would leave that to Corky.

Her eyes lifted, settled on his, and warmed. She finally spoke Romanian to him. "<Thank you so much, Vasile.>"

"<Of course.>" He inclined his head. This movement stirred some dried mud loose, and a small clod tumbled off his shoulder. "<Best I go wash myself in the shower now.>" All the dirt was making his flesh itch, as well.

He lumbered up the stairs and entered their bedroom, crossing to his clothes cabinet. He opened one of the drawers and withdrew a plain shirt and soft pants of cotton. He was finished with work for the day, and these were the clothes he wore for relaxation.

He brought these with him into the bathroom that was accessed via the bedroom—he was always mindful to emerge from the bathroom after a shower fully dressed, either in his workaday clothes or the soft shorts and shirt he wore for slumber.

Undressing, he put his filthy clothes in the sink, not on the floor or in the basket receptacle, then turned on the shower and stepped into the stall. Propping his hands against the tiled wall, he bowed his head and let the hot water spray over him, watching dark water circle down the drain.

He remained in this position until the soreness in his back and shoulders eased somewhat.

After two strong scrubbings with soap and shampoo, he finished his shower. He was just beginning to dry his body with a towel when a knock sounded.

Corky called to him through the door. "<Vasile, can you come out here, please? I need to talk to you.>"

"<Yes. But a moment.>" He made quick work of drying the rest of his body and hair, then dressed and emerged.

Corky was standing back from the door by a few paces.

He frowned.

Her eyes were red-rimmed, as if she would shed tears at the merest provocation. Or perhaps she had already been crying. "<Something is amiss?>" What could have occurred in so short a time to steal her happiness?

"<No.>"

"<But you cry.>"

"<For joy.>" Her lips formed a smile, but it was very shaky. "<What you did for me...for Mary and my former home...I... It was so...so...>" A tear trickled down her cheek...

And sank directly into his gut. "<Please, Corky, do not cry.>" He could not bear her tears. "<You thanked me already.>"

"<I owe you more than a *thank-you*.>" Her throat moved with a swallow. "<You're the first man who's ever treated me like I matter, and I...I want to hug you so much right now, but I don't even know if you'll let me.>"

He would like to hug her very much—for his own enjoyment, of course, but also because an embrace might remedy her crying.

"<If you could…aw, the hell with it. I'm just going to hug you.>" She launched herself at him.

The impact of her body against his threw him slightly off-balance. He took several steps backwards, his hands flying to her waist. Then he went motionless, seized with uncertainty. Should he embrace her in return?

Tentatively, he squeezed her waist. Her flesh was nubile and resilient, and he liked the feel of it very much.

She turned her face toward him, pressing her nose against the veins in his neck.

An electric charge darted through his brain.

She spoke in a soft tone against his throat. "<Yesterday you told me that you didn't know how to be your own man yet. But it seems to me like you've figured it out.>" Her breath caressed his flesh and stirred several strands of his long, damp hair. "<You came to my rescue with your knowledge of the land, Vasile, and no one but *you* could've done that.>"

He parted his lips but could not make any words come forth. He was struck utterly dumb by the truth of her statement about him.

Finally he managed to push out one whispered syllable. "<Yes.>" He rested his cheek against the side of her hair.

Inhaling slowly and deeply, he drew her scent into the farthest reaches of his mind. Her precious aroma was comforting and familiar and essential, like it was every night that he lay next to her in bed, but now, holding her so close, her body soft with affection and pride, there was something more…

She is my other half.

He shuddered. He felt that wholly now.

Wrapping his arms all the way around her, he gathered her close again. They both wore clothes and yet the full-body contact was profound, connecting them in a way their hug the day they kissed at the Water Park had not…not entirely. Not like this.

This hug was different.

He felt desire for her, to be sure, in the coursing vibration of his fangs and the ache of his jaw, in the heat tugging low in his belly. But there was also tenderness between them.

Maybe because she rested her cheek on his shoulder, like…

Like it was a hero who held her, not some blundering buffoon.

Like he had moved a mountain for her this night, not a mere river.

He pressed his teeth together to keep his jaw steady, poking his bottom lip with a fang by accident. "<We…>" He closed his eyes. "<This feels different between us.>"

She said, "Mmm," like she had just eaten a sweet candy treat.

Listen, Vasile, part of the problem might be that you slept through a lot of your bonding time with Corky. I mean, you scented her, yeah, but you were unconscious for days…

"<I think perchance our bond is strengthening.>"

"<Maybe it is.>" She snuggled closer, making it so he could distinctly feel the womanly shape of her thighs, the supple roundness of her bosom, and…two pebble-like points jabbed at his chest.

Another electric charge stung his brain. Those points were her nipples—they were hard. This meant—according to sex education class—that she was either cold or full of desire for him.

She did not feel cold.

His breathing quickened.

I will not have sex with Corky until I can be a man with her. It looks to me like you've figured it out.

He opened his eyes and peered down at how his arms wrapped her slender waist. Her bottom looked very ripe. His stomach knotted. "Corky?" He straightened.

"Yes?" She raised her chin and looked at him, her eyes deep clear pools of blue. "<What is it?>"

"<Will you...?>" How *did* a man ask a woman for sexual intercourse?

There's only one thing you need to do, and it'll solve every-thing.

"<Will you get naked?>"

CHAPTER FIFTY-TWO

Vasile observed Corky closely.

Her pulse came to stronger life in the veins running the length of her neck. Her breasts labored under several large intakes of air, as if she strove to gather momentum for her answer.

Had his question distressed her?

She finally smiled. "<I would love to do that.>"

A measure of relief flowed through him. He had not made an error in asking.

Her lashes swept down against her cheeks for a lingering moment, then she stepped back and gestured at their bed. "<Do you want to sit first?>"

This was a good suggestion. His legs already felt a mite unsound over the idea of seeing her bare. "<Yes. I will sit.>" He strode over to their bed and propped his bottom on the edge of the mattress.

Corky came to stand in front of him and began to work at the tie securing the waistband of her cotton pants…although her fingers did not seem entirely under her command. She could not pluck the knot apart.

He observed her efforts for several seconds, then with some surprise, he questioned, "<Are you plagued with nerves?>"

Her eyes crept up. "<Um, yes. A bit.>"

This was interesting. "<Why would that be? Is it not I who am the virgin—in all but the most literal sense?>"

"<True.>" A smile played with her mouth. "<I just want

this to go well for us. We haven't had the best start.>"

Her concern touched him—and that she, who was the experienced one, required comforting moved him to even deeper emotions.

He reached to her waistband and eased the tie from her fingers. "<If we are foolish and silly, it matters not to me. We will just laugh about it together, and be foolish and silly some more.>"

A breath hiccupped out of her. "<That sounds fine to me.>"

"<Good.>" He nimbly undid the knot, and her cotton pants sagged off her waist, exposing the narrow cotton sidebands of her under-attire. He stared at the thrust of her hipbones, and his pulse began a hard drumming against his veins.

Why he should be so enchanted by this part of her body, he did not know—except, perhaps, it was because the delicate nature of these bones was very womanly. For a surety, no blocky male hipbones were like this.

She pushed her pants down her hips, and he tracked every centimeter of the journey of this garment down the long stretch of her legs. The shapely curve of her thighs was also mesmerizing, but when she pulled off her shirt, there was something even better to observe—her belly. This part of her was sprinkled with fine, almost-not-there hairs that gave her flesh a dewy and soft-looking appearance.

He reached for her, then hesitated. "<I may touch you?>"

Her chin moved, inviting him forward. "<You can touch me however and wherever you want, Vasile. With your hands, your mouth—*anything*.>"

He sat with his palm upraised. That was quite a voucher—socialization class had never made it known that a woman would ever grant this sort of extensive permission.

Such must be one of the many inestimable benefits of the bonded union.

He laid a hand on her belly, spreading his fingers wide. Praise the Zâne, she *was* soft.

He felt her shiver.

"<I like this part of you.>"

She gazed down at him with parted lips and deep eyes, so wholly accepting of him, so authentic with her tenderness, that he made an impetuous move to embrace her. Like no better than a green and ungainly schoolboy, he just flung his arms around her and fell forward until the bridge part of his nose and his brow pressed against her exquisite belly.

He whispered, "*Comoara mea.*"

She threaded her fingers into his hair, her fingertips running ribbons of pleasure along his scalp, and whispered back, "*Dragul meu.*"

My darling.

He lifted his gaze to hers.

Her eyes were like black moons, all pupils.

The whisper in his throat turned hoarse. "<I am ready for you to show me more of yourself.>"

"<I'm ready too.>"

He straightened to watch.

She stepped out of the lump of clothes around her feet, doing this in a way that was most charming, her pretty toes pointed, her knees lifting almost like a prancing reindeer.

She reached behind herself—demonstrating an impressive dexterity of her arms—and unclasped her brassiere. With a little forward shrug of her shoulders, she sent the undergarment tumbling down her arms. It fell off her body and landed atop the lump of her cotton pants.

He stared at her breasts. His mouth became wet. He could have tried to imagine the beauty of Corky for a century and not have conjured a picture that properly honored her. Her breasts were like porcelain, though not hard like chinaware, but rather full and soft, with nipples the shade of a rose, and extra-pleasing at present, the way they stood out in proud form. But mostly, her breasts were *real* and right here in front of him—not up on a film screen.

And they were on *his* woman.

Reaching for one erect point, he gently trailed his fingertips around it.

Corky freed a rough breath, her nipple trembling and hardening some more.

His blood moved through his body in a mad rush. He feathered the backs of his curved fingers along the plump side of her breast, reveling in—

He froze.

His nostrils quivered.

This was odd. She was emitting some sort of scent. It was the same scent, to a certain degree, that she gave off when he fed on her in the night—although he was clearly not feeding on her. In addition, this aroma was much stronger.

He inhaled a better breath of her, tasting her scent at the back of his throat. It was not her fertility fragrance—as he had smelled on her at the dining table of Kimberly-Solicitor. This scent was more tangy, and as it worked its way by progressive degrees inside his head, prickles of heat spread through his man-balls.

He dropped his hand and blinked at her. *What sorcery is this?*

Corky tucked her thumbs into the narrow cotton side-bands of her under-attire and smoothed the garment down her legs, one foot kicking the underclothing free.

A growl tumbled out of him, and he stared at her woman parts with fevered eyes. The alluring scent was coming from *there*, and it was so powerful now that she was bare, he rocked back on the bed, as if hit by a firebolt from his ankle shocker, even though he wore it no more.

He could not tear his eyes away from this area of her body, it was so amazing and alluring.

He had once wondered if all woman parts were the same.

They were not.

What he was seeing on his woman was a hairless and fair area, her inner folds peeking demurely from her outer folds…although barely so. What he saw for the most part was a tantalizing slit.

And this was all the true-male side of his mind needed to see—his fangs slammed down and blood rushed in a thundering wave toward his groin. He sucked in a quick breath, but there was no pain. Just a surging, expanding, gripping pleasure in his lap.

He lowered his focus to his own crotch.

Outlined against his cotton pants was his pole, now long and rigid—much more swollen than it ever was in the mornings when he first awoke.

It had, in fact, grown into a monstrosity.

Just from seeing Corky naked.

He felt the rings around his eyes begin to spin, everything inside becoming an impulse, a surge of blood, marrow, and ancestry, a sense of a dam about to break…similar to how he had felt in Main Parlor the first time he met Corky.

When he had attacked her and scared her.

"<Please.>" His voice croaked. "<Do not fear me.>"

"<Why would I?>"

"<I perchance look like a predator at present.>" He lifted his face.

She looked at him.

"<I will not hurt you.>" He made it a vow. "<I will never hurt you.>"

"<I know. I'm not afraid of you.>"

So he took her by the wrist and pulled her forward, making sure to do so with gentle care.

She came toward him with willing splendor, the tip of her tongue drifting out to touch her bottom lip and wet it.

It was the last primal push. Everything came together— scent, dewy flesh, pebbled nipples, honest eyes, lips made for kissing, and a long road traveled—so that... "<I must...>" He started to tell her his desires, but he did not want to speak in this moment.

I must know your secret woman place in its entirety.

Reaching down to one of her knees, he curved his fingers into the delicate hollow at the back and lifted her leg, setting her foot on the bed beside his hip.

His nostrils flexed and released, and again.

He had arranged her thusly to conduct a more thorough inspection of her woman parts—what a better observation might do to his pole he was curious to determine—but a smear of glistening wetness on her inner thigh now wholly grabbed his attention.

He leaned forward, his eyes nigh crossing from moving so close to her scent, and licked it off.

"Oh, God!" crowed Corky.

His tongue tingled with her moisture. He stared at the glistening slit of her womanhood. Just heaven, this part of her was beyond amazing. "<Do I still have your permission to touch you in any manner I wish?>"

He heard her exhale in a fluttery way.

"<Because I would like to lick your woman parts now, since that area of you smells and tastes very fine to me.>" He glanced up. "<May I do this?>"

Corky crimped her eyebrows together and hummed behind compressed lips.

This was a strange response. "<Does that mean yay or nay?>"

She now gave him a vigorous nod.

"<Good.>" He leaned forward again, resting his nose against some very cushiony flesh at the top of her woman parts, then dipped his tongue into her tender slit. He smoothed his way over a small bump and curled his tongue as deep as he could.

Corky yelped, her hands flying into his hair.

He clenched his teeth as her flavor slid down his throat, lit a fire in his belly, and sent his pole into a series of violent throbs. <Upon my soul.>" His next breath emerged as a hiss. "<You are indeed a marvel.>"

She stammered, "V-Vasile…" She sounded winded for some reason. "I-I-I…"

He sat back, feeling her hands drift out of his hair.

Her cheeks were flushed and glowing, and it appeared as if her nipples were on the brink of popping off her breasts.

"<I need to lie down if you want to keep doing that.>"

Had he done something to make her unwell? "<Are you ailing of a sudden?>"

"<God, no. It's from pleasure. My knees feel weak.>"

Ah. He understood very well the feeling of unsteady knees. "<I will tend to you, my treasure. Do not worry.>" He tugged the bed coverlet down, then wrapped both hands around her waist, picked her off the floor, and swung her toward the bed, settling her on her back in the center of the mattress.

He scooted up to lie beside her and look down at her, taking in the way she gazed up at him with wide pupils and breath on her lips, her lush hair scattered across the white sheet in a mass of spun gold. She moved her bottom to adjust herself into a position of offering and temptation—her knees bent, and her legs parted just so.

His rib cage clamped hard around his lungs.

Elbowing himself downward, he shifted to kneel between her legs.

Much was displayed in her current position, and his next breath was slow in coming. Her inner folds, heretofore all but shielded by her outer folds, were now discernible. These delicate petals ran from the button that he knew—from sex education class—was her clitoris, down the entire length of her woman parts to where they hugged the pink brooch that was the opening to her body.

A rush of warm pleasure surged along the length of his pole, and he set his hands upon her bent knees. "<This pose is very enticing.>" He caressed his palms down her thighs, letting his fingers drift over her precious hipbones before he smoothed his hands back up. He repeated his caress. "<I like it very much.>"

She heaved a breath that made her nipples dance.

A sharp urgency stabbed through him. He lowered himself onto his belly between her legs. *Sweet moonlit night.* The flesh of her thighs was like cream. He edged fore and aft to situate himself perfectly. Her scent caught his brain in a hammerlock. His vision blurred, then cleared. Saliva ran off his fangs.

"<All aspects of your woman parts look so beautiful and delicious I do not know what to lick first.>"

Corky started humming again.

Chapter Fifty-Three

GOING SLOW IS HOT.

Going slow makes sex sexier.

Going slow is…is…

Corky stared at her bedroom ceiling and grabbed up two fistfuls of sheets, clenching and releasing her fingers in rhythm to the pulsation of her clitoris.

Going slow is torture!

But going slow was also necessary, if that's how Vasile wanted it. Because the last time Corky was with him, she'd been totally in charge, so letting him be his "own man" now and set the pace was an important step in their marriage.

Problem was, her husband was unwittingly driving her insane.

How was she supposed to control herself when he kept telling her all the things he loved about her and her body?

How could she be expected not to jump on him when everything he said was spoken with such rare, pure honesty?

How was she supposed to survive this agonizing pace when Vasile's touch expressed the same genuine admiration…and every inch of her that he discovered seemed a cause for celebration.

He shifted between her thighs. "<All aspects of your woman parts look so beautiful and delicious I do not know what to lick first.>"

She rolled her eyes up under her lids. *See* the way he talked to her?

Going slow is hot…

She made herself repeat the silent chant.

Going slow makes sex sexier…

She hummed a few tuneless bars under her breath. It was the only way to stop herself from making a liar out of herself by hollering, *TAKE ME NOW, YOU SEXY BEAST!*

"<This is the area where you find the most profound pleasure, is it not?>" He pressed his thumb to her clitoris.

Yow! Her clit was as sensitive as a live wire.

She tightened her fists around the sheets, aching with a quiet desperation to feel him inside her, to rush this encounter toward the deeper intimacy her body was screaming for.

Going slow makes me want to die!

"<Sex education class instructed us to give this area on the female body special care.>" He circled his thumb over her clit, once again not *purposely* driving her insane—just discovering her—but still…

A battery of moans kicked up her throat. She pressed her teeth together.

He set his large hands on either side of her body and cupped her hips. "<Your body feels like it holds lightning.>"

She gouged her nails into the sheets, probably tearing the fabric. "<That's because what you're doing feels great.>"

He paused. "<For truth?>"

"<Absolutely.>" *More, dammit, more!*

He edged forward and lay his cheek on her mons like it was a pillow, his hair—still slightly wet from his shower—spilling like velvet across her belly. "<This is a boon to hear. For I have discovered it is the most heady of powers to give you joy and pleasure.>"

A nearly unbearable pressure woke under her heart. "<Well, lucky for you,>" she said in a scratchy voice, "<that you seem to have a natural talent for it.>"

He rumbled a pleased noise, then shifted back into prime position between her legs.

In her periphery, she saw his head moving deeper into her

crotch. The mattress tilted slightly. Heat rose near her sensitive flesh. Her clit stiffened in anticipation…

And then Vasile's tongue made contact—soft, moist, gentle, awestruck.

"Oh!" She gasped and arched against a jolting current of warmth flaring at the base of her belly.

Her reaction spurred a noise of interest and curiosity from him. With the clear objective of finding out what else he could make her do, he started to devour her with gusto, his head moving rhythmically between her thighs with the steady lapping of his tongue over her clit, his long hair tickling her thighs…

Oh, God…

She hadn't expected this.

Vasile was *not* going about oral sex in any of the ways she'd learned things went.

There wasn't an ounce of vanity in this man: he wasn't doing what he was doing for praise. Or a grain of arrogance: he wasn't trying to show her what a great lover he was. And he wasn't operating off an agenda, going down on her for the express purpose of oral sex reciprocity—which just so happened to be one of Hunter's favorite moves.

With Vasile there was no showboating. No impatience masquerading as frenetic lust. No fancy tricks.

Nothing he did was for himself.

It was all about her—about *really tasting her.*

And it was the most arousing experience of her life.

Her sheath grew so heavy with cream, she felt almost faint from it. A thrilling tension fisted tighter and tighter around her clitoris as she built toward climax. Built and built…

Vasile's head came up. "<This is incredible, Corky. It is as if I can taste you clear into my man-balls. How do you do that?>"

She squeezed her eyes shut.

She had never amazed anyone in her life, but…

I amaze him.

Emotions thickened in her throat.

One smile, one laugh, one glimpse at all that resides in the deepest parts of your eyes, and nothing else matters.

She drew her tongue across her lips. "<I don't know, darling, but if you keep doing what you're doing, I'm going to have an orgasm.>"

He paused. "<Do you reference the 'pleasure explosion' sex education class taught us?>"

"<That's it.>"

"<I will continue.>"

He went at her again, his tongue smoothing over her clit in strokes of sweet agony. Her hips tensed into the grip of his hands, her entrance swelling, opening, yearning. Goosebumps rippled over her skin, her inner muscles throbbing.

"Yes," she moaned as she started to come in earnest, harder than she could've ever imagined possible. "Oh, God…oh, God…"

Her entire body shook with the power of her spasms, and she had to force herself not to lock her thighs around Vasile's head—poor guy wouldn't know what that was about.

Throwing her hands above her, she gripped the headboard, fingernails scraping the wood. Something guttural wrenched from her throat.

She careened through the last of her convulsions with her spine bowed off the mattress and her toes curling up little pleats in the sheets…until finally the spasms released her, and she flopped into a pile of limp bones, struggling for breath.

Vasile rose slowly onto his knees.

After a moment, she peeked at him through her lowered eyelids.

"<That was indeed likened to an explosion. Are you…well?>"

"<I'm great.>" Corky stretched like a cat, glowing all over with a languid satiety.

"<Is it required that I stop licking you now?>"
Her eyes popped fully open, and she gaped at him.
Her husband wanted to *keep going*?

CHAPTER FIFTY-FOUR

CORKY TEETERED UP ONTO HER elbows. "<Uh…maybe we can go back to more licking later. But right now my body wants to show you how much I care for you. So I need you to stop licking me and make love.>"

"<You refer to the sexual intercourse?>"

"<Yes. That's what I want.>"

He pinned his gaze onto her privates and frowned intently, like he was puzzling out a complicated mathematical equation. "<You are certain that is what you want to do?>"

"<Very certain.>"

He glanced down at the sizeable outline of his cock against his sweatpants, then looked again at her privates. Tendons in his throat tautened for the space of two heartbeats. "<I am sorry, but we cannot.>"

"<No?>"

"<No. We will not fit together.>"

She fought back a smile. "<We will. Don't worry about it.>"

He wasn't convinced. "<I know that this hole—>" he pointed at her privates—"<is supposed to be the opening to your body I am meant to breach. But *opening* vastly overestimates what I am seeing. Your hole is all but closed.>"

"<Oh, haha, no, it only looks that way. My body will change shape for you.>" She reached between her legs, tucked two fingers into her privates, and slightly stretched herself open to him. "<See?>"

Oh, he saw.

His eyes went black, and the rings around his irises began to spin again. He sucked air between his teeth…and then movement below his waist grabbed her attention. She checked on his crotch.

He followed the direction of her gaze.

They both watched his cock buck against his sweatpants.

He made a choked sound. "<By a starry night, what do I do?>"

"<It's all right, your penis is supposed to do that—it's lust. Take off your pants and come to me.>"

He didn't move. He looked at her, a muscle leaping in his jaw.

"<It's all right,>" she repeated. She wasn't sure if she should bring it up, but… "<We did this once before, remember? In the hospital. And you felt great inside me.>"

"<I did?>"

"<Yes.>"

"<I did not cause you discomfort?>"

"<No. Of course not. I love this part of you.>" Pushing to a sitting position, she caressed her fingertips over the hard contours of his cock through his sweatpants.

An uneven shudder ran through him.

"<It'll be fine.>" She grabbed the hem of his T-shirt and pulled it up. "<Better than fine.>" He was too tall for her to remove his shirt on her own, not while sitting, so he tugged it the rest of the way off. He then drew down his sweatpants, careful not to catch the elastic waistband on his erection.

She didn't breathe. Just stared.

Wow. The sight of Vasile naked was…

It hit her then that she'd never seen him completely naked before. Here at home, he never undressed in front of her, and the time she ravished him in the hospital, she only saw him naked below the waist.

So she wasn't prepared for how…how superbly *fit* he was. Which was dumb. He worked out every day, and she knew that. It was just…Lord. All those muscles! His smooth chest was wide and thickly defined, and his abs were cut like flagstones.

Pale and hairless—two things she never thought would be sexy, but his body rocked these qualities.

Next time you go out with him, try to get his shirt off. I'm curious to know how inked-up he is…

Well, now Corky could make a full report to Hadley.

Vasile's interlocking circular tattoos ran all the way up his sculpted right arm, over his broad shoulder, then looped back down onto his right pec.

He was both savage and beautiful…and scarred.

With her eyes, she followed the line of a raised white scar surrounded by pinhole stitching that slashed the entire breadth of his chest. Then she let her attention drift down to a knobby knot of flesh on the left side of his waist.

A shiver tinkled a string of little bells all the way down her spine.

She lay flat on the bed again. "<I want you to make love to me, my darling. So much.>"

His throat moved. But he finally took her at her word and knee-walked into position between her thighs.

"<Do you want me to help you,>" she asked, "<or do you want to guide yourself?>"

"<Guide?>

"<When you settle on top of my body, you won't be able to see my…hole, so you'll need to take your penis in your hand and place it at my entrance. Don't worry—you'll find me.>"

He nodded and encircled his cock with his fingers, breathing in deeply. He leaned over her, bracing his weight on his free arm, and maneuvered himself where he thought her opening was. He poked around, his eyes narrowed in concentration, his long hair dancing near her cheeks.

"<Let me know if you need me to——>"

He found her.

She groaned softly, tendrils of sensation coursing through her when his ridged head seated at her opening. Her legs trembled in anticipation. "<Okay, now push forward with your hips.>"

He pushed.

He slid in.

He kept going…going… *Oh!* The depth of his penetration wrung a gasp out of her.

Vasile's gaze flew to hers, the muscles on either side of his jaw going slack.

She released a single pant. "<Pretty great, isn't it?>" She grazed her fingertips over his hips. "<Keep going. In and out.>"

She felt his knees dig into the mattress beneath her butt and his hip muscles flex as he withdrew himself. He plunged in again and uttered a ragged noise.

Her throat jerked against a sudden swallow. She'd forgotten how big he felt inside her, how powerful…how perfect. A renewed flush of ecstasy spread throughout her abdomen, and her womb quickened.

Eyes squinched shut, he started to pump his hips, his tempo a little stilted at first, but then he caught on to a steady rhythm. His strokes gradually became longer and more forceful.

She gripped the ropy muscles in his forearms and held on.

His skin felt like it buzzed with an oncoming storm, a barely leashed voltage clamoring to be set free. He was—

A snarl lashed out of him.

Her eyes sprang wide.

She stared up at him through jolting vision as he continued to pound away. The hard, chiseled tendons in the muscular column of his neck were standing out in bas-relief against his flesh, and his lips were drawn back, revealing dagger-like fangs.

A spurt of instinctive fear stiffened every hair on the back of her neck. Her rising bliss began to come to a screeching halt.

That noise is vampire pleasure…

She grabbed Vasile's shoulders and pulled him down on top of her, needing to feel closer to him if she was going to convince herself that his growly noises didn't mean *dinnertime!* Tucking her face against his neck, she made herself listen more carefully to his snarls—not just react. Free from her knee-jerk survival instinct, she could now distinguish a difference between Vasile's pleasure snarl and the one that'd come out of him the day he attacked her in the parlor.

This snarl reverberated against her breasts almost like a deep purr.

I know it sounds strange at first, but you'll get used to it. In fact, you'll grow to love it.

After a few seconds her nipples peaked against the heavy pads of his chest muscles.

I will never hurt you…

Tears and sweat stung her eyes. "<You feel so great, Vasile.>" His body was solid and warm, and some of his long hair was draped across her face, smelling both soapy and feral.

"<You feel very great too,>" he choked out. "<There is an incredible pressure in my man-balls. I do not know what…what…>"

"<You're going to have an orgasm soon.>"

He moaned against her neck. His mighty back muscles flexed beneath her palms, his naked flesh sliding slickly over hers. The regular sound of his hoarse breathing in her ear spiraled her toward a second pinnacle. She opened her legs wider.

His exertions intensified, the hammering friction where their bodies were joined astonishing.

Her sheath throbbed.

She scooped her arms under his and clasped the rounded

bulk of his shoulders, holding him as close as she possibly could on the ride to the end. His cock swelled against her inner flesh as the jetting torrent of his completion began and—

He barked out in surprise. "AH!"

Then he shouted—loud enough to wake the neighbors—then his shout rolled down his throat and boiled there as a string of ecstatic growls.

His pounding release against the mouth of her womb sent her soaring into orbit number two. She cried out and clutched her knees around his driving flanks as her inner muscles contracted around him in rhythmic pulses.

With a vast moan, he shuddered all over twice more and slumped on top of her, gulping for air, his thighs and buttocks still tight.

They lay belly to belly, chest to chest, sharing breaths.

She clung to him with all her heart.

After several moments his panting quieted, and he lifted his head. His eyes were still closed, his long hair gleaming, the veins on the sides of his neck ticking with remnants of adrenaline.

He slowly opened his eyes. The spinning around his irises was just coming to a languid halt. He gazed down at her, not speaking, tongue-tied, she suspected, by this soul-shattering and monumental discovery.

Sex.

Soaring into an orbit of a different kind, she smiled. She really liked this whole *you're-amazing* thing.

"<That was...>" He stopped. He clasped both sides of her head in his large palms. "<I have no words.>"

"<Neither do I.>" She felt like she'd just handed him every star in the galaxy.

He leaned down and kissed her, his hair draping either side of her face.

She tunneled her fingers into the loose strands, gently

twining up fistfuls of it to hold onto him. She opened her mouth to his, coaxing him inside. Their tongues swept like silk over each another, soft and loving. He angled his head and pressed his tongue deeper into her mouth, then drifted over and trailed kisses along her cheek.

Her pulse skittered back to life.

His lips nuzzled her ear.

Her spine melted.

"<I forgot to bite you during intercourse.>" He raised his head to gaze at her again. "<The sex with you was too…dumbfounding for me to manage two activities at once, I think.>"

"<Don't worry about it.>" She wasn't in any hurry to be bitten again, not after his first painful bite. That bite had ended well, true, but the beginning part was so—

She gasped when Vasile shoved his face against her throat and began to drag his fangs up and down her flesh, tracing her veins. She felt a soft thrumming, then he gripped her throat between his jaws, his body suddenly crushing her into the mattress.

A spike of adrenaline sped her pulse.

The community manual said that all bites after the first one didn't hurt, but her fight-or-flight signaling system didn't seem to care. Her heart was trying to beat its way forcibly through her chest.

Vasile applied steady pressure.

She held onto his shoulders, feeling the give of her flesh, then more pressure, then—*pop*. He broke through.

She stiffened, then drooped into the mattress. *Oh, thank goodness*. It *didn't* hurt. There was only pressure, slickness against her skin, and—

"Wooooo!" Supercharged heat again!

Her pelvis lit up. Her privates clenched and released in a series of contractions.

ORGASM NUMBER THREE!

"Ooooooooo," she moaned.

When her third amazing climax finally ended, she lay in a sprawl. Warm lubrication was between her legs, seeping around where Vasile was still inside her. She couldn't move. She was absolutely and completely sapped and fuzzy-brained.

Vasile's head came up, his lips glistening, his fangs retracting. "<I see now what sweet torture it has been to have fed from your wrist these past weeks.>"

She managed to pry her lids half-open. *You've been doing…what?*

"<Feeding from your throat is like imbibing juice from a fairy chalice.>" The part of him still inside her began to thicken and lengthen.

She opened her eyes a little more. Was he getting hard again…already?

Slowly he began to move his hips, a luxurious, dreamy cadence.

"Oh, my." She threw her arms around his neck. "The votes are in," she murmured.

I can happily live the rest of my life with you as my mate.

CHAPTER FIFTY-FIVE

9:45 p.m.

VASILE STRODE UP THE STAIRSTEPS to the house where
Jacken Brun dwelled and stopped at the door. The exterior of
the Brun house was a brisk white. If this house had been in a
topside neighborhood, it would have glowed in the moonlight
like a beacon—ill-advised when a man sought to protect his
family from harm.

But since this house was not a topside house—and therefore not subject to the revealing glare of the moon—what
mattered if it all but called to an enemy?

The window to the right of the door was illuminated,
indicating that at least one person was not yet abed.

Vasile knocked and waited.

The door to the house swung open and Jacken appeared.
He was dressed in black pants of a denim material and a
simple black cotton shirt. Across his shoulders was draped a
lumpy bag that brought to mind an overgrown slug or a
mutant abscess.

"What is this growth upon you?" questioned Vasile.

Jacken glanced at his own shoulders. "It's a hot pack." He
tugged it off and tossed it aside. "Used for sore muscles. Toni
put it on me."

Ah, yes. Vasile well understood the feeling of sore muscles…although feeding on Corky this evening had been of
tremendous help for his own aches. "We dig in the riverbed
for many hours today."

"Fuckin' A," said Jacken—this was a term of exclamation

and pride. "It was a helluva job."

Vasile very much agreed. "It give Corky a great deal of happiness that we do this for her former home. She just engage in much sexual intercourse with me."

Jacken paused. "Did she?" A small muscle jumped at the edge of his mouth. "Then what the hell are you doing here?"

"I am on a journey to the town diner to collect takeaway food. But first I come here to offer thanks to you for your wise counsel. Getting my woman naked was indeed very sound advice."

"Yeah?" Jacken crossed his arms. "Good to know."

Vasile held out his hand.

Jacken glanced at it, then uncrossed his arms and shook.

"And I want to tell you that I am here to provide you advice, as well, should you ever have need of it."

"Thanks, Lazăr," said Jacken, a smile pulling at his mouth. "I might just take you up on that. You clearly know a lot of shit the rest of us don't."

Heat prickled the flesh on his nape.

Jacken was a leader of strong men and was therefore very strong himself—a compliment from him was the utmost.

Vasile coughed against a sudden itch in his throat. "Best I continue on my journey now. I learn that many hours of sexual intercourse tires the woman, so I must replenish Corky."

Jacken edged his eyebrows up. "You're not tired?"

"No."

Jacken snorted. "Newly bonded male."

Vasile frowned. "Do you mean to say this will change over time?"

"Maybe not."

"Good." Vasile took a step back from the door. "May the Zâne look upon you well this night."

"You too," said Jacken.

Vasile froze. The leader of the warriors had just wished

Vasile the luck of the fairies? Would the largesse of this night never cease?

Nodding a final farewell, Jacken closed the door.

Vasile turned and bounded down the stairsteps, trekking off toward the town diner with an abundance of vigor in his stride.

✧　✧　✧

CORKY WRENCHED OPEN ONE EYE, a task requiring enormous effort, then opened the other. She was facedown on the bed, still floating in a state of slobbering euphoria, her mouth slack, her heart rate drubbing at a beats-per-minute that could probably be classified as barely alive.

She and Vasile had made love four times.

She'd lost count of how many times she climaxed during all their lovemaking, but it was a lot. It seemed that the more times Vasile satisfied her, the more fascinated he became by all the different ways he could make her go off on a "pleasure explosion."

The man was tireless in his explorations.

Was she complaining?

No way—even though her privates were a bit sore.

Smiling with one side of her face, she blinked around the room.

Where was her husband, anyway?

She grunted herself onto her back—taking two tries to accomplish the rollover—and looked around again. Vasile wasn't anywhere, but there was a note on his pillow.

She picked it up and—*crud*. It was written in Romanian.

She'd only started learning how to read and write Romanian here in Țărână's language school, so her skills were still rudimentary.

She did understand one word, though—*mâncare*.

Food.

Did that mean Vasile was out getting something to eat?

God, she hoped so. Lunch had been her last meal, and it was now nearly ten at night.

Rolling across the bed, she swung her legs over the side and sat up, hugging the sheet to her bare breasts. Grabbing her cell phone off the nightstand, she found her husband's number, pushed the microphone icon, and spoke. "<Hey, I'm awake, and I miss you.>" She paused. *How goofy*. But she did miss him. "<How long until you come home?> She clicked off, then pushed the icon again. "<Please use voice mail instead of text. I don't understand Romanian writing.>"

She set her phone on the mattress beside her and stretched. Her whole body felt gelatinous. She gazed vaguely at three moving boxes stacked at the foot of the bed, the word *bedroom* scrawled in a black Sharpie on all sides. Her stuff had arrived from topside this morning.

Her cell beeped.

A little megaphone icon was lit up next to Vasile's phone number. She picked up her cell and pressed the icon.

Her husband's voice came out of her phone's speaker. <The diner chef tells me it will take him ten more minutes to cook my hamburger with cheese. I ordered you a salad with tuna and other vegetables since you generally don't prefer beef meat. It will then take me five minutes to walk home to you. So that is fifteen minutes total.>"

She smiled, then chuckled. So he *was* getting food.

I am a fine hunter. You'll never go hungry with me as your man...

A second message arrived from him. "<And I miss you, as well.>"

Giggling, she pushed the microphone icon. "<Okay. See you soon. And thank you so much for going out for food. I'm starving!>" If not for Vasile, she would've hibernated under the covers and just gone hungry.

He answered, "<Of course.>"

Of course. Like it was no biggie. She sent back: ♥

The message icon lit almost immediately.

She pressed it, and a scoffing noise came out of the speaker. "<What is this absurdity? Emoji symbols are silly.>"

Silly! She jammed her thumb to the microphone button. "<A heart emoji means I love you!>" She clicked off before she realized what she'd said.

Oh, Lord. She stared at her phone screen. *Do I love him?*

Moments slid by while Vasile didn't respond.

She'd never been in love before, so she wasn't sure how to tell if she was now.

Maybe it's the little things that really matter between you and Vasile too...

She drew her forefinger around the edge of her phone. Like...how sweetly unsure Vasile had been when he lifted his coffee mug to her in Kimberly's kitchen....or how embarrassed and undone he'd become by his first experience of sexual attraction to her...or the charming hesitancy he'd shown about correcting her elk misidentification at Garwald's...

She hugged her cell to her chest. He'd been expressing emotions to her all along!

And what about how he said he loved her in spite of her flaws, but then he hadn't been able to name any real ones.

He loves me.

Her phone vibrated against her breasts. She lowered it and pushed the megaphone icon.

"<Very well,>" Vasile said, his voice gruff. "<I will accept this one type of emoji.>"

She laughed. "<Good,>" she responded.

"<I'll be starting home soon.>"

"<All right, I'm going to take a shower.>" Setting her phone down, she padded naked toward the bathroom, passing the stack of moving boxes. Half the lid of the topmost box was open, and she caught a glimpse of the kind of white-and-black marble-patterned essay book she'd used for journaling when she was young.

"I'll be damned." She forgot she'd kept them.

She opened the other side of the box lid. Wow, there was a whole pile. Grabbing the one on top, she fanned through the pages with her thumb. The familiar scrawl of her handwriting flew by, except for the last few pages of the book—those were blank.

She gave up writing in her journals when she left Mary Sills' Angels for college.

She thumbed through a second time, more slowly, reading snippets of her gloomy life—the rejection and loneliness she'd endured, the self-doubt that trapped her in too many unhealthy relationships, the never-ending mistreatment she allowed from boys.

A cold feeling washed over her as she saw a theme develop before her eyes that she'd never seen before…

Polly Allred tells me not to be a cocktease, so I let a boy feel me up.

The most popular boy at the home wants me to play surf-board with him, and I end up letting him hump my butt.

Leather wants me to meet his parents on Christmas Eve, and I agree even though it's weird.

Phillip Beedman wants to use me for sexual experience, and I talk myself into wanting the same thing…

Corky's next breath left her as a jerky exhale.

Look at everything she'd *done*.

Her whole life she hadn't just been acquiescing. No, she'd been acting like some kind of skirted dancing bear, *performing* to get people to like her. Or love her.

I babysat Tweets so Sharon would like me.

I thought only good thoughts so that Mary would love me…

Actually, *everything* Corky had done for Mary was to get her foster mother to love her. But…

Corky's stomach balled into a knot.

But she'd been climbing an impossible mountain.

Because the primal bond just wasn't there.

Corky dug her fingernails into her journal.

No wonder her multiple screwups made her feel unloved. She'd learned to equate love with *doing,* so failure equaled being unlovable.

How sad was *that?*

You're so pitifully eager to please that you let me do anything to you. Have you ever stopped to consider what kind of woman that makes you…?

Flushing, she slammed her journal back in the box and continued at a stomp toward the bathroom.

But you weren't really who you were meant to be while you were topside…

She jerked to a halt.

Maybe who you really are here *is a kind and loving woman who just needs a man who won't abuse those qualities. A strong man. Like Vasile…*

*Like Vasile…*who had fallen in love with her without her having to *do* a single damned thing.

When he'd been dying, she stepped up to save his life, yes, but he'd already said he loved her.

She brought her chin up.

I am not a caretaker. I am someone who cares. *There's a big difference.*

Snatching her bathrobe off a hook on the bathroom door, she shrugged it on as she marched back to the open moving box. She grabbed her journal again and returned to her bed. Finding a pen in the nightstand drawer, she climbed on the mattress, sitting with her back against the headboard, her legs curled under her.

She uncapped the pen and opened her journal to a blank page.

I have a family now!

One brother and three sisters (well, more than three

sisters, but I'm not going to think about the others).

There's Hadley Wickstrum.

Even before she and I knew we were sisters, Hadley showed me what it's like to be part of a family. She loved me at first sight and made me feel like I belonged.

She loved me for <u>myself</u>, and that was a first major step for me to learn that I don't have to DO anything for love…although I didn't know it at the time.

Then there's Pandra Costache.

We're still getting to know each other, but I think she's already taught me some important things by example.

Like a woman can wear a Rugrats T-shirt and still be a badass.

A person can care for someone and not be a caretaker.

Soft doesn't have to equal weak.

Pandra puts a good spin on female strength.

And then there's Toni Parthen. Big sis.

She talked things through with me when I was hurting. She GAVE when I needed it and didn't expect anything in return.

She helped me to redefine myself, and I owe her big for that.

Because when she urged me to take a chance on my heart, I was able to do it.

I reached out to a man with all the care inside me, and it worked out!

He didn't stomp on me or turn me into a caretaker.

He cared back.

About him…

He's my Half-Moon Man.

I think of him that way because everything changed after he shared his half-moon story with me. There was so much to see in him that night.

Hadley once said that he's a hard guy to read.

Some people might look at him and wonder what in the world I see in him.

But that's the thing.

I do see…a softening around his mouth, relaxation near his eyes, a small dent in his cheek, a darkening in his pupils, movement around his irises…

These all mean something: a smile, affection, laughter, concern, passion.

But all of it's for me.

Only for me.

His deepest expressions are little secrets I get to hoard inside my heart.

Precious gifts that I can keep for a lifetime.

Because we are bonded forever, body and soul.

Funny thing is, a part of me got together with him to help my Half-Moon Man rise up and be everything he could be. But it ended up going the other way around.

He helped me to become whole.

No half-in, half-finished, halfway, or half-open.

He showed me how two people can be everything to each other.

And so here I am.

Thirty years old and in love for the first time to a man who completes me.

His name is Vasile Lazăr.

CHAPTER FIFTY-SIX

July
Two days later
Oțărât
5:23 a.m.

REESE SHUFFLED INTO THE TWENTY-BY-TWENTY common space his hovel shared with five other dumps and made a beeline toward the smell of coffee.

The side of the common space farthest from his crapshack was plain cave wall, and against it was shoved a three-foot long counter, which was home to a stove burner, a toaster, and a Mr. Coffee. Butting up against the left side of the counter was a fridge that periodically let out a wailing death-moan—just one of Oțărât's many *spectacular* sounds—and to the right were three Sparkletts® water containers.

The Culligan® Man apparently refused to deliver down here to the Demon Shitsburgs.

Next to the water were a half dozen stacked barrels, some labeled "supplies," others "sewage," and how un-fun would it be if those ever got confused?

Besides the risk of accidently mixing up your doodie with your donuts, life was a beach in Oțărât.

Not.

Shocking update: for a man who'd spent his entire life leading with his fists—punch first, ask *Gee, you mean you weren't serious about that?* second—Reese was super-duper fucking sick and tired of fighting.

No need to analyze his astrology chart and Myers-Briggs

Personality Test score.

He wasn't the guy in control anymore.

Point, the first: the violence here was unpredictable as fuck.

Sometimes the Om Rău would get all lazy and turn about as threatening as plain yogurt.

Other times they would light into you for any and all reasons—*Excuse me, but did you just end your sentence with a preposition? ROAR!*—and then they'd punch you with mad force.

Most of these battles ended with Reese facedown in his own drool, and—if he could gather the gumption for locomotion—eventually sacked out at Medieval Medical.

So point, the second: Reese was no longer the guaranteed victor.

His first sad defeat occurred on day three of his sojourn here when Volcano Burpee made good on his threat to go nuclear if Reese didn't bow down and impregnate Havel.

Did you fuck, Havel?

No.

DOUBLE ROAR!

Reese did his best to defend himself, but his fists might as well have been made of Nerf balls for all the good they did him. He was merked so badly he ended up in Medieval Medical for four days.

When he emerged, the forked-tail occupants of the Shitsburgs were all about letting Reese know just how much his Royal ass didn't belong here.

Outsider? Who me? Golly, I've never felt that way before.

Lots and lotsa fights went on.

He flew into every one balls-out and fuck-you, and so even though he was on an incredible losing streak, at least he'd earned the rep of being a scrapper who didn't just sit back on his frilly Royal laurels and take it.

He damned well let it be known that he would serve up a

lot of hurt on his way down to his drool nap.

The fights started to lessen.

He even made a couple of friends.

Krolan, Fade and Havel's brother—marked with two full "sleeves" of black teeth tats—deigned on occasion to hold conversations with him that didn't include the usual snarling and spitting, and Tollar, a fellow redhead but with safety pins in a lot of *duuude-that's-whack* places, became a drinking buddy.

Except, you know, a man would be wise to remember that impulse control wasn't exactly in large supply around here, especially when alcohol was involved.

Yesterday, Reese won a game of pool against Tollar, and Beelzebub broke a pool stick over the top of Reese's head.

Reese had regained consciousness in a puddle of drool *and* blood—a couple of Om Rău casually playing pool around his inert form—then dragged himself off to Medieval Medical.

He was pretty sure Gwyn kept a bed on permanent hold for him.

This morning the two ibuprofen she'd given him were no longer on point with pain relief, so he shuffled to the Mr. Coffee machine with "Babalu" playing against his skull (iconic *I Love Lucy* song. C'mon, Millennials, get with it!).

Mug in hand, he moved with care to one of two wooden picnic tables set in the middle of the common space. He sat with even more care on the bench across from Gwyn. "Hey." He sipped his coffee and stared with vacant eyes at the newspaper Ţărână sent in daily. A *paper* newspaper. Of all the things.

The first time he'd sat his duff down at Gwyn's picnic table early one morning, she had nothing but the hairy eyeball for him.

Only about two precious hours per day weren't filled with all the clatter that made Oţărât uniquely Oţărât—the constant screaming was the real asspits—so the wee hours of the morning were Gwyn's hoarded peace-and-quiet time.

She didn't want anyone intruding on it.

She dropped the attitude as soon she saw that Reese didn't want to intrude, just grab some peace himself.

He didn't talk to her. Merely drank his coffee.

And nursed his wounds.

But then one morning he alerted Gwyn to the fact that he wasn't a complete skillethead by mumbling some quote from his best bud, Nietzsche.

Gwyn herself was a smart cookie—she was a trained nurse, as well as a necessary jack-of-all-trades around this place—so she started chatting with him. He figured she enjoyed conversing with someone who was on par with her intellectually, but he also suspected she tested him on a regular basis for brain damage.

"Morning, Chuck," she said now.

This was her hilarious way of calling him a bumpkin—one of which he now resembled.

Good ol' Dr. Willard's implant had long ago fallen victim to Oṭărât's daily violence and been knocked out, leaving behind a hillbilly-style open space in the front of Reese's mouth. His hair likewise ran heavy on the huckleberry. During nearly four weeks of outgrowth, now an inch of red roots showed against the dyed black.

His appearance was rendered even more fuckdiculous by yesterday's medical ministrations—Gwyn had shaved the left side of his head to give him seven stitches.

Thanks were owed to Tollar's pool stick for that.

"How are my stitches holding up?" Gwyn's eyes tracked over him.

The woman was an interesting mix of compassion and hardass. She didn't suffer fools lightly, but those who put in a solid effort received her full attention.

"I have a butthole of a headache."

Gwyn made an *hmm* sound. "How about Havel? Will she

be in class today?"

Speaking of knockouts… Late yesterday, Havel had thrown down with Ejohn, whose arms were also tatted-up with black teeth but only on his biceps.

Of the twelve times Havel had been raped, Ejohn had doled out seven of those violations, and it was a nasty habit of his to try and dish out more.

Ejohn was—not to floor you or anything—Reese's arch-nemesis.

Any time the fuck laid a hand on Havel, Reese went berserk and whaled on him.

'Cept yesterday Ejohn used Reese's pool-stick nappy time to make a move on her.

But Havel was not one to fold at the first sign of trouble.

Same as Toni.

Same as Gwyn.

Havel went to town on Ejohn and ended up knocking him out with a brutal uppercut to the jaw, saving herself from unlucky thirteen.

Damn, gurl, those built muscles of yours really get the job done.

Reese had never met a woman who could stand up for herself better than Havel. It didn't matter who tried to mess with her—a fellow Om Rău or a bumpkin Royal Dragon—she didn't take shit off anyone.

Never one to hammer away at a pointless occupation, Reese had stopped trying to rile her a long time ago. He just hung out with her in their shared hovel. And that was when some strange weirdness happened. Like…a demon chick with built biceps and ratty dreads became his friend.

"Havel's a trooper." Reese took a reinvigorated drink of coffee. It was a decent roast, considering it sat next to a vat of poo. "She should make it to class."

Gwyn tugged a Sweet'N Low out of her front shorts pocket, the packet looking like Genghis Khan and his

Mongolian horde had trampled over it about thirty times—it was barely pink anymore. "Havel's still having trouble with her multiplication tables." Gwyn tore open the Sweet'N Low and sprinkled it into her coffee. "Can you help her with that?"

"'Course." Helping Havel with homework was actually one of his few pleasures these days. He dug watching the transformation that came over her when comprehension struck.

She'd start out with two deep creases across the bridge of her nose, struggling to understand, then her eyes would light up and she'd look at Reese like he was a god among men for helping the lightbulb go off.

Gwyn stood, crossed to the Mr. Coffee, refilled her mug, then grabbed a plastic bag from underneath the counter. She returned to the picnic table and set the bag in front of Reese with a soft *clatter*. "These are small plastic blocks you can use to demonstrate the concept of grouping," she said, sitting again. "I think Havel learns best by seeing and touching."

"Will do."

Josnic tramped into the common space, his hand wrapped around seven-year-old Dange's arm, dangling the kid off the ground by one arm. The boy's face was scrunched up, but he wasn't making any more trouble for himself by wriggling.

Josnic plunked the boy next to Gwyn on the bench and growled, "He's bothering me."

Dange buried his face in Gwyn's side. The kid was actually a spunky and precocious redhead, but when the meanie poophead leader of the Om Rău complained about being *bothered*, you tucked your face.

Dange was Josnic and Gwyn's only son together, and how Gwyn had managed to produce just *one* kid with Josnic was a mystery. Had stress dried up her eggs? Or did she actively take secret measures to prevent conception in a land of no birth control and certainly no celibacy—Gwyn was Josnic's unabashed favorite.

Volcano Burpee might make visits to various Oţărât hovels to spread his enormous seed around, but after the night's sowing was complete, he always ended up back in Gwyn's bed.

Stalking to the picnic table, Josnic slammed his butt down on the far side of Reese's bench—if this had been a teeter-totter Reese would be doing a massive pogo up to the cave ceiling right now.

Reese pinched his aching forehead. *Crap, there goes quiet time*—and why was it that he always heard "Horst Wessel Lied" play whenever Volcano Burpee came onto the scene?

Josnic grabbed the newspaper.

Gwyn stood, sending Dange scrambling underneath the table for cover. "What do you want for breakfast?" she asked Josnic.

Eggs? Bacon? A concrete block? Deadly nightshade?

Josnic grunted. "Oatmeal."

Mush? For *this* guy? "No shit?" Reese said.

Josnic snapped his focus over.

Whatever the tough, gangsta version of *oopsy-doopsy* happened to be, Reese was thinking it.

Josnic's eyes narrowed. "You've been here a month, Dragon, so—"

"Is that all?"

"So…" Josnic's backhand flashed out, clipping Reese on the kisser.

Ouch. Eyes watering, Reese rubbed a hand across his stinging lower lip—it felt like a darning needle was jammed in two inches deep. "Owie, man, you seriously just harshed my mellow."

Gwyn dumped some oatmeal into a battered pot and sighed heavily.

Right. *Don't run your mouth around the Volcano.*

"Havel is ripe again." Josnic pointed at Reese's hovel. "Get your ass in there and fuck her."

"Absolutely. I'm totally going to do that." Reese finished his coffee and stood. "Gwyn wants plumbing, doesn't she? I'm definitely getting her some plumbing with my dick."

Setting the pot on the stove burner, Gwyn side-eyed Reese.

Josnic opened the newspaper. "Each month you refuse, I'll beat you harder."

Harder…than *last* time? Stomach bile sloshed clear into the back of Reese's teeth.

"Until one day I kill you," Josnic added with casual indifference.

Hmm. Maybe he should've grabbed the Frightmare Homey Knife out of his sock drawer when he had the chance.

Then again, maybe not.

"Get off me!" a woman shrieked.

Furniture crashed. A door slammed.

Siofranna barreled into the common space, Olacar hot on her heels. Olacar grabbed Siofranna by her long ponytail and yanked her back.

The newlyweds—together a month now—were constantly at war over how much sex to have. Olacar wanted it all the time. Siofranna pretty much didn't want his mitts on her much at all.

Siofranna swung around and socked Olacar in the face, screaming again.

Reese pressed his thumb and forefinger against his closed lids.

Just another day in the neighborhood…

Striding to the counter, Reese splashed the dregs of his coffee into the refuse bucket, set his mug in the wash basin, then made a quick escape from the loud marital strife. He strode toward his hovel after first grabbing the bag of blocks.

More shouting rose from an adjacent common area. It was of the MEET ME THERE LATER! YEAH! OKAY! variety. But it was still noise.

Reese set his forehead against the doorjamb of his hovel, his eyes mashed closed, and stood still for a long moment. Finally, he pushed inside.

Havel's lashes parted sleepily at him. One of her eyes was swollen and black.

He set the bag of blocks on the spindly desk, then slipped into bed behind her and spooned his body around hers.

"You're back early from morning coffee," she observed in a gravelly tone.

Her morning voice was huskier than her normal voice and always lit his undershorts on fire. Bending forward, he tucked his face against her neck and stayed that way for a few breaths. She always smelled strongly of sweat—no showers here, remember?—but he liked it. The scent wasn't bad, and it was *her*. "Josnic showed up and ordered me to have sex with you."

Havel rolled onto her back, the sleepiness clearing from her gaze. "Are you going to?"

Reese kissed the tip of her nose. "Wish I could."

"Reese…" Havel's brow wrinkled. "Josnic's going to hurt you bad if you don't have sex with me."

He gave her a one-shouldered, *shit-happens* shrug but suddenly didn't feel like leaving their hovel for the rest of the day.

"Why won't you?" Havel asked.

"You know why."

"I know you said that you don't want to leave a kid of yours behind, but you're staying here anyway."

That little factoid tightened Reese's throat. When he'd agreed to stay in Oţărât, he never imagined he was consigning himself to the Demon Shitsburgs *forever*.

But the way he saw it, he was caught in a particularly gnarly Catch-22—he couldn't leave until he knocked up Havel, and if he knocked up Havel he couldn't leave.

And that was punk as fuck.

Because if there was one place on earth that could eventually break Reese, it was Oţărât.

Falling onto his back, he locked his hands behind his head and stared without seeing at the ceiling.

CHAPTER FIFTY-SEVEN

Same day
Topside
San Diego County Courthouse, Dept. 10
Night court
6:26 p.m.

VASILE COULD NOT BELIEVE A douche-man worse than Reese Terrella existed on this planet, but the reprobate Hunter Scott equaled, if not surpassed, Reese in this area.

The derisive sneer Hunter had aimed at Corky as she and Kimberly entered the door into the courthouse room called Department Ten told Vasile all he needed to know about the fopdoodle.

Wretched imposter. The foul male was not even a huntsman by trade, just stupidly named as such. He was, in fact, the solicitor in competition with Corky this day, as well as her former paramour.

Upon seeing the fopdoodle, Vasile determined that he would not be able to sit mindfully by and keep from strangling the man during the court proceedings—more sneers would surely be forthcoming—and so he opted to remain in the outer hallway, guarding against the arrival of the daughters of Zalina.

None of whom showed up, thank the Zâne.

But while no witches abounded, there were a great number of Regular Humans bustling hither and yon, which made Vasile dart his focus around to many places. He had never been near to so many non-vampires, and it assaulted his nerves, knowing how much care he must put toward watching himself.

He must not show his fangs, even retracted.

He must not show the spinning in his eyes, should his battle vision overtake him.

He must not allow anyone to see his warding tattoos activate, should he come under threat. For this last, he had donned his coat of a lightweight material as concealment.

Still, it was a heavy burden, having to monitor so many of his mannerisms, that when he took a position against the wall next to a machine that dispensed water in an arching stream, he could not help but wear a heavy scowl.

Persons who sought to quench their thirst at this water-dispensing machine took one look at his expression and went off to find their relief elsewhere.

The door to Department Ten swung open, and Vasile straightened from the wall.

But it was only Sedge Stănescu.

Community rule stated that no warrior could go topside alone. So Dev and Thomal accompanied Vasile today, and since Kimberly was with Corky at the San Diego Courthouse, Sedge came as well.

The blond warrior now approached Vasile with a huge grin spread across his face—albeit he pressed the back of his fist against his mouth to cover his fangs.

"Remind me never to piss off your wife," said Sedge to Vasile as he came to a stop in front of him. "She just totally crushed that guy in there."

Vasile felt the beats of his heart trip one over the other. "Corky succeed in putting the river decree back in place?"

"Yep." Sedge smiled again. "And the other lawyer dude was not happy about it. You should have seen the look on—"

The door to Department Ten opened again.

Now it was Corky and Kimberly who exited, both women carrying satchels, both women smiling and chatting.

Behind them the hunter-douche emerged, his eyes boring baleful holes into the back of Corky.

Vasile did not like this look at all. He flexed his fists at his sides and took a step forward.

"Not yet, Lazăr." Dev was standing next to Vasile, doing something called "scrolling" on his cellular phone. But even though his eyes were lowered, Dev was clearly observing everything. "Watch what goes down first."

Thomal said in addition, "See if Corky can handle this on her own—she needs to." He was standing near to a pillar, trying to use the shadow cast by the large pole to conceal himself as much as possible from women, who enjoyed staring at him nonstop.

The hunter-douche snapped at Corky, "This isn't over, Catherine."

Vasile swung back around to watch matters unfold. A fire built in his chest despite the advice of Dev and Thomal. It took much effort not to lunge at the ill-mannered imposter and bite his skull.

Corky stopped and turned toward her opponent, Kimberly doing the same beside her. "It *is* over, Hunter. Sorry."

Hunter scoffed. "Do you really think some flimsy environmental statute is going to stop me from—"

"You *will*," interceded Corky, "prompt your client to cease and desist all harassment of Mary Sills, and that includes enjoining Rand Resources to drop the false allegations against her."

"Allegations? Harassment?" Hunter shrugged all this away. "I don't recall hearing you prove any of that."

"I don't have to, Mr. Scott. Because if you don't do what I say, I'll bring you up on fraud charges."

Hunter went very still. Then he laughed. "You're insane."

"Am I?" Corky smiled, although she showed no teeth. "It's always raised red flags to me that Rand Resources would pay off Reuben's mortgage. Seems excessive, doesn't it?"

Kimberly nodded smartly.

Hunter did not reply.

"So I did more digging, and I found out that the lending institution Rand *supposedly* used isn't regulated by any official governing body. Guess what that means?" Corky arched her brows. "The lender is fraudulent."

Hunter still did not speak, but now he made his spine go rigid as a javelin.

Corky continued. "Rand Resources, in point of fact, never paid off Reuben's loan." Her expression flattened and her eyes cooled. "You forged the mortgage discharge papers, Hunter."

The imposter-douche narrowed his eyes even as his face drained. "You tell anyone that, and I'll see you disbarred." He took a step closer. "Are you forgetting that I have you for breaking client confidentiality?"

"My colleague will be happy to bring charges against you." Corky nodded toward Kimberly. "So you can stuff your threats."

Hunter hissed. "Who the hell do you think you are?"

Kimberly said to Corky, "Let's go."

Hunter grabbed Corky by the arm. "You little bitch."

Vasile whirled on Dev. *He touches her!*

"Yeah. Go now." Dev nodded. "Just watch your fucking face—Regulars are around."

Lips seamed and eyes hooded, Vasile stalked toward Corky.

Kimberly saw the way he approached and moved back a step.

Hunter curled his upper lip into that loathsome sneer again. "You're nothing but a two-bit—"

"I am husband to Corky." Vasile stopped beside Corky and spoke to the hunter-douche in a low snarl. "If you do not unhand her this moment, I will squeeze your face in my fist until I break your jaw in several places."

Hunter took on the expression of a dumbfounded sheep.

"Husband?"

Vasile set a hand on the shoulder of this despised man—for the douche still held Corky—and dug his fingers into the muscles there.

Hunter widened his eyes into very large circles. The leather satchel he held fell out of his hand.

"Do not doubt the veracity of the threat I make to you." Vasile pressed harder, his fingers gouging through the material of the fancy coat the douche wore.

Hunter sucked in a breath, so sharply and deeply that a button popped off his fancy coat. "Fuck! Ouch!" He released Corky. "Okay! Okay! Now let go of me!"

Vasile removed his hand.

The hunter-douche reeled backwards by several paces.

Vasile turned to Corky. <Are you okay?>"

She gave him a gleaming look from beneath her lashes. "<I am, thank you.>" Then she faced Hunter again. "Inform Mr. Meyerston that he still needs to make payments to his bank so he doesn't inadvertently default on his loan. And rein in your client, like I said, or you'll end up doing jail time—or at the very least, you'll be fined to the hilt."

Hunter just stood in place, massaging the shoulder Vasile had damaged.

"Do we have a deal?" asked Corky.

"Yes," retorted Hunter. He bent over, snatched up his satchel, and marched off.

They watched him leave the building, then Kimberly wandered over to Sedge.

Corky turned toward Vasile.

Vasile gazed down upon her and cupped her cheek. "<My congratulations to you, Treasure. You won.>"

"<Hah! I did, didn't I?>" She brushed her fingertips lightly beneath one of his eyes. "<Even better, I get to discover another expression of yours.>"

"<Indeed? What is that?>"

"<Pride.>"

"<Ah. I *am* proud of you.>"

She gave him a smile full of sparkles.

This was the utmost of her smiles.

"<Are you ready to go home?>" asked Corky.

Home. He brushed his thumb across her cheekbone. She had done a remarkable job fashioning their abode into one of those. "<Yes.>"

They stepped apart and strolled over to the others.

Dev smiled at Corky, though not too widely. "Kimberly just told us how you wiped the floor with your opposition. Nicely done."

"Thanks."

"Hell," said Thomal. "Now I'm wishing I'd gone into the courtroom with Stănescu, watched how you—"

The cellular phone Thomal wore on his belt made a cricket chirp. He angled the phone screen toward him, as if he just meant to glance at it, then he stiffened.

"Holy shit!" He wrenched the cellular phone out of its holder and gaped down at the screen. "Alex found my sister!"

Are you a fan of The Community Series?

There are _so many_ ways you can help get the word out about these stories!

Yes, a written review is the gold standard, but <u>rating anonymously with stars</u> is also very helpful—and it's easy to do! And of course, word of mouth is the best of the best…so please _tell a friend_.

Thank you so much for your help, and see ya at next month's newsletter.

✧　✧　✧

<u>Book 6 in The Community Series, CURSE CASTERS, coming soon!</u>

Do the witches continue to be a threat…will Nicolae and Hadley ever get together…what is in store for Reese and Havel?

Will the Costaches' long-lost sister accept her new vampire brothers?

And will the next person to join the community shock you…?

There's still plenty more excitement coming your way in The Community Series!

Don't miss a single thrilling moment.
Go to https://tracytappan.com/contact to sign up for my newsletter.

With each newsletter you'll earn a chance to win a Community Series mug in my monthly giveaway!

RIDERS
TRACY TAPPAN
THE COMMI
BREED
TRACY TAPPAN

About the Author

Tracy Tappan is a bestselling and award-winning author of gritty romance and the creator of the Choose A Hero Romance™ reading experience, a brand-new concept in storytelling where the reader controls the ending. You can find out more about this exciting new trend at www.choosea hero.com.

Tracy's books in paranormal and military romance have earned both bronze and gold medals in the Readers' Favorite contests, have finaled for the USA Book News and Kindle Book Awards, and won both the HOLT Medallion and the Independent Publishers Book Award (IPPY) bronze medal for romance.

Tracy holds a master's degree in Marriage, Family, Child Counseling (MFCC), loves to play tennis, enjoys a great glass of wine, and talks to her Labrador like he's a human (admittedly, the wine drinking and the dog talking probably go together).

A native of San Diego, Tracy is married to a former Navy helicopter pilot, who retired after thirty years of service. He and Tracy spent over ten years living in Rome, Italy, in the diplomatic corps.

Visit her website and join the gang on her monthly newsletter for giveaways, publication updates, and other fun and sexy news. www.tracytappan.com.